UNLOCKING HER
SURGEON'S HEART

BY
FIONA

H OY'S
ET

BY
TINA BECKETT

MILLS
BOON
&

MIDWIVES ON-CALL

Welcome to Melbourne Victoria Hospital—
and to the exceptional midwives
who make up the Melbourne Maternity Unit!

These midwives in a million work miracles on a daily
basis, delivering tiny bundles of joy into the arms of their
brand-new mums!

Amidst the drama and emotion of babies arriving
at all hours of the day and night, when the shifts are over,
somehow there's still time for some sizzling
out-of-hours romance…

Whilst these caring professionals might come face-to-
face with a whole lot of love in their line of work, now
it's their turn to find a happy-ever-after of their own!

Midwives On-Call

*Midwives, mothers and babies—
lives changing for ever…!*

Eight special stories to collect and treasure:

**These titles are also available in eBook format
from www.millsandboon.co.uk**

UNLOCKING HER SURGEON'S HEART

BY
FIONA LOWE

Published in Great Britain 2015
by Mills & Boon, an imprint of Harlequin (UK) Limited,
Eton House, 18-24 Paradise Road, Richmond, Surrey, TW9 1SR

© 2015 Harlequin Books S.A.

Special thanks and acknowledgement are given to Fiona Lowe for her contribution to the *Midwives On-Call* series

ISBN: 978-0-263-24717-6

Harlequin (UK) Limited's policy is to use papers that are natural, renewable and recyclable products and made from wood grown in sustainable forests. The logging and manufacturing processes conform to the legal environmental regulations of the country of origin.

Printed and bound in Spain
by CPI, Barcelona

Dear Reader,

Usually writing a book is a relatively solitary job, but when you're writing a novel which is part of a series written by a group of authors it comes with a lovely sense of camaraderie. The *Midwives On-Call* series was no exception. Way back in the day, I worked as a midwife. I loved it. There is something so precious and special about delivering a baby. For a few hours you're part of people's lives as they experience one of their most momentous events. It's an honour and a privilege. One of the births that stands out in my memory is delivering twins on Christmas Day. I've also been on the other side of delivery—the woman giving birth—and I still remember with great fondness the midwives who delivered my sons.

In *Unlocking Her Surgeon's Heart* Lilia is a dedicated midwife in a small coastal town. She loves her work but to a certain extent she's hiding behind it. Her world is small and safe—which is how she wants and needs it to be. The arrival of an arrogant and grumpy city surgeon is something to be endured for four short weeks and she's endured worse—so how hard can it possibly be?

Noah is in the final months of his surgical fellowship, and being sent to the tiny township of Turraburra is his worst nightmare. He's chosen surgery so he doesn't have to talk to patients, but his boss at the Melbourne Victoria Hospital has other ideas. Noah starts counting down the hours until he can leave from the moment he arrives, and he surely doesn't need or want the enigmatic midwife's opinion on his rusty communication skills. As the weeks go by Noah not only discovers his bedside manner, but exactly what's been missing in his life. Can he convince Lilia to take the biggest risk of her life and love him?

I hope you enjoy Lilia and Noah's story. For photos, back story and information about the series, as well as my other books, please join me at www.fionalowe.com. You can also find me at Facebook, Twitter, Pinterest, and of course you can catch me by email at fiona@fionalowe.com

Happy reading!

Fiona x

Dedication

To my fellow Mills & Boon® Medical Romance™ authors.
You're all amazing and talented women.
Thank you for the support, the laughs and the fun times
when we were lucky enough to meet in person.

Always an avid reader, **Fiona Lowe** decided to combine her love of romance with her interest in all things medical, so writing Mills & Boon® Medical Romance™ was an obvious choice! She lives in a seaside town in southern Australia, where she juggles writing, reading, working and raising two gorgeous sons with the support of her own real-life hero!

Books by Fiona Lowe
Mills & Boon® Medical Romance™

**Visit the author profile page at
millsandboon.co.uk for more titles**

CHAPTER ONE

'WANT TO CLOSE?'

Noah Jackson, senior surgical registrar at the Melbourne Victoria Hospital, smiled behind his mask as he watched the answer to his question glow in the eyes of his surgical intern.

'Do I support The Westies?' Rick Stewart quipped, his eyes alight with enthusiasm. His loyalty to the struggling Australian Rules football team was legendary amongst the staff, who teased him mercilessly.

'For Mrs Levatti's sake, you need to close better than your team plays,' Noah said, knowing full well Rick was more than capable.

There'd be no way he'd allow him to stitch up his patient unless he was three levels above competent. The guy reminded him of himself back in the day when he'd been an intern—keen, driven and determined to succeed.

'Thanks, team.' Noah stepped back from the operating table and stripped off his gloves, his mind already a long way from work. 'It's been a huge week and I've got the weekend off.'

'Lucky bastard,' muttered Ed Yang, the anaesthetist. 'I'm on call for the entire weekend.'

Noah had little sympathy. 'It's my first weekend off in over a month and I'm starting it at the Rooftop with one of their boutique beers.'

'I might see you there later,' Lizzy said casually.

The scout nurse's come-hither green eyes sparkled at him, reminding him of a previous good time together. 'Everyone's welcome,' he added, not wanting to tie himself down to anyone or anything. 'I'll be there until late.'

He strode out and headed purposefully towards the change rooms, savouring freedom. Anticipation bubbled in him as he thought about his hard-earned weekend of sleeping in, cycling along the Yarra, catching a game at the MCG, eating at his favourite café, and finally seeing the French film everyone was talking about. God, he loved Melbourne in the spring and everything that it offered.

'Noah.'

The familiar deep voice behind him made him reluctantly slow and he turned to face the distinguished man the nursing staff called the silver fox.

'You got a minute?' Daniel Serpell asked.

No. But that wasn't a word an intern or registrar ever said to the chief of surgery. 'Sure.'

The older man nodded slowly. 'Great job on that lacerated liver on Tuesday. Impressive.'

The unexpected praise from the hard taskmaster made Noah want to punch the air. 'Thanks. It was touch and go for a bit and we almost put the blood bank into deficit but we won.'

'No one in this hospital has any doubt about your surgical abilities, Noah.'

Something about the way his boss hit the word *surgical* made Noah uneasy. 'That's a good thing, right?'

'There are nine areas of competency to satisfy the Royal Australasian College of Surgeons.'

Noah was familiar with every single one of them now that his final surgical exams were only a few months away. 'Got them all covered, Prof.'

'You might think that, Noah, but others don't agree.' He reached inside his jacket and produced a white envelope with Noah's name printed on it.

'What's this?'

'Your solution to competency number two.'

'I don't follow.'

The prof sighed. 'Noah, I can't fault you on technical skills and I'd trust you to operate on me, my wife and my family. You're talented with your patients when they're asleep but we've had complaints from your dealings with them when they're awake.' He cleared his throat. 'We've also had complaints from staff.'

Noah's gut clenched so tight it burned and the envelope in his hand suddenly developed a crushing weight. 'Is this an official warning?'

'No, not at all,' the prof said genially. 'I'm on your side and this is the solution to your problem.'

'I didn't know I had a problem,' he said, not able to hide his defensiveness.

The professor raised a brow. 'And after this, I hope you won't have one either.'

'You're sending me on a communications course?' The idea of sitting around in a circle with a group of strangers and talking about feelings appalled him.

'Everything you need to know is in the envelope.

Just make sure you're ready to start at eight o'clock on Monday morning.' He clapped a hand on Noah's shoulder. 'Enjoy your weekend off.'

As his boss walked away, Noah's anxiety ramped up ten notches and the pristine, white envelope now ticked like an unexploded bomb. Not wanting to read it in public, he walked quickly to the doctors' lounge, thankfully finding it empty. He ripped open the envelope and scanned the brief letter.

> *Dear Dr Jackson*
> *Your four-week rotation at the Turraburra Medical Clinic commences on Monday, August 17th at eight a.m. Accommodation, if required, is provided at the doctor's flat located on Nautalis Parade. Collect the key from the real estate agent in Williams Street before noon, Saturday. See the enclosed map and tourist information, which we hope will be of assistance to you.*
>
> *Enjoy your rotation in Turraburra—the sapphire of South Gippsland.*
> *Nancy Beveridge*
> *Surgical Trainee Placement Officer.*

No. No way. Noah's intake of breath was so sharp it made him cough. This could *not* be happening. They couldn't do this to him. Not now. Suddenly, the idea of a communications course seemed positively fun.

Relax. You must have read it wrong. Fighting the red heat of rage that was frantically duelling with disbelief, he slowly reread the letter, desperately hoping he'd misunderstood its message. As his eyes scrolled left to right and he slowed his mind down to read each and every word, it made no difference. The grim message the black and white letters told didn't change.

He was being exiled—sent rural—and the timing couldn't be worse. In fact, it totally sucked. Big time. He had less than six months before he sat his final surgical examinations and now more than ever his place was at the Victoria. He should be here, doing cutting-edge surgery, observing the latest technology, attending tutorials and studying. Always studying. He should *not* be stuck in a country clinic day in, day out, listening to the ramblings of patients with chronic health issues that surgery couldn't solve.

General practice. A shudder ran through him at the thought. There was a reason he'd aimed high and fought for his hard-earned place in the surgical programme, and a large part of it was to avoid the mundane routine of being a GP. He had no desire at all to have a long and ongoing connection with patients or get to know their families or be introduced to their dogs. This was blatantly unfair. Why the hell had he been singled out? Damn it, none of the other surgical registrars had been asked to do this.

A vague memory of Oliver Evans bawling him out months ago flickered across his mind but surely that had nothing to do with this. Consultants yelled at registrars from time to time—usually during moments of high stress when the odds were stacked against them and everyone was battling to save a patient's life. Heated words were exchanged, a lot of swearing went down but at the end of the day it was forgotten and all was forgiven. It was all part of the cut and thrust of hospital life.

Logic immediately penetrated his incredulity. The prof had asked him to teach a workshop to the new interns in less than two weeks so this Turraburra couldn't be too far away from downtown Melbourne. Maybe he was just being sent to the growth corridor—the far-flung edges of the ever-growing city, the outer, outer 'burbs. That wouldn't be too bad. A bit of commuting wouldn't kill him and he could listen to his training podcasts on the drive there and back each day.

Feeling more positive, he squinted at the dot on the map.

His expletive rent the air, staining it blue. He'd been banished to the back of beyond.

Lilia Cartwright, never Lil and always Lily to her friends, stood on a whitewashed dock in the ever-brightening, early morning light. She stared out towards the horizon, welcoming the sting of salt against her cheeks, the wind in her hair, and she smiled. 'New day, Chippy,' she said to her tan and white greyhound who stared up at her with enormous, brown, soulful eyes. 'Come on, mate, look a bit more excited. After this walk, you'll have another day ahead of you of lazing about and being cuddled.'

Chippy tugged on his leash as he did every morning when they stood on the dock, always anxious to get back indoors. Back to safety.

Lily loved the outdoors but she understood only too well Chippy's need for safe places. Given his experiences during the first two years of his life, she didn't begrudge him one little bit, but she was starting to think she might need a second dog to go running with to keep fit. Walking with Chippy hardly constituted exercise because she never broke a sweat.

Turning away from the aquamarine sea, she walked towards the Turraburra Medical Centre. In the grounds of the small bush nursing hospital and nursing home, the glorious bluestone building had started life a hundred and thirty years ago as the original doctor's house. Now, fully restored, it was a modern clinic. She particularly loved her annexe—the midwifery clinic and birth centre. Although it was part of the medical centre, it had a separate entrance so her healthy, pregnant clients didn't have to sit in a waiting room full of coughing and hacking sick people. It had been one of the best days of her career when the Melbourne Midwifery Clinic had responded to her grant application and incorporated Turraburra into their outreach programme for rural and isolated women.

The clinic was her baby and she'd taken a lot of time and effort in choosing the soothing, pastel paint and the welcoming décor. She wanted it to feel less like a sterile clinic and far more like visiting someone's home. In a way, given that she'd put so much of herself into the project, the pregnant women and their families were visiting her home.

At first glance, the birthing suite looked like a room in a four-star hotel complete with a queen-sized bed, side tables, lounge chairs, television, bar fridge and a roomy bathroom. On closer inspection, though, it had all the important features found in any hospital room. Oxygen, suction and nitrous oxide outlets were discreetly incorporated in the wall whilst other medical equipment was stored in a cupboard that looked like a wardrobe and it was only brought out when required.

The birth centre didn't cater for high-risk pregnancies—those women were referred to Melbourne, where they could receive the high-tech level of care required for a safe, happy and healthy outcome for mother and baby. The Turraburra women who were deemed to be at a low risk of pregnancy and childbirth complications gave birth here, close to their homes and families. For Lily it was an honour to be part of the birth and to bring a new life into the world.

As Turraburra was a small town, it didn't stop there either. In the three years since she'd returned home and taken on the position of the town's midwife, she'd not only delivered a lot of babies, she'd also attended a lot of children's birthday parties. She loved watching the babies grow up and she could hardly believe that those first babies she'd delivered were now close to starting three-year-old kinder. As her involvement with the babies and children was as close as she was ever likely to get to having a family of her own, she treasured it even more.

Lily stepped into the main part of the clinic and automatically said, 'Morning, Karen,' before she realised the receptionist wasn't behind her desk. Karen's absence reminded her that a new doctor was starting today. Sadly, since the retirement of their beloved Dr Jameson two years ago, this wasn't an uncommon occurrence. She remembered the fuss they'd all made of the first new doctor to arrive in town—ever hopeful he'd be staying for years to come—but he'd left after three months. Seven other doctors had followed in a two-year period and all of the staff, including herself, had become a bit blasé about new arrivals. The gloss had long faded from their hope that *this one* might actually stay for the long term and grand welcoming gestures had fallen by the wayside.

Turraburra, like so many rural towns in Australia, lacked a permanent doctor. It did, however, have more than its fair share of overseas and Australian general practitioner trainees as well as numerous medical students. All of them passed through the clinic and hospital on short stays so they could tick their obligatory rural rotation off their list before hot-footing it back to Melbourne or Sydney or any other major capital city.

The cultural identity that to be Australian was to be at one with the bush was a myth. Australia was the most urbanised country in the world and most people wanted to be a stone's throw from a big city and all the conveniences that offered. Lily didn't agree. She loved Turraburra and it would take a major catastrophe for her to ever live in Melbourne again. She still bore the scars from her last attempt.

Some of the doctors who came to Turraburra were brilliant and the town begged them to stay longer, while others were happily farewelled with a collective sigh of relief and a long slug of fortifying beer or wine at the end of their rotation. Lily had been so busy over the weekend, delivering two babies, that she hadn't had time to open the email she'd received late on Friday with the information about 'doctor number nine'. She wondered if nine was going to be Turraburra's lucky number.

Chippy frantically tugged at his leash again. 'Yes,

I know, we're here. Hang on a second.' She bent down and slid her hand under his wide silver and indigo decorative collar that one of the patients had made for him. It was elegant and had an air of Russian royalty about it, showing off his long and graceful neck. She released the clip from the leash and with far more enthusiasm than he ever showed on a walk, Chippy raced to his large, padded basket in the waiting room and curled up with a contented sigh.

He was the clinic's companion dog and all the patients from the tiny tots to the ninety-year-olds loved and adored him. He basked in the daily stroking and cuddles and Lily hoped his hours of being cosseted went some way towards healing the pain of his early life at the hands of a disreputable greyhound racer. She stroked his long nose. 'You have fun today and I'll see you tonight.'

Chippy smiled in the way only greyhounds can.

She crossed the waiting room and was collecting her mail from her pigeonhole when she heard, 'What the hell is that thing doing in here?'

She flinched at the raised, curt male voice and knew that Chippy would be shivering in his basket. Clutching her folders to her chest like a shield, she marched back into the waiting room. A tall guy with indecently glossy brown hair stood in the middle of the waiting room.

Two things instantly told her he was from out of town. Number one: she'd never met him. Number two: he was wearing a crisp white shirt with a tie that looked to be silk. It sat at his taut, freshly shaven throat in a wide Windsor knot that fitted perfectly against the collar with no hint of a gap or a glimpse of a top button.

The tie was red and it contrasted dramatically with the dark grey pinstriped suit.

No one in Turraburra ever wore a suit unless they were attending a funeral, and even then no man in the district ever looked this neat, tailored, or gorgeous in a suit.

Gorgeous or not, his loud and curt voice had Chippy shrinking into his basket with fear. Her spine stiffened. Working hard at keeping calm and showing no fear, she said quietly, 'I could ask you the same question.'

His chestnut-brown brows arrowed down fast into a dark V, forming a deep crease above the bridge of his nose. He looked taken aback. 'I'm *supposed* to be here.'

She thought she heard him mutter, 'Worse luck,' as he quickly shoved a large hand with neatly trimmed nails out towards her. The abrupt action had every part of her urging her to step back for safety. *Stop it. It's okay.* With great effort she glued her feet to the floor and stayed put but she didn't take her gaze off his wide hand.

'Noah Jackson,' he said briskly. 'Senior surgical registrar at Melbourne Victoria Hospital.'

She instantly recognised his name. She'd rung her friend Ally about him when she'd first heard he was meant to be coming but Ally had felt that there was no way he'd ever come to work at Turraburra. At the time it had made total sense because no surgery was done here anymore, and she'd thought there had just been a mistake. So why was he standing in the clinic waiting room, filling it with his impressive height and breadth?

She realised he was giving her an odd look and his hand was now hovering between them. Slowly, she let her right hand fall from across her chest. 'Lilia Cart-wright. Midwife.'

His palm slid against hers—warm and smooth—and then his long, strong fingers gripped the back of her hand. It was a firm, fast, no-nonsense handshake and it was over quickly, but the memory of the pressure lingered on her skin. She didn't want to think about it. Not that it was awful, it was far from that, but the firm pressure of hands on her skin wasn't something she dwelled on. Ever.

She pulled her hand back across her chest and concentrated on why Noah Jackson was there. 'Has the Turraburra hospital board come into some money? Are they reopening the operating theatre?'

His full lips flattened into a grim line. 'I'm not that lucky.'

'Excuse me?'

'I haven't come here as a surgeon.'

His words punched the air with the pop and fizz of barely restrained politeness, which matched his tight expression. Was he upset? Perhaps he'd come to Tur-raburra for a funeral after all. Her eyes flicked over his suit and, despite not wanting to, she noticed how well it fitted his body. How his trousers highlighted his narrow hips and sat flat against his abdomen. How the tailored jacket emphasised his broad shoulders.

Not safe, Lily. She swallowed and found her voice. 'What have you come as, then?'

He threw out his left arm, gesticulating towards the door. 'I'm this poor excuse of a town's doctor for the next month.'

'No.' The word shot out automatically—deep and

disbelieving—driven from her mouth in defence of her beloved town. In defence of the patients.

Turraburra needed a general practitioner, not a surgeon. The character traits required to become a surgeon—a driven personality, arrogance and high self-belief, along with viewing every patient in terms of 'cutting out the problem'—were so far removed from a perfect match for Turraburra that it was laughable. What on earth was going on at the Melbourne Victoria that made them send a surgical registrar to be a locum GP? Heaven help them all.

His shoulders, already square, vibrated with tension and his brown eyes flashed with flecks of gold. 'Believe me, Ms Cartwright,' he said coldly, 'if I had things my way, I wouldn't be seen dead working here, but the powers that be have other plans. Neither of us has a choice.'

His antagonism slammed into her like storm waves pounding against the pier. She acknowledged that she deserved some of his hostility because her heartfelt, shock-driven 'No' had been impolite and unwelcoming. It had unwittingly put in her a position she avoided— that of making men angry. When it came to men in general she worked hard at going through life very much under their radar. The less she was noticed the better, and she certainly didn't actively set out to make them angry.

She sucked in a breath. 'I'm just surprised the Melbourne Victoria's sent a surgeon to us, but, as you so succinctly pointed out, neither of us has a choice.' She forced herself to smile, but it felt tight around the edges. 'Welcome to Turraburra, Dr Jackson.'

He gave a half grunting, half huffing sound and

swung his critical gaze back to Chippy. 'Get the dog out of here. It doesn't belong in a medical clinic.'

All her guilt about her own rudeness vanished and along with it her usual protective guard. 'Chippy is the clinic's therapy dog. He stays.'

Noah stared at the tall, willowy woman in front of him whose fingers had a death grip on a set of bright pink folders. Her pale cheeks had two bright spots of colour on them that matched her files and her sky-blue eyes sparked with the silver flash of a fencing foil. He was still smarting from her definite and decisive 'No'. He might not want to work in this godforsaken place but who was she to judge him before he'd even started? 'What the hell is a therapy dog?'

'He provides some normalcy in the clinic,' she said, her tone clipped.

'Normalcy?' He gave a harsh laugh, remembering his mother's struggle to maintain any semblance of a normal life after her diagnosis. Remembering all the hours they'd spent in numerous medical practices' waiting rooms, not dissimilar to this one, seeking a cure that had never come. 'This is a medical clinic. It exists for sick people so there's nothing normal about it. And talking about normal, that dog looks far from it.'

She pursed her lips and he noticed how they peaked in a very kissable bow before flushing a deep and enticing red. Usually, seeing something sexy like that on a woman was enough for him to turn on the charm but no way in hell was he doing that with this prickly woman with the fault-finding gaze.

'Chippy's a greyhound,' she snapped. 'They're supposed to be svelte animals.'

'Is that what you call it?' His laugh came out in a snort. 'It looks anorexic to me and what's with the collar? Is he descended from the tsars?'

He knew he was being obnoxious but there was something about Lilia Cartwright and her holier-than-thou tone that brought out the worst in him. Or was it the fact he'd spent the night sleeping on the world's most uncomfortable bed and when he'd finally fallen asleep the harsh and incessant screeching of sulphur-crested cockatoos at dawn had woken him. God, he hated the country.

'Have you quite finished?' she said, her voice so cool he expected icicles to form on her ash-blonde hair. 'Chippy calms agitated patients and the elderly at the nursing home adore him. Some of them don't have anyone in their lives they can lavish affection on and Chippy is more than happy to be the recipient of that love. Medical studies have shown that a companion pet lowers blood pressure and eases emotional distress. Like I said, he absolutely stays.'

An irrational urge filled him to kick something and to kick it hard. He had the craziest feeling he was back in kindergarten and being timed out on the mat for bad behaviour. 'If there's even one complaint or one flea bite, the mutt goes.'

Her brows rose in a perfect arc of condescension. 'In relative terms, Dr Jackson, you're here for a blink of an eye. Chippy will far outstay you.'

The blink of an eye? Who was she kidding? 'I'm here for seven hundred and twenty *very* long hours.'

Her blue eyes rounded. 'You actually counted them?'

He shrugged. 'It seemed appropriate at three a.m.

when the hiss of fighting possums wearing bovver boots on my roof kept me awake.'

She laughed and unexpected dimples appeared in her cheeks. For a brief moment he glimpsed what she might look like if she ever relaxed. It tempted him to join her in laughter but then her tension-filled aura slammed back in place, shutting out any attempts at a connection.

He crossed his arms. 'It wasn't funny.'

'I happen to know you could just have easily been kept awake by fighting possums in the leafy suburbs of Melbourne.'

Were they comrades-in-arms? Both victims of the vagaries of the Melbourne Victoria Hospital that had insisted on sending them to the back of beyond? A bubble of conciliation rose to the top of his dislike for her. 'So you've been forced down here too?'

She shook her head so quickly that her thick and tight French braid swung across her shoulder. 'Turraburra is my home. Melbourne was just a grimy pitstop I was forced to endure when I studied midwifery.'

He thought about his sun-filled apartment in leafy Kew, overlooking Yarra Bend Park. 'My Melbourne's not grimy.'

Again, one brow quirked up in disapproval. 'My Turraburra's not a poor excuse for a town.'

'Well, at least we agree on our disagreement.'

'Do you plan to be grumpy for the entire time you're here?'

Her directness both annoyed and amused him. 'Pretty much.'

One corner of her mouth twitched. 'I guess forewarned is forearmed.' She turned to go and then spun back. 'Oh, and a word to the wise, that is, of course, if you're capable of taking advice on board. I suggest you do things Karen's way. She's run this clinic for fifteen years and outstayed a myriad of medical staff.'

He bit off an acidic retort. He hadn't even met a patient yet but if this last fifteen minutes with Ms Lilia Cartwright, Midwife, was anything to go by, it was going to be a hellishly long and difficult seven hundred and nineteen hours and forty-five minutes in Turraburra.

CHAPTER TWO

'I'M HOME!' LILY CALLED loudly over the blare of the TV so her grandfather had a chance of hearing her.

A thin arm shot up above the top of the couch and waved at her. 'Marshmallow and I are watching re-runs of the doctor. Makes me realise you don't see many phone boxes around any more, do you?'

Lily kissed him affectionately on the top of his head and stroked the sleeping cat as Chippy settled across her grandfather's feet. 'Until the mobile phone reception improves, I think Turraburra's phone box is safe.'

'I just hope I'm still alive by the time the national broadband scheme's rolled out. The internet was so dodgy today it took me three goes before I could check my footy tipping site.'

'A definite tragedy,' she said wryly. Her grandfather loved all sports but at this time of year, with only a few games before the Australian Rules football finals started, he took it all very seriously. 'Did you get down to the community centre today?'

He grunted.

'Gramps?' A ripple of anxiety wove through her that he might have driven to the centre.

Just recently, due to some episodes of numbness in his feet, she'd reluctantly told him it wasn't safe for him to drive. Given how independent he was, he'd been seriously unhappy with that proclamation. It had taken quite some time to convince him but he'd finally seemed to come round and together they'd chosen a mobility scooter. Even at eighty-five, he'd insisted on getting a red one because everyone knew red went faster.

It was perfect for getting around Turraburra and, as she'd pointed out to him, he didn't drive out of town much anyway. But despite all the logic behind the decision, the 'gopher', as he called it, had stayed in the garage. Lily was waiting for him to get sick of walking everywhere and start using it.

'I took the gopher,' he said grumpily. 'Happy?'

'I'm happy you went to your class at the centre.'

'Well, I couldn't let Muriel loose on the computer. She'd muck up all the settings and, besides, it was my day to teach the oldies how to edit photos.'

She pressed her lips together so she didn't laugh, knowing from experience it didn't go down well. He might be in his eighties but his mind was as sharp as a tack and he was young at heart, even if his body was starting to fail him. She ached when she thought of how much he hated that. Losing the car had been a bitter blow.

The 'oldies' he referred to were a group of frail elderly folk from the retirement home. Many were younger than him and made him look positively spry. He was interested in anything and everything and involved in the life of the town. He loved keeping abreast of all the latest technology, loved his top-of-the-range digital camera and he kept busy every day. His passion and enthusiasm for life often made her feel that hers was pale and listless in comparison.

He was her family and she loved him dearly. She owed him more than she could ever repay.

'Muriel sent over a casserole for dinner,' he said, rising to his feet.

'That was kind of her.' Muriel and Gramps had a very close friendship and got along very well as long as she didn't touch his computer and he didn't try to organise her pantry into some semblance of order.

He walked towards the kitchen. 'She heard about the Hawker and De'Bortolli babies and knew you'd be tired. No new arrivals today?'

Lily thought about the tall, dark, ill-tempered surgical registrar who'd strode into her work world earlier in the day.

You forgot good looking.

No. Handsome belongs to someone who smiles.

Really? Trent smiled a lot and look how well that turned out.

She pulled her mind back fast from that thought because the key to her mental health was to never think about Trent. Ever. 'A new doctor's arrived in town.'

His rheumy, pale blue eyes lit up. 'Male or female?'

'Sorry, Gramps. I know how you like to flirt with the female doctors but this one's a difficult bloke.' She couldn't stop the sigh that followed.

His face pulled down in a worried frown. 'Has he done something?'

Since the nightmare of her relationship with Trent, Gramps had been overprotective of her, and she moved to reassure him. 'No, nothing like that and I'm stronger now. I don't take any crap from anyone any more. I just know he's not a natural fit for Turraburra.'

'We're all entitled to one bad day—give the poor guy a minute to settle in. You and Karen will have him trained up in the Turraburra ways in no time flat.'

I wish. 'I'm not so sure about that, Gramps. In fact, the only thing I have any confidence about at all is that it's going to be a seriously long month.'

Noah stood on the town beach, gulping in great lung-fuls of salt air like it was the last drop of oxygen on the planet. Not that he believed in any of that positive-ions nonsense but he was desperate to banish the scent of air freshener with a urine chaser from his nostrils. From his clothes. From his skin.

His heart rate thundered hard and fast like it did after a long run, only this time its pounding had nothing to do with exercise and everything to do with anxiety. Slowing his breathing, he pulled in some long, controlled deep breaths and shucked off the cloak of claustrophobia that had come out of nowhere, engulfing him ten minutes earlier. It had been years since something like that had happened and as a result he'd thought he'd conquered it, but all it had taken was two hours at the Turraburra nursing home. God, he hated this town.

He'd arrived at the clinic at eight to be told by the efficient Karen that Tuesday mornings meant rounds at the nursing home. He'd crossed the grounds of the hospital where the bright spring daffodils had mocked him with their cheery and optimistic colour. He hadn't felt the slightest bit cheery. The nurse in charge of the nursing home had given him a bundle of patient histories and a stack of drug sheets, which had immediately put paid to his plan of dashing in and dashing out.

Apparently, it had been three weeks since there'd been a doctor in Turraburra and his morning was consumed by that added complication. The first hour had passed relatively quickly by reviewing patient histories. After that, things had gone downhill fast as he'd examined each elderly patient. Men who'd once stood tall and strong now lay hunched, droop-faced and dribbling, rendered rigid by post-stroke muscle contractions. Women had stared at him with blank eyes—eyes that had reminded him of his mother's. Eyes that had told him they knew he could do nothing for them.

God, he hated that most. It was the reason he'd pursued surgery—at least when he operated on someone, he usually made a difference. He had the capacity to heal, to change lives, but today, in the nursing home, he hadn't been able to do any of that. All he'd been able to do had been to write prescriptions, suggest physiotherapy and recommend protein shakes. The memories of his mother's long and traumatic suffering had jeered at the idea that any of it added to their quality of life.

He'd just finished examining the last patient when the aroma of cabbage and beef, the scent of pure soap and lavender water and the pervading and cloying smell of liberally used air freshener had closed in on him. He'd suddenly found it very hard to breathe. He'd fled fast—desperate for fresh air—and in the process he'd rudely rejected the offer of tea and biscuits from the nurses.

He knew that wouldn't grant him any favours with

the staff but he didn't care. In six hundred and ninety-six hours he'd be back in Melbourne. Pulling out his smartphone, he set up a countdown and called it T-zero. Now, whenever the town got to him, he didn't have to do the mental arithmetic, he could just open the app and easily see how many hours until he could walk away from Turraburra without a backward glance.

The fresh, salty air and the long, deep breaths had done the trick and, feeling back in control, he jogged up the beach steps. Sitting on the sea wall, he took off his shoes to empty them of sand.

'Yoo-hoo, Dr Jackson.'

He glanced up to see a line of cycling, fluoro-clad women—all who looked to be in their sixties—bearing down on him fast. The woman in front was waving enthusiastically but with a bicycle helmet on her head and sunglasses on her face he didn't recognise her.

He gave a quick nod of acknowledgment.

She must have realised he had no clue who she was because when she stopped the bike in front of him, she said, 'Linda Sampson, Doctor. We met yesterday morning at the corner store. I gave you directions to the clinic and sold you a coffee.'

Weak as water and undrinkable coffee. 'Right, yes.'

'It's good to see you're settling in. Turraburra has the prettiest beach this side of Wilson's Promontory, don't you think?'

He opened his mouth to say he didn't really have a lot of experience with beaches but she kept right on talking. 'The town's got a lot to offer, especially to families. Are you married, Dr Jackson?'

'No.' He banged his sandy shoe against the sea wall

harder than necessary, pining for the anonymity of a big city where no one would think to stop and talk to him if he was sitting on the sea wall at the Middle Park beach.

His life had been put on hold once already and he had no intention of tying himself down to another human being, animal or fish. 'I'm happily single.' If he'd hoped that by telling her that it would get the woman to back off, he was mistaken.

'There's a fine line between happily single and happily coupled up,' Linda said with the enthusiastic smile of a matchmaker. 'And you're in luck. There are some lovely young women in town. The radiographer, Heather Barton, is single.'

One of the other women called out, 'Actually, she's dating Emma Trewella now.'

'Is she? Well, that explains a lot,' Linda said with a laugh. 'Still, that leaves the physiotherapist. She's a gorgeous girl and very into her triathlons. Do you like sports, Doctor?'

He stared at her slack-jawed. Had he been catapulted backwards in time to 1950? He couldn't believe this woman was trying to set him up with someone.

'Or perhaps you'd have more in common with the nurses?' Linda continued. 'I'm sure three of them aren't dating anyone at the moment...'

The memory of ringless white hands gripping pink folders and sky-blue eyes sparking silver arcs shot unbidden into his mind.

'Lucy, Penny and...' Linda paused, turning towards her group. 'What's the name of the pretty nurse with the blonde hair?'

Lilia. He tied his shoe laces with a jerk and reminded

himself that he wasn't looking to date anyone and even if he had been, he most certainly wasn't going to date her. Despite her angelic good looks, her personality was at the opposite end of the spectrum. He wouldn't be surprised if she had horns and carried a pitchfork.

'Grace,' someone said. 'Although is she truly blonde?'

Noah stood up quickly, dusting his black pants free of sand. 'That's quite an extensive list, Linda, but I think you've forgotten someone.'

She shook her head, the magpie deterrent cable ties on her helmet swinging wildly. 'I don't think I have.'

'What about the midwife?'

He thought he heard a collective intake of breath from the other women and Linda's smile faltered. 'Lily's married to her job, Doctor. You're much better off dating one of the others.'

The words came with an undercurrent of a warning not to go there. Before he could ask her why, there was a flurry of ringing bike bells, called farewells and the group took off along the path—a bright slash of iridescent yellow wobbling and weaving towards the noon sun.

Lily stared at the appointment sheet and groaned. How could she have forgotten the date? It was the midwifery centre's bi-monthly doctor clinic. Why had the planets aligned to make it this month? Why not next month when Noah Jackson would be long gone and far, far away? The luck of the Irish or any other nationality was clearly not running her way today. She was going to have to work in close proximity with him all afternoon. Just fantastic…not!

As the town's midwife, Lily operated independently under the auspices of the Melbourne Midwifery Unit. When a newly pregnant woman made contact with her, she conducted a preliminary interview and examination. Some women, due to pre-existing medical conditions such as diabetes or a multiple pregnancy, she immediately referred to the obstetricians at the Victoria or to the Dandenong District Hospital but most women fitted the criteria to be under her care.

However, it wasn't her decision alone. Like the other independent midwife-run birth units it was modelled on, all pregnant Turraburra clients had to be examined by a doctor once in early pregnancy. Lily scheduled these appointments to take place with the GP on one afternoon every two months. Today was the day.

Her computer beeped with an instant message from Karen.

Grumpy guts is on his way. Good luck! I've put Tim Tams in the kitchen. You'll need three after working with him all afternoon.

Karen had been having a whinge in the tearoom earlier in the day about Dr Jackson. She'd called him cold, curt and a control freak. Lily was used to Karen getting defensive with new staff members who questioned her but she couldn't believe Noah Jackson could be quite as bad as Karen made out. She'd offered Karen chocolate and wisely kept her own counsel.

'You ready?'

The gruff tone had her swinging around on her office chair. Noah stood in the doorway with his sleeves rolled up to his elbows and one hand pressed up against the doorjamb—muscles bunched and veins bulging. A flicker of something momentarily stirred low in her belly—something she hadn't experienced in a very long time. Fear immediately clenched her muscles against it, trying to force it away. For her own safety she'd locked down her sexual response three years ago and it had to stay that way.

Unlike yesterday, when Noah had looked like the quintessential urban professional, today he was rumpled. His thick hair was wildly wind-ruffled, his tie was stuffed in between the third and fourth buttons of his business shirt and his black trousers bore traces of sand. Had he spent his lunch break at the beach? She loved the calming effects of the ocean and often took ten minutes to regroup between clinic sessions. Perhaps he wasn't as stuck up as she'd first thought. 'Been enjoying the beach?'

Shadows crossed his rich chocolate eyes. 'I wouldn't go so far as to say that.'

She tried hard not to roll her eyes. Perish the thought he might actually find something positive about Turraburra. *Stick to talking about work.* 'Today's clinic is all about—'

'Pregnant women. Yeah, I get it. You do the obs, test their urine and weigh them and leave the rest to me.'

I don't think so. She stood up because sitting with him staring down at her from those arcane eyes she felt way too vulnerable. Three years ago she'd made a commitment to herself that she was never again going to leave herself open to be placed in a powerless position with another human being. Even in low heels she was closer to his height.

'These women are my patients and this is a rubber-stamping exercise so they can be part of the midwifery programme.'

His nostrils flared. 'As the *doctor*, isn't it my decision?'

Spare me from non-team-players. 'I'm sorry, I thought you were a surgical registrar but suddenly you're moonlighting as an obstetrician?'

His cheekbones sharpened as he sucked in a breath through his teeth and she reeled in her fraying temper. What was it about this man that made her break her own rules of never reacting? Of never provoking a man to anger? Of never putting herself at risk? She also didn't want to give Noah Jackson any excuse to dismiss her as *that crazy midwife* and interfere with her programme.

'I take that back. As Turraburra's midwife, with five years' experience, anyone I feel doesn't qualify for the programme has already been referred on.'

His gaze hooked hers, brimming with discontent. 'So, in essence, this clinic is a waste of my time?'

'It's protocol.'

'Fine.' He spun on his heel, crossed the hall and disappeared into the examination room.

She sighed and hurried in after him.

'Bec,' she said to the pregnant woman who was sitting, waiting, 'this is Dr Jackson, our current locum GP. As I explained, he'll be examining you today.'

Bec Sinclair, a happy-go-lucky woman, gave an expansive smile. 'No worries. Good to meet you, Doc.'

Noah sat down behind the desk and gave her a brisk

nod before turning his attention to the computer screen and reading her medical history. He frowned. 'You had a baby eight months ago and you're pregnant again?'

Bec laughed at his blatant disapproval. 'It was a bit of a surprise, that's for sure.'

'I gather you weren't organised enough to use contraception.'

Lily's jaw dropped open. She couldn't believe he'd just said that.

Bec, to her credit, didn't seem at all fazed by his rudeness. 'It was a dodgy condom but no harm done. We wanted another baby so the fact it's coming a year earlier than planned is no biggie.' She leaned towards the desk, showing Noah a photo of her little boy on her phone. 'Lily delivered Harley, and Jase and I really want her to deliver this next one too.'

'It will be my pleasure. Harley's really cute, isn't he, Noah?' Lily said, giving him an opening for some chit-chat and hoping he'd respond.

Noah ignored her and the proffered photo. Instead, he pushed back from the desk, stood and pulled the curtain around the examination table. Patting it with his hand, he said, 'Up you get.'

Bec exchanged a look with Lily that said *Is this guy for real?* before rising and climbing up the three small steps.

Lily made her comfortable and positioned the modesty sheet before returning to stand by Bec's head. Noah silently listened to her heart, examined her breasts and then her abdomen. Lily kept up a patter, explaining to Bec everything that Noah was doing because, apparently, he'd turned mute.

When the examination was over and Bec was back in the chair, Noah said, 'Everything seems fine, except that you're fat.'

Bec paled.

'What Dr Jackson means,' Lily said hurriedly, as she threw at him what she hoped was a venomous look, 'is that you're still carrying some weight from your last pregnancy.'

'That's not what I meant at all.' Noah pulled up a BMI chart, spun the computer screen towards Bec and pointed to the yellow overweight zone where it met the red obese one. 'Right now, you're just below the border of obese. If you're not careful during this pregnancy, you'll tip into the red zone. That will put you at risk of complications such as gestational diabetes, pre-eclampsia and thrombosis. There's also an increased risk that the baby may end up being in a difficult position such as breech. All of those things would make you ineligible to be delivered by Lilia at the birth centre.'

'I want to have my baby here,' Bec said, her voice suddenly wobbly.

'Then make sure you exercise and eat healthy foods. It's that simple.' Noah turned to Lily. 'I assume you have information for your patients about that sort of thing.'

'I do,' she managed to grind out between clenched teeth. 'If you come with me, Bec, I'll give the pamphlets to you now as well as the water aerobics timetable. It's a fun way to exercise and there's a crèche at the pool.'

She escorted Bec from the room and gave her all the information, along with small packet of tissues. 'Come and see me tomorrow and we'll talk about it all then in greater detail. Okay?'

Bec nodded and sniffed. 'I kinda knew I'd got big but it was hard hearing it.'

Lily could have killed Noah. 'I'm so sorry.'

'Don't be. It's not your fault.' Bec gave a long sigh. 'I guess I needed to hear it.'

She gave Bec's shoulder a squeeze. 'Only in a kinder way.'

'Yeah.' Bec took in a deep breath. 'I didn't know being heavy could make things dangerous for me and the baby, and I guess it's good that he told me because I don't want to have to go to Melbourne. I know Mandy Carmichael's preggers again and she's pretty big. Maybe we can help each other, you know?'

Lily smiled encouragingly. 'That sounds like a great plan.'

As Bec left, Karen buzzed her. 'Kat Nguyen's rescheduled for later today so you've got a gap.'

As Lily hung up the phone she knew exactly what she was going to do with her free half-hour, whether she wanted to take that risk or not.

Noah glanced up as Lily walked back into the office alone. Her face was tight with tension and disapproving lines bracketed her mouth, pulling it down at the edges. An irrational desire to see her smile tugged at him and that on its own annoyed him. So what if a smile made her eyes crinkle at the edges with laughter lines and caused dimples to score her cheeks? So what if a smile made her light up, look happy and full of life and chased away her usual closed-off sangfroid? Made her look pretty?

He tried to shake off the feeling. It was nothing to

him whether she was happy or not. Whether she was a workaholic or not, like the ladies at the beach had told him. Whether she was anything other than the pain in the rear that she'd already proved to be. He didn't have time in his life for a woman who was fun, let alone one with dragon tendencies. 'Where's the next patient?'

She crossed her arms. 'She's running late.'

He'd already pegged her as a person who liked things to go her own way and a late patient would throw out her schedule. 'So that's why you're looking like you've just sucked on a lemon. Surely you know nothing in the medical profession ever runs on time.'

Her eyes rounded and widened so far he could have tumbled into their pale, azure depths. 'Are you stressed or ill?'

'No,' he said, seriously puzzled. 'Why would you say that?'

She walked closer to the desk. 'So you're just naturally rude.'

Baffled by her accusations, he held onto his temper by the barest of margins. That surprised him. Usually he'd have roared like a lion if a nurse or anyone more junior to him had dared to speak to him like this. 'Where's all this antagonism coming from? Did something happen to upset you while you were out of the room?'

'Where's all this coming from?' Incredulity pushed her voice up from its usual throaty depths. 'You just told Bec Sinclair she's fat.'

He didn't get why she was all het up. 'So? I said that because she is.'

She pressed her palms down on the desk and as she leaned in he caught the light scent of spring flowers and something else he couldn't name. 'Yes, but you didn't have to tell her quite so baldly. Do you ever think before you speak?'

Her accusation had him shooting to his feet to rectify the power balance. 'Of course I do. She needed to know the risks that her weight adds to her pregnancy. I told her the truth.'

Her light brown brows hit her hairline. 'You're brutally blunt.'

'No. I'm honest with them.'

She shook her head back and forth so fast he thought she'd give herself whiplash. 'Oh, no, you're not getting away with that. There are ways of telling someone the truth and you're using it as an excuse to be thoughtless and rude.'

She'd just crossed the line in the sand he'd already moved for her. 'Look, Miss Manners,' he said tersely. 'You don't have the right to storm in here and accuse me of being rude.'

Her shoulders rolled back like an Amazon woman preparing for battle. 'I do when it affects *my* patients. You just reduced the most laid-back, easygoing woman I know to tears.'

A pang of conscience jabbed him. Had he really done that? 'She was upset?'

She threw her hands up. 'You think? Yes, of course she was upset.'

He rubbed his hand over the back of his neck as he absorbed that bit of information. 'I didn't realise I'd upset her.'

Lily dropped into the chair, her expression stunned. 'You're kidding me, right?'

No. Man, he hated general practice with its touchy-feely stuff and rules that he hadn't known existed. He was a surgeon and a damn good one. He diagnosed problems and then he cut them out. As a result, he gave people a better quality of life. It was a far easier way of dealing with problems than the muddy waters of internal medicine where nothing was cut and dried and everything was hazy with irrational hope.

He and his mother had learned that the hard way and after that life-changing experience he'd vowed he would always give his patients the truth. Black was black and white was white. People needed information so they could make a choice.

The prof's voice came out of nowhere, echoing loudly in his head. *We've had complaints from your dealings with patients when they're awake.*

His legs trembled and he sat down hard, nausea churning his gut. Was this the sort of thing the prof had been referring to? Propping his elbows on the desk, he ran his hands through his hair and tried to marshal his thoughts. Did Lilia actually have a point? Was his interpretation of the facts blunt and thoughtless?

He instantly railed against the idea, refusing to believe it for a moment. *We've had complaints.* The prof's words were irrefutable. As much as he didn't want to acknowledge it, *this* was the reason he'd been sent down here to Turraburra. It seemed he really did have a problem communicating with patients. A problem he hadn't been fully aware of until this moment. A problem that was going to stop him from qualifying as a surgeon if he didn't do something about it.

'Noah?'

There was no trace of the previous anger in her voice and none of the sarcasm. All he could hear was concern. He raised his eyes to hers, his gaze stalling on the lushness of her lips. Pink and moist, they were slightly parted. Kissable. Oh, so very kissable. What they would taste like? Icy cool, like her usual demeanour, or sizzling hot, like she'd been a moment ago when she'd taken him to task? Or sweet and decadently rich? Perhaps sharply tart with a kick of fire?

The tip of her tongue suddenly darted out, flicking the peak of her top lip before falling back. Heat slammed into him, rushing lust through him and down into every cell as if he were an inexperienced teen. Hell, he had more control than this. He sucked in a breath and gave thanks he was sitting down behind a desk, his lap hidden from view.

He shifted his gaze to the safety of her nose, which, although it suited her face, wasn't cute or sexy. This brought his traitorous body back under control. He didn't want to be attracted to Lilia Cartwright in any shape or form. He just wanted to get this time in Turraburra over and done with and get the hell out of town. Get back to the security of the Melbourne Victoria and to the job he loved above all else.

Her previously flinty gaze was now soft and caring. 'Noah, is everything okay?'

Everything's so far from okay it's not funny. Could he tell her the real reason the Victoria had sent a surgeon to Turraburra? Tell her that if he didn't conquer this communication problem he wouldn't qualify? That ten years of hard work had failed to give him what he so badly wanted?

For the first time since he'd met her he saw genuine interest and empathy in her face and a part of him desperately wanted to reach out and confide in her. God knew, if he'd unwittingly upset a patient and been clueless about the impact of his words, he surely needed help.

She'll understand.

You don't know that. She could just as easily use it against me.

He'd fought long and hard to get this far in the competitive field of surgery without depending on anyone and he didn't intend to start now. That said, he'd noticed how relaxed she was with her patients compared to how he always felt with them. With Bec Sinclair, she'd explained everything he'd been doing, chatting easily to her. She connected with people in a way he'd never been able to—in a way he needed to learn.

He had no intention of asking her for help or exposing any weakness, but that didn't mean he couldn't observe and learn from her. *Don't give anything away.* Leaning back, he casually laced his fingers behind his head. 'Do you have any other fat pregnant women coming in today?'

Wariness crawled across her high cheekbones. 'There is one more.'

'Do you concede that her weight is a risk to her pregnancy?'

'Yes, but—'

'Good.' He sat forward fast, the chair clunking loudly. 'This time you run the consultation, which means you're the one who has to tell her that her weight is a problem.'

She blinked at him in surprise and then her intelligent eyes narrowed, scanning his face like an explosives expert looking for undetonated bombs. 'And?'

'And then I'll critique your performance like you just critiqued mine. After all, the Victoria's a teaching hospital so it seems only fair.'

He couldn't help but grin at her stunned expression.

CHAPTER THREE

LILY TURNED THE music up and sang loudly as she drove through the rolling hills and back towards the coast and Turraburra. As well as singing, she concentrated on the view. Anything to try and still her mind and stop it from darting to places she didn't want it to go.

She savoured the vista of black and white cows dotted against the emerald-green paddocks—the vibrant colour courtesy of spring rains. Come January, the grass would be scorched brown and the only green would be the feathery tops of the beautiful white-barked gum-trees.

She'd been out at the Hawkers' dairy farm, doing a follow-up postnatal visit. Jess and the baby were both doing well and Richard had baked scones, insisting she stay for morning tea. She'd found it hard to believe that the burly farmer was capable of knocking out a batch of scones, because the few men who'd passed through her life hadn't been cooks. When she'd confessed her surprise to Richard, he'd just laughed and said, 'If I depended on Jess to cook, we'd both have starved years ago.'

'I have other talents,' Jess, the town's lawyer, said without rancour.

'That you do,' Richard had replied with such a look of love and devotion in his eyes that it had made Lily's throat tighten.

She'd grown up hearing the stories from her grandfather of her parents' love for each other but she had no memory of it. Somehow it had always seemed like a story just out of reach—like a fairy-tale and not at all real. Sure, she had their wedding photo framed on her dresser but plenty of people got married and it ended in recriminations and pain. She was no stranger to that scenario and she often wondered if her parents had lived longer lives, they would still be together.

Although her grandfather loved her dearly, she'd never known the sort of love that Jess and Richard shared. She'd hoped for it when she'd met Trent and had allowed herself to be seduced by the idea of it. She'd learned that when a fairy-tale met reality, the fall-out was bitter and life-changing. As a result, and for her own protection, and in a way for the protection of her mythical child, she wasn't prepared to risk another relationship. The only times she questioned her decision was when she saw true love in action, like today.

Her loud, off-key singing wasn't banishing her unsettling thoughts like it usually did. Ever since Noah Jackson had burst into Turraburra—all stormy-eyed and difficult—troubling thoughts had become part of her again. She couldn't work him out. She wanted to say he was rude, arrogant, self-righteous and exasperating, and dismiss him out of her head. He was definitely all of those things but then there were moments when he looked so adrift—like yesterday when he'd appeared genuinely stunned and upset that his words had distressed Bec Sinclair. She couldn't work him out.

You don't have to work him out. You don't have to work any man out. Remember, it's safer not to even try.

Except that momentary look of bewilderment on his face had broken through his *I'm a surgeon, bow down before me* facade, and it had got to her. It had humanised him and she wished it hadn't. Arrogant Noah was far more easily dismissed as a temporary thorn in her side than thoughtful Noah. The Noah who'd sat back and listened intently and watched without a hint of disparagement as she'd talked with Mandy Carmichael about her weight was an intriguing conundrum.

She braked at the four-way intersection and proceeded to turn right, passing the *Welcome to Turraburra* sign. She smiled at the '+1' someone had painted next to the population figure. Given the number of pregnant women in town at the moment, she expected to see a lot more graffiti over the coming months. Checking the clock on the dash, she decided that she had just enough time to check in on her grandfather before starting afternoon clinic.

Her phone beeped as it always did when she drove back into town after being in a mobile phone reception dead zone. This time, instead of one or two messages, it vibrated wildly as six messages came in one after another. She immediately pulled over.

11:00 Unknown patient in labour. Go to hospital. Karen.

11:15 Visitor to town in established labour in Emergency. Your assistance appreciated.
N. Jackson.

'What have you done with the Noah Jackson I know and despair of?' she said out loud. The formal style of Noah's text was unexpected and it made Karen's seem almost brusque in comparison. The juxtaposition made her smile.

11:50 Contractions now two minutes apart. Last baby I delivered was six years ago. Request immediate assistance.
NJ.

12:10 Where the bloody hell are you?!
N.

'And he's back.' Although, to give Noah his due, she'd be totally stressed out if she was being asked to do something she hadn't done in a very long time. She threw the car into gear, checked over her shoulder and pulled off the gravel. Three minutes later she was running into Emergency to the familiar groans of a woman in transition.

For the first time since arriving in Turraburra, Noah was genuinely happy to see starchy and standoffish Lilia Cartwright, Midwife. 'You don't text, you don't call,' he tried to joke against a taut throat. Trying to stop himself from yelling, *I'm freaking out here and where the hell have you been?*

'Sorry,' she said breezily. 'I was out of range.'

'Seriously?' Her statement stunned him. 'You don't have mobile reception when you leave town? That's not safe for your patients. What if a woman delivers when you're not here?'

'Welcome to the country, Noah. We'd love to have the communications coverage that you get in the city but the infrastructure isn't here.'

'How can people live like this?' he muttered, adding yet another reason to his long list of why country life sucked.

'I always let Karen know where I am and a message gets to me eventually.'

'Oh, and that's so very reassuring.'

She rolled her eyes. 'I'm here now so you can stop panicking.'

Indignation rolled through him. 'I. Do. Not. Panic.'

'I'm sure you don't when you're in your beloved operating theatre, but this isn't your area of expertise and it's normal to be nervous when you're out of your comfort zone.'

Her expression was devoid of any judgement. In fact, all he could read on her face was understanding and that confused him. Made him suspicious. If surgery had taught him anything it was that life was a competition. Any sign of weakness would and could be used to further someone else's career. He'd expected her to take this as another opportunity to show him up. Highlight his failings, as she'd done so succinctly yesterday. He'd never expected her to be empathetic.

As she pulled on a disposable plastic apron she flicked her braid to one side, exposing her long, creamy neck.

He was suddenly engulfed by the scent of apples, cherries and mangoes, which took him straight back to the memories of long-past summers growing up and fruit salad and ice cream.

Regret that midwives no longer wore gowns slugged him hard. Back in the day he would have needed to tie her gown and his fingers would have brushed against that warm, smooth skin. His heart kicked up at the thought, pumping heat through him.

What are you doing? She's so not your type and you don't even like her.

That was true on all fronts. He limited his dating to women who were fun, flirty and only interested in a good time. A good time that ended the moment they planned beyond two weeks in advance. Somehow he got the feeling that Lilia wasn't that type of woman.

With the apron tied, she lifted her head and caught him staring at her. Her fingers immediately brushed her cheeks. 'What? Do I have jam or cream on my mouth from morning tea?'

'No.' Embarrassment made the word sound curt and sharp and she tensed. He instantly regretted his tone and sighed. 'Sorry. Can I please tell you about your patient?'

'Yes.' She sounded as relieved as him. 'Fill me in.'

Happy to be back in familiar territory, he commenced a detailed patient history. 'Jade Riccardo, primigravida, thirty-seven weeks pregnant. She's been visiting relatives in town and arrived here an hour ago in established labour. Foetal heart rate's strong and, going on my rusty palpation skills, the baby's in an anterior position. Her husband's with her but they're both understandably anxious because they're booked in to have the baby in Melbourne.'

A long, loud groan came from the other side of the door. 'Sounds like she's going to have it in Turraburra and very soon.' Lilia grinned up at him, her dimples diving deep into her cheeks and her eyes as bright as a summer's day. She was full of enthusiastic anticipation while he was filled with dread. She tugged on his arm. 'Come on, then. Let's go deliver a baby.'

The heat of her hand warmed him and he missed it when she pulled it away. He followed her into the room and introduced her. 'Jade, Paul, this is Lilia Cartwright, Turraburra's midwife.'

Jade, who was fully in the transition zone, didn't respond. She was on all fours, rocking back and forth and sucking on nitrous oxide like it was oxygen.

Paul was rubbing Jade's back and he threw a grateful look to both of them. 'Are you sure everything's okay? She's doing a lot of grunting.'

Lilia smiled. 'That's great. It means she's working with her body and getting ready to push the baby out.' She rested her hand on Jade's shoulder. 'Hi, Jade. I know this is all moving faster than you expected and it's not happening where you expected, but lots of babies have been born in Turraburra, haven't they, Noah?'

'Yes.'

She rolled her eyes.

Beads of sweat pooled on Noah's brow. Her resigned look spoke volumes, telling him he was failing at something. He looked at the husband, whose face was tight with worry. 'Lots of babies,' he echoed Lilia, practising how to be reassuring and hoping he could pull it off.

'It might not be Melbourne but you're in good hands.'
Lilia's hands.

Paul visibly relaxed. 'That's good to know.'

Lilia placed one hand on Jade's abdomen and her other on her buttocks. 'With the next contraction, Jade, I want you to push down here.'

Jade groaned.

'Your tummy's tightening. I can feel one coming now.'

Jade sucked on the nitrous oxide and then pushed, making a low guttural sound.

Lilia pulled on gloves. 'You're doing great, Jade. I can see some black hair.'

Paul stroked Jade's hair, his face excited. 'Did you hear that, honey?'

Contraction over, Jade slumped down onto the pillows. 'I can't do this.'

'You're already doing it, Jade,' Lilia said calmly. 'Every contraction takes you closer to holding your baby in your arms.'

Noah, feeling as useless as a bike without wheels, did what he knew best—busied himself with the surgical instruments. He snapped on gloves, unwrapped the sterilised delivery pack, set out the bowl, the forceps and scissors, and added the cord clamps, all the while listening to Lilia's soothing voice giving instructions and praising Jade.

They developed a rhythm, with Paul encouraging Jade, Lilia focusing on the baby's descent and Noah checking the baby's heartbeat after each contraction. Each time the rushing sound of horses' hooves sounded, Paul would grin at him and he found himself smiling back. With each contraction, the baby's head moved down a little further until twenty minutes later it sat bulging on the perineum, ready to be born.

'I think you're going to have your baby with the next contraction,' Lilia said as her fingers controlled the baby's head. 'Pant, Jade, pant.'

Jade tried to pant and then groaned. 'Can't.' With a loud grunt, she pushed. A gush of fluid heralded the baby's head, which appeared a moment later, its face scrunched and surprised.

'The baby's head is born. Well done,' Lilia said.

'Our baby's nearly here, honey,' Paul's voice cracked with emotion. 'I can see the head.

'I want it to stop,' Jade sobbed. 'It's too hard.'

Noah looked at the sweaty and exhausted woman who'd endured an incredibly fast and intense labour. She was so very close to finishing and he recalled how once he'd almost stopped running in a marathon because his body had felt like it had been melting in pain. A volunteer had called out to him, 'You've done the hard yards, mate, keep going, the prize is in sight.' It was exactly what he'd needed to hear and it had carried him home.

'The hard work's over, Jade,' he said quietly. 'You can do this. One more push.' He caught Lilia's combined look of surprise and approval streak across her face and he had a ridiculous urge to high-five someone.

Jade's hand shot out and gripped Noah's shoulder, her wild eyes fixed on his. 'Promise?'

'Promise.'

'Noah's right, Jade,' Lilia confirmed. 'With the next contraction, I'll deliver the baby's shoulders and the rest of him or her will follow.'

'Okay. I can feel a contraction *noooooow*.' Jade pushed.

A dusky baby slithered into Lilia's arms and something deep down inside Noah moved. It had been years since he'd been present at a birth and he'd forgotten how amazing it was to witness the arrival of new life into the world.

Lilia clamped the umbilical cord before asking the stunned father, 'Do you want to cut the cord, Paul?'

'Yes.' With shaking hands, Paul cut where Lilia indicated and then said, with wonder in his voice, 'It's a little girl, Jade.'

Noah rubbed the baby with a towel and took note of her breathing and colour and muscle tone so he could give an Apgar score for the first minute of life. The baby hadn't cried but her dark eyes were bright and gazing around, taking in this new world. A lump formed in his throat and he immediately tried to get rid of it because emotion opened a guy up to being weak and vulnerable.

'I'm going to pass the baby between your legs, Jade,' Lilia said. 'Are you ready?'

'My arms are shaking and I'm getting another contraction.'

Paul took the baby, cradling her in his arms while Lilia delivered the placenta. As she examined it, Noah helped Jade roll over. 'In an hour we can transfer you to the midwifery unit. You'll be a lot more comfortable there.'

Paul reverently passed his daughter to his wife. 'Meet Jasmine.'

Silent tears rolled down Jade's cheeks as she unwrapped the baby and counted her fingers and toes. 'Hey, sweetie, I'm your mummy.'

Noah stepped back, moving to the corner of the room and standing next to Lilia, who was breathing deeply. He glanced at her. Her beautiful blue eyes shone with unshed tears but her face was wreathed in a smile. She was luminous with joy and it radiated from her like white light.

With a jolt, he realised this was the first time he'd ever seen her look truly happy. It called out to him so strongly that his body leaned in of its own accord until his head was close to hers and her fresh, fruity perfume filled his nostrils. He wanted to wrap his arms around her, kiss her long and slow and harvest her jubilation. Keep it safe.

Get a grip. You're at work and this is Lilia, remember? The ice queen and dragon rolled into one.

Shocked at what he'd almost done, he covered by saying quietly so only she could hear, 'You did an amazing job. It was very impressive.' The words came out rough and gruff and he jerked his head back, putting much-needed distance between them.

'Thanks.' She blew her nose. 'Sorry. I'm a bit of a sook and it gets to me every time.'

He took in the new family—their love and awe swirling around them in a life-affirming way. It both warmed and scared him. 'I guess I can understand that.'

She tilted her head and gave him a long, considering look. 'I'm glad. You did okay yourself.'

In his world, okay didn't come close to being good enough. 'Just okay?'

She laughed. 'Fishing for compliments, Noah?'

He found himself smiling at her directness. 'I might be.'

'Then let me put it this way. You did better today than you did yesterday.'

That didn't tell him very much at all. 'And?'

'And empathy doesn't come easily to you.'

She walked back to the bed to do a mother and baby check and he let his gaze drop to admire the swing of her hips. Part of him hated that she'd worked out he struggled to be naturally sympathetic and another part of him was glad. All of it added together discombobulated him, especially his response to her. How could he be driven to madness by her one minute and want to kiss her senseless the next?

Suddenly surviving four weeks in Turraburra just got harder for a whole different set of reasons.

Two days later Lilia waved goodbye to the Riccardos, who were keen to get back to Melbourne with Jasmine. She'd arranged for the district nurse to visit them so they'd have help when Jade's milk came in and to cover the days before the maternal and child health nurse visited. As she closed off the file, an unusual wistfulness filled her. She was used to farewelling couples but usually she knew she'd see them again around town and she'd be able to watch the baby grow. She hoped the Riccardos would call in the next time they were in town and visiting relatives, so she could get her little Jasmine fix. She really was a cute baby.

Lily had been beyond surprised when Noah had called in first thing this morning, insisting on doing a discharge check. She'd assumed he'd handed Jade and Jasmine's care over to her the moment she'd stepped into Emergency and he'd said, 'Can I tell you about *your* patient?' Even though she'd seen him try really hard to connect with Jade and Paul during the fast labour, she'd thought he probably much preferred to be far away from such patient intimacy.

Apparently, she'd been wrong.

He'd spent ten minutes with the Riccardos but in reality it had been way more of a cuddle of Jasmine than a discharge check. Always taut with tension, as if he needed to be alert and ready for anything, Noah had seemed almost relaxed as he'd cradled the swaddled baby—well, relaxed for him anyway. She'd been transfixed by the image of the tiny newborn snuggled up against his broad chest and held safely in his strong arms—his sun-kissed skin a honey brown against the white baby shawl.

The idea of arms providing shelter instead of harm burrowed into her mind and tried to set up residence. For a tempting moment she allowed it to. She even let herself feel and enjoy the tingling warmth spinning through her at the thought of Noah's arms wrapped around her, before she rejected all of it firmly and irrevocably. Entertaining ideas like that only led her down a dangerous path—one she'd vowed never to hike along again. It was one thing for other people to take a risk on a relationship but after what had happened with Trent she wasn't ever trusting her judgement with men again.

At almost the same time as she'd locked down her wayward body and thoughts Noah had quickly handed the baby back to Jade, stood abruptly, and with a brisk and brief goodbye had left the room. Paul had commented in a puzzled voice, 'I guess he needs to see a patient.'

Lily, who'd been busy getting her own emotions back under control, had suspected Noah had experienced a rush of affection for the baby and hadn't known how to process it. Like her, he probably had his reasons for avoiding feeling too much of anything and running from it when it caught him unawares.

Time to stop thinking about Noah Jackson.

Shaking her shoulders to slough off the unwanted thoughts, she set about preparing for her new mothers' group that was meeting straight after lunch. She was talking to them, amongst other things, about immunisation. Too many people took for granted the good health that life in Australia afforded them and didn't understand that whooping cough could still kill a young child.

'Ah, Lily?'

She glanced up to see Karen standing in the doorway. Karen rarely walked all the way back here to the annexe, preferring instead to use the intercom. The medical secretary ran the practice her way and she liked to have all the 'i's dotted and the 't's crossed.

Lily racked her brain to think if she'd forgotten some vital piece of paperwork but came up blank. 'Hi, Karen. Whatever I did wrong, I'm sorry,' she said with a laugh. 'Tell me how to fix it.'

Karen shook her head. 'It's not about work, Lily. The hospital just called and your grandfather's in Emergency.'

Gramps! No. Her hand gripped the edge of her desk as a thousand terrifying thoughts closed in on her. At eighty-five, any number of things could have happened to him—stroke, heart attack, a fall. She didn't want to consider any of them.

Karen shoved Lily's handbag into her arms and pushed her towards the door. 'You go to the hospital and don't worry about work. I'll call all the new mums and cancel this afternoon's session.'

'Thanks, Karen, you're the best.' She was already out the door and running down the disabled entry ramp. She crossed the courtyard gardens and entered the emergency department via the back entrance, all the while frantically praying that Gramps was going to be okay.

Panting, she stopped at the desk. 'Where is he?'

'Room one,' Bronwyn Patterson, the emergency nurse manager, said kindly, and pointed the direction.

'Thanks.' Not stopping to chat, she tugged open the door of the resus room and almost fell through the doorway. Her grandfather lay on a narrow trolley propped up on pillows and looking as pale as the sheet that covered him. 'Gramps? What happened?'

He took in her heaving chest and what was probably a panicked look on her face and raised his thin, bony arm. 'Calm down, Lily. I'm fine.'

She caught a flicker of movement in the corner of her eye and realised Noah was in the room. He raised his head from studying an ECG tracing and his thoughtful gaze sought hers.

'Hello, Lilia.'

There was a slight trace of censuring amusement in his tone that she'd just barged into the room and completely ignored him. She knew if she'd done that to her, she'd have been critical of him. 'Hello, Noah. How's my grandfather?'

'He fainted.'

The succinct words made her swing her attention back to her grandfather. 'Did you eat breakfast?' Her fear and concern came out as interrogation.

'Of course I ate my breakfast and I had morning tea,' he said grumpily, responding to her tone. 'When have you ever known me to be off my tucker? And before you ask, I took all my tablets too. I just stood up too quickly at exercise class.'

You're lucky you didn't break a hip. She noticed a wad of gauze taped to his arm and a tell-tale red stain in the centre. 'What happened to your arm?'

'Just a superficial cut. Don't get all het up.' He wriggled up the pillows and glared at her in a very un-Gramps way. 'Isn't there a baby you need to go and deliver?'

She sat down hard on the chair next to him, pressing her handbag into her thighs. 'I'm not going anywhere until I know you're okay.'

'Fine, but don't fuss.' Her usually easygoing grandfather crossed his arms and pouted.

'Let me know when both of you want my opinion,' Noah said drily.

Her grandfather laughed, his bad mood fading. 'You didn't tell me this one's got a sense of humour, Lily.'

I didn't know he did. She wanted to deny she'd ever spoken about Noah at home but there'd be no point given it was obvious she'd discussed him with her grandfather. Embarrassment raced through her and she could feel the heat on her face and knew she was blushing bright pink.

Noah shot her a challenging look. 'I'm not sure your

granddaughter would agree with your assessment of my sense of humour, Mr Cartwright.'

'Call me Bruce, Doc. Now, why did I faint?'

'Your heart rate's very slow.'

'That's good, isn't it? Means I'm fit for my age?'

Lily put her hand on Gramps's and waited for Noah to explain. She hoped he was able to do it using words her grandfather could understand and do it without scaring him.

Noah held up the tracing strip. 'The ECG tells me there's a block in the electrical circuitry of your heart, in the part that controls how fast it beats. When the message doesn't get through, your heart beats too slowly and not enough blood is pumped out. That makes you faint.'

Bruce looked thoughtful. 'Sounds like I need some rewiring.'

This time Noah laughed. 'More like a new starter motor but, yes, some wires are involved. It's called a pacemaker and it's a small procedure done by an electrophysiologist at a day-stay cardiac unit. I can refer you to the pacemaker clinic in Melbourne.'

'Is there anywhere closer?' Bruce asked.

Lily expected Noah to give his usual grunt of annoyance that a country person would want to use a country hospital.

Noah rubbed the back of his neck. 'There's a clinic at Dandenong, which is closer to Turraburra. I could refer you there if you don't want to go all the way to the centre of the city.'

She blinked. Was this the same doctor from the start of the week?

'Well, that all sounds reasonable,' Bruce said, squeezing her hand. 'What do you think, Lily? It will be easier for you if I don't go to Melbourne, won't it?'

Her throat thickened with emotion. Even when her grandfather was sick, he was still putting her first. 'It's your choice, Gramps.'

'Dandenong it is, then.'

'Can I get you anything?' she asked, wanting to focus on practical things rather than the surging relief that she wouldn't have to take him to Melbourne.

'A cup of tea and some sandwiches would be lovely, sweetpea.'

She felt Noah's gaze on her and a tingle of awareness whooshed across her skin. Looking up, she found his dark, inscrutable eyes studying her in the same intense way she'd noticed on other occasions. As usual, with him, she couldn't tell if it was a critical or a complimentary gaze, but its effect made her feel hot and cold, excited and apprehensive, and it left her jittery. She didn't like jittery. It reminded her far too much of the early days with Trent when lust had drained her brain of all common sense. She wasn't allowing that to happen ever again.

'Is it okay for Gramps to have some food?'

Noah seemed to snap out of his trance. 'Sure, if you can call what the kitchen here serves up food,' he said abruptly. He scrawled an order on the chart and left the room.

'See what I have to put up with, Gramps?' she said, feeling baffled that Noah could go from reasonable to rude in a heartbeat.

'He seems like an okay bloke to me. Now, go get me those sandwiches and some cake. A man could starve to death here.'

CHAPTER FOUR

NOAH FOUND LILY sitting in the staff tearoom in the emergency department. *Her name is Lilia*, he reminded himself sharply.

When his phone had woken him at three that morning with an emergency call, it had pulled him out of a delicious dream where he'd been kissing her long, delectable and creamy neck. He'd woken hard, hot and horrified. Right then he'd vowed he was only ever using her formal and full name. It wasn't as pretty or as soft as Lily and that made it easier to think of her as a one-sided equation—defensive and critical with hard edges. He didn't want to spend any time thinking about the talented midwife, the caring granddaughter and the very attractive woman.

Doing that was fraught with complications given they sparked like jumper leads if they got within a metre of each other. Hell, they had enough electricity running between them to power Bruce Cartwright's heart. Working in Turraburra was complication enough given the closeness of his exams. He wasn't adding chasing a woman who had no qualms speaking her mind, frequently found him lacking and gave no sign he was anything more to her than a doctor she had to put up with for four long weeks.

She intrigues you.

No, she annoys me and I'm not pursuing this. Hell, he didn't pursue women any more, full stop—he didn't have to. Since qualifying as a doctor, women had taken to pursuing him and he picked and chose as he pleased, always making sure he could walk away.

Seriously, can you hear yourself?

Shut up.

Needing coffee, he strode to the coffee-machine and immediately swore softly. The pod container was empty.

'Do you need to attend a meeting for your coffee addiction?' Lilia asked with a hint of a smile on her bee-stung lips as she handed him a teabag.

'Probably.' He filled a mug with boiling water. 'I suppose I should be happy you didn't tell me to put money in a swear jar.'

Her eyes sparkled. 'Oh, now, there's an idea. With you here filling it ten times a day, I could probably go on a cruise at the end of the month.'

He raised his brows at her comment. 'And if I instigated a sarcasm jar, so could I.'

'Touché.' She raised her mug to her mouth and sipped her tea, her brow furrowed in thought. 'Thanks for picking up Gramps's heart block so fast.'

He shrugged, unnerved by this almost conciliatory Lilia. 'It's what I'm paid to do.'

She rolled her eyes. 'And he takes a compliment so well.'

He wasn't touching that. 'Your grandfather's not doing too badly for eighty-five.'

Shadows darkened the sky blue of her eyes. 'He's not doing as well as he has been. I've noticed a definite slowing down recently, which he isn't happy about. As you saw, he's an independent old coot.'

He jiggled his teabag. 'Does he live alone?'

She shook her head. 'No. I live with him.'

He thought about the two long years he'd been tied to home, living and caring for his sick mother. Eight years may have passed since then, but the memories of how he'd constantly lurched between resentment that his life was on hold and guilt that he dared feel that way remained vivid. It still haunted him—the self-reproach, the isolation, the feelings of uselessness, the overwhelming responsibility. 'Doesn't living with your grandfather cramp your style?'

She gave him a bewildered look and then burst into peals of laughter, the sound as joyous as the ringing bells of a carillon. 'I don't have any style to cramp. Besides, I've been living with him since I was four. My parents died fighting the bush fires that razed the district twenty-seven years ago.'

'That must have been tough for you.'

She shrugged. 'I was two when it happened and, sure, there were times growing up when I wondered if my life might have been different if my parents had lived, but I never lacked for love. Somehow Gramps not only coped with his own grief at losing his son and daughter-in-law but he did a great job raising me.'

She sounded very together for someone who'd lost both parents. 'He's a remarkable man.'

'He is.' She gave a self-deprecating grimace. 'Even more so for not dispatching me off to boarding school when I was fifteen, running wild and being particularly difficult.'

'One of those times you were wondering about what life would have been like if your parents were still alive?'

She tilted her head and her gaze was thoughtful. 'You know, you may be right. I never thought about it that way. All I remember is playing up and testing Gramps.'

He found himself smiling. 'I can't imagine you being difficult.'

Her pretty mouth curved upwards, its expression ironic. 'Perhaps we both need a sarcasm jar.'

Her smile made him want to lean in close so he could feel her breath on his face and inhale her scent. He immediately leaned back, desperate to cool the simmering attraction he couldn't seem to totally shut down, no matter what he did.

Stick to the topic of work. 'The insertion of the pacemaker should be straightforward but, even so, you need to give some thought to what happens if he continues to go downhill.'

Her plump lips pursed as her shoulders straightened. 'There's nothing to think about. He cared for me so I'll care for him.'

He drummed his fingers against the tabletop, remembering his own similarly worded and heartfelt declaration, and the inevitable fallout that had followed because he'd not thought any of it through. His life had become hijacked by good intentions. 'How will you work the unpredictable hours you do and still manage to care for him?'

Her chin tilted up. 'I'll find a way.'

'Really?' Memories of feeling trapped pushed down

on him. 'What happens when you're called out to deliver a baby in the middle of the night and Bruce can't be left home alone? What happens when you have a woman in labour for longer than a few hours? You could be gone for two days at a time and what happens then? You haven't fully thought it through.'

Lily watched Noah become increasingly tense and fervent and she couldn't fathom where his vehemence was coming from. Despite his slight improvement with patients, this was a man who generally saw people in terms of disconnected body parts, not as whole people with thoughts and feelings and a place in a family and community. Why was he suddenly stressing about something that didn't remotely concern him.

'I live in a community that cares, Noah. People will help.'

'Good luck with that,' he muttered almost bitterly, his cheekbones suddenly stark and bladed.

His chocolate-brown eyes, which for the last few minutes had swirled with unreadable emotions, suddenly cleared like a whiteboard wiped clean. His face quickly returned to its set professional mask—unemotional. With his trademark abruptness, he pushed back his chair and stood.

'I have to get back to work. I'll call Monash and try and get your grandfather transported down there this afternoon for the procedure tomorrow morning. Hopefully, he'll be home by five tomorrow night.'

'Thanks, Noah.'

'Yeah.'

The terse and brooding doctor was back, front and

centre, and she had the distinct feeling he'd just returned from a very dark place. 'Is everything okay?'

'Everything's just peachy,' he said sarcastically as he tossed a two-dollar coin in her direction. 'Choose a charity for the S jar.'

One side of his wide mouth pulled up wryly and she found herself wishing he'd smile again, like he had when he'd teased her about being difficult. Those rare moments of lightness were like treasured shafts of sunshine breaking through cloud on a dark and stormy day. They lit him up—a dark and damaged angel— promising the hope of redemption. His smiles made her smile. Made her feel flushed and giddy and alive. They reminded her that, despite everything, she was still a woman.

No man is who he seems. Remember Trent? He hid something so dark and dangerous from you that it exploded without warning...

And she knew that as intimately as the scars on her back and shoulder. She'd been sensible and celibate for three years without a single moment of temptation. Now wasn't the time to start craving normality—craving the touch of a man, especially not a cantankerous and melancholy guy who did little to hide his dark side.

She reminded herself very firmly that Noah would be gone in three weeks and all she had to do to stay safe and sane was to keep out of his way. He was general practice, she was midwifery. As unusual as this week had been for them to be intersecting so often at work, it was thankfully unlikely to continue.

He spun around to leave and then turned back, slapping his palm to the architrave as he often did when a thought struck him. Again, the muscles of his upper arms bulged. 'Lilia.'

A rush of tingling warmth thrummed through her. Somehow, despite his usual taciturn tone, he managed to make her full name sound soft, sweet and, oh, so feminine. 'Ye—' Her voice caught on the word, deeply husky. She cleared her throat, trying to sound in complete control instead of battling delicious but dangerous waves of arousal. 'Yes?'

'You got the agenda for the quarterly meeting at the Victoria?'

It had pinged into her inbox earlier in the day and she'd done what she always did when it arrived. Ignored it until she couldn't ignore it any longer. 'I did.'

'So you're going?'

She sighed. 'Yes. It ticks me off, though. The secretary who sets the agenda is utterly Melbourne-centric and has no clue of what's involved for people who have to travel. She always sets the meetings to start at nine in the morning, making me battle peak-hour traffic on top of a pre-dawn start.'

'So go up to Melbourne the night before,' he said reasonably.

'No.' She heard the horror in her voice and saw a flash of recognition on his face that he'd heard it too. She backpedalled fast. 'I've got a prenatal class the night before.'

'Fair enough. I'll pick you up at five, then.'

'I beg your pardon?'

He sighed. 'I can't get away early either so there's no point in both of us driving up independently. Carbon footprint, parking issues and all that.'

Panic simmered in her veins. 'I might not be able to go after all. Gramps might need me.'

He folded his arms. 'You just finished telling me there were plenty of people you can call on to keep an eye on him and this is one of those times. You know you can't miss the meeting and that it makes perfect sense for us to drive up together.'

No, no, no, no, no. She wanted to refuse his offer but she would look deranged if she insisted on driving up herself. The urge to go and rock in a corner almost overwhelmed her. She didn't know which was worse—spending two four-hour stretches in Noah's luxury but small European sports car—where there'd be no escape from his woodsy scent, his penetrating gaze and all that toned and fit masculinity—or the fact the first leg of the journey was taking her back to Melbourne, the place of her worst folly. A place full of shadows and fears where her past could appear at any moment and suck her back down into the black morass she'd fought so hard to leave.

Either way, no matter how she came at it, all of it totally sucked.

Noah opened the car door and slid back inside the warmth, surprised to find Lilia still asleep. They'd left Turraburra two hours ago in the dark, the cold and the spring fog, when the only other people likely to be awake had been insomniacs and dairy farmers.

She'd greeted him with a tight and tired smile and had immediately closed her eyes and slept. At first he'd spent far too much time glancing at her in the predawn light. Asleep, she'd lost the wary look she often wore and instead she'd looked soft and serene. And kissable. Far too kissable.

To distract himself, he'd connected his MP3 player and listened to a surgical podcast. The pressure of the looming exams was a permanent part of him and the time in the car was welcome revision time. Turraburra had kept him so busy that he hadn't found much time for study since he'd arrived, adding to his dislike of the place.

Lilia stirred, her eyes fluttering open and a sleep crease from the seat belt marking her cheek. 'What time is it?'

'Seven. I've got coffee, fruit and something the bakery calls a bear claw.'

'Yum. Thanks, that was thoughtful.'

'It's who I am,' he said, teasing her and wanting to see her smile.

'And there's another two dollars for the children's leukaemia fund,' she said with a laugh. Her usually neat braided hair was out today, flowing wildly over her shoulders. She tucked it behind her ears before accepting the coffee. 'Where are we?'

'Cranbourne.' He clicked his seat belt into place, feeling the buzz of excitement flicker into life as he pulled onto the highway and saw the sign that read 'Melbourne 60km'.

'We'll be in East Melbourne by eight-thirty with time to park and make it to the meeting by nine.'

'Great.'

The tone of her voice made him look at her. 'You just matched my donation to the sarcasm jar.'

'Who knew we were both so philanthropic,' she said caustically, before biting into her bear claw.

'Do you always wake up grumpy?'

She wiped icing sugar from her lips. 'Only when the smell of Melbourne's smog hits my nostrils.'

'Well, your bad mood isn't going to dent my enthusiasm,' he said as he changed lanes. 'I can't wait to step inside the Victoria.'

'What about sitting in snarled traffic just to get there?'

'You really are Ms Snark, aren't you?' He grinned at her, perversely enjoying the fact that their individual happiness was proportional to the proximity of their respective homes. Using it as much-needed protection and reminding himself that no matter how much his body craved her, they were a total mismatch.

'We won't be sitting in a traffic jam. I know every side street within a five-kilometre radius of the hospital. My favourite way is through Richmond.'

'That's ridiculous,' she said, her fingers suddenly shredding the white paper bag that had contained the pastry. 'That way you've got traffic lights and trams.'

He rolled his eyes. 'You've just described most of the inner city.'

'Exactly. Just *stay* on the toll road and use the tunnel,' she said tightly, her words lashing him. 'It will get us there just as fast.'

A bristle of indignation ran up his spine. 'And suddenly the country girl's an expert on Melbourne?'

Her eyes flashed silver blue. 'On your first day I told you I did my Master's in midwifery here but you were too busy being cross to listen.'

He ignored her jibe. 'So how long did you live here?'

'Two years.' Her bitter tone clashed with the love he knew she had for midwifery and this time he did more than just glance at her. Her face had paled to the colour of the alabaster statue of mother and child that graced the foyer of MMU and her usually lush mouth had thinned to a rigid and critical line. The paper bag in her lap was now a series of narrow strips. What the hell was going on?

Don't ask. Don't get involved, remember? No emotions means no pain. Whatever's upsetting her is her thing. Let it be. It's nothing to do with you.

Her hand shot from her lap and she turned on the radio as if she too wanted to change the subject. The raucous laughter of the breakfast show announcers filled the silence between them and both of them allowed it.

Noah couldn't stop smiling as the reassuring familiarity of the Melbourne Victoria hospital wrapped around him like a child's blankie. He loved it all, from the mediocre coffee in the staff lounge to the buzz of the floor polisher being wielded by a cleaner.

The moment he'd pulled into his car space he'd been suffused with such a feeling of freedom he'd wanted to sing. Lilia, on the other hand, had looked as if she'd seen a ghost but once inside the hospital she'd perked up. They had different schedules across the day and had agreed to meet at six o'clock in the foyer. He'd gone direct to the doctors' lounge in the theatre suite like a puppy panting for a treat.

Unluckily for him, the first person he saw was Oliver Evans.

'Noah.' The surgeon greeted him coolly. 'How's Turraburra?'

It's purgatory. Certain that Oliver had been a big part of the reason he'd been sent to the small country town, he kept his temper leashed, drawing on willpower born from his sheer determination to succeed. He was half ticked off and half grateful to the guy but, even so, he still thought that with his exams so close he could have worked on his communication skills here at the Victoria, instead of being shunted so far south.

'It's coastal. The beach is okay.'

'And the people? Emily introduced me to the midwife down there once. She seemed great.'

'She's certainly good at her job but she's seriously opinionated.'

'Not something you're known for,' Oliver said, with an accompanying eye-roll. 'She sounds like the perfect match for you.'

It was a typical comment from a happily married family man and it irked him. 'I've got exams looming, a private surgical practice to start and no interest in being matched up with anyone.'

'Shame. I remember her as intelligent, entertaining and with a good sense of humour, but then again I don't have to work with her.' He picked up a file. 'Talking about work, I imagine you're missing operating. I've got a fascinating case today if you want to scrub in and observe.'

Interest sparked. 'What is it?'

'Jeremy Watson, the paediatric cardiologist from

The Deakin is inserting a stent into the heart of Flick Lawrence and Tristan Hamilton's baby. Are you in?'

Eagerness and exhilaration tumbled through him at the chance to be part of such intricate and delicate in utero surgery. He almost said, 'Hell, yeah,' but memories stopped him. Oliver standing in front of an open lift. Oliver yelling at him about a little girl with Down's syndrome. Oliver telling him to get some people skills.

This surgery wasn't taking place on just any baby—it was the unborn child of Melbourne Victoria's paediatric cardiologist. If Noah failed to acknowledge that, he knew he'd be kicked to the kerb, and fast. 'This is a pretty personal case, Oliver. Tristan and Flick are staff. How will they feel about me scrubbing in?'

Oliver gave him a long, assessing look before his stern mouth softened. 'They'll be happy to know they're in the hands of talented doctors.' He shoved papers at Noah's chest. 'Read up on the procedure so you know exactly what's required of you. We don't want Jeremy taking any stories back to The Deakin about our team not being up to scratch. I'll see you in Theatre Five at one.'

Lily's head spun after a morning of meetings. She craved to feel fresh air and sunshine on her skin instead of artificial lighting and to feel earth underneath her feet instead of being six floors up in the air. A sandwich in the park across the road from the hospital was the perfect solution.

Are you sure? What if Trent walks past?

Stop it! You're being irrational. A. Melbourne is a city of four million people. B. Trent doesn't work at

*the Melbourne Victoria. C. Richmond is far enough
away for this not to be his local park. D. He doesn't
even know you're in Melbourne and, for all you know,
he might have left for Queensland, like he always said
he would.*

She hauled in deep breaths, trying desperately to
hold onto all the logic and reason that half her brain quietly told her, while ignoring the crazy la-la her paranoia
had going on. She hated that she had the same conversation with herself every time she came to Melbourne.
It was one of the reasons why she limited her visits to
the city to the bare minimum.

*It's been three years and this has to stop. Lunch in
the park will be good for you. It's the same as when
you have lunch at the beach in Turraburra. You need
the natural light—it will boost your serotonin and it's
good for your mental health.*

Still feeling jittery, she decided to take the service
elevator. It gave her the best chance of making it down
to the ground floor without running into anyone she
knew. People who would implore her to join them for
lunch in the cafeteria. She pressed the 'down' button
and waited, watching the light linger on level one, the
operating theatre suite.

'Lily?' Isla Delamere, looking about seven months
pregnant, walked easily towards her *sans* waddle and
leaned in to kiss her on the cheek. 'I thought it was you.'

Lily hugged her friend. 'Look at you. You look fantastic.'

'Thanks.' Isla rubbed her belly with a slightly distracted air. 'I'm just starting to feel a bit tired by the
end of the day and Alessi has gone from dropping

occasional hints that I should be giving up work to getting all macho and protective.' She laughed. 'But in a good way, you know, not a creepy way.'

Sadly, Lily understood the difference only too well. 'When do you start mat leave?'

'Next month.' A smile wreathed her face. 'I can't wait to set up the nursery and get organised.'

'That sounds like fun,' Lily said sincerely. She was shocked then to feel a flutter of something she didn't want to acknowledge as a tinge of jealousy.

The sound of voices floated out from the office—the crisp and precise tones of a female British accent contrasting sharply with a deeply male and laconic Aussie drawl. Neither voice sounded happy.

Emergencies excepted, Lily was used to the MMU being a relatively tranquil place. 'What's going on?'

'Darcie and Lucas. Again.' Isla's brows shot skyward. 'They spit and hiss like territorial cats when they get within five metres of each other. All of us are over it.' She laughed. 'We think they should just get on with it and have sex. You know, combust some of that tension so the MMU can go back to the calm place it's known for.'

Lily thought about the tension that shimmered between her and Noah and immediately felt the hot, addictive heaviness between her legs. 'You really think having sex would work?'

'I have no clue but if it means Darcie and Lucas could work together in harmony, I'd say do it. They'd make an amazing obstetric team.'

Working in harmony...

Stop it! Now you're totally losing your mind. Don't even go there.

'You okay, Lily?' Isla asked, clicking her fingers. 'You've vagued out on me.'

She forced a laugh. 'Sorry, I was thinking about sex and the occupational health and safety implications.'

'As long as no ladders are involved, it's probably fine,' Isla quipped, then her face sobered. 'Lily, if you're not busy, can you do me a favour?'

You really need ten minutes in the park out of this artificial light so you can get through the rest of the day. The thought of being in the park and Trent finding her there sent her heart into panicky overdrive. 'I'm not busy, Isla. How can I help?'

'I hate this so much, Lily.' Tristan Hamilton leaned his head against the glass that separated them from Theatre Five, gazing down at his wife's draped and prostrate form on the operating table. The only thing not covered in green was Flick's pregnant belly.

'It must be so hard.' Lily put her hand on the Melbourne Victoria's neonatal cardiothoracic surgeon's shoulder, struck by the sobering thought that today he wasn't a doctor, just a scared and anxious father-to-be. 'It's especially difficult when you're the one used to being in charge and in control so let's look at the positives. Oliver's an expert in utero surgeon and you and Jeremy Watson share that award for the ground-breaking surgery the two of you did on the conjoined twins. Just like you, he's one of the best. Flick and the baby are in great hands.'

Isla had explained to Lily how she'd desperately

wanted to support both Tristan and Flick by being here and how she and Alessi had discussed it. They'd both felt strongly that it would be difficult enough to cope with the fact their baby was undergoing life-threatening surgery without their support person being heavily pregnant with a healthy baby. Isla had asked Lily to stay with Tristan throughout the operation, saying, 'He says he doesn't need anyone with him but he does, and you're perfect because you're always so calm.'

Lily had immediately thought about her chaotic reactions to Noah, which were the antithesis of calm, but she hadn't voiced them because it hadn't been the time or place. People needed her. They needed her to be the person they thought she was—serene and unflappable. No one knew how hard she'd worked to cultivate that aura of tranquillity for her own protection.

Now she was doing as Isla asked, staying with Tristan during the surgery, and she was glad. The guy was understandably stressed and she was more than happy to help.

The operating theatre was full of people scrubbed and wearing green gowns, unflattering blue paper hats and pale blue-green masks. Their only visible distinguishing features were their eyes and stance. She recognised Ed Yang, the anaesthetist, by his almond-shaped eyes, Oliver Evans's by his wide-legged stance, and Jeremy Watson by his short stature and nimble movments, but she didn't recognise the back of the taller doctor standing next to him.

'Oliver is using ultrasound to guide Jeremy's large-gauge needle into Flick's abdomen. It will pierce the uterus before going directly into the baby's heart,' Tristan said, as if he was conducting a teaching session for the interns.

If talking was going to help him get through this then Lily was more than happy to listen.

'Of course the risks are,' he continued in a low voice, 'rupture of the amniotic sac, bleeding through the insertion site, the baby's heart bleeding into the pericardial sac and compressing the heart.' His voice cracked. 'And death.'

Lily slid her hand into his and squeezed it hard. 'And the best-case scenario is the successful insertion of the stent and a healthy baby born at term.'

'Who will still need more surgery.'

Lily heard the guilt and sadness in his voice. 'But the baby will be strong enough to cope with it. Most importantly, unlike you, he or she is unlikely to need a heart transplant. You know it's a different world now from when you were born and your baby is extremely fortunate to have the best doctors in the country.'

'You're right. She is.' He gave her a grateful smile. 'We're having a little girl. We found out during the tests.'

'That's so exciting.'

'It is.' A slow smile wove across his face. 'I thought I didn't need anyone here with me today but I was wrong. Thanks for being here, Lily.'

'Oh, Tris, it's an honour. All I ask is for a big cuddle when she's born.'

'It's a deal.' He suddenly muttered something that sounded like, 'Thank God.'

'Tris?'

He grinned at her. 'The stent's in. Both my girls have come through the surgery with flying colours.'

'Fantastic.' She noticed the assistant surgeon suddenly raising both of his arms away from the surgical field as if he were a victim of an armed hold-up. He stepped back from the table. 'What's happening?'

'That's the surgical registrar. The operation's almost over and he's not required any more.'

As the unknown surgeon walked around, he glanced up at the glass. A set of very familiar brown eyes locked with hers. She stifled a gasp. *Noah.*

The Swiss chocolate colour of his eyes was familiar but she didn't recognise anything else about them. Gone was the serious, slightly mocking expression that normally resided there and in its place was unadulterated joy. His eyes positively sparkled, like fireworks on New Year's Eve.

Her heart kicked up, her knees sagged and lust wound down into every part of her, urging her dormant body to wake up. Wake up and dare to take a risk—live on the wild side and embrace it—like she'd often done before life with Trent had extinguished that part of her.

No. Not safe. You must stay safe.

Panic closed her eyes but the vision of his elation stayed with her—vibrant and full of life—permanently fused to her mind like a brand.

It scared the hell out of her.

CHAPTER FIVE

'MAN, THAT WAS a great day,' Noah said, smoothly changing through the gears as he took yet another bend on the narrow, winding and wet road back to Turraburra.

'I'm glad,' Lilia said with a quiet smile in her voice.

'Why?'

She sighed. 'Are you always so suspicious of someone being happy for you?'

He glanced at her quickly before returning his gaze to the rainy night, the windscreen wipers working overtime to keep the windshield clear. 'Sorry, but you have to admit we don't exactly get along.'

'That's true, I guess, but today I saw you in a new light.'

'Should I be worried?' he said, half teasing, half concerned.

'I guess I saw you on your home turf and I've never seen you look like that before. You looked happy.' Her fingers tangled with each other on her lap. 'You've really missed the Victoria and surgery, haven't you?

'Like an amputee misses his leg.' He shot her an appreciative glance, one part of him both happy and surprised that she'd drawn the connections. 'Couldn't you feel the vibe of the place? Being part of world-class surgery is my adrenalin rush.

'It bubbles in my veins and I love it. What you saw today, when Jeremy inserted that stent into the Hamilton-Lawrence baby's heart, is cutting-edge stuff. It's an honour and a privilege to be part of it and I want to be part of it. I didn't work this hard for this long to spend my life stuck in a backwater.'

'Let me take a wild stab in the dark that you're talking about a place like Turraburra.'

'Exactly. By the way, you owe another two dollars to the S jar,' he said lightly, then he sobered. 'But, seriously, doesn't it frustrate you on some level that you're so far away from the centre of things?'

'Not at all,' she said emphatically, the truth in her voice ringing out loud and clear in the darkness of the car.

'I can't believe you didn't even have to think about that for a second.'

'How is it any different from me asking you if being in Melbourne frustrates you on any level?'

He nodded thoughtfully. 'Fair point.'

'Noah, babies have been coming into the world in pretty much the same way for thousands of years so, for me, the joy comes from helping women, not from feeling the need to be constantly chasing new and exciting ways of doing things.'

He thought of his mother. 'There's nothing wrong with wanting to discover new techniques and new ways of doing things. It's how we progress, find cures for diseases, better ways of treating people.'

'I never said there was anything wrong with it.' She

suddenly pointed out the window and yelled, 'Wombat! Look out.'

His headlights picked up the solid black shape in the rain, standing stock-still on the road, right in the path of the car. He pulled the steering-wheel hard, swerving to avoid hitting and instantly killing the marsupial. Lilia's hands gripped the dash, stark white in the dark as the car heaved left. The tyres hit the gravel edge of the road and the car fishtailed wildly.

Don't do this. He braked, trying to pull the car back under control, but in the wet it had taken on its own unstoppable trajectory. The back wheels, unable to grip the gravel, skidded and the next moment the car pulled right, sliding across the white lines to the wrong side of the road. White posts and trees came at them fast and he hauled the wheel the other way, driving on instinct, adrenalin and fear.

The car suddenly spun one hundred and eighty degrees and stopped, coming to an abrupt halt and facing in the opposite direction from where they were headed. The headlights picked up shadows, the trees and the incessant rain, tumbling down from the sky like a wall of water. The wombat ambled in front of the car and disappeared into the bushes.

Noah barely dared to breathe while he did a mental checklist that all his body parts still moved and that he was indeed, alive. When reality pierced his terror, his half-numb fingers clumsily released his seat belt and he leaned towards Lilia, grabbing her shoulder. 'Are you okay?'

'I…I…' Her voice wobbled in the darkness. 'I

thought for sure we'd slam into the trees. I thought we were dead.'

'So did I.' He flicked on the map reading light, needing to see her.

Her eyes stared back at him, wide and enormous, their blue depths obliterated by huge black discs. 'But we're not.'

'No.' He raised his right hand to her cheek, needing to touch her, needing to feel that she was in one piece. 'We're safe.'

'Safe.' She breathed out the word before wrapping her left hand tightly around his forearm as if she needed to hold onto something.

Her heat and sheer relief collided with his, calling to him, and he dropped his head close in to hers, capturing her lips in a kiss of reassurance. A kiss of mutual comfort that they'd survived unscathed. That they were fine and here to live another day.

Her lips were warm, pliant and, oh, so gloriously soft. As he brushed his lips gently against them, he tasted salt and sugar. God, he wanted to delve deep and taste more. Feel more.

He suddenly became aware she'd stilled. She was neither leaning into the kiss nor leaning back. She was perfectly motionless and for a brief moment he thought he should pull away—that his kiss was unwelcome— but then she made a raw sound in the back of her throat. Half moan, half groan, it tore through him like a primal force, igniting ten long days of suppressed desire.

He slid one hand gently around her neck, cupping the back of it and tilting her head. He deepened the kiss while he used his other hand to release her seat belt.

Her arms immediately slid up around his neck and she met his kiss with one of her own.

If he'd expected hesitation and uncertainty, he'd been wrong. Her tongue frantically explored his mouth as if she had only one chance to do so, branding him with her heat and her taste, and setting him alight in a way he'd never known. His blood pounded need and desire through him hot and fast, and his breathing came short and ragged. He wanted to touch her and feel her, wanted her to touch and feel him. Hell, he just wanted her.

His talented surgical fingers, usually so nimble and controlled, fumbled with the buttons on her blouse. Lilia didn't even try to undo his buttons—she just ripped. Designer buttons flew everywhere and then her palms pressed against his skin, searing him. Her lips followed, tracing a direct line along his chest to his nipples. Her tongue flicked. Silver spots danced before his eyes.

Somehow he managed to rasp out, 'Need more room.' Shooting his seat back, he hauled her over him. As she straddled him, her thighs pressed against his legs and she leaned forward, lowering her mouth to his again. Her hair swung, forming a curtain around their heads, encasing them in a blonde cocoon and isolating them from the real world. It was wild and crazy as elbows and knees collided with windows, the steering-wheel and the handbrake. A small part of him expected her to jolt back to sanity, pull back and scramble off him.

Thank God, it didn't happen.

He'd never been kissed like it. She lurched from ingénue to moments of total control. Her mouth burned hot on his and her body quivered against him, driving him upward to breaking point. She matched his every move with one of her own, and when he finally managed to unhook her bra she whipped off his belt. When he slid his hand under her skirt, caressing the skin of her inner thighs, she undid his fly. When he cupped her, she gripped him.

She rose above him a glorious Amazon—face flushed, eyes huge, full breasts heaving—and he wanted nothing more than to watch her fly. 'God, you're amazing.'

'Shush.' Lilia managed to sound the warning. She didn't want compliments, she didn't want conversation—she didn't want to risk anything being said that might make her think beyond this moment. She'd spent years living a safe and bland life and tonight she could have died. In this moment she needed to feel alive in a way she hadn't felt in years. The woman she'd once been—the one life had subjugated—broke through, demanding to be heard. She had Noah under her, his hands on her, and she was taking everything he offered.

'No condoms,' he said huskily. 'Sorry. Hope this will do.' His thumb rotated gently on her clitoris as his fingers slid inside her, moving back and forth with delicious and mind-blowing pressure.

She swayed against him, her hands moving on him trying to return the favour, but under his deft and targeted ministrations they fell away. Sensations built inside her, drowning out everything until nothing existed at all except pleasure. Sheer, glorious, pleasure. It caught her, pushing her upwards, pulling her forward, and spinning her out on an axis of wonder until she exploded in a shower of light far, far away from everything that tied her to her life.

As she drifted back to earth, muscles twitching, chest panting, she caught his sparkling eyes and deliciously self-satisfied grin.

What have you done?

The enormity of what had just happened hit her like a truck, sucking the breath from her lungs and scaring her rigid.

If Lily hadn't known better she would have said she'd drunk a lot of tequila and today's headache was the result of a hangover. Only she knew she hadn't touched a drop of alcohol yesterday or today. All she wanted was to desperately forget everything about last night's drive home from Melbourne, but sadly it was all vividly crystal clear, including her screaming Noah's name when she'd come.

She ruffled her dog's ears. 'Oh, Chippy, I've been so sensible and restrained for so long, why did I have to break last night? Break with Noah?'

But break she had—spectacularly. How could she have put herself at risk like that? Left herself open to so many awful possibilities?

It was Noah, not a mass murderer.

We don't know that.

Oh, come on!

She blamed Isla's suggestion that people should have sex to defuse tension, Noah's look of utter joy in the operating theatre, which had reached out and deliciously wrapped around her, and finally, to cap it all off, their near-death experience. All of it had combined, making her throw caution to the wind. But despite how she was trying to justify her actions, the only person she could blame was herself. She'd spent all night wide awake, doing exactly that.

Gramps had even commented at breakfast that she looked in worse shape than he did. Since the insertion of his pacemaker he was doing really well and had a lot more energy than he'd had in a long time. For that she was grateful. She was also grateful that she hadn't seen Noah all morning.

Last night, after she'd scrambled off his lap in a blind panic and had said, 'Don't say a word, just drive,' he'd done exactly that. When he'd pulled up at the house just before eleven, he'd leaned in to kiss her on the cheek. She'd managed to duck him and had hopped out of the car fast. Using the door as a barrier between them, she'd thanked him for the ride and had tried to walk normally to the front door when every part of her had wanted to run. Run from the fact she'd just had sex in a car.

Dear God, she was twenty-nine years old and old enough to know better. She'd kept the wild side of herself boxed up for years and she still couldn't believe she'd allowed it to surface. Not when she had the physical evidence on her body constantly reminding her of the danger it put her in.

She lined her pens up in a row on her desk and straightened the files in her in-box. Yesterday was just a bump in the road of her life and today everything went back to normal. Normal, just like it had been for the last three years. Like she needed it to be. Safe. Controlled. Restrained. Absolutely drama-free.

A hysterical laugh rose in her throat. She should probably text Isla, telling her that sex didn't reduce tension at all. If anything, it made things ten times worse.

She dropped her head in her hands. She had to work with Noah for the next two and a half weeks and all the time he would know that if he tried, it barely took any time at all for him to strip away her reserve and reduce her to a primal mess of quivering and whimpering need. She'd unwittingly given him power over her—power she'd vowed no man would ever have over her again. Somehow she had to get through seventeen days before she could breathe easily again.

To keep her chaotic thoughts from ricocheting all over her brain, she decided to check her inventory for expired sterilised equipment and drugs nearing their use-by dates. There was nothing like order and routine to induce calm.

She was halfway through the job when a knock on her door made her turn.

'May I come in?'

Noah stood in the doorway in his characteristic pose of one hand pressed against the doorjamb, only this time he looked very different. Gone was the suit and tie he'd worn during his first week and a half in Turraburra. Today his long legs were clad in chinos and his chest, which she now knew was rock-hard muscle, was covered in a green, pink, blue and orange striped casual shirt. His brown curls bounced and his eyes danced. He looked…relaxed.

Her heart leaped, her blood pounded and tingles of desire slammed through her, making her shimmer from top to toe. If her body had been traitorously attracted to the strung-out Noah, it was nothing compared to its reaction to the relaxed Noah.

Distance. Keep your distance. 'I'm pretty busy, Noah. Did you need something?'

His mouth curved up in a genuine smile that raced to his eyes. 'I figured, seeing as we've done things back to front and had sex first, we should probably go out to dinner.'

'I...I don't think that's a good idea,' she said hurriedly, before her quivering body overrode her common sense and she accepted the unexpected invitation. 'And we didn't actually have sex,' she said, feeling mortified that she'd been the one to have the orgasm while he'd been left hanging.

His brows rose. 'I'm pretty certain what we did comes under the banner of sex.'

The irony of what she'd said wasn't lost on her, given she always put a lot of emphasis in sex ed classes with the local teenagers on the fact that sex wasn't just penetration. 'Either way, it was a mistake so why compound it by going on a date?'

'A mistake?' The words came out tinged with offence and a flare of hurt momentarily sparked in his eyes before fading fast. 'If it was a mistake, why did you have sex with me?'

She didn't meet his gaze. 'I panicked.'

'You panicked?'

She heard the incredulity in his voice and it added to the flash of hurt she'd seen. She felt bad and it made her tell him the truth. 'I'd just had a near-death experience and I hadn't had sex in a very long time.'

'So you used me?'

Her head jerked up at the slight edge in his voice. 'Oh, and you didn't use me?'

A look of distaste and utter indignation slid across his face and two red spots appeared on his cheeks as if she'd slapped him. 'No! I don't use women. What the hell sort of a man do you think I am?'

A kernel of guilt burrowed into her that because of Trent's role in her life she'd offended him, but she wasn't about to explain to him why. 'Look, we're adults. You don't need to appease your conscience by buying me dinner. What happened happened and now we can just forget about it and move on.'

'I don't want to forget about it,' he said softly, as he moved towards her.

Panic had her pulling a linen skip between them but he put his hands on either side of it and leaned in close. 'Do you?'

His soft words wound down into her, taunting her resolve. *I have to forget.*

He suddenly straightened up and opened his hands out palms upward in supplication. 'Come to dinner, Lily. You never know, we might actually enjoy each other's company.'

'I really don't think—'

'I promise you it will just be dinner.' He gave a wry smile. 'Sex is an optional extra and totally your choice. I'm not here to talk you into or out of it.'

She stared at him, trying desperately hard to read him and coming up blank. Why was he was doing this? Why was he being so nice? She sought signs of calculation but all she could see was genuineness. It clashed with everything she wanted to believe about him— about all men—only she got a sense that if she said no, she'd offend him. Again. 'Okay, but I'm paying.'

His jaw stiffened. 'I'm not an escort service. We'll go Dutch.'

The memory of him stroking her until she'd come made her cheeks burn hotly. 'I guess…um…that's fair.'

Shoving his hands in his pockets, he said, 'I'd offer to pick you up but that would probably upset your independent sensibilities. Emergencies and babies excepted, how does seven at Casuarina sound?'

She was so rusty at accepting invitations that her voice came out all scratchy. 'Seven sounds good.'

He shot her a wary smile. 'Cheer up. You never know, you might just enjoy yourself.'

Before she could say another word, he'd turned and left.

Please, let a baby be born tonight. Please.

But, given her luck with men, that was probably not going to happen.

CHAPTER SIX

NOAH FULLY EXPECTED Lily to cancel. Every email and text that had hit his phone during the afternoon he'd opened with that thought first and foremost in his mind. Now, as he sat alone in the small restaurant, he fingered his phone, turning it over and over, still waiting for the call to come. He caught sight of his countdown app and opened it. Four hundred and fifty-six hours left in Turraburra. Almost halfway.

Why are you even here in this restaurant? That thought had been running concurrently with *She will cancel.* He had no clue why he'd insisted they have dinner. It wasn't like he'd never taken the gift of casual sex before and walked away without a second glance. Granted, he'd not actually hit the end zone last night, but watching Lilia shatter above him had brought him pretty damn close. And it had felt good in a way he hadn't experienced in a long time.

Something about her—the wildness in the way she'd kissed him, the desperation in the way she'd come and then her rapid retreat into herself afterwards had kick-started something in him. A desire to get to know her more. A vague caring—something he'd put on ice years ago.

It confused him and dinner had seemed a way of exorcising both the confusion and the caring. Hell, her reaction to his dinner invitation had almost nuked the caring on the spot. He'd never had a woman so reluctant to accept his invitation and it had fast become a challenge to get her to accept. He refused to be relegated to the category of *a mistake*. He checked his watch. Seven-ten p.m.

'Would you like a drink, Dr Jackson?' Georgia Brady asked, as she extended the black-bound wine list towards him.

Noah had recently prescribed the contraceptive pill for the young woman and had conducted the examination that went along with that. He was slightly taken aback to find she was now his waitress. 'I think I'll wait, thanks.'

'Who are you waiting for?'

'Lilia Cartwright,' he answered, before he realised the inappropriateness of the question. Small towns with their intense curiosity were so not his thing. 'Aren't there other customers needing your attention?'

Georgia laughed as she indicated the virtually empty restaurant. 'Thursday nights in Turraburra are pretty quiet. Are you sure Lily's coming? It's just she never dates.'

'It's a work dinner,' he said quickly, as a crazy need to protect Lilia from small-town gossip slugged him.

Georgia nodded. 'That makes more sense. Oh, here she is. Hi, Lily.'

* * *

Lily stood in the entrance of the restaurant and slipped off her coat, wondering for the thousandth time why she was there. Why she hadn't created an excuse to cancel. That was the one drawback of a small town. Without a cast-iron reason it was, oh, so easy to be caught out in a lie because everybody knew what everyone was doing and when they were doing it. So, here she was. She'd eat and leave. An hour, max.

Plastering on a smile, she walked forward and said, 'Hi, Georgia,' as she took her seat opposite Noah, who'd jumped to his feet on her arrival. 'Noah.'

He gave her a nod and she thought he looked as nervous as she felt.

'If this is a work dinner, will you want wine?' Georgia asked.

'Yes.'

Noah spoke at exactly the same moment as she did, his deep 'Yes' rolling over hers.

They both laughed tightly and Georgia gave them an odd look before going to fetch the bottle of Pinot Gris Noah ordered.

Lily fiddled with her napkin. 'This is a work dinner?'

Noah grimaced. 'Georgia was giving me the third degree about my date and as the town believes you're married to your job, I thought it best not to disabuse them.'

She stared at him, stunned. 'How do you know the town thinks I'm married to my job?'

'Linda Sampson told me on my first day,' he said matter-of-factly, before sipping some water. 'So are you?'

She didn't reply until Georgia had finished pouring the wine, placed the bottle in an ice bucket by the side of the table and left. 'I love my job but I also love Gramps, Chippy and bushwalking. Plus, I'm involved as a volunteer with Coastcare so I live a very balanced life,' she said, almost too emphatically. 'It's just that Linda wants to marry off every single woman in town.'

'And man,' Noah said, with a shake of his head. 'The first day I was here she ran through a list of possible candidates for me, despite the fact I'd told her I wasn't looking.'

'Why aren't you looking?' The question came out before she'd censored it.

His perceptive gaze hooked hers. 'Why aren't you?'

So not going there. She dropped her gaze and sipped the wine, savouring the flavours of pear and apple as they zipped along her tongue. 'This is lovely.'

'I like it. The Bellarine Peninsula has some great wineries.'

'You mean there are times you actually leave Melbourne voluntarily?' she teased.

He grinned. 'I've been known to when wine's involved.'

'There's a winery an hour away from here.'

'This far south?'

She smiled at his scepticism. 'They only make reds but the flavours are really intense. You should visit. You get great wine, amazing views across Wilson's Prom and wedge-tailed eagles.'

His eyes, always so serious, lightened in self-deprecation. 'I guess I should have read the tourist information they sent me after all.'

She raised her glass. 'To the hidden gems of Turraburra.'

'And to finding them.' He clinked her glass with his, his gaze skimming her from the top of her forehead, across her face and down to her breasts and back again.

A shiver of need thundered through her and she hastily crossed her legs against the intense throb, trying to quash it. She gulped her wine, quickly draining the glass and then regretting it as the alcohol hit her veins. *Stick to pleasantries.* 'The eye fillet here is locally grown and so tender it melts in your mouth.'

'Sounds good to me,' he said, as he instructed Georgia that he wanted his with the blood stopped. When the waitress had refilled their glasses, removed the menus and departed for the kitchen, he said, 'I saw your grandfather this morning for his check-up. He's a new man.'

'He is. Thanks.'

He gave a wry smile. 'Don't thank me. Thank the surgeon who inserted the pacemaker and fixed the problem.'

'A typical surgeon's response. Noah, you made the diagnosis so please accept the thanks.' She fiddled with the base of her glass and sought desperately for something to say that was neutral. 'So you know I grew up in Turraburra, what about you?'

He took a long drink of his wine.

Her curiosity ramped up three notches. 'Is it a secret?'

'No. It's just not very interesting.'

'Try me.'

'West of Sydney.'

She thought about his reaction to Turraburra and wondered if he'd grown up in a small town. 'How west? Orange? Cowra?'

'Thankfully, not that far west.' He ran his hand through his curls as if her questions hurt. 'I grew up in a poverty-stricken, gossip-ridden town on the edge of Sydney. Not really country but too far away to be city. I hated it and I spent most of my teenage years plotting to get out and stay out.'

She thought about her own childhood—of the freedom of the beach, of the love of her grandfather and the circle of care from the town—and she felt sad for him. 'Do your parents still live there?'

He shook his head. 'I was a change-of-life baby. Totally unexpected and my mother was forty-four when she had me. They're both dead now.'

She knew all about that. 'I'm sorry.'

'Don't be.'

The harshness of his reply shocked her. 'You're glad your parents are dead?'

A long sigh shuddered out of him and he suddenly looked haggard and tired. 'Of course not, but I'm glad they're no longer suffering.'

'So they didn't die from old age?'

'Not exactly.' He cut through the steak Georgia had quietly placed in front of him. 'My father died breathless and drowning in heart failure and my mother...' He bit harshly into the meat.

His pain washed over Lily and she silently reached out her hand, resting it on top of his. He stared at it for a moment before swallowing. 'She died a long and protracted death from amyotrophic lateral sclerosis.'

Motor neurone disease. 'Oh, God, that must have been awful.' She caught a flash of gratitude in his eyes that she understood. 'Did you have a good nursing home?'

'At the very end we did but for the bulk of two years I cared for her at home.' His thumb moved slowly against her hand, almost unconsciously, caressing her skin in small circular motions.

Delicious sensations wove through her, making her mind cloud at the edges. She forced herself to concentrate, working hard to hear him rather than allowing herself to follow the bliss. 'That's…that's a long time to care for someone.'

His mouth flattened into a grim line as he nodded his agreement. 'It is and, to be honest, when I took the job on we didn't have a diagnosis. I just assumed she'd need a bit of help for a while until she got stronger. I had no clue it would play out like it did, and had I known I might have…'

She waited a beat but he didn't say anything so she waded right on in. 'When did she get sick?'

'When I was nineteen. With illness, no timing is ever good but this totally sucked. I was living in Coogee by the beach, doing first-year medicine at UNSW and loving my life. It was step one of my plan to get out and stay out of Penrington.'

She thought of what he'd said about growing up in a poverty-stricken town. 'Because doctors are rarely unemployed?'

'That and the fact I was sixteen when my father died. I guess it's an impressionable age and I used to daydream that if I'd been a doctor I could have saved him.'

He gave a snort of harsh laughter. 'Of course, I now know that no doctor could have changed the outcome, but at the time it was a driving force for me to choose medicine as a career.'

A stab of guilt pierced her under the ribs. She'd so easily assigned him the role of arrogant surgeon—a guy who'd chosen the prestigious speciality for the money—that she'd missed his altruism. 'You must have needed a lot of help to balance the demands of your study with helping your mum.'

He shook his head. 'My parents never had a lot of money and Mum gave up work to care for Dad in his last weeks of life. By the time she got sick, there wasn't any spare cash for a paid carer and there wasn't a lot of choice.'

'What did you do?'

He pulled his hand away from hers and ripped open the bread roll, jerkily applying butter. 'I deferred uni at the end of first year and took care of her.'

She thought about her own egocentric student days. 'That would have been a huge life change.'

His breath came out in a hiss. 'Tell me about it. I went from the freedom of uni where life consisted of lectures and parties to being stuck back in Penrington, which I'd thought I'd escaped. Only this time I was basically confined to the house. I spent a lot of time being angry and the rest of it feeling hellishly guilty as I watched my strong and capable mother fade in front of me.'

There weren't many nineteen-year-olds who'd take on full-time care like that and this was Noah. Noah, who seemed so detached and closed off from people.

She struggled to wrap her head around it. 'But surely you had some help?'

He shrugged. 'The council sent a cleaner every couple of weeks and a nurse would visit three times a week, you know the drill, but the bulk of her care fell to me.' He took a gulp of the wine before looking at her, his eyes filled with anguish. 'Every day I was haunted by a thousand thoughts. Would she choke on dinner? Would she aspirate food into her lungs? Would she fall? Would she wake up in the morning?'

Lily heard the misery and grief in his voice and her heart wept. This brisk, no-nonsense, shoot-from-the-hip doctor—the man who seemed to have great difficulty empathising with patients—had nursed his mother. 'I… That's… It…'

'Shocks you, doesn't it?' he said drily, accurately gauging her reaction. 'Part of it shocks me too but life has a way of taking you to places you never expected to go.'

He returned to eating his meal and she ate some of hers, giving him a chance to take a break from his harrowing story. She was certain he'd use the opportunity to change the subject and she knew she'd let him. She was familiar with how hard it was to revisit traumatic memories, so it came as a surprise when he continued.

'You really don't learn a lot more than anatomy and some physiology in first-year medicine and I truly believed we'd find a doctor who could help Mum.' His hand sneaked back to hers, covering it with his warmth. 'We went from clinic to clinic, saw specialist after specialist, tried three different drug trials and nothing changed except that Mum continued to deteriorate. In all those months, not one person ever said it was hopeless and that there was no cure.' His mouth curled. 'I've never forgiven them for that.'

'And yet you still had enough faith to return to your studies and qualify as a doctor?'

'I became a surgeon,' he said quietly but vehemently. 'Surgery's black and white. I see a problem and I can either fix it or I can't. And that's what I tell my patients. I give it to them straight and I *never* give them false hope.'

And there it was—the reason he was so direct. She'd been totally wrong about him. It wasn't deliberate rudeness—it came from a heartfelt place, only the message got lost in translation and came out harsh and uncaring. 'There's a middle line between false hope and stark truth, Noah,' she said quietly, hoping he'd actually hear her message.

He pulled his hand away. 'Apparently so.'

Her hand felt sadly cool and she struggled not to acknowledge how much she missed his touch.

Noah helped Lily into her coat, taking advantage of the moment to breathe in deeply and inhale her perfume. All too soon, her coat was on and it was time for him to open the front door of Casuarina and follow her outside onto the esplanade. The rhythmic boom of the waves against the sand enveloped them and he had to admit it had a soothing quality. He glanced along the street. 'Where's your car?'

She thrust her hands into her coat pockets, protecting them against the spring chill. 'I walked.'

'I've got mine. I can drive you home.'

Her eyes widened for a second and he caught the moment she recalled exactly what had happened the last time they had been in his car. Sex. The topic they'd both gone to great lengths to avoid talking about tonight. The one thing he'd told her was her choice.

He didn't want her to bolt home alone so he hastily amended his offer. 'Or I can walk you home, if you prefer.'

She tilted her head and studied him as if she couldn't quite work him out and then she gave him a smile full of gratitude. 'Thanks. A walk would be great.'

'A walk it is, then.' She could go from guardedly cautious to sexy in a heartbeat and it disarmed him, leaving him wondering and confused. With one of her hands on her hip, he took advantage of an opportunity to touch her and slid his arm through hers. 'Which way?'

She glanced at his arm as if she was considering if she should allow it to remain there but she didn't pull away. 'Straight ahead.'

The darkness enveloped them as they strolled out of the pool of light cast by the streetlamp. Unlike Melbourne, there weren't streetlights every few houses—in fact, once you left the main street and the cluster of shops on the esplanade there were very few lights. He glanced up into the bright and cluttered Milky Way. 'The stars are amazing here.'

'The benefits of barely any light pollution. Are you interested in astronomy?'

He mused over the question. 'I'm not saying I'm not interested, it's just I've never really given it much thought.'

'Too busy working and studying?'

'You got it.'

She directed them across the street and produced a torch from her pocket as they turned into an unpaved road. 'How far away are you from taking your final exams?'

'Six months,' he said, trying really hard to sound neutral instead of bitter and avoid yet another city-versus-country argument.

She stopped walking so suddenly that his continued motion pulled her into his chest and her torch blinded him. 'What's wrong? Did you leave something at the restaurant?' he asked, seeing floaters as he turned off the torch.

'Six months?' Her voice rose incredulously. 'That close?' Her hands gripped his forearms. 'Noah, you should be in Melbourne.'

Her unexpected support flowed into him. 'You won't get an argument from me.'

'So why are you here?'

Her voice came out of the dark, asking the same question she'd posed almost two weeks ago. Back then he'd dodged it, not wanting to tell her the truth. Admitting to frailties wasn't something he enjoyed doing. Then again, he hadn't told anyone in a very long time about the dark days of caring for his mother and although he'd initially been reluctant, telling Lily the story at dinner hadn't been the nightmare he'd thought it would be.

Don't expose weakness.

She'll understand.

Hell, she'd hinted at dinner that she suspected so what was the point in avoiding the question? He sucked in a deep breath of sea air and found his fingers playing with strands of her hair. 'The chief of surgery believes if I sat the communication component of my exams now, I'd fail. He sent me down here for a massive increase in patient contact when they're awake.'

Her fingers ran along the lapel of his jacket and then she took the torch back from him, turning it on. Light spilled around them. 'Do you think you're improving?'

God, he hoped so. He'd been trying harder than he ever had before but it didn't come easily. 'What do you think?'

She worried her bottom lip.

He groaned as his blood pounded south. 'Lily, please don't do that unless you want me to kiss you.'

'Sorry.'

Her voice held an unusual trace of anxious apology, which immediately snagged him. 'Don't be sorry. But, seriously, do you think I'd pass now?'

She sighed. 'Do you promise not to yell?'

'Come on, Lily,' he said bewildered, 'I'm asking for your opinion. Why would I yell?'

She gave a strangled laugh. 'Because what I'm about to say may not be what you want to hear.'

He gently tucked her hair behind her ears, wanting to reassure her. 'I've been watching you for a week and a half and you have a natural gift with people. I want and need your opinion.'

She was quiet for a moment and when she spoke her voice was soft and low. 'I think you're doing better than when you arrived.'

Her tone did little to reassure him. 'But?'

'But you're not quite there yet.'

Damn it. Every part of him tightened in despair and he ploughed his hands through his hair. He'd thought what he was doing was enough and now that he knew it wasn't, he had no clue what else he could try.

She reached up, her hand touching his cheek. 'I can help, Noah.'

The warmth of her hand dived into him, only this time, along with arousal, came something else entirely. He didn't know how to describe it but hope was tangled up in it. 'How?'

Her hand dropped away and she recommenced walking as if she'd regretted the intimate touch. 'It's no different from surgery.'

'It's hugely different from surgery,' he said, nonplussed.

'I meant,' she said kindly, 'it's a skill you can learn.'

'And you're willing to teach me? Why?'

She paused outside a house whose veranda lamp threw out a warm, golden glow. When she looked up at him he caught a war of emotions in her eyes and on her pursed lips. 'Because, Noah, despite not wanting to and despite all logic, I like you.'

He should be affronted but the words made him smile. 'Aw, you're such a sweet talker,' he teased. 'Does this mean I'm no longer a mistake?'

She tensed. 'Goodnight, Noah.'

Crazy disappointment filled him that she was going to turn and disappear inside. He wasn't ready to let her go just yet. 'Lily, wait. I'm sorry.' He wanted her back in his arms and to kiss her goodnight but he had the distinct impression that if he pulled her towards him she'd pull right back. The woman who'd thrown caution to the wind last night had vanished like a desert mirage.

He shot for honesty. 'I had a good time tonight.'

She fiddled with her house key. 'So did I. Thanks.'

'You're welcome.' He suddenly gave in to an over-whelming urge to laugh.

Her chin instantly jutted. 'What's so funny?'

'This.' He threw out his arms, indicating the space between them. 'A first date after we've touched each other in amazing places and I've almost come just watching you fall apart over me. Yet I'm standing here on your grandfather's veranda like an inexperienced teenager, wondering if I'm allowed to kiss you good-night.'

Her feet shuffled, her heels tapping on the wooden boards. 'You still want to kiss me, even though you know nothing else is going to happen?'

Something in her quiet voice made goose-bumps rise on his arms. 'Lily, what's going on?'

'Nothing. Just checking.'

The words came out so sharply they whipped him. The last thing he expected was for her to step in close, wrap her arms around him, rise up on her toes and press her lips to his.

But he wasn't complaining. His arms tightened around her as he opened his mouth under hers. Orange and dark chocolate rushed him, tempting him, addict-ing him, and he moaned softly as his blood thundered pure pleasure through his veins. It hit his legs and he sat heavily on the veranda ledge of the old Californian bungalow, pulling her in close, loving the feel of her breasts and belly pressing against him.

She explored his mouth like a sailor in uncharted waters—flicking and probing, marking territory—each touch setting fire to a new part of him until he was one united blaze, existing only for her. The frenzied exploration slowly faded and with one deep kiss she stole the breath from his lungs.

A moment later, wild-eyed and panting, she swung out of his arms and opened the front door.

'Lily,' he croaked, barely able to see straight and struggling to construct a coherent sentence, 'not that I'm complaining, but somehow I think I still owe you a kiss.'

A wan smile lifted the edge of her mouth. 'Not at all. Goodnight, Noah.'

As the door clicked shut softly, he had the craziest impression that he'd just passed some sort of a test.

CHAPTER SEVEN

LILY CLOSED THE DOOR behind her and sagged back against it.

What on earth were you thinking?

I wasn't thinking at all.

And that was the problem. What had started out as a kiss to test if what Noah had said about sex being her choice was really true had almost culminated in something else entirely. Thank goodness they'd been on Gramps's front veranda—that had totally saved her.

She pushed off the door and headed to the bathroom to splash her burning face and body with cold, cold water. Damn it, she should never have agreed to dinner. She could rationalise her reaction in the car last night as a response to trauma. She had no such luxury tonight. Dinner had been a huge mistake. If she hadn't gone to dinner she wouldn't have seen a vulnerable side to a guy she'd pegged as irritable and difficult. She desperately needed to see him as arrogant, irascible, opinionated, unfeeling and short-sighted, because that gave her a buffer of safety. Only he really wasn't any of those things without good reason and *that* had decimated her

safety barrier as easily as enemy tanks rolling relent-
lessly into a demilitarised zone.

At dinner he'd been the perfect gentleman and he'd
walked her home, and—this still stunned her—he'd
asked her permission to kiss her goodnight. He was
all restraint while she… *Oh, God.* She groaned at the
memory and studied herself in the bathroom mirror.

Face flushed pink, pupils so large and black they almost obliterated the blue of her irises, and her hair wild
and untamed, framing her cheeks. She looked like an
animal on heat. One kiss and she'd been toast. Toast on
fire, burning brightly with flames leaping high into the
air. Feeling alive for the first time in, oh, so long, and
she both loved and feared the feeling.

Why fear it? He kept his word.

And that scared her most because it tempted her to
trust again.

'You're looking tired,' Lily said to Kylie Ambrose as
she took her blood pressure. 'Are you getting any rest?'

'With three kids? What do you think?'

Lily wrapped up the blood-pressure cuff. 'I think that
as tomorrow's Saturday you need to get Shane to take
the kids out for the day and you need to sleep.'

'Shane's working really hard at the moment, Lily.
He needs to rest too.'

Lily's pen paused on the observation chart and she
set it down. 'Shane's not six months pregnant, Kylie.'

'Can you imagine if guys got pregnant? They'd have
to lie down for the whole nine months.' Kylie's laugh
sounded forced. 'You know tomorrow's the footy so he
can't mind them.'

'Sunday, then,' Lily suggested, with a futility she didn't want to acknowledge.

Despite the fact she was both taller and fitter than Shane Ambrose, he was the sort of man she avoided. He reminded her too much of Trent—the life of the party, charming and able to hold a crowd in the palm of his hand, flirting shamelessly with all the women of the town while Kylie, so often pregnant, stood on the sidelines and watched.

'Shane insists that Sunday's family day,' Kylie said in a tone that brooked no further comment. 'I promise I'll catch up on some sleep next week.'

'Great,' Lily said, stifling a sigh and knowing it was unlikely to happen. 'Your ankles are a little puffy so I want to see you next week too.'

'Shane's not going to like that.'

Memories of Trent trying to control her made Lily snap. 'Tell Shane if he has a problem with the care you're receiving, he can come and talk to me and Dr Jackson.' And she'd tell Noah that Shane Ambrose was the one person he didn't have to be polite with. In fact, she'd love it if he gave the man some of his shoot-from-the-hip, brusquely no-nonsense medical advice.

Kylie immediately backpedalled. 'That's not necessary, Lily. Of course Shane wants the best for me and the kids.'

Lily wasn't at all sure Shane Ambrose wanted the best for his family but she felt bad for being short with Kylie. 'If it helps, bring the kids with you to the appointment. Karen and Chippy can keep them entertained while I see you.'

Kylie gave her a grateful look. 'Thanks, Lily. Not everyone understands.'

Lily understood only too well and that was the problem.

Noah heard the click-clack of claws on the floor and turned to see Chippy heading to his basket. 'Hey, boy, what are you doing here on a Saturday?'

The dog wandered over to him, presenting his head to be patted. It made Noah smile. When he'd arrived he'd thought the idea of a dog in a medical practice was ridiculous but two weeks down the track he had to agree that Chippy had a calming effect on a lot of the patients. 'Where's your owner, mate?'

'Right here.'

He spun around to see Lily wearing three-quarter-length navy pants, a cream and navy striped top and bright red ballet flats—chic, casual, weekend wear. She looked fresh and for Lily almost carefree. Almost. There was something about her that hovered permanently—a reserve. An air of extreme caution, except for the twice it had fallen away spectacularly and completely. Both times had involved lust. Both times he'd been wowed.

He hadn't seen her since Thursday night when she'd kissed him like he was the last man standing. He'd thought he'd died and gone to heaven. As a result, his concentration had been hopeless yesterday, to the point that one of the oldies in the nursing home had asked him if he was the one losing his memory.

With a start, he realised he was staring at her. 'You look good.' The words came out gruff and throaty. 'Very nautical.'

She shrugged as if the compliment unnerved her. 'It's the first sunny day we've had this season so I hauled out the spring clothes to salute the promise of summer.'

'As you're here on a Saturday, I guess that means you have a labouring woman coming in?'

'No. I'm here to help you, like I promised.'

Confusion skittered through him. 'But I got the book you left in my pigeonhole and I've read it.' It was a self-help guide that he'd forced himself to read and had been pleasantly surprised to find that, instead of navel-gazing mumbo-jumbo, it actually had some reasonable and practical suggestions. 'Is there more?'

'Yes.' Her mouth curved up into a smile. 'This is Noah's Practical Communication Class 102.'

'I guess that's better than 101,' he grumbled.

'That's the spirit, Pollyanna,' she said with a laugh, as her perfume wafted around him.

He wanted so badly to reach out and grab her around the waist, feel her against him and kiss those red, ruby lips. He almost did, but three things stopped him.

Number one: he was at work and a professional.

There's no one else here yet so it would be okay.

Shut up.

Number two: after two nights of broken sleep and re-living their exhilarating and intoxicating random hook-ups, he'd decided that the best way to proceed with Lily was with old-fashioned dating. Not that he really knew anything about that because his experience with women came more under the banner of hook-ups rather than dating, but his month in Turraburra was all about firsts.

Number three: Karen chose that moment to march

through the door like the Pied Piper, with half a dozen patients trailing in behind her.

If he was brutally honest with himself, this was the *only* reason he didn't give in to his overwhelming desire to kiss Lily until she made that mewling sound in the back of her throat and sagged against him.

'No rest for the wicked, Doctor,' Karen said briskly, dumping her bag on the desk. 'Mrs Burke is up first.'

Smile, eye contact, greeting. He recalled the basics from the book. Smiling at the middle-aged woman, he said, 'Morning, Mrs Burke. Glorious day today.'

'For some perhaps,' she said snarkily as she stomped ahead of him down the hall.

'Deep breath, Noah,' Lily said quietly, giving his arm a squeeze before they followed their patient into the examination room.

His automatic response was to read Mrs Burke's history but as he turned towards the computer screen Lily cleared her throat. He stifled a sigh and fixed his gaze on his patient. 'How can I help you today, Mrs Burke?'

'You can't.' She folded her arms over her ample chest. 'Not unless you can pull any strings with the hospital waiting lists.'

'What procedure are you waiting for?'

'Gall bladder.'

'You're—' He stopped himself from saying, 'fair, fat and forty', which was the classic presentation for cholelithiasis. 'How many attacks have you had?'

'One. I thought I was having a heart attack but, according to the hospital in Berwick, one attack doesn't qualify as urgent so I'm on the waiting list. It's been three months and now on top of everything I have shocking heartburn. I feel lousy all the time.'

He tapped his pen, running through options in his head. 'Is there any way you can afford to be a private patient?'

'Oh, right. I'm just waiting around for the hell of it.'

Frustration dripped from the words and he was tempted to suggest she donate to the sarcasm jar.

'I think Dr Jackson is just covering all the bases,' Lily said mildly.

Surprise rocked him. Had she just defended him? Or was she just worried he was going to be equally rude back to Mrs Burke? Ordinarily, he would have said what he always said to patients attending the outpatient clinic at the Melbourne Victoria, which was, 'You're just going to have to wait it out,' and then he'd exit the room quickly. Only that wasn't an option in Turraburra.

Try reflective listening. The self-help book had an entire chapter on it, but Noah wasn't totally convinced it worked. 'I understand how frustrating it must be—'

'Do you really?' Claire Burke's eyes threw daggers at him. 'With that car you drive and the salary you earn, I bet you have private health insurance.'

He wanted to yell, *I'm a surgical registrar. Plumbers earn more than I do at the moment and my student debt is enormous,* but he blew out a breath and tried something he'd never done before. He gave a tiny bit of himself. 'I grew up in a family who couldn't afford insurance, Claire,' he said, hoping that by using her first name it might help defuse some of her anger. 'I can treat your heartburn and I'll make a call on Monday to find out where you are on the surgical waiting list. I will try and see if I can move you along a bit.'

He knew the chance of getting her moved up the list was about ten thousand to one. It frustrated him because the crazy thing was that an elective cholecystectomy was routine laparoscopic surgery. He could have operated on her but in Turraburra he didn't have access to any operating facilities.

You will in two weeks. The thought cheered him. 'Would you be able to go to East Melbourne for surgery if that was the only option?'

'I'll go anywhere.' Claire's anger deflated like a balloon as she accepted the prescription for esomeprazole. 'Thanks, Doctor. I appreciate that you took the time to listen.'

He saw her out and then turned to face Lily. 'You have no idea how much I wanted to tell her she was rude and obnoxious.'

Lily laughed. 'We all want to do that. The important thing is that you didn't.' She raised her hand for a high-five. 'You managed empathy under fire.'

He grinned like a kid let loose in a fairground, ridiculously buzzed by her praise. 'Empathy is damn hard work.'

'It will get easier.' She steepled her fingers, bouncing them gently off each other. 'I do have one suggestion for you, though. Get into the habit of giving the medical history a brief scan before you go and get the patient. That way you're not tempted to read it and ignore them when they first arrive.'

'First I have to show empathy and now you're asking

me to take advice as well?' he said with a grin. 'It's a whole new world.'

'Sarcasm jar?' she said lightly.

'I'll pay up on behalf of Claire Burke.' He clicked on the computer, bringing up the next patient history. 'Mr Biscoli, seventy-three and severe arthritis.'

'He's a honey and will probably arrive with produce from his garden for you.'

'It says here he's on a waiting list for a hip replacement.' Noah frowned. 'How long since the Turraburra hospital closed its operating theatre?'

'Five years. It's crazy really because the population has grown so much since then. Now we have a lot of retirees from Melbourne who come down here to live just as they're at an age where they need a lot more health services. The birth centre had to fight hard to exist because we can't push through double doors for an emergency Caesarean section, which is why the selection criteria are so strict.'

Noah leaned over to the intercom. 'Karen, on Monday can you do an audit on how many clinic patients are on surgical waiting lists, please?'

'I can do that, Doctor,' Karen said, sounding slightly taken aback.

'Thanks.' He released the button and leaned back, watching Lily. He laughed at her expression. 'I've just surprised you, haven't I?'

'You do that continually, Noah,' she said wryly.

'I'm taking that as a good thing.'

'I never expected any less.' She laughed and smile lines crinkled the edges of her eyes. She almost looked relaxed.

God, she was gorgeous and he wanted time to explore this thing that burned so hotly between them. He checked his watch as an idea formed and firmed. 'Emergencies excepted, I should be out of here by twelve-thirty. Let's have lunch together. We can put together a picnic and you choose the place. Show me a bit of Turraburra I haven't seen.'

Somewhere quiet and secluded so we can finish what we started the other night.

Based on previous invitations, he expected protracted negotiations with accompanying caveats and he quickly prepared his own strategic arguments.

'Sounds great.'

He blinked at her, not certain he'd heard correctly. 'So you're up for a picnic?'

Her eyes danced. 'Yes, and I know the perfect place...'

He was already picturing a private stretch of beach or a patch of pristine rainforest in the surrounding hills, a picnic rug, a full-bodied red wine, gourmet cheeses from the local cheese factory, crunchy bread from the bakery and Lily. Delectable, sexy Lily.

'The oval. Turraburra's playing Yarram today in the footy finals.'

Her words broke into his daydream like a machete, splintering his thoughts like kindling. 'You're joking, right?'

'About football?' She shook her head vehemently. 'Never. Turraburra hasn't won against Yarram in nine years but today's the day.'

And that's when it hit him—why she'd so readily accepted his invitation. They weren't going to be alone at all. They'd be picnicking with the entire town.

* * *

Lily wrapped the black and yellow scarf around Noah's neck. 'There you go. Now you're a Tigers fan.'

He gave a good-natured grimace. 'This wasn't quite what I had in mind when I suggested a picnic. Tell me, are you truly a football fan or are we here because you don't want to be alone with me?' His face sobered to deadly serious. 'If you don't want to build on what's already gone down between us, please just tell me now so I know the score and I'll back off.'

This is your absolute out. Her heart quivered at the thought. It should be an easy decision—just say no— but it wasn't because nothing about Noah was as clear-cut as she'd previously thought.

Why are you being so nice, Noah?

Trent had been nice at the start—charming, generous and, unbeknownst to her at the time, calculatingly thoughtful. She already knew Noah was a far better man than Trent. He had a base honesty to him. A man who put his studies on hold to care for his dying mother wasn't selfish or self-serving. A man who confessed to his guilt about finding it so much harder than he'd thought it would be and yet hadn't walked away from it was a thousand times a better man than Trent.

She tied a loose knot in the scarf for the sheer reason that it gave her an excuse to keep touching him. 'I'm a die-hard footy fan to the point that I'll probably embarrass you by yelling at the umpire. And…' She hauled in a fortifying breath and risked looking into those soulful brown eyes that often saw far too much. 'I like being alone with you. It's just that I don't trust myself.'

He caught her hand. 'We're both adults, Lily. Having

sex doesn't mean a lifelong commitment. It can just be fun.'

Fun. It had been fun and good times that had landed her in the worst place she'd ever been in her life and she wasn't going back there. 'That's what scares me.'

'Fun scares you?' He frowned down at her and then pulled her into him, pressing a kiss to her hair.

He smelled of sunshine and his heart beat rhythmically against her chest. She didn't want to move.

He stroked her back. 'Let's just enjoy the match, hey?'

He could have done a million things—told her she was being silly, urged her to tell him why, cajoled her to leave the game and go and have the sort of fun they both wanted, but he didn't do any of those things. She fought the tears that welled in her eyes at his understanding. 'Sounds good to me.'

He kept his arm slung casually over her shoulder as they watched the second quarter and she enjoyed its light touch and accompanying warmth. It felt delightfully normal and it had been for ever since she'd associated normal with a guy.

The aroma of onions and sausages wafted on the air from the sausage sizzle. Farm and tradies' utes were parked along the boundary of the oval and families sat in chairs while the older kids sat on the utes' cabs for a bird's-eye view. The younger ones scampered back and forth between their parents and the playground. She recognised the Ambrose girls playing on the slide and glanced around for Kylie, but she couldn't see her.

The red football arced back and forth across the length of the oval many times, with the Turraburra Tigers and the Yarram Demons fighting it out. When

Matty Abrahams lost possession of the ball to a Demons player, who then lined up for a set shot at goal, Noah yelled, 'Chewy on your boot!'

She laughed and nudged him with her hip. 'Look at you. Next you'll be eating a pie.'

He grinned down at her, his eyes dancing. 'I never said I didn't enjoy football. I may have grown up in New South Wales in the land of rugby league, but since coming to Melbourne I've adopted AFL. I get to games when I can.'

The man was full of surprises. The Turraburra crowd gave a collective groan as the ball sailed clearly through the Demons's goalposts, putting them two goals ahead.

The whirr of Gramps's gopher sounded behind her, followed by the parp-parp of his hooter. 'Hi, Gramps, I thought you were watching from the stands with Muriel?'

'I was and then Harry Dimetrious told me he'd seen you down here so I thought I'd come and say hello.'

'Good to see you out and about, Bruce,' Noah said, extending his hand.

Bruce shook it. 'You seem to be enjoying yourself, Doc,' he said shrewdly. 'I know you'll be on your best behaviour with my granddaughter.'

'Gramps!' Lily wanted to die on the spot.

Noah glanced between the two of them, his expression amused and slightly confused. He squeezed her hand. 'I like to think I'm always on my best behaviour with women, Bruce.'

Gramps assessed him with his rheumy but intelligent eyes. 'Long may it stay that way, son.'

Desperate to change the subject lest Noah ask her

why, when she was almost thirty, her grandfather was treating him like they were teenagers, she saw a Demons player holding onto the ball for longer than the rules allowed. 'Ball,' she screamed loudly. 'Open your eyes, Ump! Do your job!'

Noah laughed. 'I think she's more than capable of standing up for herself, Bruce.'

She stared doggedly at the game, not daring to look at her grandfather in case Noah caught the glance.

By half-time the Turraburra Tigers trailed by fifteen points. 'Cheer up,' Noah said. 'It's not over until the final siren. I saw a sign in the clubrooms that the Country Women's Association are serving Devonshire tea. Come on, my shout.'

Still holding her hand, they walked towards the clubrooms and she felt the eyes of the town on her.

'Hey, Doc.' Rod Baker, her mechanic, pressed his hand against Noah's shoulder. 'You know Lily's special, right?'

Lily's face glowed so hotly she could have fried eggs on her cheeks. Before she could say a word, Noah replied without a trace of sarcasm, 'Without a doubt.'

'Just as long as you know,' Rod said, before removing his hand.

When she'd suggested the footy to him, she'd never anticipated Noah's public displays of affection. Granted, they'd done a lot more than handholding in his car and the other night she'd kissed him so hard she'd seen stars, but in a way it had been private, hidden from other people's eyes. She'd never expected him to act as if they were dating.

Not that she didn't like it. She really did but it put

her between a rock and a hard place. If she pulled her hand away it would make him question her, and if she didn't then the town would.

A movement caught her eye and she saw Kylie Ambrose being pulled to her feet by her husband. 'Kylie, you okay?' she called out automatically, a shiver running over her skin.

'She's fine,' Shane said. 'Aren't you, love?'

'Yes,' Kylie said, brushing down her maternity jeans but not looking up. 'I just tripped over my feet. You know, pregnancy klutz.'

'I think I should just check you out,' Lily said, 'Just to make sure you and the baby are fine.'

'For God's sake, Lily,' Shane said. 'You were a panic merchant at school and you're still one.'

Before she could say another word, Noah stepped forward. 'I'm Dr Noah Jackson, Kylie. Were you dizzy before you fell?'

'Kylie's healthy as a horse, aren't you, love,' Shane said, putting his arm around his wife.

'She's also pregnant,' Noah said firmly. 'Have a seat on the bench, Kylie, and I'll check your blood pressure.'

Lily expected Kylie to object but she sat and started pulling up her sleeve, only to flinch, stop and tug it back down before pushing up the other sleeve.

Was she hiding something? Not for the first time, Lily wondered if she should tell Kylie a little something about her own past. 'Did you hurt your arm, Kylie?'

'No. It's just this one's closer to the doc.'

And it was. Two minutes later Noah declared Kylie's blood pressure to be normal, Shane teased his wife about having two left feet, and Lily felt foolish for allowing her dislike of Shane to colour her judgement. She really must stop automatically looking for the bad in men. Good guys were out there—Noah and her grandfather were perfect examples of that—and although Shane wasn't her type of guy, it didn't make him a bastard.

'We still have time for those scones,' Noah said, putting his hand gently under her elbow and propelling her into the clubrooms.

Linda Sampson served them with a wide smile. 'Lily, it's lovely to see you out and about.'

'I'm always out and about, Linda,' she said, almost snatching the teapot out of the woman's hands.

'You know what I mean, dear,' Linda continued, undeterred by Lily's snappish reply. 'Treat her nice, Dr Jackson.'

Lily busied herself with pouring tea and putting jam and cream on the hot scones. When she finally looked up, Noah's gaze was fixed on her.

'The town's very protective of you.'

'Not really. Have a scone.' She pushed the plate towards him.

'At first I thought all these warnings and instructions were about me. That I'd ruffled a few feathers.'

'I'm sure that's it,' she said desperately. 'But word will get around fast that you've improved out of sight. Claire Burke's a huge gossip and after this morning she'll be singing your praises.'

He didn't look convinced. 'The thing is, the more I think about it, every piece of advice I've been given is about you.' He leaned forward. 'Why is the town protecting you?'

'They're not.' She gulped her tea.

'Yeah, they are, and I can't afford any negative reports about me getting back to the Melbourne Victoria.'

Something inside her hurt. 'I guess we should stop whatever this is, then.'

His eyes darkened with a mix of emotions. 'That's not what I'm suggesting at all.'

She stood up, desperate to leave the claustrophobic clubrooms, leave the game, and leave the eyes of the town. 'Let's get out of here.'

He grabbed a scone and followed her outside as she half walked, half ran, able to outrun the eyes of the town but not the demons of her past.

'Where are we going?' Noah finally asked as they passed through the gates of the recreation reserve.

'Your place.'

CHAPTER EIGHT

THE MOMENT NOAH closed his front door Lily's body slammed into his, her hand angling his head, and then she was kissing him. *Yes!* His body high-fived and he was instantly hard. This was it—what he'd been dreaming about for days was finally going to happen. He was about to have sex again with Lily. He was so ready that he risked coming too soon.

Her lips and tongue roamed his, stealing all conscious thought. Nothing existed except her touch, her scent and her taste. Her wondrous, glorious, intoxicating taste that branded itself onto every part of his mouth. He went up in flames in a way he'd never done before.

She kicked off her shoes and then pulled his T-shirt over her head, sighing as she pressed her hands to his chest. 'I've been wanting to do that for hours.'

He pulled her T over her head and smiled at the filmy lace bra that hid nothing. 'You're gorgeous.'

She seemed to almost flinch and then she dropped her head and kissed his chest before licking his hard and erect nipples. For a second he lost his vision.

'Let's go have some fun,' she said, glancing around. Her gaze landed on the kitchen bench.

'Oh, yeah.' As he moved towards the kitchen his brain suddenly fired back into action. *Fun scares me.*

His body groaned. *Don't do this to me. Now is not the time to start thinking and acting like a girl.*

But try as he might, he couldn't banish Lily's words from his head. *Fun scares me.*

He thought about the time in the car when she'd let go of all restraint and how she was doing it again with such intensity, as if she was trying to forget something.

It was a mistake.

That's what she'd said last time and for some un-fathomable reason he didn't want to have sex and then watch her run again.

Why? Usually that's exactly what you want—wish for even. But today it felt wrong. He didn't want to have Lily close up on him again and he knew as intimately as he knew himself that he sure as hell didn't want to be considered a mistake.

He held her gently at arm's length. 'I want so badly to have sex with you right now that it hurts.'

She grinned, her eyes wild. 'I'm glad.'

He stared down into her bluer-than-blue eyes and regret hammered him so hard it hurt to breathe. 'But I'm not having sex with you until you tell me what's going on.'

Panic spread through Lily's veins, pumping anxiety into every cell. She opened her mouth to say, 'Noth-ing is going on,' but immediately closed it. As much as she didn't want to tell him anything, he didn't deserve lies. Her brain whirred, trying to find a way to give him enough to satisfy him without opening the floodgates to a past she refused to allow back into her life.

She scooped up their shirts from the floor and threw his at him. 'Put that on so you don't distract me,' she said, trying to joke. It came out sad.

He silently obliged and by the time she'd pulled her T over her head he too was fully dressed. She'd hit the point of no return. *Say it fast and it won't hurt so much.* 'The town's protecting me because I was married.'

'You were married?' His echoing tone was a combination of horror and surprise.

'I was.' The memory of those pain-filled twenty-four months dragged across her skin like a blunt blade.

'And you're a widow?'

I wish. Oh, how I wish. She was tempted to say yes, but Turraburra knew that wasn't true. Although only her grandfather knew the full story about her marriage, everyone else knew she'd come home a faded version of her former self and without a husband. She was sure they'd speculated and talked about it amongst themselves, but instead of asking her what had happened, they'd circled her in kindness. 'No. I'm divorced.'

He looked seriously uncomfortable. 'Sorry.'

I'm not. She shrugged. 'It is what it is.'

'Am I the first guy since…?'

At least she could give him the absolute truth to one question. 'Virtually. There was one drunken episode the day my divorce came through but nothing since.' She wrung her hands. 'I'm sorry about my erratic behaviour,' she said, hoping the topic was almost done and dusted because she wasn't prepared to tell him any more. 'My libido's been dormant for so long and you've exploded it out of the blocks. I guess it scared me and I'm really sorry for saying you were a mistake. You're not at all, but you don't need to panic. I'm not looking for anything serious. We can enjoy whatever this is for what it is.' *Please.*

His keen gaze studied her and for a heart-stopping moment she thought he was going to ask her more questions. Questions she didn't want to answer. Information she never wanted him to know.

He wrapped his arms gently around her and pulled her into him, pressing a kiss to her forehead. 'As much as I find the out-of-control Lily a huge turn-on and sex in a car and on a kitchen counter reminds me I'm not past spontaneity, I want to make love to you in a bed. I want to be able to see you and touch you without the risk of either of us getting injured. I want your first time in a long time to be special.'

She hastily dropped her head onto his chest, hiding an errant tear that had squeezed out of her eye and was spilling down her cheek. *Oh, Noah, why do you have to be so caring?* But before she could overthink things he ran them down the hall to the bedroom.

'Sorry,' he said with an embarrassed grin as he pulled her into the room. 'I'd have made the bed if I'd thought I had a chance of being in it with you.'

She laughed. 'I only make mine on laundry day.'

'But I bet you do hospital corners.' He whipped off his shirt. 'I believe we were up to here when we hit pause.'

She gazed at his taut abdominal muscles, delineated pecs and a smattering of brown hair and sighed. 'I remember.'

'You're overdressed.' As his hands tugged on the hem of her shirt she raised her arms and let him pull it off. 'As much as I love pretty underwear, this has to go as well.' His fingers flicked the hooks on her bra and the straps fell across her shoulders.

As she stood there half-naked in the afternoon light without the cover of darkness, she suddenly felt extremely vulnerable and exposed. She dived for the bed, pulling at the sheet for cover, but it came away in her hand. 'And you don't do hospital corners at all, do you?'

He laughed. 'Obviously not very well but that's in my favour today.' He rolled her under him, gazing at her appreciatively. 'No hiding your beauty under sheets, Lily.' He lowered his mouth to her left breast and suckled her.

A flash of need—hot, potent and addictive—whooshed through her so fast and intense that she cried out and her hands rose to grip his shoulders.

He paused and raised his head, a slight frown on his face. 'You okay.'

'More than okay.'

His smile encapsulated his entire face. 'Excellent, but tell me if something's not working for you.'

He was killing her with kindness and she didn't know how to respond so she did what she always did when she got scared—she took control. Pulling his head down to her mouth, she kissed him, only this time he kissed her back. Hot, hard, sensual and electrifying, his mouth ranged over hers while his hands woke up the rest of her body.

She was hot but shivery, boneless with need yet taut with it too. She wanted his touch to go on for ever and at the same time she screamed for release. She ran her fingers through his hair, down his spine and across his hips. She soaked him in—the strength of his muscles, the hardness of his scapula, the dips between his ribs, the rough and smooth of his skin—all of him. Her legs tangled with his until he'd moved down her body and she could no longer reach them. By the time his mouth reached the apex of her thighs, she was writhing in pleasure, burning with bliss and aching in emptiness.

'Noah.'

He raised his head. 'Yes?'

'As much as I appreciate your focused ministrations, I feel I owe you after last time.'

'No hurry,' he said lazily. 'We've got all afternoon.' He dropped his head and his tongue flicked her.

Her pelvis rose from the bed as her hands gripped the edge of the mattress. 'What…what if I want to hurry?'

'You sure?' His voice was as ragged as hers.

'God, yes.'

He moved, reaching for a condom, but she got there first. 'Let me.'

'Next time,' he grunted, plucking the foil square out of her hand.

'How do you want to do this?'

'I want to see you.'

She cupped his cheek. 'So do I.'

She tilted her hips and with her guidance he slowly moved into her. Slick with need, she welcomed him with a sob. 'I'd forgotten how good it could feel.'

'Let me remind you.'

He kissed her softly and she wrapped her legs high around his hips, moving with him, feeling him sliding against her, building on every delicious sensation he'd created previously with his mouth and hands. She spiralled higher and higher towards a peak that beckoned. Pleasure and pain morphed together and she screamed as she was flung far out of herself. Suspended for a moment in waves of silver and grey, she hovered before falling back to the real world.

Noah, moving over her, his face taut with restraint and his breath coming hard and fast, finally shuddered against her. She wrapped her arms around him as he came and she realised with a jolt that, once again, he'd put her needs first. No man had ever done that for her once, let alone twice.

It's just sex, remember.

It could only ever be sex.

Noah's blood pounded back to his brain and he quickly realised his limp and satiated body was at risk of flattening Lily. He kissed her swiftly on the lips, before rolling off her and tucking her in beside him. 'That was wonderful. Thanks.'

'Right back at you.' Her fingers trailed down his sternum.

He drew lazy circles on her shoulder. 'So how long has it been?'

'If I told you that I'd lose my air of mystery,' she said lightly.

Her tone didn't match the sudden tension around her mouth. 'Fair enough.' He wanted to know what was going on but most of him didn't want to lose the golden glow that cocooned them both. 'Let me just say, though, for the record, you haven't forgotten a thing.'

She gave a snort of embarrassed laughter. 'Thank you, I think.'

'I can't believe you're blushing,' he teased her. 'You're a conundrum, Lil.'

Her body went rigid. 'Don't ever call me that.'

Like the strike of an open palm against skin, her tone burned. 'Duly noted.'

She sighed and pressed a kiss to his chest. 'I'm sorry. I just hate that contraction of my name. It's so short that it's over before it's started. All my friends call me Lily.'

He wasn't exactly certain what he was to her or what he wanted to be. Lover? Yes. Colleague? Yes. 'Do I qualify as a friend?'

'A friend with benefits.'

A zip of something resembling relief whizzed through him with an intensity that surprised him. Usually, at this point, the snuggling with a woman was starting to stifle him and he was already planning his exit strategy.

'I need the bathroom,' she said, sitting up with her back to him.

Jagged, pale pink scars zigzagged over her shoulder and across her back. He automatically reached out to touch them. 'What happened here?'

She flinched then utterly stilled.

'Lily?'

'I fell through a plate-glass window. I'll be right back.' He expected her to elaborate on how the accident had happened but she didn't say anything more. He watched her disappear into the bathroom. When she returned and kissed him soundly, he totally forgot to ask.

* * *

Lily was pottering around the kitchen, supposedly cooking an omelette—something she did most Sunday nights—only tonight she was struggling to remember how to do it. She was struggling to remember anything prosaic and everyday. Usually by this time on a Sunday evening she had her list drawn up for the coming week, her work clothes washed and ironed, and if a baby wasn't on the way she was ready to sit down and relax.

Not tonight. Every time she tried to focus on something her brain spun off, reliving Noah's mouth on her body and his gentle hands on her skin—and they were always gentle—yet they could make her orgasm with an intensity she'd never experienced. Sure, she'd had sex before, thought it had been good even, and then when everything with Trent had started to change in ways she'd never anticipated—irrevocably and devastatingly final—it had taken the joy of sex with it.

It was a shock to discover she now craved sex with a passion that scared her. To crave sex was one thing—and in one way she was fine with that. What she didn't want was to crave Noah. She didn't want to crave any man because it left her wide open to way too much pain and grief.

Don't overthink this. Like Noah said, it's just temporary and for fun. It has a definite end date in less than two weeks when life returns to normal. Enjoy it and bank it for the rest of your life.

And she was enjoying it. They'd spent Saturday afternoon in bed and then she'd been called in to deliver a baby. Noah had visited the midwifery unit on Sunday morning to do the mother and baby discharge check and had brought with him pastries from the bakery and coffee he'd made himself. Once they'd waved goodbye to the Lexingtons and their gorgeous baby, they'd taken a walk along the beach and ended up in his bed. Again.

Distracted, she stared at the egg in her hand before glancing into the bowl, consciously reminding herself how many eggs she'd already cracked. The ding-dong of the doorbell pealed, its rousing noise rolling through the house. Before she could say, 'I wonder who that is?' her grandfather called out, 'I'll get it.'

A moment later she heard, 'Hello, Doc.'

Her hand closed over the egg and albumen oozed through her fingers. *Noah? What was he doing here?*

His deep and melodic voice drifted down the hall, friendly and polite. 'Call me Noah, Bruce.'

'Right-oh. Come on in, then.' Footsteps made the old floorboards creak and then her grandfather called out, 'Lily, you've got a visitor.'

By the time she'd washed her egg-slimed hand, Noah's height and breadth was filling the small kitchen. 'Uh, hi,' she said, feeling ridiculously self-conscious because the last time she'd seen him he'd been delectably naked.

Now he was dressed deliciously in soft, faded jeans and a light woollen V-neck jumper, which clung to him like a second skin. She swallowed hard, knowing exactly how gorgeous the chest under the jumper was and what it tasted like. 'I…I thought you were studying?'

He put the bottle of wine he was holding on the bench. 'I was but your grandfather called and invited me to dinner. I have to eat so I thought…' He suddenly frowned. 'You knew I was coming, right?'

She shook her head slowly, wondering what her grandfather was up to. In three years he'd never invited someone around without telling her and he'd never once invited a man under the age of sixty. 'Ah, no. Gramps kept that bit of information to himself.'

'If it's a problem, I can go.'

Was it a problem? 'You being here's not a problem but I might need to have a chat with Gramps.'

He rounded the bench and reached for her. 'I'm glad he invited me.'

She stepped into his embrace, enjoying how natural it felt to be in his arms yet at the same time worried that it did. 'You say that now, but you have no clue if I can cook.'

His thumbs caressed her cheeks and his often serious eyes sparkled in fun. 'It's a risk I'm willing to take. I mean, how bad can it be?'

She dug him in the ribs. 'For that, you're now my kitchen hand.'

He grinned. 'I'm pretty handy with a knife.'

She pushed the chopping board towards him. 'In less than two weeks you'll be back operating,' she said, as much to remind herself as to remind him. 'How many hours away is that?' she teased, remembering his first day in Turraburra.

He pulled his phone out of his pocket. 'Two hundred and ninety-four hours and three minutes, twelve seconds.'

'Seriously? You've got an app?'

He had the grace to look sheepish. 'I was pretty ticked off when I first arrived here.'

'Were you?' She couldn't help laughing. 'I had no clue.'

'And that takes the total of the sarcasm jar to one hundred and forty dollars.' He got a self-righteous glint in his eye. 'You've now put more money in it than me.'

'That's a bit scary. That jar was for your problem, not mine.'

He gave her a look that said, *You can't be serious.* 'You use sarcasm like a wall.'

Did she? Before Trent, she hadn't been sarcastic at all. Then again, she hadn't been wary and fearful either. The fact Noah had noticed she used sarcasm to keep people at a distance worried her. She plonked an onion on the chopping board to change the subject. 'Dice this.'

'About the app.' He started peeling the onion. 'When I arrived I was taking my frustrations out on the town. I thought I was being singled out from the other surgical registrars and being punished for no good reason.' His warm eyes sought hers. 'It took you to show me I had a problem and that I really needed to be down here. I've hardly looked at the app since our trip back from Melbourne.'

Trent had destroyed personal compliments for her—she never completely trusted them and Noah's sat uneasily. 'But you must be happy that your time's more than half over. That you'll be back in Melbourne soon?'

'Put it this way…' He slid the diced onion off the board and into her warmed and oiled pan. He stepped in behind her, his body hugging hers, 'I have a strong feeling the next twelve days are going to fly by.'

They settled into companionable cooking—he stood next to her, sautéeing the fillings for the omelettes—and his arm brushed hers as he moved, his warmth stealing into her and settling as if it had a right to belong. He asked her about the music she liked, the books she enjoyed—the usual questions people asked as they got to know each other. It was so very conventional. Normal. Terrifying.

'I've set the table,' Gramps announced, as he walked into the kitchen.

'I'm just about ready to serve up,' Lily said, pulling warmed plates out of the oven.

Bruce picked up the bottle of wine. 'This is a good drop, Noah,' he said approvingly. 'Might be a bit too good for eggs, though.'

'Never.' Noah smiled. 'I think it will go perfectly with our gourmet omelettes.'

'In that case, I'll open her up.' Gramps, who loved big, bold, Australian red wines, gave Lily a wicked wink before cracking the seal on the bottle. By the time they sat down at the table he'd poured three glasses. 'Cheers.'

'*Salute*,' Noah said easily.

It was a surreal moment and Lily silently clinked her glass against the other two, not knowing what to say. She was struck by the juxtaposition that Trent, whom she'd married, had never sat down to a meal in her grandfather's house and now Noah, who was nothing more than a wild and euphoric fling, was at the table, sharing their casual Sunday night meal. It was nothing short of weird.

Despite her discombobulation, conversation flowed easily around the table and both Noah and Gramps drew her into the chatter. Slowly, she felt herself start to relax. When the plates were cleared, Bruce suggested they play cribbage.

'Gramps, Noah has to study and—'

'I'm rusty, Bruce,' Noah cut across her, 'but, be warned, I used to play it a lot with my father before he got too sick to hold a hand.'

Bruce clapped his hand on Noah's shoulder in a gesture of understanding. 'Tell you what. I'll give you a couple of hands to warm up then but then it's on for young and old.'

Noah laughed. 'That's a fair deal.'

Lily stared at him, once again flummoxed by his thousand sides—so many that he kept hidden from view. With his tailored clothes, his city sophistication and penchant for gourmet foods and wine, no one would ever guess that he loved footy and played cards. 'Do you play other games?'

'Does the Pope have an art collection?' He gave her a grin. 'My parents didn't have a lot of money but we had an annual beach camping holiday for two weeks every summer. If it rained and I couldn't surf, we'd play cards and board games. You name it, I've played it.'

'Me too,' she said, remembering her own childhood summers and Gramps teaching her the card game Five Hundred, 'but I bet you played to win.'

'Of course.' A bewildered look crossed his face. 'Why else would you play?'

This was pure Noah. 'Oh, I don't know. What about for the sheer enjoyment of it and the company?'

He shuffled the deck of cards like a professional. 'It is possible to do both.'

'The man's right, Lily,' Gramps said, rubbing his hands together. 'Enough of the talk, let's play.'

Over the next hour Lily watched, fascinated as the two men battled it out both determined to win. Despite the heady competition and the good-natured trash and table talk, a lot of laughter and fun ensued. It had been a long time since she'd seen her grandfather quite so animated.

To Gramps's delight, he beat Noah by the barest of margins. 'You'll have to come back another time and try again.'

Noah rose to his feet and shrugged into his jacket with a smile. 'Next time we'll play poker.'

Bruce shot out his hand. 'You're on.'

Lily walked Noah outside. 'It was generous of you to give up your evening and play cards with Gramps.'

A slight frown marred his forehead. 'You think I was just being polite?'

'Playing cards with an old man? Yes, I do.'

He sighed. 'Lily, surely you know me well enough to know that I wouldn't have accepted Bruce's invitation for dinner or cards if I didn't want to.'

But that was the problem—every time she thought she had him worked out he'd go and do something totally unexpected. Every time it happened it humanised him for her, making her think way beyond the sexy guy and skilled lover. Making her want to hope.

And that scared her more than anything.

CHAPTER NINE

NOAH STRODE ALONG the main street, eating his ham and salad baguette as he went and enjoying the sunshine on his face. Unlike his first week in Turraburra, when he'd actually sat on a park bench and taken in the ocean view, today he was walking directly from the bakery to the clinic, because his morning visit to the nursing home had run a long way over time.

He'd got distracted with the birthday morning tea for Mrs Lewinski, who was celebrating her one-hundredth birthday. The local press had been there and the staff had put on a party with balloons, mugs of tea, a cream-filled sponge cake and bingo. It was Mrs L.'s favourite game and it had seemed wrong not to stay and play one game with her. He'd lost.

His week had been a busy one—Lily had been right about word getting out. His third week in town had passed so fast he could hardly believe it was Friday.

'Dr Jackson. Dr Jackson, slow down.'

He turned towards the female voice and saw Claire Burke hurrying towards him. 'Hi, Claire, great day, isn't it?'

'Yes, it is!' Unlike the scowling woman she'd been

last Saturday, now she was positively beaming. 'Karen just called me and told me the news. I can't believe it. I really thought you were just spinning me a line the other day to placate me. I never expected you to be a miracle-worker.' She pushed a carton of eggs into his hands. 'These are free-range eggs from my chooks as a thank-you.'

He accepted the eggs. 'You're welcome, and I'm not a miracle-worker. I just made a few phone calls and spoke with my boss at the Melbourne Victoria. I suggested to him that as the hospital had sent me down here to work, it was only right and proper that I finish the work I started. I'll be removing your gall bladder on my first day back in Melbourne.'

'Well, the fact I'll be operated on in eleven days is a miracle to me and I'm not your only happy patient, Dr Jackson. Rita Hazelton and Len Peterken told me their news too.'

Noah matched her smile. 'Like I said, I'm happy to be able to help.' And he meant it.

In his telephone conversation with the prof, the experienced surgeon had been hesitant about the idea of Noah bringing back a patient load with him from Turraburra. Noah had surprised himself at how passionately he'd pushed for the surgical cases. He always saw his surgery in terms of making a difference but, seeing people in their home environment, those differences were even starker.

His life in Melbourne, his income and his access to services had given him a certain amount of immunity to his past. It was easier to forget the difficult stuff but his time in Turraburra had brought back a lot of memories—life in a town without services and hard-working people in low-paid jobs who couldn't afford health insurance. The reminder that he'd lost contact with his roots came with a shot of middle-class guilt and going in to bat for four patients had seemed a valid way of easing it. It surprised him just how much pleasure he was getting out of being able to help.

'We all thought you were a bit of a cold fish, Doctor,' Claire said, her tone bemused, 'but you've totally surprised us, in a good way.'

Thank you? It was time to go. 'It's been good talking to you, Claire, but I need to get back to the clinic. Thanks for the eggs.'

He arrived back to find Lily sitting at Reception with a huge box of vegetables. He leaned in for a quick kiss. 'Are you starting a food bank?'

She laughed and kissed him back. 'Actually, they're for you, along with this tub of honey, a leg of lamb and some filleted flathead. The town loves you.'

He gave a wry smile. 'Claire Burke just told me the town thought I was a bit of cold fish when I first arrived.'

Lily dropped her face in her hands before looking up at him. 'She seriously said that after you've just organised her surgery?'

'It's okay. I know she meant it as a compliment and we both know I wasn't exactly enthusiastic when I first arrived. The funny thing is, Turraburra grows on you.'

A stricken look crossed her pretty face. 'But Melbourne's better, right?'

'Melbourne is without a doubt the absolute best.' He hauled her to her feet, wrapping his arms around her waist. 'Do you want to come over for dinner tonight and help me eat some of this stuff?'

Her brows rose teasingly. 'Cook it, you mean?'

'Well, if you're offering...'

She laughed. 'How about you barbecue the fish and I'll make ratatouille with the veggies. Deal?'

'Deal.' He glanced around and with no sign of Karen or the afternoon session patients he kissed her long and hard, loving the way she slumped against him. 'And just maybe you could stay the *whole* night?'

Shadows rolled across her usually clear eyes. 'It's not like I have a lot of control over that. Women have a habit of going into labour in the early hours of the morning.'

Only he knew irrespective of a labouring woman, Lily always left his bed before dawn. 'Is it your grandfather?'

'Is what my grandfather?'

'The reason you always leave.'

She spun out of his arms. 'I'm a grown woman, Noah. Gramps doesn't question my comings and goings.'

So why do you leave? He didn't know why it bugged him so much that she did, because in the past he'd always been the one to depart first. In fact, he'd made sure his trysts with women occurred at their place or in a hotel so that he could always make his exit when it suited him. With Lily, staying at her grandfather's house was out of the question so they used his flat. He couldn't say exactly why he wanted her to stay a whole night but he did know that when she rolled away from him, swung her legs out of bed and padded out of the room, a vague hollowness filled him.

An idea pinged into his head—the perfect solution

to this problem. 'You have this weekend rostered off, right?'

She nodded. 'Someone's down from MMU this afternoon through Sunday. Why? Do you want to visit that winery I told you about?'

He caught her hands and drew her back in close. 'Better than that.'

She gazed up at him, her expression quizzical. 'Better than a studio room high in the gum trees with a view clear to Tasmania?'

He grinned. 'Yep.'

Her eyes sparkled with excitement. 'Where?'

'My place.'

'Um, Noah, the hospital flat doesn't come close to the accommodation at the winery.'

He shook his head. 'No, I mean *my* place. Come and spend the weekend with me in Melbourne.'

Her eyes dimmed. 'Oh, I don't th—'

'Yes,' he said enthusiastically. 'Come and experience *my* world. Let me show you my Melbourne. We can go to the Queen Vic market for the best coffee in the country, take in the exhibition at the National Gallery, see a show at the Melbourne Theatre Company, anything you want.'

She stiffened in his arms. 'No.'

The quiet word carried gravitas. He tucked some hair behind her ears. 'Why not?'

'I don't like Melbourne.'

He kissed her hair. 'But you've never had me as a tour guide before.'

She pulled away. 'It's not like I haven't seen or done those things before, Noah. None of it's new to me.'

Her quick dismissal of his idea felt like a slap in the face. 'So you'll spend the weekend at the winery where you've been before but you won't come to Melbourne?'

She shrugged. 'What can I say? I'm a country girl.'

Her dismissive manner was at odds with her usual interest in things. 'Aren't you at all curious about seeing my place?'

She sucked in her lips. 'Not really, no.'

Her rejection flared a jagged, white-hot pain, which burned him under his ribs. *No.* His hand rubbed the spot. It had been a long time since he'd felt something like that and he hated it was back. Hated that he'd allowed himself to care enough to be hurt. 'So this thing between us doesn't extend beyond Turraburra?'

She stared at him, her face filling with pity. 'Noah, you were the one who said sex doesn't have to mean a lifelong commitment. I took you at your word. We enjoy each other while you're here and then we go back to our lives.'

His own words—ones he'd always lived by when it came to women and sex—suffocated him with their irony. For the first time in his life he didn't want to walk away. Lily made him laugh, she called him on his arrogant tendencies and as a result he'd become a better doctor and a better person. She understood him in a way no one else ever had, and because of that he'd opened up to her, telling her more about this life than he'd told anyone.

He wanted a chance to explore this relationship, an opportunity to see where it would take them. Hell, he wanted more than that. He wanted to come home to

Lily, tell her about his day, bounce ideas off her, and hear about her day.

I love her.

His breath left his lungs in a rush, leaving him hauling in air against cramping muscles. *No, I do not love her. I can't love her.*

He didn't have time to love anyone, didn't want to love anyone, and he didn't want to feel tied down to another person. Loving meant caring and caring meant his life wasn't his own to do as he pleased.

It's already happened, mate. That empty feeling when she leaves the bed—that's love.

Wanting to show her Melbourne—that's love.

Wanting her to share your life—that's love.

He ran his hands through his hair but the ragged movement morphed into something else. Panic eased, replaced by a desperate need to tell her exactly how he felt. 'What if I told you that when I said all that stuff about commitment I truly believed it, but getting to know you has changed everything?'

'Noah, I—'

'Shh.' He pressed his finger gently to her lips. 'I want to take this to the next level. I want commitment, exclusivity, the complete deal. I want us to be a couple because I've fallen in love with you.'

A look of pure horror crossed her face and she brought her arms up in front of her like a protective shield. 'You don't love me, Noah.'

He opened his hands palms up, hoping the gesture would reassure her. 'It's a surprise to me too but I most definitely do love you.'

'No.' Her voice rose, tinged with a sharp edge. 'You don't.'

Every cell in his body tensed and he worked hard at keeping a leash on his temper. 'Don't tell me—' he immediately dropped his slightly increased volume '—what I think and feel.'

Her face blanched, suddenly pinched. 'Don't yell at me.'

He stared at her, confused. 'You think that's yelling?' He laughed, trying to make a joke to lighten the moment. 'If you think that's yelling, don't come near my operating theatre when a patient's bleeding out.'

'And that's so very reassuring.'

Her sarcasm—her default defensive setting— whipped him, burning his skin. Bewildered, he reached for her, needing to touch her and fix this. How had his declaration of love landed him in emotional quicksand?

She ducked his touch. 'People don't fall in love in three weeks, Noah, they just think they do. You're a doctor. You know about hormones and lust. You've seen the MRI films of the effect of lust on the brain but it's not love.' Her face implored him to understand. 'Think about it. You arrived here angry and disenfranchised, like an alien from another planet, and I made you feel good. You're projecting those feelings onto me but it's not love.'

The logical side of his brain grappled with her argument while his bruised heart quivered, telling him she was wrong. Very, very wrong. 'If it was only lust, I wouldn't be thinking past the next time we had sex or a week from today, but I am. What we have is so much more than sex, Lily, you know it too. I've never felt this way about anyone and for the first time in my life I want to try. We have a shot at a future and it starts with me showing you my real life.'

Her mouth flattened into a grim line. 'I glimpsed it when we spent the day at the Melbourne Victoria.'

'My life's more than just the hospital.'

Her brows rose. 'You're a surgical registrar about to sit your part-two exams. Your life is work and study.'

He immediately jettisoned that line of argument, knowing he couldn't win it, and tried something else. 'I've had the luxury of getting to know you. You invited me into your world and last Sunday, cooking with you and then playing cards with Bruce, was really special.'

'Gramps invited you, Noah, not me. Don't read more into it than country hospitality.'

Her words hit with the force of a king punch and he gripped the reception desk. Something was definitely off. He scanned her face, searching for clues that told him why she was behaving this way. Sure, she had moments of whipping sarcasm but he'd never known her to be so blunt. So mean.

He sighed and tried again. 'All I'm asking is for one weekend, Lily. After all, you've lived in Melbourne so you know one night won't kill you.'

Her already pale face turned ashen and her pupils dilated so fast that the beautiful blue vanished under huge, ebony discs.

A shiver ran over his skin. 'Lily? What's wrong? You look like you've just seen a ghost.'

Her chin shot up and she shook her head. 'I'm sorry, Noah. There's no point me coming to Melbourne with you because we have an end date. My home is here and yours is in the city. These last few weeks have been great but that's all they can ever be. An interlude. We agreed to that and you can't change the rules on me now.'

Incredulity flooded him. 'You're letting geography get in the way of something that could be amazing?'

She folded her arms over her chest, as a slight tremor rippled across her body. 'Geography has *nothing* to do with it, Noah.'

'I know something's going on, something I don't understand. Please tell me what it is so I can help. Whatever it is, together we can fix it.'

She closed her eyes for a moment and when she opened them again their emptiness chilled him. She swallowed. 'There's nothing to fix, Noah.'

'Why?'

'Because I don't love you.'

His lunch turned to stone in his stomach. 'Well, there's nothing ambiguous about that answer.'

'No. There's not.' She wrung her hands. 'I'm sorry it couldn't be different.'

'You're sorry?' Feelings of foolishness curdled with hurt and despair. 'Am I supposed to be grateful you threw me that bone, because, let me tell you, I'm not.' He tapped his chest directly over his heart. 'This hurts.'

Lily heard Noah's anguish and it tore at her, shredding her heart. She'd never intended to hurt him but he wanted more of her than she was able to give. Loving him was too much of a gamble. It would open her up to a huge risk and she'd worked way too hard at rebuilding her life to chance losing everything all over again. 'I said I was sorry.' And she truly meant it.

'Yeah. I heard.' The deep words rumbled around her,

vibrating in controlled anger that flicked and stung her like the tail of a switch. 'Did sorry cut it with your ex-husband?'

She gasped as his bitter words spun her back in time. *I'm sorry, Trent. I apologise. I was wrong.* Fighting for control, she managed to grind out, 'This has *nothing* to do with my marriage.'

His expression turned stony. 'I wouldn't know, seeing as you've never told me anything about it.'

Fear and embarrassment rose on a river of acid, scalding the back of her throat. *And I'm never going to tell you.* 'There's nothing to tell. I was young and stupid. I had a whirlwind, high-octane romance with all the trimmings—flowers, chocolates, horse-and-carriage rides and a proposal straight out of a Hollywood movie. I thought I'd found my great love and I got married. Turned out it was neither great nor love, just lust, and it wore off fast. For Trent, it wore off even faster.' *If you'd been a better wife, I wouldn't have had to look elsewhere.*

She sucked in a steadying breath to push the memory of Trent's vicious voice away. 'It turns out the affair I discovered he was having was actually his third since we got married. I filed for divorce. End of story.'

His keen and piercing eyes bored through her. 'So you were young, you made a mistake and, just like that, you're not prepared to take a second chance?'

Panic skittered through her. She had to stop him asking questions, digging and probing, in case he got close to the truth. *Do what it takes to stop him.*

Her gut rolled. The only choice she had was to hurt him. 'We're too different, Noah. We'd never work so there's no point trying. Believe me, when I tell you that I'm saving us the heartache.'

'You're wrong.'

No, I'm so very right. 'I have to get back to work.'

'Of course you do.' He swiped his phone. 'Don't worry. I've only got one hundred and seventy-two hours left in town and then I'll be out of your hair. I'm sure we can avoid each other if we try hard enough.' His generous mouth thinned to a hard line. 'Believe me, I'll be trying.'

With his back straight and his shoulders rigidly square, he walked away from her before disappearing into his office.

As she stood staring at the closed door, desolation hit her and, like an arrow slicing through the bullseye on a target it pierced her straight in the solar plexus. Searing pain exploded into every cell, setting up a vibrating agony of wretchedness. She'd just wounded a good and decent man to save herself.

She doubled over in agony. Playing it safe had never hurt so much.

By Monday morning, back in Turraburra after the weekend, Noah struggled not to hate Lily. He'd spent his two days in Melbourne, preparing for his return the following Saturday. Once he'd lodged the necessary paperwork for the Turraburra patients at the Victoria and booked the operating theatre, he'd concentrated on doing all his favourite things. He'd gone to a game at the MCG, he'd run through Yarra Park, bought coffee beans from his favourite deli to replenish his Turraburra supply, and he'd spent Saturday night at the Rooftop. He'd hated every minute of it.

At the footy, he'd kept turning to tell Lily something, only to find she wasn't there, and later, at the Rooftop, his usual coterie of flirting nurses and interns had seemed bland and two-dimensional. For the first time since arriving in Melbourne six years ago, his shiny and beloved city had seemed dull and listless.

He blamed Lily. He didn't belong in Turraburra but now Melbourne didn't seem like home either.

In his more rational moments he could see that perhaps by telling her he loved her he'd caught her by surprise and rushed her. But it was her reaction to his declaration that hurt most. It was one thing not to love him. It was another to be aghast at the thought and look utterly shocked and horrified by it. She'd looked at him as if he was a monster instead of a deluded guy who'd stupidly fallen in love.

He glanced at the two tins on his desk filled with home-baked lamingtons and shortbreads and at a small cooler that contained a freshly caught salmon—all gifts from grateful patients. The irony was that Turraburra had embraced him. He had more fresh produce than he could eat, Chippy had taken to sleeping under his desk, and the biggest surprise of all was that Karen was throwing him a going-away party. Everyone loved him, except the one person he wanted and needed to have love him back.

He picked up the phone for the tenth time that day, determined to call Bruce and ask him about Lily's marriage—to try and get the real story. He set the receiver back onto the cradle just like he had the nine other times. He didn't have the right to stress an eighty-five-year-old man with a heart condition, and deep down he knew it wasn't Bruce's story to tell.

He thumped the table with his fist. Why wouldn't Lily tell him?

Accept it, buddy. There is no story, she just doesn't love you.

Not possible. But even his well-developed sense of self had started to doubt that shaky belief.

We're too different. He shook his head against the thought as he'd done so often over the weekend. They shared so much in common—love of footy, medicine, sense of humour—the list went on. The only thing they really disagreed on was country versus city living and surely there was a way to negotiate on that? But if she didn't love him there was nothing to negotiate.

The intercom buzzed, breaking into his circular thoughts. 'Yes, Karen?'

'Looks like you might get to do some stitching. Lachy Sullivan's cut his hand climbing over a barbed-wire fence and it's nasty. He's waiting in the treatment room.'

'On my way.' He had ninety-eight hours to fill and with any luck this might just kill sixty minutes.

CHAPTER TEN

LILY'S HEAD ACHED. Her day had started at three-thirty a.m. with Sasha Ackers going into labour. Baby Benjamin, the third Ackers child, had arrived by breakfast, knowing exactly how to suck. From that high point the day had gone downhill fast.

On her postnatal rounds, she'd got a flat tyre in a mobile phone dead zone and, unable to call for assistance, she'd fallen in the mud, trying to use the wheel brace to loosen the wheel lugs. She'd been late back for clinic and had spent the afternoon trying to claw back time, but today every pregnant woman was teary and overwhelmed. She felt much the same way.

The only good thing about the day was the fact she hadn't run into Noah. She wasn't up to facing those brown, angst-ridden eyes that accused her of being a coward. At this point she was just counting down the days until Turraburra returned to being the safe refuge it had always been for her.

All she wanted to do was go home and fall into bed, and that was exactly what she was going to do now Sasha had insisted on an early discharge twelve hours after the birth. Sasha claimed her own bed was more comfortable than the birth centre's and, with her mother minding the other children, home was more peaceful.

Karen had closed the clinic at seven and so all Lily had to do was set the security sensor. As she started entering the numbers a frantic banging made her jump. Someone was pounding on the external doors.

'Hello?' a female voice called out. 'Please, help me.'

Lily rushed to the door, threw the lock and opened it. The woman fell into her arms and she staggered backwards into the waiting room and the light. 'Kylie? Are you in labour?'

Kylie's head was buried in her shoulder but Lily heard a muffled, 'No.'

She automatically patted her back. 'What's wrong?'

The woman raised her head. Black bruising spread across her face like tar and congealed blood sat in lumps on her split bottom lip.

Oh, God. Panic swooped through her. She knew only too well what this meant—all her worst fears about Shane Ambrose had come true. *Safety first. Lock the door. Now!*

In her haste, she almost pushed Kylie into a chair. 'Sorry, I just have to…' Her hands trembled as she bolted the door and started pulling chairs across the doorway.

'What are you doing?'

'Keeping you safe.' *Keeping us safe.* 'From Shane.'

Kylie shook her head quickly. 'No, you've got it all wrong, Lily. Shane wouldn't hurt me on purpose. This…' she gingerly touched her lip '…was a misunderstanding. He was tired and I shouldn't have let the kids annoy him.'

You brought this on yourself, Lily. You only have yourself to blame.

The past thundered back in an instant, bringing fear and chaos. She wanted to put her hands over her head and hide, only she couldn't. Kylie needed her. She needed to deal with this situation. She needed to make Kylie understand that the devil she knew was worse than the devil she didn't.

She kneeled down so she was at eye level with the trembling woman. 'Did he hit you?'

Kylie's mouth stayed shut but her eyes filled with tears.

'He has no right to do that, Kylie. Did he hit you anywhere else? In the stomach?'

'He…he didn't mean to hurt the baby.'

Nausea made her gag and she hauled in deep breaths against a closing throat. *Hold it together. You can do this.* Every part of her screamed to call the police but triage came first—check the baby, check Kylie, call the police. She extended her shaking hand. 'Come with me.'

Like a compliant child, Kylie allowed herself to be led to the treatment room and she got up onto the emergency trolley. Lily handed her an ice-pack for her face then helped Kylie shuffle out of her yoga pants. Two bright red marks the size of a fist stained the skin of her pregnant belly.

Fury so strong blew through Lily taking the edge off her fear.

'Is…is there any bleeding?' Kylie asked, her voice so soft and quiet that Lily could barely hear her.

'Your undies are clean.' Only that didn't mean there wasn't any bleeding. Her hands carefully palpated

Kylie's abdomen and the woman flinched. The area was tight. 'Does this hurt?'

'A bit.'

Lily turned on the hand-held Doppler and the baby's heartbeat thundered through the speakers. The heartbeat was way too fast.

'Oh, thank God.' Kylie immediately relaxed, falsely reassured by the sound.

'Kylie, I'm going to put in an IV and call Dr Jackson.'

The woman's face paled. 'Why? What's wrong?'

Lily opened her mouth to reply but the loud sound of fists banging on the door made her freeze.

'Kylie! Are you in there?' Shane's voice sounded frantic and filled with concern.

Kylie struggled to sit up.

'No.' Lily shook her head as she gently pushed Kylie back against the pillows. Snapping a tourniquet around her arm, she said, 'Stay there.'

'Kylie, honey, I know you're in there,' Shane cajoled. 'I'm worried about you.'

'He's not coming in here,' Lily said, sounding a lot more certain than she felt. She forced her fingers not to tremble as she palpated Kylie's arm for a vein.

'But he's my husband,' Kylie whispered, fear filling her voice. 'I made a commitment to him.'

Hearing the words she'd once spoken tore her heart. She understood the power of strong memories—those of a loving, caring man duelling with the new version of the one who inflicted pain. All types of pain—emotional, financial, sexual and physical—that left a woman blaming herself and questioning everything she believed through a fog of devastated self-esteem. Pain that was *always* followed by recanting, declarations of love and the promises of *never again*.

'Kylie, loving husbands don't put your life and the life of your unborn baby in danger. I have a duty of care to protect you and your baby and that means that right now Shane's not coming anywhere near you.' The cannula slid straight into the vein and she connected up the saline drip.

Kylie slumped as tears poured down her face. 'Th-thank you, Lily.'

'Kylie.' Shane's charming and caring voice was fast developing an edge. 'I just want to check that you're okay. Come on, darl, let me in.'

'I'm scared,' Kylie whimpered, as her hand gripped Lily's arm with bruising force. 'Can you talk to him? Please?'

Don't poke the dragon. 'I'm not sure that's—'

'I know him, Lily,' Kylie implored. 'He won't leave until he knows I'm okay.'

She felt herself caving. 'Okay, but you stay here. Do not get off the trolley.'

Kylie released her hand, nodding her acquiescence.

Lily walked slowly back to the foyer, already regretting her offer. When she arrived at the front doors she didn't open them. 'Shane,' she said, trying to sound calm and dispassionate as her heart thundered in her chest so hard it threatened to leap into her mouth. 'Kylie needs medical attention. I will call you as soon as Dr Jackson's seen her.'

'I want to be with her.'

'I know you do but...*forgive me, Noah*...Dr Jackson wants to see her on her own. As soon as he's made his diagnosis, we'll call. For now, it's best if you go home and wait.'

'You stuck-up bitch.' Shane's charm vanished as he continued to scream at her, calling her names no one should ever have to hear. His poisonous words slid through the cracks in the old building, sneaking under the window seals, their vitriol a living, thriving beast with intent to harm. 'Open the goddamn door now, before I kick it in.'

Lily, you're scum. Lily, you're useless. You're a worthless whore. You ruined my life.

The past bore down on her so hard she gasped for breath, trying to force air into rigid lungs. The edges of her mind started to fuzz.

'Lily, I'm scared.'

Kylie's voice penetrated her panic making her fight back against the impending darkness. *I'm a good person. Kylie needs my help. I have to protect Kylie and the baby.*

Somehow her trembling hands managed to press in Noah's number on her phone.

As his rich, warm voice came down the line, the crack of a gun going off had her diving for safety. With her belly on the floor and adrenalin pouring through her, she commando-crawled for cover under the reception desk.

'Lily?' Noah's voice was frantic. 'What's happening?'

The sound of crashing glass deafened her.

'Get the police. Come to the clinic,' she whispered, barely able to speak against the terror that was tightening her throat. 'Kylie Ambrose is bleeding.'

She left the phone connected, hoping against hope

that Noah would use the landline to call the police and keep his mobile connected to hers. That he'd stay on the line and be her lifeline.

He's already your lifeline.

The thought pierced her with its clarity and she gasped. Over the past few weeks Noah, with his love and caring, had brought her back into the world. Noah, who argued with her but never punished her if she disagreed with him. Noah, who loved her but didn't want to control her. Noah, who hadn't run from the hard, hurtful facts that he had a communication problem or blamed her but had worked to change how he dealt with people. How many men would do that?

Some. Not that many. He was one of life's good guys—truly special—and she'd tossed him aside, too scared to trust her future to him because of the fear scumbags like Trent and Shane Ambrose had instilled in her. And for what? A hysterical laugh threatened to burst out of her. She was back to hiding again.

I don't love you, Noah. She shoved her fist in her mouth at the memory of what she'd said to him, biting down on her knuckles to stop herself from crying out in pain. Fear had driven those words from her mouth and she'd do anything to have the chance to take them back.

The crunch of glass under boots boomed in the silence—threatening, ominous and terrifying—taking her back to another dark night and shattered glass. *You survived that and you'll survive this. You have to live so you can save Kylie and tell Noah that you love him.*

The footsteps got closer. Louder. A moment later Shane Ambrose was towering over her with a gun pointed straight at her. 'Next time, bitch, open the bloody door.'

His arrival turned her panic to ice. Now she knew what she was dealing with. Trent had taught her the unpredictability of men and this whole event was all about power. She'd told Shane he couldn't come inside the clinic so to show her he was the one in charge— the man in control— he'd broken in to teach her a lesson. If she wanted to get out of this situation in one piece, she had to do what she'd vowed she'd never do again.

She agreed. 'Yes, Shane.'

He grunted. 'That's more like it. I'm taking Kylie home.'

She kept her gaze fixed on his hateful face and concentrated on keeping her voice toneless and even. 'Kylie's bleeding, Shane. If you take her home, she'll die.'

The gun wavered. 'Don't bullshit me.'

She swallowed, praying that she could get through to him on some level. 'You're holding a gun at my head, Shane. You hold all the cards here, you have all the control. Why would I lie to you?'

'Shane, it's Ross Granger.' The police sergeant's voice, loud and distorted by a megaphone, carried into the clinic from outside. 'I know you're in there, mate, and you've got a gun. We got a call from the clinic saying Kylie and the baby need the doctor. He's here but we need you to come to the door first and bring the gun.'

Shane's cold eyes assessed her. 'Take me to Kylie and don't do anything stupid because I'm right behind you.'

Forcing her jelly legs to carry her, she walked straight to the treatment room. She'd expected the pregnant woman to be sitting up, quivering and terrified, but instead she was lying on her side. 'Kylie?'

Her eyes fluttered open and her hands pressed her belly. 'Hurts.'

Lily opened the IV full bore and checked her blood pressure. It was dangerously low. 'She's bleeding, Shane. She needs a Caesarean section or she and the baby will die.'

The bravado of the cowardly man faltered for a moment. 'Get the doctor.' The gun rose again. 'No police.'

'I have to get in there now, Sergeant.' Noah paced up and down outside the clinic, frantic with worry. 'Gunshots have been fired, there's a pregnant woman who's at risk of bleeding out, a baby who might die, and there's Lily…' His voice cracked on her name. Some crazy guy had his Lily bailed up with a gun.

'Doctor, you can't go in until Ambrose is disarmed. I can't risk any more lives. I've got the medical evacuation helicopter and skilled police negotiators on the way.'

'We don't have time to waste—'

The clinic door opened and Lily stood in the doorway with Shane. He had one of his hands clamped on her arm and the other held the gun pointing at a pale and silent Lily.

'Get the doctor,' Shane yelled.

As if reading Noah's mind, the sergeant said, 'Noah, wait.'

But he wasn't waiting any longer and he bounded forward. Better that he be inside with some control than outside with none. No way in hell was he leaving Lily alone with that bastard. As he approached, Shane stepped back to allow him to pass.

Noah made his second split-second decision for the

day—he decided to just be the doctor and not mention the gun. 'Where's Kylie?'

Shane waved the gun towards the treatment room. 'You have to save her.'

Relatives often said that to him, only they weren't usually holding a gun. 'I'll do my best but I might need more medical help.'

'No one else is comin' in here,' Shane said with a menacing growl.

Noah strode directly to the treatment room. 'Lily,' he said firmly, hating how terrified she looked. He wanted to wrap her in his arms and keep her safe but gut instinct told him not to. Men like Shane Ambrose considered women inferior. Noah needed to keep the bastard on side. 'What's Kylie's BP?'

'Ninety on forty-five,' she replied, her voice oddly emotionless. 'She needs a Caesar but we can't do it here.'

'We don't have a choice,' he said grimly. 'If I don't operate, she dies. We may not have operating theatre conditions but at least we have antibiotics and plasma expander. What about surgical instruments?'

Her eyes widened in momentary surprise before filling with confirmation. 'I can put together an emergency set from the clinic supplies and we have a cautery pen, but I've never given an anaesthetic before.'

'I'll talk you through it. We can do this.' He sounded way more confident than he felt. What he was about to do was combat surgery, only he was a very long way from a war zone. He glanced at the gun. Maybe not.

Calling out instructions to Lily for the drugs he needed, he quickly intubated the barely conscious Kylie.

As Lily took over the bagging, he administered the muscle relaxant and that's when reality hit him. They were short one set of hands. He needed another nurse but he couldn't ask anyone to step into this dangerous situation and even if he could, Shane wasn't going to allow it.

He glanced at Shane and the gun. The fact the guy had insisted Noah save his wife made him hope he wanted her to live. 'Shane, can I call you Shane?'

The man nodded. 'Yeah.'

'See how Lily is pressing that bag in and out, giving Kylie oxygen? Do you think you can do that?'

His eyes narrowed. 'Why can't the bitch do it?'

Every part of Noah wanted to dive at Ambrose's throat but he needed the low-life's help and right now saving Kylie came ahead of trying to disarm the creep. 'There's a big chance the baby is going to have trouble breathing when it's born and Lily has the skills to care for it. I'm not asking you to put the gun down. You can bag her one-handed.'

'Fair enough.' Shane sat down at his wife's head and took over from Lily, the gun still in his other hand.

Lily walked over to Noah, her face impassive like she was on automatic pilot. He got the sense she'd gone somewhere deep inside herself to get through this. He surreptitiously squeezed her hand. 'Time to gown up.'

'Time to gown up,' she repeated softly, saying the words like a mantra. 'We can do this. You can do this.'

Her belief in him slid under him like a flotation device, holding him up out of the murky depths of fear. He was operating in a makeshift operating theatre on a woman who might die on the table, a baby who might be born dead, and he was doing it all in the presence of an unpredictable guy holding a gun.

Don't go there.

Panic didn't belong in surgery and as the mask, gown and gloves went on, everything superfluous to the surgery fell away.

Quickly draping Kylie's abdomen, he picked up the scalpel. 'Making the incision. Have the retractors ready.'

A minute and half later he was easing the baby out of the uterus. Lily double-clamped the cord and he cut it, separating the baby from Kylie.

'He's blue.' Shane's panicked eyes followed Lily as she carried the baby to the cot and gave him oxygen. 'Is he alive?'

God, he hoped so, but right now he was battling with keeping the surgical field free of blood and he needed another pair of hands.

'He's got a pulse,' Lily said, relief clear in her voice. 'Come on, little guy, breathe.' A moment later the baby gave a feeble cry.

'That's my boy. Finally after three useless girls I get a son.' The pride in his voice was unmistakable.

Noah almost lost it. He wanted to vault the table and take the guy down. Instead, he bit his tongue to stop the fury that boiled in him from spilling over and putting him and Lily in even more danger.

The baby's cry thankfully got stronger. One saved. One to go. He battled on, trying to find the bleeder in a surgical field awash with blood.

The automatic blood pressure machine beeped wildly, the sound screaming danger and flashing terrifyingly low numbers. He refused to allow Kylie to die.

'Lily, put up another bag of plasma expander, administer oxytocin and re-glove. I need you here with suction. Now.'

A stricken look flared in Lily's eyes as she placed the cot next to Shane and he understood her dilemma. This bastard had caused this mess and now they had to depend on him.

'Please, Shane, will you watch the baby to make sure he doesn't stop breathing?' Lily said evenly and devoid of all the fear that burned in her eyes. 'Your wife and son need you.'

'Of course they need me,' he said, his shoulders straightening with warped pride. 'They depend on me for everything.'

Noah could only imagine the chilling smile that Shane's surgical mask was hiding. The complicated web of emotions that was domestic violence was anathema to him. How could men profess to love a woman and children and yet cause so much damage and pain? If he had his way, after all of this was over, he'd be appearing in court, giving evidence against this man and hoping he got jail time.

First things first. Save Kylie, disarm Ambrose.

The reassuring and tantalising whirring noise of the emergency evacuation helicopter sounded overhead and Noah prayed Kylie would get the chance to use its services.

Lily adjusted the suction and more blood bubbled up.

He swore quietly and cauterised another bleeder. He held his breath. *Please, let that be the last one.* They had limited supplies of plasma expander and Kylie's heart would only pump if it had enough circulating volume to push through it.

The field stayed miraculously clear.

He raised his eyes to Lily's, whose glance said, *Thank you.*

The blood-pressure machine stopped screaming but they weren't out of the woods yet. 'Shane, Kylie needs blood and she needs to be evacuated to an Intensive Care Unit in Melbourne the moment I've stitched her up.'

'And my son?' he asked, his gaze fixed on his new-born baby.

'He needs to be examined by a paediatrician,' Lily said quietly.

'Why?' Ambrose's eyes darted between Lily and Noah. 'Is something wrong?'

'He seems okay,' Lily said, 'but we just like to be thorough.'

'Shane,' Noah said, seeing a potential weak spot in their captor, 'we want your son to have the best medical care possible.'

'Damn right. Get over here and squeeze this bag.' Shane kept the gun pointed firmly on Lily as he used the phone to call the police sergeant, demanding that the emergency medical staff meet them at the front doors.

'How much longer are you going to take, Doc?'

'Five minutes.'

Shane put his finger against the baby's palm and grinned when his son's fingers closed tightly around it. 'Strong little beggar, like his dad.'

'Does he have a name?' Lily asked.

Noah's gaze jerked up from closing the muscle layer

of Kylie's abdomen. For the first time Lily sounded herself, as if this were a totally normal childbirth scenario.

'Jed,' Shane said.

'A good choice. A strong name for a fighter,' Lily said almost conversationally.

Lily, what are you doing?

'Look, he's looking for a drink,' Shane said. 'Kylie always breastfeeds them.'

Not this time, buddy. Noah struggled with the normality of the conversation. It was like Shane had conveniently forgotten that his violence had put his wife and child in mortal danger. 'I've finished.' Noah set down the scissors. 'Shane, she needs to go now.'

'What about the baby?' Shane asked, still keeping the gun trained on both of them.

'Can you please bring him?' Lily started walking backwards, still bagging Kylie.

Noah manoeuvred the trolley through the wide treatment room doors wishing he could read Lily's thoughts.

'Don't try anything,' Shane said, keeping the gun trained on the both of them as the police and medical evacuation team met them at the front door.

Noah gave a rapid handover, finishing with, 'She needs blood five minutes ago.'

As the flight nurse relieved Lily of the bagging job and the trolley disappeared out the door, Shane grabbed Lily by the arm, pulling her away from Noah. She stumbled backwards.

Noah's heart flipped and he held up his hands. 'Shane—'

'You go with Kylie, Doc. I trust you.'

No way in hell. 'What about the baby, Shane? I thought you wanted him checked out too?'

'Lily knows about babies and she'll do until you send a baby doctor in.'

'I'll be fine, Noah,' Lily said so softly he barely heard, but her gaze—full of love—loudly implored him to leave. To take this opportunity for his own safety.

His heart ripped into two. She loved him. Despite what she'd told him, despite sending him away, she loved him. What should have been the most wonderful news now rocked him with its devastating irony.

The gun moved directly to Noah's chest. 'Get out, Doc. Right now.'

Noah felt one of the police officer's hands wrap around his upper arm. 'Do as he says, Dr Jackson.'

At that moment the baby, who'd been quiet for so long, started to cry.

'Shane, do you want to hold your son?' Lily asked quietly. 'Give him a bottle?'

Shane hesitated, his hand tightening on the gun. Noah, backing slowly out of the door, could see the man's mind working out all the logistics. 'You pick him up and give him to me.'

Lily did exactly as he asked and settled the baby in the crook of his arm.

Shane jiggled his arm to try and sooth the crying baby but Jed, now awake and hungry, wouldn't be silenced. He kicked his little legs, destabilising his position in his father's arm, and Shane, momentarily distracted, moved his gun-holding hand to adjust the baby.

The baby screamed.

Lily moved.

172 UNLOCKING HER SURGEON'S HEART

No! Noah watched, horrified, as she slammed the side of her hand into Shane's wrist.

Shane roared. The gun dropped and somehow Lily had it in her hands. Noah threw himself forward, grabbing Shane before he could do anything to Lily.

The police poured into the building, guns raised, and immediately surrounded Shane. Noah relinquished his grip on the man, stepping back as a police officer took the baby and another handcuffed Shane.

Lily sank to her knees, the gun falling from her hands.

Noah ran to her, wrapping his arms around her, holding her tightly, convinced she was going to vanish any second. He frantically kissed her hair, her face and stroked her back. 'You're safe. You're very safe. It's over, Lily.'

Her huge, blue eyes sought his. 'We're...both...safe.'

'We are.'

Her body shook violently in his arms and the next moment she vomited all over the floor.

CHAPTER ELEVEN

LILY OPENED HER eyes, recognising the bright pattern of Noah's quilt. Vague memories of him telling the police she was in no fit state to give a statement and then being cradled in his arms slowly dribbled back.

'Hey,' Noah said softly. 'Welcome back.'

She turned to find him staring down at her, his face full of concern. Despite the fact she'd stupidly told him she didn't love him, despite the hurt and pain she'd inflicted on his heart, he'd never left her side all night. It overwhelmed her. 'What…what time is it?'

'Seven. You've been asleep for eight hours.'

'Gramps?' Panic gripped her. 'Is he okay? Does he know where I am?'

Understanding crossed his face. 'Bruce is fine. He's relieved you're safe and he knows you're with me, getting the best medical care possible.' He stroked her cheek. 'I said I'd call him when you woke up.'

She still felt half-asleep. Her limbs hung like lead weights and her brain struggled to compute, feeling like it was drowning in treacle. 'What did you give me?'

'A mild sedative. I promise it will wear off quickly but you needed it. It was really important that you sleep.' He squeezed her hand. 'Any nightmares?'

'No.' She shook her head and struggled up to rest against a bank of pillows before accepting the steaming mug of tea. 'But I know the drill about nightmares. They'll come later.'

His lovely mouth grimaced. 'The trauma counsellor wants to see us both later today and it's important we go.'

His matter-of-fact words pierced her, reminding her that he'd been through the same awful experience. She squeezed his hand. 'What about you? Did you sleep? Are you okay? You had a gun pointed at you, just like me.'

'I'm okay.' He brushed her forehead with his lips. 'I was more scared for you than for myself.'

She didn't understand. 'Why?'

His incisive gaze studied her. 'Shane Ambrose's vitriol was centred squarely on you.'

'Yeah. He's a misogynist.' She stared into the milky tea. 'You have the immunity of a Y chromosome.'

'And I hated every minute of it,' he said, his voice cracking with emotion. 'I would have given anything to change places with you and when you karate-chopped him my heart almost stopped. You could have been shot.' He stroked her hair. 'Promise me you'll never scare me like that again.'

Tears welled up in her eyes. His love flowed into her like a life force, giving her hope that, despite all her fears, she hadn't lost him. But before she could hope too much she owed him the truth. 'Shane was distracted by the baby and I saw a chance and took it. I had to take it for Kylie and for you. For me. I've spent too many years being scared.'

Worry lines creased his forehead. 'Scared? I don't

understand. What you did was one of the bravest things I've ever seen.'

She shook her head. 'That wasn't brave, it was just instinctive survival. I've got a Ph.D in that, courtesy of my marriage.'

His face filled with compassion. 'Perhaps you need to tell me about that.'

She met his warm brown gaze. 'There's no perhaps about it, Noah. There are things you need to know about me, things I should have told you but I was too ashamed to tell you because I've always considered it my dirty little secret.' She licked her dry lips. 'Yesterday, when I had a gun pointed at my heart, I realised I should have told Kylie the story of my marriage weeks ago. I should have told you.'

She gulped down her tea and told him fast. 'You know how I said I'd fallen through a plate-glass window? Well, I didn't exactly fall.'

Noah's skin prickled and flashes of the stoic, non-confrontational Lily from yesterday hammered him, making his gut roll. 'My God, Lily, he pushed you?'

Her gaze seemed fixed on a point on the quilt. 'It was the night I left him. I was stupid. Despite his affairs, despite everything he'd done, I thought I owed him an explanation as to why I was leaving, why I was breaking a vow and a promise I'd made in good faith two years earlier.' Her sad gaze met his. 'But I learned there's no such thing as a rational conversation with an irrational person who thinks that you're his property. His chattel.'

He had the primal urge to kill the unknown man. 'You have nothing to be ashamed about, Lily,' he said, keen to reassure her. 'And neither does Kylie or any other woman in the same situation. These men are sick. Even if I hadn't known that before, yesterday sure as hell taught me.'

'Thanks.' She gave him a wry smile. 'On one level, I knew that Trent's behaviour wasn't my fault but when you're cut off from friends and family, doubt sneaks in and it strips away your self-esteem so slowly that you're not even sure it's going until it's gone. If you're told often enough that you're useless, hopeless, a disappointment, and that everything is your fault, then you slowly start to believe it.'

'Please, believe me, you're none of those things, Lily,' he said gruffly, as a thousand feelings clogged his throat.

She patted his hand as if he was the one needing reassurance. 'I know,' she said softly. 'I truly do.'

'So this Trent.' He spat out the name. 'Please, tell me he got charged for almost killing you.'

'Yes, and there's an intervention order in place against him but I find it hard to trust it. I know that's stupid because he's never once tried to break it.' She wrung her hands. 'Other women aren't so lucky.'

Slowly, things started to make sense to him. Her tension in the car the day they'd driven to Melbourne, her refusal to spend the weekend with him, her accusation that he was yelling when he'd only been emphatic. 'All of this happened when you lived in Melbourne, didn't it?'

'Yes.' Her eyes pleaded with him to understand. 'I met Trent in Melbourne a few months before I started my Master's of midwifery. He dazzled me with romantic gestures, poetic words and gifts. He had a way of making me feel incredibly special, as if I was the cen-

tre of his world. It was his suggestion that we elope because—' she made air quotes with her hands '—there's
nothing more romantic.'

Her hands fell back in front of her. 'As it turned out,
I married him for worse, with two strangers as wit-
nesses in the Melbourne registry office. It should have
been my first clue about things to come. How he'd work
really hard at separating me from my few friends and
Gramps.'

He slid his hand into hers. 'When did things start to
change?'

'When I started my midwifery lectures. We'd only
been married for five weeks and the first four weeks
of our marriage was our honeymoon, backpacking in
Vietnam and Cambodia. He resented the time I needed
to study. If I got engrossed in an essay and was late
with dinner, he'd fly off the handle. Initially, I put it
down to low blood sugar and him being tired and hungry after work.'

She barked out a short, derisive laugh. 'I wish it
could have been that simple but it was so far from simple it made complicated look easy. The first time I
stayed late for a delivery he refused to believe I'd been
at work all that time. He called me a slut, told me he
knew I was sleeping with one of the registrars, and the
more I denied it, the more he accused me of sleeping
around. Although I didn't know it at the time, the irony
was that he was the one having affairs.

'From that night he insisted on driving and collecting
me when I had hospital placements. One night I accepted
drinks after work with a group of fellow student midwives
to celebrate someone's birthday and he locked me out of

the house for two hours. After that, he started to control our money. He took over the grocery shopping and re-stricted the amount of money I could access to a tram fare. Without access to cash, it was impossible to attend any social get-togethers and if you say no to invitations often enough, people stop issuing them.'

He was battling to make sense of why his strong-willed Lily had found herself in this situation. 'Why didn't you tell someone what was happening?'

'This is the hardest thing for people to understand. I was a small-town girl in a big city with no close friends and in a new course. Every time I got close to making a friend, Trent would sense it and find a way to destroy it.' She squeezed his hand. 'Domestic violence is insidi-ous, Noah. Because your filter is clouded by love and you're not expecting someone who professes to love you to hurt you, you're in the middle of it before you realise. He effectively marooned me on an island of fear.

'I threw myself into study and work and managed to qualify. I was the team member who took on any extra shifts on offer to avoid being at home.'

'But didn't he hate that?'

She gave him a pitying glance. 'Noah, there's no logic to his behaviour. As much as he hated me not being at home where he could control me, he enjoyed the freedom my absences offered him. He still took me to and from work so he knew exactly where I was. One afternoon I came down with a high fever and work bundled me into a taxi and sent me home early. I found Trent in bed with a woman who had long blonde hair and blue eyes, just like me. She could have been my double. That night I told him I was leaving him.'

He kissed the back of her hand, hating how much she'd been through.

Her voice took on a flat tone as if remembering the trauma of being flung through a glass door was too much. 'I had five days in hospital to think about what I was going to do. The police and the social worker at the Royal helped me take out an intervention order and they even managed to get my clothes out of the flat. As much as I loved working at MMU, the thought of staying in Melbourne was just too awful so I gave notice on the pretext of being homesick. They suggested I apply for a grant for a birth centre to operate down here. I came back to Turraburra, back to Gramps and love, and I slowly recovered.'

Noah's chest hurt from a mixture of pure, hot anger at Trent for his brutal treatment of her and agonising pain that Lily had endured the slow demise of her marriage, her confidence and everything she'd believed she had a right to enjoy. 'You rebuilt your life. That takes incredible resilience and courage.'

She shrugged. 'There were days I thought I couldn't do it but adopting Chippy helped. He's my kindred spirit. He knows what it's like to live in fear. Although no one apart from Gramps knows the real story, the town knew my marriage had failed and they wrapped me up in their care and I concentrated on staying safe.'

'Given what you'd been through, that makes sense.'

She gazed up at him, her eyes filled with shadows. 'I thought it made sense too and I'd convinced myself

I had a full and happy life because it was so much better than what I'd had with Trent. It was all working just fine until you arrived and suddenly it was like waking up from a long hibernation and feeling sunshine on my skin for the first time in for ever. You brought me out into the light and showed me what I'd been living had only been half a life. You showed me what my life could truly be.'

Noah held his breath. Since the moment last night when Lily had looked at him with such love shining in her eyes, along with a desperate need to protect him, he'd been waiting and hoping she'd tell him she loved him. Only now he'd learned exactly what she'd been through in Melbourne and on top of yesterday's trauma, which would have brought everything back in Technicolor, he wasn't going to rush her. He needed to give her time and he was going to take things very, very slowly. Take things one tiny step at a time so he never lost her again.

Exhaustion clung to Lily. Telling her story was always like being put through the emotional wringer, but if she and Noah were to have a chance at a future, he needed to know what she'd been through and how the remnants still clung to her. She swallowed hard, knowing what she said next was vitally important. She had to get it right, had to try and make Noah understand why she'd behaved the way she had when he'd told her he loved her.

'All those wonderful feelings I experienced with you both awed and terrified me. Part of me wanted them badly, while another part of me rejected them out of fear.' She grabbed both his hands, needing to touch him, needing him to feel her love for him in case her words let her down. 'Even though I know on every level possible that you're nothing like Trent, me giving in to those feelings felt like I was stepping off a cliff and free-falling without a safety net. When you told me you loved me, I panicked. I said awful and hurtful things, things that aren't true, just so you'd leave.'

She gulped in a breath as bewildered tears poured down her cheeks. 'And despite me breaking your heart, you still came and risked your life for me, Kylie and the baby. I've been so stupid. I've let that awful secret ruin my chance at happiness with you and I'm so sorry.'

His earnest gaze hooked hers. 'I'm still here, Lily. It's not over until the fat lady sings.'

She gulped in breaths. The time had come for her to put her heart on the line. 'I love you so much, Noah. Can you forgive me and risk loving me too?'

'I love you, Lily,' he said so softly she almost didn't hear. 'That never stops.'

The three little words that had sent her into a tailspin four days ago now bathed her soul in a soothing, life-affirming balm. She cupped his stubbled cheek with her palm, still struggling to understand. 'How can you love me so unconditionally when I've hurt you so much?'

His brown eyes overflowed with tenderness. 'Because you're you. You're a good person, Lily. You're kind, generous and no-nonsense, and, oh, so very good for a grumpy-bum like me.'

A puff of laughter fell from her lips. 'You overheard Karen?'

His mouth twitched. 'I might have.'

She smiled and fingered his shirt, secure in his love for her. 'You can be grumpy from time to time but, then again, so can I.'

'I'm a lot less grumpy than I was now I have you in my life.' He kissed her tenderly on the forehead. 'And talking about *our* life, after what happened on Friday I don't want to rush you into any decisions. I especially don't want to after yesterday.'

Her heart ached and sang at the same time. 'We *both* experienced yesterday, Noah.'

His face tensed with the memory. 'We did and we need to go to counselling so it doesn't hijack our lives. We go for as long as it takes. I want you to feel safe, to feel loved and secure. We can get through this together, Lily. We'll find our way to be a united couple, no matter what it takes.'

His heart beat under her hand—strong, steady and reassuring—and she needed to pinch herself that he was part of her life. This wonderful man who understood that rushing into things was the worst thing for her. 'Taking things slowly sounds like a perfect idea.'

He let out a long breath and she realised he'd been scared she might freak out again at the idea of them being a couple. Her heart cramped and she moved to reassure him. 'Exactly how slowly are we taking this? We can still have sex, right?'

He grinned. 'Absolutely. And do fun stuff together like picnics and visiting wineries and—'

She smiled up at him. 'So we're dating?'

The last vestiges of tension on his face faded away. 'Dating and having sex sounds great.'

And it did. It sounded fantastically normal. 'Lots of

good times and wonderful experiences and time to really get to know each other.'

She laid her head on his chest and closed her eyes, feeling his love and warmth seeping into her.

'Lily?'

'Hmm…?'

He wound strands of her hair around his fingers. 'I have to go back to Melbourne in a few days.'

She stifled a sigh. 'I know. You have that pesky exam to study for and pass with flying colours.'

'And you hate coming to Melbourne.'

She bit her lip. She hated that those last vestiges of her marriage, which still clung to her, could hurt him. 'I'm going to get better at that. I know Trent's never breached the intervention order here or in Melbourne and, who knows, he might not even live there any more. I'll be asking the counsellor to help me over this last stumbling block because I want to enjoy being in Melbourne again. I want to feel comfortable there, with or without you.'

'That's great but it's not quite what I meant.' His hand stalled on her hair and hesitancy entered his voice. 'Days off excepted, I'll be working in Melbourne and you'll be down here, delivering pregnant women.'

'You're sounding worried.'

'I know we're dating and I'm fine with that but I'm just checking we're on the same page. I know I said I didn't want to rush you and I don't, but we're an exclusive couple, right?'

She propped herself up fast, resting on one elbow with her heart so full it threatened to burst. 'We are most definitely an exclusive couple. I'll take down any woman who so much as bats her eyelashes at you. I won't allow anyone to steal you away from me.'

His eyes, so full of love, gazed down at her. 'That could be the sexiest thing you've ever said to me.'

She laughed. 'Really? I'm sure I can do much better than that.'

He raised a brow as a smile raced from his lips to the corners of his eyes. 'I dare you.'

She leaned up and whispered in his ear. He sucked in a sharp breath before lowering his head to kiss her gently and reverently, as if he was worried he might hurt her. She knew he'd never intentionally do that and she wanted the Noah who'd made love to her before he'd learned what had happened to her in Melbourne.

Wrapping her arms around his neck, she pressed herself against him, kissing him back hard—needing to feel, needing to lose herself in wonder and banish the past, banish yesterday and everything they'd been through.

He groaned and immediately rolled her over, his mouth and hands loving her until she was a quivering mess of glorious sensation. 'Noah,' she panted, 'now.'

When he slid inside her, she knew she was home. This amazing man was her safety and her security. With him, she could take risks, say what she believed, challenge him, but most importantly she could be herself. As the wave to bliss caught them they rode it together, embracing life and forging a new future.

Later, as she lay in his arms, a peace she'd never known before trickled through her. She knew without equivocation that no matter what life threw at them, if they faced it hand in hand and side by side, they could and would come out the other end not only stronger but together. She couldn't wait to start.

EPILOGUE

'THERE'S PLENTY OF food in the freezer so, please, don't feel you have to cook,' Lily told Karen as she ran through her list. 'Gramps and Muriel are happy to take the kids for two hours tomorrow, which is about as much as they can handle in one hit, but it gives you a break and—'

'Just go already,' Karen said, with an indulgent smile. 'Anyone would think this was the first time you'd left Ben and Zoe with me. Just be back here by five tomorrow or I'll turn into a pumpkin.'

'Who's turning into a pumpkin?' Noah asked, appearing in the kitchen doorway holding a curly blonde toddler and with a pre-schooler whose arms were clamped tightly around his legs.

'Ka! Ka!' Zoe squealed, putting her arms out towards Karen with delight.

'Let's go and see my new puppy,' Karen said with a broad smile as she lifted Zoe into her arms then put her hand out to coax the reluctant Ben to let go of his father's legs.

As Lily watched Karen and the children disappear out the back door she pinched herself yet again to remind herself how blessed and lucky she was. Who would have known underneath all of Karen's pedantic office rules and terse texts there lurked a woman who adored messy children. She turned to Noah, who was at the sink, sponging something sticky off his shirt. 'I've got a surprise for you.'

Noah dropped the cloth onto the sink and caught her around the waist, gazing down at her. 'I love surprises. Promise it involves me having my wife to myself for a couple of hours?'

She stroked the distinguished strands of silver hair that had appeared at his temples. Six years had passed since he'd told her he loved her and if anything that look of adoration that flared in his eyes whenever he looked at her had deepened. 'I promise you it's better than that.'

'How can it be better than that?'

'Well, first of all it's thirty-six hours with me and it's in Melbourne with tickets to that new show you wanted to see.'

His face lit up. 'Are you serious?'

She laughed at his enthusiasm. 'But wait, there's more. We're having dinner at our favourite restaurant and—'

He tightened his arms around her, pulling her in close against him so his heat flowed through her. 'Tell me you booked at the Langdon.'

She laughed and slid her fingers between the buttons on his shirt, her fingertips caressing his chest. 'I booked the spa room at the Langdon.'

He groaned with pleasure as his lips sought hers,

kissing her long and hard. 'It's a shame we've got a long drive and we're not there right now.'

'Everything comes to those who wait,' she teased.

He stroked her hair. 'Not that I'm not appreciative of this amazing weekend you've planned for us but now you've got me worried that I've forgotten some important date. I know it's not my birthday or your birthday and it's definitely not our wedding anniversary so...?'

She rested her head on his shoulder the way she liked to do, loving the feeling of being cocooned in care. 'It's five years since you officially became Mr Jackson, General Surgeon, and we polished your new brass plaque and opened the surgical practice in Bairnsdale.'

'Is it?' He ran his hand through his hair as if he couldn't believe it. 'The time's gone so fast.'

Five years ago she'd offered to go to Melbourne to live but he'd been adamant he was coming to join her in the country. 'No regrets?'

'Not a single one. It was the best decision I ever made. With my one day a fortnight at the Victoria I get to keep up to date with the latest techniques, and with my patient load down here I get plenty of chances to refine them. The practice has grown so fast that I need another general surgeon to join me.' His eyes lit up. 'And I just got an email with some fabulous news.'

She tapped him on the chest. 'Don't keep me in suspense. Spill.'

'With the rural medical course at the uni being affiliated with the hospital, you're looking at the new associate professor of surgery.'

With a squeal of delight, she threw her arms around his neck. An aging Chippy, resting in his basket, looked up in surprise to see what all the noise and fuss was about. 'That is so fantastic. Congratulations. I'm so proud of you.'

'Thanks, but it's because of you.'

'No, it's because of all your hard work.'

'Let's agree it's both.' He gave her a quick kiss on the nose. 'All those years ago I thought that being sent to Turraburra was the worst thing that could have ever happened to me but in reality it was the very best thing. I was embraced by a community in a way I'd never experienced in Melbourne and I learned there's something intrinsically special about being able to give back.' He cupped her cheeks. 'And then there was you. You and the kids are what I'm most proud of in my life. You're the best thing that ever happened to me.'

Her throat thickened with emotion as his love circled her. 'And you and the children are the best thing that's ever happened to me. We've been so blessed.'

'We have. And although I love Zoe and Ben more than life itself, they're exhausting on a scale that makes back-to-back surgeries look like a walk in the park.' He grabbed her hand and tugged her towards the door. 'Let's not waste another moment of our thirty-five hours and fifty minutes of freedom.'

She laughed. 'You're not going to set a countdown app on your phone, are you?'

He gave a sheepish grin. 'No need. By the end of breakfast tomorrow both of us will be desperate to come straight home to see the kids.'

'We're pretty hopeless, aren't we?'

He kissed her one more time. 'True, but I wouldn't have it any other way.'

And neither would she.

* * * * *

HER PLAYBOY'S
SECRET

BY
TINA BECKETT

Published in Great Britain 2015
by Mills & Boon, an imprint of Harlequin (UK) Limited,
Eton House, 18-24 Paradise Road, Richmond, Surrey, TW9 1SR

© 2015 Harlequin Books S.A.

Special thanks and acknowledgement are given to Tina Beckett
for her contribution to the *Midwives On-Call* series

ISBN: 978-0-263-24717-6

Dear Reader,

Have you ever met someone and formed an instant opinion—only to be forced to revise that opinion once you get to know them? That's the case when obstetrician Darcie Green meets gorgeous Lucas Elliot for the first time. Sparks fly, and she soon labels him a playboy of the worst kind, only interested in one thing. Darcie has no intention of joining the throngs of female patients and co-workers who seem to hang on his every word. What she *doesn't* realise, however, is that Lucas uses his flirtatious charm to conceal a painful family secret and his real reason for becoming a midwife.

Thank you for joining Lucas and Darcie as they tiptoe around their attraction and try their best to avoid repeating the mistakes of the past. And maybe, *just maybe*, this very special couple will discover what love and loyalty really mean. I hope you enjoy reading their story as much as I loved writing it!

Love

Tina Beckett

Dedication

To those who dare to chase their dreams

Born to a family that was always on the move, **Tina Beckett** learned to pack a suitcase almost before she knew how to tie her shoes. Fortunately she met a man who also loved to travel, and she snapped him right up. Married for over twenty years, Tina has three wonderful children and has lived in gorgeous places such as Portugal and Brazil.

Living where English reading material is difficult to find has its drawbacks, however. Tina had to come up with creative ways to satisfy her love for romance novels, so she picked up her pen and tried writing one. After her tenth book she realised she was hooked. She was officially a writer.

A three-times Golden Heart finalist, and fluent in Portuguese, Tina now divides her time between the United States and Brazil. She loves to use exotic locales as the backdrop for many of her stories. When she's not writing you can find her either on horseback or soldering stained-glass panels for her home.

Tina loves to hear from readers. You can contact her through her website or 'friend' her on Facebook.

Books by Tina Beckett

Mills & Boon® Medical Romance™

**Visit the author profile page at
millsandboon.co.uk for more titles**

PROLOGUE

One week ago

IT WAS A curse heard around the world. Or at least around the ward of the Melbourne Maternity Unit.

Everyone on the ward went silent and several heads cranked around to see what the normally easygoing Lucas Elliot could possibly be upset about.

Darcie Green already knew—had braced herself for this very moment, wondering what his reaction would be.

Now she knew.

Still facing the rotation roster hanging on the far wall, Lucas didn't move for several seconds. Then, as if he couldn't quite believe what his eyes were telling him, one finger went to the chart, dragging across it to follow the line that matched dates with names.

She cringed as he muttered yet again, slightly lower this time. A few sympathetic glances came her way as people went back to their jobs. Isla Delamere, her former flatmate—now heavily pregnant—mouthed, "Sorry," as she tiptoed out of firing range.

A perfect beginning to a stellar day. She rolled her eyes.

Nine months in Australia and Darcie was just beginning to feel a part of the team. Except for Lucas's very vocal reaction at having the rota that matched hers, that was. He'd evidently not seen the list until just now.

Did he even know she was standing not seven meters behind him at the nurses' station? Probably not.

Then again, it was doubtful he would even care.

It wasn't as if she felt any better about having to spend an entire rotation with the handsome senior midwife. She just hadn't been quite as "loud" in expressing her displeasure.

Yes, she'd given him an earful about his periods of tardiness a few months back. But that had been no reason to call her an uptight, snooty, English…

Her eyes closed before the word formed, a flash of hurt working through her yet again.

Was the thought of being paired with her so hideous that he had to make sure everyone on the ward knew what he thought of her?

Evidently.

And why not? Her fiancé hadn't minded letting a whole chapel full of wedding guests know that he'd fallen in love with her best friend, who just so happened to be her maid of honor. Tabitha had promptly run over to him, squealing with delight, and thrown herself into his arms, leaving Darcie standing there in shock.

And, yes, Robert had called her uptight as well, right before he'd dropped the bomb that had ended their engagement.

Lucas's left hand went to the back of his neck, head bending forward as he massaged his muscles for a moment. When he finally turned around his eyes swept the area, going right past her before retracing his steps and pausing.

On her.

Then his left brow quirked, a rueful smile curving his lips. "Sorry. Heard that, did you?"

Was he serious? "I imagine there were very few who didn't."

He moved forward, until he was standing in front of her—all six feet of him. "I bet you did some name-calling of your own when you saw the rotation." His smile faded. "Unless you requested we work this one together."

Sure. That's just what she would have done, left to her own devices.

She forced her chin up. "No, I didn't request it, but it doesn't bother me, if that's what you mean. I've had worse assignments." Before she could congratulate herself on keeping her response cool and measured, even when her insides were squirming with embarrassment, he gave her a quick grin.

"Touché, Dr. Green. Although since you almost had me fired the last time we interacted, I assume your 'worse assignment' didn't fare quite as well."

Since the assignment she'd been referring to had had to do with returning hundreds of wedding gifts courtesy of her ex, it would appear that way. "I don't know about that. I think he feels *quite* lucky not to have to deal with my—how did you put it?—'uptight English ways' any more."

Lucas's gaze trailed over her face, but instead of whipping off a sharp retort he leaned in closer. "Then maybe you should consider some behavior modification courses."

Although the words were made in jest—at least she thought they were—they still stung. Darcie pulled the edges of her cardigan around herself to combat the chill spreading from her heart to the rest of her body and then forced every muscle in her chin go utterly still, so he wouldn't see the wobble. "You're right. Maybe I should."

His head tilted, and he studied her for a minute longer. He reached out a hand as if to touch her, before lowering it again. "Hey. Sorry. I was teasing."

Maybe, but a part of what he'd said was true. Men did seem to find her "chilly and distant"—words her ex had also used to describe her during the last troubled weeks of their engagement. And he had been right. Compared to her, Tabitha was warm and bubbly and anything but distant.

Darcie couldn't help the way she was made, though, could she? She dragged her thoughts back to the man in front of her. She hadn't tried to be unreasonable during their confrontation a few months ago, whatever Lucas might have thought. Was asking someone to be prompt and to keep his mind on his job so unreasonable?

Well, she didn't really have her mind on the job right now either.

"Don't worry about it." She fastened the buttons on her cardigan to keep from having to hold onto it and drew herself upright. "I'm sure, if we both remain professional, we'll come off this rotation relatively unscathed."

He gave her a dubious-looking smile. "I'm sure we will."

As he strode away, his glance cutting back to the chart and giving a shake of his head that could only be described as resigned, she realized that was the problem. Neither of them seemed able to maintain a calm professionalism around the other.

Two fortnights. That's all it was. Just because her rota corresponded with his, it didn't mean she had to stick to his side like glue. She could do this.

Doubt, like a whisper of smoke that curled round and round until it encased its victim, made her wonder if her ex-fiancé's cutting words were the hardest things she would ever face. She'd thought so at one time.

But as Lucas ducked around a corner and out of sight, she had a terrible suspicion she could be facing something much worse.

CHAPTER ONE

Present day

"CORA? WHAT'S WRONG, sweetheart?"

Lucas leaned a shoulder against the wall outside the birthing suite as his niece's voice came over the phone, dread making his blood pressure rise in steady increments. Every time he thought his brother was through the worst of his grief, he'd go on yet another binge and undo all the work he'd accomplished during therapy.

He took a quick glance down the hall. The coast was clear.

Lucas had worked hard over the last week to make sure his personal life didn't interfere with his job. As angry as he'd been at Darcie for giving him a public flogging over being late for work a couple of months ago, she'd been right. It was why he'd hired a childminder to help with Cora's care. Burning the candle at both ends was not only unwise, it could also be dangerous for his patients.

Had his parents still been alive, they would have been happy to help. But it had been almost ten years since the car accident that had taken their lives.

His niece's voice came through. "Nothing's wrong. I just called to tell you what Pete the Geek did today."

Cora's Belgian sheepdog. Muscles he hadn't been aware he'd contracted released all at once. "Can you tell me later, gorgeous? I'm working right now."

"Oh, okay. Sorry, Uncle Luke. Are you coming for dinner tonight?"

"I wouldn't miss it, sweetheart." He smiled, unable to resist the pleading note in her voice. "What are we having?"

"Prawns!"

Cora's birth was what had propelled him to change his career path from plastic surgery to midwifery. The lure of a glamorous life filled with beautiful women had faded away in a moment when Felix's wife had gone into labor unexpectedly. Lucas had delivered his own niece in the living room of his brother's home. As he'd stared down at the tiny creature nestled in his hands, Cora had blinked against the light and given a sharp wail of protest that had melted his heart. Seven years later, she still had the power to turn him into a soppy puddle of goo, especially since he and Felix were now the only family she had left.

He needed to get off the phone, but the ward was quiet—none of his patients were laboring at the moment. He cradled the device closer to his ear. "Prawns, eh? What's the occasion?"

She giggled. "Just because."

"You're going to spoil me." His chest tightened at how happy she sounded. He'd take this over those *other* phone calls any day.

"Oh," his niece said, "make sure you bring some briquettes for the barbie. Daddy forgot them at the store."

Felix had forgotten quite a few things lately. But at least he seemed to be pulling out of his current well of depression.

Footsteps sounded somewhere behind him, so he moved to end the conversation.

"Okay, Cora, I will. Looking forward to tonight."

"Me too. Love you bunches."

"Love you even more, sweetheart. Bye." He ended the call, only to have the very person he'd been hoping not to encounter stalk past him, throwing an icy glare his way.

Lucas sighed. The woman did seem to pop up at just the wrong time. He slid the phone into his pocket and decided to go after her. He had no idea why, but he liked trying to get a rise out of her. Within five steps he'd caught up with her. Matching her pace, he glanced to the side.

Not good. The obstetrician's lips were pressed together into a thin line, her expression stony.

He pushed forward anyway, throwing her what he hoped was a charming smile. "Were you looking for me?"

Her expression didn't budge. "I was, but I can see you're busy."

"Just taking a short breather between patients. What was it you wanted?"

She glanced at him, her eyes meeting his for a mere second. "Is Isla scheduled to see you this week?"

Isla Delamere was one of his colleagues as well as a friend.

"Yes, did you want to be there for her appointment?"

Her chin edged up in a way he was coming to recognize. "I'd planned to be. She's my patient as well."

Okay, he'd gotten a rise out of her, but not quite the kind he'd been hoping for.

He moved ahead of her and planted himself in her path before she could reach the door to the staff lounge. Why he was bothering he had no idea, but something in him wanted to knock down a block or two of that icy wall she surrounded herself with. "Listen, Dr. Green—Darcie—I know we got off on the wrong foot somehow, but can we hit the reset button? We have three weeks of our rotation left. I'd like to make them pleasant ones, if at all possible. What do you say?"

The tight lines in her face held firm for another moment, and he wondered if she was going to strike him dead for daring to use her first name. Then her eyes closed, and she took a deep breath. "I think I might be able to manage that." The corners of her mouth edged up, creating cute little crinkles at the outer edges of her eyes. "If we both try very hard."

Something in Lucas's chest shifted, and a tightening sensation speared through his gut. Had he ever seen the woman smile? Not that he could remember, and certainly never at him. The transformation in her face was...

Incredible.

He swallowed. That was something he was better off not thinking about.

Three weeks. He just had to get through the rest of this rotation. From what he understood, Dr. Green had only been seconded to MMU for a year, then she'd head back to England. He did some quick calculations. She had, what…three months left? Once their rotation was over she'd be down to two, which meant it was doubtful they'd be paired together again. He gave an internal fist pump, trying to put his whole heart into it. It came off as less than enthusiastic.

Because you still have these three weeks to get through.

He gave her another smile. "I think I can manage it as well."

"Well, good. Now that that's settled, when is Isla's appointment?"

He checked his schedule. "Next Wednesday at two."

Darcie pulled her phone out and scrolled through a couple of screens before punching some buttons. "I don't have anyone scheduled at that time, so I'll be there." She gave him another smile—a bit wider this time—and the wobble in his chest returned. And this time he noticed the crinkles framed eyes that were green. A rich velvety color. Sparkling with life.

Her lips were softer too than they had been earlier. Pink, delicate, and with just a hint of shine.

The tightening sensation spread lower, edging beneath his waistband.

What the hell? Time to get out of here.

"Great. See you later." He turned and started back the way he had come, only to have her voice interrupt him.

"Don't forget to call for a consult if anything unusual comes up."

He stiffened at the prim tone. "Yes, I know the protocol, thank you."

When she didn't respond, he turned around and caught something…hurt?…in the depths of those green eyes, and maybe even a hint of uncertainty. In a flash, though, it winked out, taking with it any trace of her earlier smile and, very possibly, their newborn peace accord.

While that bothered him on a professional level, it was what he'd seen in her expression in that unguarded moment that made him want to cross over to her and try to understand what was going on in her head. He didn't. Instead, he chose to reiterate his comment in a less defensive way. "I'll ring if I need you."

Then he walked away. Without looking back. Praying the next weeks sped by without him having to make that call.

That man should wear a lab coat. A long one.

Darcie tried not to stare at the taut backside encased in dark jeans as he made his way back down the hall, but it was hard. No matter how much she tried to look anywhere but there, her peripheral vision was still very much engaged, keeping track of him until he finally turned down a neighboring corridor.

The thread of hurt from his curt response still lingered, just waiting for her to tug on it and draw it tighter. Why had he acted so put out to have her assistance on a case?

Was it the professional rivalry that sometimes went on between midwives and obstetricians?

She sagged against the wall, pressing her fingers against her temples and rubbing in slow, careful circles to ward off the migraine that was beginning to chomp at the wall of her composure.

What was it about Lucas that put her on edge?

The fact that he was a man in a field dominated by women?

Or was it the fact that all the expectant mums who came through the doors clamored to be put on his patient list? Despite the run-ins they'd had over the past nine months, Senior Midwife Lucas seemed quite capable of doing his job with an ease and efficiency that only enhanced his good looks.

And they were good.

She tried to dredge up an unflattering image, like the time he'd come in late for work, dragging his fingers through his wavy hair, his rumpled clothes the same ones he'd had on when he'd left the previous afternoon. Nope. He'd been just as attractive then as the first time she'd laid eyes on him.

Ugh. She disliked him for that most of all.

Or maybe it was all those secretive phone calls she'd caught him making when he'd thought he'd been alone. Oh, those were definitely over the top. So many of them, right in the middle of his shift.

And he wondered why she was outraged when he came in late or took little side breaks to indulge in whispered conversations.

Could she be jealous?

She straightened in a flash. *No!* Just because Robert had decided she wasn't enough "fun", it didn't mean she should go ballistic over any man who wanted to indulge in a bit of pillow talk on the phone.

Maybe it wouldn't bother her so much if he didn't

use the same flirty tones when in conversation with the MMU staff and his patients. The tone he turned on this "Cora" person—a kind of I'm-not-willing-to-commit-but-I-still-want-you-at-my-beck-and-call attitude that grated on Darcie's nerves. Especially after the way her ex had led her down the rosy path, only to dump her for her maid of honor—who, actually, *was* a lot of fun to be with.

She sighed and went into the lounge to get a strong cuppa that she hoped would relieve the steady ache in her head and keep it from blooming into something worse.

As soon as she moved into the space, she knew it was a mistake. Lucas, it seemed, was the main topic of conversation among the cluster of four nurses inside.

"I swear one of his patients this morning had on false eyelashes. While in labor!" Marison Daniels blinked rapidly, as if trying to imitate what the woman had done. They all laughed.

If Darcie had hoped to slide by them, grab her tea and tiptoe back out of the room unseen, that hope was dashed when the nurse next to Marison caught Darcie's eye and gave the jokester a quick poke in the ribs with her elbow. The laughter ceased instantly.

Oh, Lord. Her face burned hotter than the kettle she'd just switched on.

"Sorry. Didn't mean to interrupt."

"You didn't interrupt," Marison assured her. "I was just headed back to the ward."

The others all echoed the same thing.

With a scurry of feet and tossing of rubbish, the four headed out.

Just what she needed. To be reminded that she was still very much an outsider when it came to certain things—like being allowed to let her hair down with the rest of them.

No, the pattern had been set from the moment she'd got off the plane. Oh, she'd made friends and people were nice enough, but to let her in on their little jokes? That didn't happen very often, except with Isla.

Worse, she'd even overheard Lucas making fun of her English accent while on one of his phone calls to Cora. It hadn't been in a mean way, he'd just repeated some of her colloquialisms with a chuckle, but it made her feel self-conscious any time she opened her mouth around him. So she made sure she spoke to him as little as possible. And now that they were sharing a rota, she was still struggling to maintain that silence.

Not that it was going to be possible forever.

She could still picture the confident way he strode through the hallways of the ward, his quick smile making itself known whenever he met a patient. She wrinkled her nose. More than one expectant mum would have probably given her left ovary to bat long sexy lashes and claim the child she was carrying was Lucas Elliot's.

Including his current paramour, Cora?

Probably, but not *her*. She was done with men like him.

Her fiancé had been handsome and attentive. Until he hadn't been. Until he'd grown more and more distracted as their engagement had progressed.

Now she knew why.

And Lucas had Cora. She was not about to smile and flirt with a man who was taken. She wasn't Tabitha.

She packed leaves into the tea ball and dropped it into a chunky mug—a gift from her dad to remind her that her favorite footballers resided in England and to not let herself get swept away by a handsome face, especially one who lived halfway round the world.

Lucas's quirked brow swam before her eyes, and she let out an audible groan, even as she poured boiling water into her cup. No matter how good looking he was or how elated she'd been to see the momentary confusion cross his expression when she'd smiled at him, she did not need to become like False-Eyelash Lady—the one Marison had carried on about.

There'd be a real corker of a reaction if someone caught her mooning after him. Or staring after him, like she'd done earlier.

She bounced her tea ball in the water and watched as the brew grew darker and darker, just like her thoughts. What she needed was to stay clearheaded. Like he'd said, they had three more weeks together.

He wanted them to be pleasant ones. She finished adding milk and sugar to her cup and then discarded the used tea leaves, rinsing the ball and leaving it on a towel for the next person who needed it.

"Pleasant" she could do, but that had to be the extent of it. Maybe she should be grateful for all those calls to Cora…maybe she should even hope the relationship stayed the course. At least for the next few weeks.

Which meant she would not go out of her way to put him at ease or cut him any slack if he came in late again. Neither would she give the man any reason to

look at her with anything other than the casual curiosity his eyes normally held.

And once those three weeks were up?

Life would go back to the way it had been before
they'd found themselves joined at the hip.

Joined at the hip. She gave a quick grin. That was
one place she and Lucas would never be joined, even if
the idea did create a layer of warmth in her belly. But it
was not going to happen. Not in this lifetime.

With that in mind, she took a few more sips of the
sweet milky brew, then, feeling fortified and ready to
face whatever was out there, she headed off to see her
next patient in what was proving to be a very interesting morning.

CHAPTER TWO

FELIX WASN'T AT HOME.

Arms loaded with items for their dinner, Lucas set everything down in the kitchen. "Where is he?"

Chessa, the childminder, shrugged and said in a quiet voice, "He went out an hour ago, saying he needed to buy prawns, and hasn't come back yet."

Damn. "And where's Cora?"

"Outside with Pete." The young woman's brow creased. "Should I be worried? He's been good for the last few weeks, but he did put some bottles of ale in the fridge. I haven't seen him drink anything, though."

"It's okay. It's not your job to watch him. If he ever fails to come home before you're supposed to leave, though, call me so I can make sure Cora is taken care of."

"I would never leave her by herself, Mr. Elliot." The twenty-five-year-old looked horrified.

"I know you wouldn't. I just don't want you to feel you have to stay past your normal time."

The sliding door opened and in bounded Pete the Geek in a flash of brown and white fur, followed closely by Cora, whose red face said they'd been involved in some sort of running game. The dog came over and sat in front of him, giving a quick woof.

Lucas laughed and reached in his pocket for a treat. "Well, you're learning."

He and Cora had been working on teaching Pete not to leap on people who walked through the door. By training him to sit quietly in front of visitors, they forestalled any muddy paw prints or getting knocked down and held prisoner by an overactive tongue. The trick seemed to be working, although if the tail swishing madly across the tile floor was any indication, Pete was holding himself in check with all his might.

Kind of like *him* when Darcie had smiled at him as he'd left the hospital?

Good thing he had more impulse control than Cora's dog.

Or maybe Darcie was training him as adeptly as Cora seemed to be training Pete.

"He wants his treat, Uncle Luke."

Realizing he'd been standing there like an idiot, he tossed the bacon-flavored bit to Pete and then bent down to pet him. "I think he's gained ten kilos in the last week."

He squatted and put an arm around both his niece and her dog.

Cora kissed him on the cheek, her thin arms squeezing his neck. "That's just silly. He doesn't weigh that much."

"No?" He gave her a quick peck on the forehead, grimacing when Pete gave his own version of a kiss, swiping across his eyebrow and half his eye in the process. "Okay, enough already."

He couldn't hold back his smile, however, despite the niggle of worry that was still rolling around inside him.

Where the hell was his brother?

Standing, he kept one hand on Pete's head and smiled at the minder. "Would you try ringing his mobile phone and seeing how long he'll be while I fire up the barbie and get it ready? I don't know about everyone else but I'm starving."

His voice was light, but his heart weighed more than the dog at his feet.

"Of course," Chessa said. "I'll bring you some lemonade in a few minutes."

As he was preparing the grill, she came out with a glass and an apologetic shake of her head. "There was no answer, but I left a voice mail."

"Thank you. Luckily I brought some prawns with me, just in case. Feel free to stay and eat with us, if you'd like."

She smiled. "Thanks, but if it's all the same to you, I think I'll head back to my flat. Do you need anything else?"

"No, I think we're good."

Twenty minutes later he had the briquettes going while Cora and Pete—worn out from a rough-and-tumble game of tug of war—lounged in a hammock strung between two gum trees, the dog's chin propped on his niece's shoulder. Both looked utterly content. Rescuing Pete had been the best thing his brother had ever done for his daughter, unlike a lot of other things since his wife's tragic death. In fact, the last four years had been a roller coaster consisting of more lows than highs—with the plunges occurring at lightning speed.

He went in and grabbed the package of prawns and some veggies to roast. Just as he started rinsing the shellfish, the front door opened and in came his brother. Bleary, red-rimmed eyes gave him away.

Perfect. Lucas already knew this routine by heart.

"Was our cookout tonight?" his brother asked, hands as empty as Lucas's stomach. "I forgot."

His molars ground against each other as he struggled with his anger and frustration. Was this what love and marriage ultimately led to? Forgetting that anyone else existed outside your own emotional state? Felix had a daughter who needed him, for God's sake. What was it going to take to make him look at someone besides himself? "Cora didn't forget."

His brother groaned out loud then mumbled, "Sorry."

"I'm just getting ready to throw it all on the barbie, so why don't you get yourself cleaned up before you go out there to see?"

The first two steps looked steady enough, but the next one swayed a bit to the left before Felix caught himself.

"Tell me you're not drunk."

"I'm not."

"Can you make it to your bedroom on your own?" The last thing Lucas wanted was for Cora to come in and see her father like this, not that she hadn't in the past. Many times.

Felix scowled. "Of course I can." He proceeded to weave his way down the hallway, before disappearing into one of the rooms—the bathroom.

Looks like you're spending the night on your brother's couch once again, mate.

Lucas had impressed on Cora the need to call him if her father ever seemed "not himself." The pattern was bizarre with periods of complete normalcy followed by bouts of depression, sometimes mixed with drinking. Not a good combination for someone taking anti-depressant medication.

He made a mental note to ask Felix if he was still taking his pills, and another note to make sure he arrived at work…on time! As he'd found out, it was tricky getting Cora off to school and then making the trek to the hospital, but if the traffic co-operated it could be done.

Otherwise that hard-won peace treaty would be shredded between pale English fingers.

Strangely, he didn't want that. Didn't want to disappoint her after he'd worked so hard to turn things around between them. Didn't want to lose those rare smiles in the process. So yes. He would do his damnedest to get to the hospital on time.

And between now and then he'd have to figure out what to do about his brother. Threaten him with another stint in rehab? Take away his car keys?

He cast his eyes up to the ceiling, trying not to blame Melody for allowing his brother to twine his life so completely around hers that he had trouble functioning now that she was gone.

Lucas never wanted to be in a position like that. And so far he hadn't. He'd played the field far and wide, but he still lived by two hard and fast rules: no married women and no long-term relationships. As long as he could untangle himself with ease the next day, he was happy. And he stuck to women who felt the same way.

No hurt feelings. And definitely no burning need to hang around and buy a house with a garden.

Finishing up the veggies, he faintly caught the sound of the shower switching on, the *poof* from the on-demand water heater confirming his thoughts. Good. At least Felix was doing something productive. He opened the refrigerator, pulled out the ale in the door and popped the top on every single bottle. Then he took a long gulp of the one in his hand, before proceeding to pour the rest of the contents down the drain, doing the same with every other bottle and then placing the lot in the recycle bin. If the beer wasn't here, Felix couldn't drink it, right?

Not that that stopped him from going out to the near-est pub, but at least that took some effort, which he hoped Felix didn't have in him tonight.

Lucas went outside and loaded the prawns into a cooking basket and set it over the fire, then arranged the vegetables next to them on the grate. Cora's empty glass of lemonade was next to his full one. She was still sprawled on the hammock and it looked like both she and Pete were out for the count. If only he could brush off his cares that easily, he might actually get a full night's sleep.

But maybe tonight would be different. He'd learned from experience that the fold-out cot in the spare room was supremely uncomfortable. He was better off just throwing a quilt over Melody's prized couch and set-tling in for the night there.

And he would wake up on time. He absolutely would.

And he'd arrive at work chipper and ready to face the day.

He hoped.

Something was wrong with Lucas.

He'd come through the doors of the MMU with a frown that could have swallowed most of Melbourne. She'd arrived at work armed with a smile, only to have him look right past her as if she didn't exist.

Ha! Evidently she'd been wrong about his reaction. Because there was nothing remotely resembling attraction in the man's eyes today. In fact, his whole frame oozed exhaustion, as did the two nicks on the left side of his strong jaw. He'd muttered something that might have been "G'day." Or it might just as easily have been "Go to hell."

She was tempted to chase him down and ask about his evening, but when she turned to do so, she noticed that the back of his shirt was wrinkled as if he'd... Her gaze skimmed down and caught the same dark jeans he'd worn yesterday.

Her stomach rolled to the side. The staff all had lockers, and the last time he'd come in like this he'd used the hospital's shower and changed into clean clothes. That's probably what he was headed to do right now.

The evidence pointed to one thing. That he'd spent the night with "Cora" or some other woman.

The trickle of attraction froze in her veins.

None of your business, Darcie.

Just leave the man alone. If she made an issue of this,

they would be back where they'd started: fighting a cold war that neither one of them would win.

But why the hell couldn't he drag himself out of his lover's bed in time to go home and shower before coming to work?

Unless he just couldn't manage to tear himself away from her.

An image emerged from the haze that she did her best to block. Too late. There it was, and there was no way to send it back again—the one of Lucas swinging his feet over the side of the mattress, only to have some faceless woman graze long, ruby fingernails down his arm and whisper something that made him change his mind.

She shook her head to remove the picture and forced herself to get back to work.

Just as she did so she spied one of her patients leaning against the wall, her hands gripping her swollen belly. Margie Terrington, an English transplant like herself, had just come in yesterday for a quick check to make sure things were on track. They had been.

At least until now. From the concentration on her face and the grey cast to her skin, something wasn't right. Darcie glanced around for a nurse, but they were still tending to the morning's patients. Darcie hurried over.

"Margie? Are you all right?"

Her eyes came up. "My stomach. It's cramping. I think it's the baby."

"Let's get you into a room."

Alarm filled her. No time to check her in or do any of the preliminaries. This was the young woman's second pregnancy. She'd miscarried her first a little over a year ago, and she was only seven months along with this one. Too soon. The human body didn't just go into labor this early unless there was a problem.

Her apprehension grew, and she sent up a quick prayer.

Propping her shoulder beneath Margie's arm, they headed to the nearest exam room. One of the nurses came out of a room across the hall, and Darcie called out to her. "Tessa, could you come here?"

The nurse hurried over and got on the other side of their patient.

"Once I get her settled, can you see if you can find Lucas? He arrived a few minutes ago, so he might be in the lounge or the locker area. Let him know I might need his help."

"Of course."

The patient was sweating profusely—Darcie could feel the moisture through the woman's light maternity top. Another strike against her. If she had some kind of systemic infection, could it have crossed the placenta and affected the baby? A thousand possibilities ran through her mind.

Pushing into the exam area, the trio paused when Margie groaned and doubled over even more. "Oh, God. Hurts."

"Do they feel like contractions? Are they regular?" They finally got her to the bed and helped her up on it.

"I don't know."

Tessa scurried around, getting her vitals, while Darcie tried to get some more information. What she learned wasn't good. Margie had got up and showered like normal and had felt fine. Forty minutes later she'd got a painful cramp in her side—like the kind you got while running, she'd said. The pain had grown worse and had spread in a band across her abdomen. Now she was feeling nauseous, whether from the pain or something else, she wasn't sure. "And my joints hurt, as if I'm getting the flu."

Could she be?

As soon as Tessa called out the readings, the nurse went out to get the patient's chart and to hunt down Lucas.

"Let's get you into a robe and see what's going on."

"Wait." Margie groaned again. "I think I'm going to be sick."

Grabbing a basin, she held it under her patient's mouth as she heaved. Nothing came up, though.

"Did you eat breakfast?" Darcie started to reach for a paper towel, only to have Lucas arrive, chart in hand. He took one look at the scene and anticipated what she was doing. Ripping a couple of towels from the dispenser, he glanced at her in question. "What've you got?"

"This is Margie Terrington from Southbank. She's cramping. Pain in the joints. Nausea."

"Contractions?"

"I'm not sure. I'm just getting ready to hook her up to the monitor."

He tilted his head. "Theories?"

"None." She laid a hand on the young woman's shoulder. "Are you up to telling Lucas what you told me?"

Even as she asked it, Margie's face tightened up in a pained grimace, and she gave a couple of sustained breaths, dragging air in through her nose and letting it out through her mouth. A second or two later she nodded. "Like I told you, I took a shower this morning. Then I started getting these weird sensations in my side."

"What kind of weird?"

"Like a pulled muscle or something." She stiffened once again. She gritted out, "But now my whole stomach hurts."

"Where's the father?" Lucas asked.

"He's at work. I—I didn't want to worry him if it's nothing."

Lucas frowned. "I think he should be here." He glanced at Darcie. "Can you get her hooked up while I ring him?"

If anything, Margie looked even more frightened. "Am I going to lose this baby too?"

Darcie's heart ached for the woman, even as her brain still whirled, trying to figure out what was going on. "Let us do the worrying, love, can you do that?"

"I think so." She wrote her husband's phone number on a sheet of paper and handed it to Lucas.

While he was gone, Darcie got Margie into a hospital gown and snapped on a pair of gloves. Then she wrapped the monitor around her patient's abdomen. Wow, she was really perspiring. So much so that it had already soaked through the robe on her right side.

And her abdominal muscles were tight to the touch. "Are you having a contraction right now?"

Margie moaned. "I don't know."

She started up the machine and the first thing she heard was the quick *woompa-woompa-woompa-woompa* of the baby's heart. Thank God. Even as that thought hit, a hundred more swept past it. A heartbeat didn't mean Margie's baby wasn't in distress, just that he was alive.

She stared at the line below the heart rate that should be showing the marked rise and fall of the uterus as it contracted and released. It was a steady line.

Placing her hand on Margie's abdomen again, she noted the strange tightness she'd felt before. But it seemed more like surface muscles to Darcie. Not the deep, purposeful contraction of a woman's uterus.

Lucas came back and glanced at the monitor. "Your husband's on his way."

"Thank you." Another moan, and her hands went back to her stomach.

Lucas sat next to the bed and held the patient's hand, helping guide her through the deep breathing.

"She's not contracting." Darcie's eyes were locked on the monitor where a series of little squiggles indicated that something was happening, but it was more like a series of muscle fasciculations than the steady rise and fall she would expect to see. Could she have flu, like Margie suspected?

"When did you start sweating like this?"

Lucas's voice drew her attention back. He eased Margie's robe to the side and stared at the area where moisture was already beading up despite just having been exposed to the chilly air of the ward. Strange. Although Margie was perspiring everywhere—Darcie gave a quick glance at her face and chest above the gown—there was a marked difference between her moist upper lip and her right side, where a rivulet of liquid peaked and then ran down the woman's swollen belly.

"I don't know. An hour after my shower? Right about the time I started to hurt."

He peered at her closer. "You said you took a shower. Did you feel anything before or after it? A sting…or a prick maybe?"

A prick? Darcie stared at him, trying to figure out where he was going with this.

"No."

"Where did the pain start exactly?"

Margie pressed her fingers right over the area that was wet from perspiration.

He muttered something under his breath then glanced up at Darcie. "I need to make a quick phone call."

"What?" Outrage gathered in her chest and built into a froth that threatened to explode. Surely he was not going to make a personal call right now.

As if he saw something in her face, he reached out and encircled her wrist. "I want her husband to check on something at the house before he comes here," he said in a low voice.

The anger flooding her system disappeared in a whoosh as she stared back at him.

Margie's panicked voice broke between them. "What's wrong?"

"I'm not sure yet. But I don't think you're in labor."

"Then what?"

"I think you may have been bitten by a redback," Lucas said.

"A what?" Margie asked.

"It's one of our most famous residents," he said. "It's a spider. A nasty one at that."

A redback! Darcie had heard of them but had never

encountered one, and since she wasn't from Australia, it had never dawned on her that Margie could have been envenomed by something. Her patient was also from England. She'd probably never thought of that possibility either.

She glanced at Lucas. "Are they that common?"

"Quite." He patted Margie's hand. "If that's the case we have antivenin we can give you, which should help."

"If it is a bite, will it hurt the baby?" She gritted her teeth and pulled in another deep breath.

"I think we've caught it at an early stage." His gaze went back to the monitor, which Darcie noted still held steady. "I want to have your husband check the towel and your bathroom."

The patient's eyes widened. "I used the walk-in shower in the guest bathroom this morning. I almost never use that one because it's quite a long way from the bedroom. But my mother is due to fly in to help with the house and baby in a few weeks, and I thought I could tidy things and scrub the shower stall down as I was bathing."

"I'm just going to pull Dr. Green into the hallway for a moment. I'll send the nurse in to sit with you."

Once they were outside the room, and Lucas had rung the husband, asking him to shake out the towel and examine the bathroom, she spun toward him. "A redback. Are you sure?"

"Pretty sure. Most Australians know what to look for, but no one else would. I've seen this once before. A redback bite that comes in looking like preterm labor."

She sagged against the wall. "God. I would have never checked for that. I didn't see a bite. Didn't even think to ask."

"You wouldn't have. And as for the bite mark…" He shrugged. "Small fangs, but they pack quite a wallop."

He gave a smile that looked as tired as she suddenly felt.

"Can we give antivenin to her during pregnancy?"

"We've given it before. I can't recall anyone having a bad reaction, unless the patient is allergic to the equine immunoglobulin in the serum." He sighed. "There've been some conflicting reports recently about whether or not the antivenin actually works, but I've seen enough evidence to tell me it's worth a shot. Especially since she's miscarried once already."

Lucas's mobile phone buzzed, and he glanced at the screen. "It's him. Let's hope this is the answer we're looking for."

He punched a button asking a few questions before assuring the man that she should do well with the antivenin and telling him they'd be awaiting his arrival.

"He found the redback. It was still in the towel. A big one, from the sound of it." He dragged his fingers through his hair. "I'll need you to sign off on the medication. We'll go the intravenous route rather than administering the antivenin intramuscularly, since that's more favored at the moment."

"Of course." She closed her eyes with a relieved laugh. "God, I could kiss you right now. I never in a million years would have got that diagnosis right."

A few seconds of silence met her comment.

Hell. Had she really just said that? About kissing him?

Evidently, because when she dared to look at him again a thread of confused amusement seemed to play across his face. "I don't think now would be appropriate, do you, Dr. Green? But later…" He let his voice trail off in a way that gave her no question that he was definitely open to whatever later meant.

What? Hadn't he just come to work this morning all rumpled and sexed up?

Sexed up? Was that even a real expression?

Whether it was or not wasn't the point. It was unbelievable that he would roll out of one woman's bed and be ready and willing to kiss a second one. A perfect stranger, actually, since they barely knew each other.

Not likely, you jerk.

She gave the haughtiest toss of her chin she could manage and fixed him with a cold glare. "It's a figure of speech, Lucas, in case you haven't heard. I was just happy to know that Margie's symptoms have an explanation and a treatment. But get this straight. As grateful as I am for your help, I had no intention of *really* kissing you. Now…or ever. I have no interest in being part of a love triangle. Been there. Done that."

Before she could scurry away in horror over that last blooper, he murmured, "I stand corrected on the kissing, although you totally had me for a moment or two. But I'm intrigued by this supposed love triangle you envision us in. Care to enlighten me as to who the third party might be, or do I have no say in the matter?"

Was he serious?

She wanted to hurl Cora's name at him. Instead, by some superhuman force of will, she clamped her jaws shut before they had a chance to issue any other crazy statements. Then, without another word, she swung back into their patient's room to give her the news about the redback.

At least he hadn't asked her about the been-there-done-that part of her rant, because no one needed to hear her sad tale about the wedding that almost had been. Or the woman who'd stolen her fiancé's heart when he was supposed to be madly in love with her.

Since when had she become so reckless with her words?

Just like the ruby stripe on the infamous redback that warned of dire consequences to those who came in contact with it, the answer to her last question was inscribed with words that were just as lethal: Lucas Elliot.

He made her forget about everything but his presence.

The thing was, she had no idea how to go about scrubbing him—or the image of their lips locking in a frenzy of need—from her mind and finishing out the rest of her time in Australia in relative peace.

But she'd better figure out an antivenin that would work against his charm and inject herself with it. As soon as she possibly could.

CHAPTER THREE

"How's Cora?"

Isla settled herself on the paper-lined exam table like a pro, despite the burgeoning evidence of her pregnancy.

A week after they'd successfully treated the redback spider victim, Darcie had somehow managed to keep her tongue to herself.

Ugh. Now, why did that thought sound so raunchy?

And why was it that every time she was around Lucas her mind hadn't quite stopped doing mental gymnastics over every word the man uttered, turning them over and over and looking for hidden meanings?

There weren't any, and he hadn't brought up the subjects of kissing, love triangles, or anything else of a personal nature, for which she was extremely grateful.

Here Isla was, though, bringing up the one person she had no desire to hear about.

Lucas's supposed lover.

As if hearing her thoughts, he glanced at her before looking back at their patient. "She's great. Wants me to buy her a sports car."

Darcie's eyebrows shot up, even though she tried to keep her facial features frozen into place. The woman had actually asked him to buy her a car? A pool of distaste gathered in the pit of her stomach. Just what kind of women did the man hang out with?

Isla, though, instead of castigating Lucas and telling him to kick the tramp to the curb, laughed as if she found that idea hilarious.

"Did you tell her she has to be tall enough to reach the pedals first?"

Her brain hit the rewind button and played those words over twice. Either he was dating a very short woman or...

"Yep. I also told her she has to be old enough to have her driving permit. So I'm safe for a few years."

Darcie couldn't help it. The words just came out. "Cora's not of legal age?"

"He hasn't talked your ear off about her yet? Wow." Her former flatmate blew out a breath. "She's his niece. And she gives him quite a bit of grief. Isn't that right, Lucas?"

The man in question studied Darcie as if he couldn't quite grasp something. "That's right, and..." The pupils in his eyes grew larger. "Oh, Darcie, I'm almost afraid to ask. Who did you think she was?"

"I—I..." She stammered around for a second then finally gave up.

He made a tutting sound then his lips curved. "I think I see. A love triangle, wasn't it? I don't know if I should be insulted or flattered."

"I just thought, she was—"

"My girlfriend?"

Isla's voice cut in. "Would someone like to clue me in on what you two are going on about? What's this about a love triangle?"

"It's nothing."

Lucas spoke at the exact same time she did. He then laughed, while Darcie's face flamed.

Their patient looked from one to the other of them. "Oh, this is definitely *not* nothing. But…" she patted her belly "…someone is starting to use my bladder as his own personal football. So unless you want to take a break while I visit the loo, maybe we should get on with this."

"Of course." Lucas pulled out his measuring tape and stretched it over the bulge of Isla's belly, writing the results on her chart. "Right on schedule. At this rate I think the baby will weigh in at a little over seven pounds. The perfect size for a first baby."

"Thank goodness, because right now my stomach looks to be the size of a football." She gave a light laugh. "I guess that's why this little guy feels like he's training for the World Cup."

"Anything out of the ordinary? Contractions?"

"No. Nothing. I feel great." She glanced at Darcie. "Except I have to break our date for the beach this afternoon. Someone called off sick, and they've asked me to fill in."

"Don't worry about it. Some other time."

"I know, but I promised to take you to see some sights, and with everything with Alessi and the baby, time has just slipped away." Isla slid a look at Lucas. "Aren't you two on the same rota?"

A pit lodged in her stomach. "Yes, why?"

"Well, because…" She gave the midwife a wide smile. "Would you mind going in my place? Darcie and I were going to make a list of things for her to see and do. If she puts it off too much longer, she'll go back to England without having visited anything."

Her unease morphed into horror. "Isla, I'm sure he has other things to do with his off time than go to the beach."

"Actually, I'm free once our shift is over." The smile he gave her was much slower than Isla's and held a touch of challenge that made her shiver. "I'll be happy to help her make her list. And maybe even tick an item or two off of it. Since we *do* have the same rota. Unless she doesn't trust me, for some reason."

Isla skimmed her hands over her belly and gave a sigh that sounded relieved. "Of course she trusts you. That would be brilliant, Lucas. At this point, I would only slow her down."

They were making plans that she hadn't even agreed to. And go to the beach with Lucas? See those long legs stretched out on the sand beside hers? A dull roar sounded in her ears as panic set in.

"I'll be fine—"

A quick knock sounded before she could blurt out the rest of her sentence, that she would be fine on her own, that she didn't need company.

Sean Anderson, one of the other obstetricians, poked his head into the room. "Sorry, guys, they told me Isla was here." He looked at the patient, his expression unreadable. "One of your teen mums-to-be projects is at the nurses' station, asking for you. And after that your father wants to speak with you about your sister. I have a few questions about her myself."

Poor Isla. Not exactly the kind of thing one wanted to deal with when heavily pregnant.

Charles Delamere—Isla's father and the head of the Melbourne Victoria Hospital—had given her friend nothing but grief over her older sister's mad dash to England and the reasons behind it. Sean hadn't been far behind in the question department. But according to Isla, she'd promised Isabel that she would never reveal her secret to anyone. Especially not to Sean, since his coming to the hospital nine months ago had been what had sent Isabel running for the door in the first place.

She tried to avoid the other man's gaze as much as possible, until Isla sat up and grabbed her hand. "Would you come with me, since you wanted to know more about the teen mums program?"

Her eyes said it all. She didn't want to be alone with Sean in case he grilled her again about Isabel. Darcie wouldn't have known about any of this except that Isabel's sudden departure had left an opening at both the MMU and in the Delameres' luxurious penthouse flat, which she'd shared with Isla until her friend's marriage to Alessandro.

Darcie had been all too happy to take Isabel's place, since she knew what it was like to run from something. In Darcie's case, it had been the right decision. In Isabel's, she wasn't so sure.

Isla hadn't told her much, but she knew Isabel was keeping something big from Sean. Maybe it was time for her to tell him the truth and see what happened.

But that wasn't her decision to make.

"Of course I'll come with you. It'll give me a chance to meet someone who's in the program."

As Isla threw her a grateful look and slid off the bed, Lucas, who'd been listening to their conversation without a word, wrapped his fingers around Darcie's wrist. "I'll meet you by the entrance after work. This'll give us a chance to discuss some things as well."

Like how she'd somehow managed to leap to the conclusion that his niece was some floozy that kept him out late at night and caused him to have a flippant attitude about work? Heavens, she'd misjudged the man, and she wasn't exactly sure how to make it right. But going to the beach with him was the last venue she would have chosen. For the life of her, though, she couldn't think of a way to get out of it. "If you're sure."

"More than sure." His thumb glided across the inside of her wrist, the touch so light she was almost positive she'd imagined it, if not for the cheeky grin that followed. Then he released her. "Give me a ring when you're done."

"'Kay."

Once out the door, she went with Sean and Isla to the waiting area, her shaking legs and thumping heart threatening to send her to the floor. It took several deep breaths to get hold of herself.

It turned out the expectant mum was there to introduce Isla to a friend of hers—also a teen, also pregnant—who wanted to be included in the teen mums program. Darcie's heart ached over these young women who found themselves facing the unthinkable alone. She glanced at her friend, who greeted the newcomer with a smile, handing her a brochure that explained the enrolment process for TMTB. Darcie might not be able to understand what they went through, but Isla and Isabel understood all too well. Her chest grew tighter as she noticed Sean still standing behind them.

Oh, the tangled webs.

Once the girls were off on their way, Sean stepped forward. Holding up a hand, Isla stopped him in his tracks. "Don't ask, Sean. I can't tell you." She hesitated, and her mouth opened as if she was going to say something else then stopped.

All the heartache with Robert came rushing back, and Darcie realized how much simpler it would have been if he'd told her the truth when he'd first realized he loved someone else, rather than dragging out the process. If he hadn't kept his feelings for Tabitha a secret, maybe things would have been easier on all involved.

That thought propelled her next words.

"Maybe you should call Isabel and ask her yourself," she suggested, grabbing Isla's hand and giving it a quick squeeze of reassurance. She was half-afraid Isla would smack her for sticking her nose where it didn't belong.

Sean's blue eyes swung toward her. "I tried when I heard she was leaving, but she wouldn't take my calls."

Instead of cutting her off, Isla nodded, wrapping her arm around Darcie's as if needing to hold onto something. "Maybe, Sean…maybe you should just go there. If you're standing in front of her, she can't ignore you."

"Go to England?" he asked.

That was a fantastic idea.

Lucas had planted himself in Darcie's path a couple of weeks ago, and she'd been forced to stand there while he'd had his say. Maybe Sean should do the same. Once everything was out in the open, they could decide what to do with the truth. Or at least Isabel would be forced to tell him to his face that she wanted nothing to do with him. Somehow Darcie didn't think that's what the other woman would say when it came down to it. But, whatever happened, it was up to the two of them to hash things out. It wasn't Isla's responsibility, and she shouldn't have to act as intermediary, especially with a baby on the way. The last thing she needed was any added stress.

"I can give you her address, if you promise not to tell her where you got it," Isla added.

"My contract at the hospital *is* almost up." He dragged a hand through his hair, tousling the messy strands even more. "I'll have to think about it."

Isla's chin angled up a fraction of an inch. "I guess it comes down to whether or not you really want to know why she left, or how much you might come to regret it if you never take the chance and ask."

"I'll let you know if I need that address." With that, he strode down the hallway as if the very hounds of hell were hot on his heels.

Darcie sighed. "Do you think he will?"

"I don't know. Maybe the better question would be… if he *should*."

Why had he agreed to take her to the beach?

Lucas paused at the entrance to the car park to roll down the long sleeves of his shirt and button the cuffs against the cool air—or maybe he was gearing up for battle.

Having seen Darcie's face go pink when she'd realized Cora was his niece and not his lover had made something come to life inside him…as had her comment about a love triangle. The fact that she'd envi-

sioned herself with him in that way was so at odds with
how she'd always treated him that her flippant words
had intrigued him. As had the thought of seeing her
outside her own environment. Would the woman he'd
come to view as an English rose—beautiful skin, green
eyes, and a set of thorns that would pierce the toughest
hide—turn into someone different once she stepped off
hospital property?

That was why he'd agreed. If she was going to make
any kind of transformation, he wanted to be there to
see it.

He glanced back inside the hospital as he waited. It
was spring in Melbourne, and the air definitely bore a
hint of that as it had been warmer than usual. Hence
Isla's suggestion of going to one of the beaches hadn't
seemed too crazy. In fact, the temperature was still
holding at almost nineteen degrees, and the sun was just
starting to ease toward the horizon, so they wouldn't
need jackets. Although in Melbourne that could change
at any time.

"Hi, sorry I'm late," Darcie said in a breathless voice
as the automatic doors closed behind her. "I wanted to
grab a cardigan."

She'd done more than that. She'd changed from her
dark trousers and white blouse into a long gauzy white
skirt and a knit turquoise top that crossed over her chest
in a way that drew attention to her full curves. Curves
that made his mouth go dry.

The transformation begins.

He swallowed, trying to rid himself of the sensation.
He'd expected her to let her hair down in a figurative

sense. He hadn't expected to see those soft silky strands grazing the upper edges of her breasts.

That he was still staring at.

Forcing his eyes back to her face, where the color of her shirt made her eyes almost glow, he blinked back to reality. "Don't worry about it. Do you want to take the car or ride the tram?"

"Oh, the tram, please. I haven't ridden it to the beach yet, and it sounds like fun."

When he'd called the house, Chessa had said Felix was home and was grilling burgers on the barbie. When he'd tensely asked the childminder if he seemed "okay" she'd answered yes. For once he appeared clearheaded.

Thank God. The last thing he wanted to do was skip out on his date with Darcie and ruin his reputation with her all over again.

Nope. This was not a date. Something he needed to remember.

"How do you usually get to the beach, then? Taxi?"

She glanced at him as they headed for the nearest tram station. "I haven't actually been yet. I hear they're beautiful."

"You haven't been to any of them?" Shock made him stop and look at her. Isla had mentioned taking her to see some sights, but surely she'd at least visited some of Melbourne's famed beaches.

"Nope. No time. That's why Isla suggested starting there and making a list of some other things."

They started walking again. Hell, she'd been here how long? Nine months? "Well, I'm glad she mentioned it, then. We can get a snack at one of the kiosks if you want. The beaches are prettier in the morning, though."

Maybe he should take her to see the sun rise over the ocean. Those first rays of light spilling onto the water and sand made them flash and glitter as if waking from a deep slumber.

Like him?

Of course not. He wasn't asleep. He was purposeful. Conscious of every move he made and careful to keep his heart far from anything that smacked of affection…or worse. He'd seen firsthand what had happened with Felix and Cora when Melody had died. He never wanted anyone to have to explain to a child of his the things he'd had to explain to his niece. That her father was very sad that her mother had gone away.

You mean she died.

Cora had said the words in her no-nonsense, too-adult-for-her-age manner that made his heart contract.

His niece needed him for who knew how long. He wouldn't do anything that would jeopardize his ability to be there for her.

Especially not for love.

That wasn't true. "Love" was exactly why he'd decided to remain single. He needed to expend all his emotional energy on a little girl who desperately needed a dependable, stable adult. Something that Felix couldn't be. At least not yet.

Buying their tickets, he eased them over to the queue, where a few people waited for the next tram to arrive.

Darcie's soft voice came through above the sound of nearby traffic. "I owe you an apology."

He glanced over in surprise to see her hands clasped in front of her, her eyes staring straight ahead. "For what?"

"For chastising you for being late all those months ago. I thought you were…that Cora was…" She shrugged.

The tram, with its bright splashes of color, pulled to a halt as he processed her words. They both got on and grabbed an overhead strap, since all the seats were full. As they did so, he suddenly saw the whole situation through Darcie's eyes. If she truly had thought his niece was a woman, then all those times he'd come rushing into work after sleeping on his brother's couch had to look pretty damning when viewed through that lens.

He stepped closer to prevent anyone from hearing and leaned down. "I should have explained, but I thought it was—"

"None of my business. And it wasn't. If I had questions, I should have asked you directly."

Whether the reasons had been valid or not, she'd been right in expecting him to be prompt and ready to work when it was time for his assigned shift. "I should have tried harder."

Except that sometimes there'd been no way to do that. He'd had to take Cora to school on mornings that Felix had been recovering from a bender or, worse, when he hadn't come home for the night. There'd been that worry on top of having to care for his niece. There had been days he probably shouldn't have come in to work at all. Except his sense of duty had forced him to march in there—late or not—and do what he'd promised to do.

After a while, though, all those promises had begun to bump into one another and fight for supremacy. His niece had to come first. And he would make no apologies for that.

The tram started up and Darcie lurched into him for a second. He reached out with his free hand to steady her, but she recovered, pulling away quickly and clearing her throat. "Does your niece live with you?"

His grip tightened slightly on the handhold, but he forced his voice to remain light. "She lives with my brother, but I help out with her every once in a while."

That was the understatement of the year. But he loved Cora. He'd give his life for her if he had to.

Sensing she was going to ask another question, he added. "Her mom died of cancer a few years ago."

She glanced up at him. "I'm so sorry, Lucas."

So was he. But that didn't change anything. "Thank you." He braced himself to go around a curve, and Darcie—not anticipating the shift—bumped into him once again. This time the contact sent a jolt of awareness through him. He just prevented himself from anchoring her against him, and instead changed the subject. "So how is it that you haven't seen any of our beaches? As busy as you are, surely you could have managed one side trip."

"It's no fun on my own." She gestured at the sights outside the tram, which were racing by with occasional stops to pick up or let off passengers.

With Isla busy building her own life, Lucas had never stopped to wonder how Darcie was faring now that she had the Delamere flat all to herself. That made him feel even worse. "You should have asked someone at the hospital to go with you."

"It's okay. I understand how busy everyone is."

Their bodies connected once more, and this time he couldn't help but reach out to make sure she didn't stumble or hit the passenger on her other side. She didn't object, instead seeming to lean in to brace her shoulder against his chest. Or that could just be his damned imagination since the contact seemed to be burning a hole through his shirt. Whatever it was, he was in no hurry to let her go again. Except they were nearing the Port Melbourne Beach, which was one of the best locales for a newbie tourist. "Let's get off at this one."

When the tram stopped, he reached for her hand and guided her to the nearest door. Stepping down and waiting for her to do the same, he glanced around. "I want to get a notebook."

"What for?" she asked, brushing her skirt down her hips.

"To make that list Isla mentioned."

She reached into her bag and pulled out a small spiral-bound pad. "I have this if that would work."

"Perfect. We can sit down and put our heads together."

She paused then said, "Oh, um…sure, that would be great. But you really don't have to go with me to see the city."

It was said with such a lack of enthusiasm that he smiled. "I told Isla I would. Besides, I want to. It'll be one way for me make amends."

"Are you sure? If anyone needs to make amends, it's me."

He allowed his smile to grow as he took the notepad from her and headed toward the paved footpath that led to the beach. "You were just trying to avoid that love triangle you mentioned."

Darcie laughed, a low throaty sound that went

straight to his groin and lodged there. "For all I knew, it could have been a love hexagon…or octagon."

"Hmm, that might be a little ambitious even for someone like me."

"Someone who jumps from woman to woman?"

He shook his head. "Nope. I don't jump. I just don't stick around long enough to make any kind of angles—triangular or otherwise."

And if that didn't make him sound like a first-class jerk, he didn't know what did. "That didn't come out exactly right."

"It's okay. I understand. You're just not interested in serious relationships. Same here."

"Really? No serious relationships back in England?"

"Not at the moment."

"So there was someone?" The pull in his groin eased, but a few other muscles tensed in its place. Why did the idea of her being with someone else put him on edge?

"I was engaged. I'm not any more."

Those seven words were somehow more terrible than if she'd gone through a long convoluted explanation about why she and her fiancé had come to their senses and realized they weren't meant to be together. They spoke of heartbreak. And pain.

All the more reason for him to stay out of the dating pool.

"I'm sorry it didn't work out."

"Me too."

So she still loved the guy? She must. What the hell had her fiancé done to her?

He reached down and squeezed her hand, and instead of letting go he held on as they reached the wide footpath that ran along the far edge of the beach where other people strolled, jogged or rolled by on skates or bicycles.

"Wow, it's busy for so late in the afternoon," she said.

"It's a nice day. Do you want to walk in the sand or stick to the path?"

"Definitely the sand. Let me take my shoes off." Stepping to the side and grasping his hand more tightly, she kicked off one sandal and then the other, reaching down to pick them up and tuck them into the colorful tote bag she carried. "Your turn."

He let go of her hand long enough to remove his loafers and peel off his socks, shoving them into his shoes. He then tucked the notebook under his right arm so he could hold his shoes with the same hand.

Once their feet hit the sand their fingers laced back together as if by magic, and Darcie made no move to pull away.

She was a visitor. Alone, essentially, and dealing with a broken engagement. He was offering friendship. Nothing more.

And if she offered to drown her sorrows in his arms?

All the things that had gone soft suddenly headed back in the other direction.

Hell, Lucas, you've got to get a grip.

It might have been better if she'd never shown him her human side. Because it was doing a number on him. Okay, so he could show her some things. Maybe he'd invite Cora along for the ride. He could make sure his niece was being cared for and have a built-in chaperone should his libido decide to put in more appearances.

Darcie stopped halfway to the shoreline, her arm brushing his as she took in the sights around her.

"What's that ship?" She motioned to where the *Spirit* was docked, waiting on its next round of travelers, its large sleek shape a normal part of the landscape here at the beach.

"It carries passengers and vehicles across to Tasmania. Maybe that's first thing we should put on your list."

"Maybe."

Darcie's hair flicked around her face in the breeze from the surf, the long strands looking warm and inviting in the fading rays of the sun. His fingers tightened around his shoes, trying to resist the urge to catch one of the locks to see if it was as silky as it appeared. Good thing both of his hands were occupied at the moment.

"It's lovely here," she murmured.

It was. And he wasn't even looking at the water. Why had he never noticed the way her nose tilted up at the end, or the way her chin had the slightest hint of an indentation? And the scent the wind tossed his way was feminine and mysterious, causing a pulling sensation that grew stronger by the second.

"I agree." He forced his eyes back to the shoreline and started walking again. "Are you hungry? We could grab something and sit on the sand. Then we could start on that list while we eat."

She reached up and pushed her hair off her face with her free hand. "That sounds good. I should have brought an elastic for my hair."

"I like it down."

Green eyes swung to meet his. She blinked a couple of times. "It's not very practical."

"Neither are a lot of things." Why was he suddenly

spewing such nonsense? He motioned to a nearby vendor. "How about here?"

They bought some ice-cream bars and ate them as they strolled a little further down the beach. By the time they'd finished they'd come across an area that wasn't packed with people. "Can we stop?" she asked.

"I didn't think to bring a blanket."

"It's fine." Dropping her shoes and bag onto the soft sand, she sat cross-legged, covering her legs with her skirt. Then she propped her hands behind her hips and lifted her face to the sky. She released a quiet exhalation, a sound that spoke of letting go of tension…along with a hint of contentment.

She was still transforming—losing some of those hard, brittle edges she had at the hospital. Maybe they were simply a result of working long hours with little or no downtime. Because right now she was all soft and mellow, her billowing skirt and bare feet giving her a bohemian, artsy flare he'd never have equated with Dr. Darcie Green. And he liked it. The hair, the pale skin, the casual way she'd settled onto the sand, curved fingers burrowing into it. That firm behind that had bumped against him repeatedly as they'd ridden the tram.

The list! Think about something else. Anything else.

He opened the notebook and riffled through pages of notes from what must have been a medical seminar until he came to a blank sheet. He drew a pen from his shirt pocket. "So what would you like to see or do while in Australia?"

Her eyes blinked open but she didn't look at him. Instead, she stared out at Port Phillip Bay instead. "Mmm. Travel to Tasmania on that ship we saw?"

His pen poised over the paper as she paused for a second.

"Do some shopping. Visit a museum." Her brows knitted together as she thought. "See some of the parks. Go to a zoo."

She glanced his way, maybe noticing he wasn't writing. Because he was still too damn busy looking at her.

He shook himself. "Those are all safe things—things every tourist does. You should have at least one or two things that are a little more dangerous."

"Dangerous?" Her eyes widened just a touch.

"Not dangerous as in getting bitten by a redback but dangerous as in fun. Something you never would have done had you remained in England. Something outrageous and wild." He leaned a little closer. "Something you'll probably never get a chance to do again."

There was silence for a few seconds then her gaze skimmed across his lips and then back up, her cheeks turning a luscious shade of pink.

Oh, hell. He was in deep trouble. Because if the most outrageous thing she could picture doing was pressing her mouth to his… Well, he could top that and add a few things that would knock her socks—and the rest of her clothes—right off.

"What are you thinking?"

She shook her head. "Nothing."

"Darcie." His voice came out low and gruff. "Look at me."

Her face slowly turned back toward him.

"If I write, 'Kiss a non-triangular Aussie' on this list, would you consider that wild and dangerous?"

There was a long pause.

"Yes," she whispered.

His gut spun sideways. He hoped to God he'd heard what he thought he'd heard, because he was not backing away from this. His brain might have come to a standstill, but his body was racing forward at the speed of light.

He set the notebook on the sand, one hand coming up to cup her nape. "Do you want to tick at least one thing off that list before we leave this beach? Because you have a willing member of the male Aussie contingent sitting right next to you."

"You?"

"Me."

He reeled her in a little closer, his senses coming to life when her eyes slowly fluttered shut.

He would take that as a yes.

His body humming with anticipation, Lucas slowly moved in to seal the deal.

CHAPTER FOUR

HE TASTED LIKE ice cream.

Darcie wasn't quite sure how it happened, but that tram ride must have messed with her head, muddled her thinking, because somehow Lucas was kissing her, his mouth sliding over hers in light little passes that never quite went away.

That was good, because once the contact stopped the kiss would be over.

And that was the last thing she wanted.

There were people walking on the path not ten meters behind them, but it was as if she and Lucas were all alone with just the beach and the sound of the surf to keep them company.

His lips left hers, and she despaired, but he was back in less than a second, the angle changing, the pressure increasing just a fraction. Her arms started trembling from holding herself upright, and as if sensing her struggle he eased her down, hand beneath her head until she touched the sand.

The flavor of the kiss changed, going from what she feared might be a quick peck—the thing of friends or family members—to a full-on assault on her senses... a *kiss*.

If he was out to prove that Aussie men were hot-blooded, he'd done that. He'd more than done that. There was a raw quality to Lucas that she didn't understand but which she found she liked. As if he were a man on the edge—struggling to keep things casual but wanting, oh, so much more.

So did she.

Darcie opened her mouth.

The kiss stilled, and she wondered if she'd gone too far or if he was trying to process what to do at this point.

You said wild and dangerous. I'm laying myself open to it so, please, don't make me sorry.

He didn't. His tongue dipped just past her lips, sliding across the edge of her upper teeth before venturing further in. Her nerve endings all came to life at once, nipples tightening, gooseflesh rising on her arms.

Maybe she could tick that item off her list multiple times…right here, right now.

She wound her arms around his neck, reveling in the sense of urgency she now felt in his kiss. His free hand went to her waist and tightened on it, his thumb brushing across her ribs in a long slow stroke.

Then he withdrew, pulling back until he was an inch from her mouth.

"Damn." His curse brushed across her lips, but he didn't sound angry. Not like he had when he'd seen the rotation schedule. More like surprised.

He sat up, using the hand behind her head to help her up as well. "We'd better start actually making that list or it's never going to get done."

Who cared about some stupid list?

His jotting things down, though, gave her a chance to

compose herself. Well, a little. Because nothing could have prepared her for that kiss. Not her relationship with Robert or any of her past dating experiences.

Lucas was… She wasn't sure what he was. But he was good.

She glanced over at the sheet of paper where he'd made a list of about ten things. "Kiss an Aussie" was first on the list, but the tick mark he'd made beside it was now scratched through.

"I thought we were going to cross that off."

The look he gave her was completely serious. "We can't tick something off a list that didn't exist at the time it happened."

"We can't?"

"No." His eyes went dark with intent. "Because if you want to experience a real Aussie kiss, it has to be behind closed doors—with no audience to distract you."

Distracted? Who'd been distracted? Certainly not her.

But if he wanted to kiss her again—like that—she was more than willing to play along.

He scrawled a couple more words.

"Hey, wait a minute. I never said I wanted to bungee jump."

"Dangerous, remember?"

"But—"

"I have a friend who used to have a bungee-jumping business. He closed it last year but still lets friends take a dive from time to time. And I promised Cora—my niece," he reminded her with a smile, "that she could come out and watch me do a jump."

It was her turn to be surprised. "You bungee jump?"

"I have to get my adrenaline pumping somehow, since I don't have any love triangles to keep me busy."

That was something she didn't even want to think about, because she might end up volunteering if she wasn't careful.

She wouldn't mind meeting his niece, though. And it wasn't like *she* had to jump.

"Okay, I'll go. But I don't promise I'm going to do anything but watch."

"Oh, no, gorgeous, you're going to do a whole lot more than that. I promise."

Why had he invited her on his and Cora's day out?

Because he'd been too strung out on kissing her two days ago to think clearly when he'd written that item on her so-called list. She and Cora had been chatting the whole trip, with Darcie twisted around in her seat in order to talk to her. Why couldn't Cora have hated her on sight?

But she hadn't. And her "Are you Uncle Luke's girlfriend?" had turned Darcie's face the color of pink fairy floss. She hadn't freaked out, though. She'd simply shaken her head and said that she was just a friend.

Huh. He couldn't remember any friends kissing him the way she had.

And it had shocked the hell out of him. Prim and proper Darcie Green had something burning just beneath the surface of those cool English features. He had the singe marks on his brain to prove it.

As they stood on the edge of the tower suspended over a deep pool of water, Cora bounced up and down with excitement but Darcie looked nervous. "You don't have to do this, you know," he murmured.

"Are you sure it's safe? What if…?" She nodded toward Cora.

He understood. What if something happened in front of his niece? And maybe it hadn't been the smartest thing to bring her up here to watch. But she'd been begging to watch him do one of his jumps for a while now.

"Max Laurel is an engineer and a friend." He glanced over at where a stick-straight figure was adjusting some fittings. "He has his PhD in physics. I trust him. And at a hundred feet her tower isn't very high. Even if the bungee-cord snaps, there's a safety line. If that fails as well, I'll just go into the water."

He gave her a quick smile. "Like I told you earlier, he only does it for friends, he's not open to the public any more."

"What happens when you finish the jump?"

"Max will lower me the rest of the way into the water, and I'll undo the cables and swim to the side." He understood her nerves, but compared to what had happened between them back at the beach this felt pretty tame. No way was he about to admit that to her, though.

Neither was he planning on being the Aussie she checked off her list, despite his words to that effect.

Strung out on kisses.

Yep, there was no better way to put it than that. But it had to stop now. Because he had a feeling things could get out of hand really quickly with Darcie for some reason. And not just for him. She'd just come out of a bad relationship and he didn't want her to get the idea that anything serious could come of them being tossed together at work and for a few outside excursions. He had enough on his plate with Felix and Cora to risk complicating his life any further.

"You ready, Luke?" his friend asked.

"I am. Can you hold on just a minute?"

Going down on his haunches in front of his niece, he put his hands on her shoulders. "Are you sure you're okay with this? I don't want you to be scared."

"No way! As soon as I'm old enough, I'm going to do it too."

Lucas had told her she had to wait until she was eighteen before attempting it. He wanted to make sure her bones and joints were strong enough to take the combination of her weight and the additional force that came from the jump. He smiled at her bravado, though. "Then let's get this show on the road."

"Darcie is going to jump too, isn't she?"

He glanced up at the woman in question. "Depends on how brave she's feeling."

"I'm only feeling half-brave. Is that enough?"

The fact that she was here, at the top of the tower, said she was more than that. She could have backed out of the trip altogether and he wouldn't have stopped her. But here she was. "More than enough."

"I'll cheer you on," promised Cora. "I wish Daddy had come, though."

Lucas hadn't told Darcie why he helped so much with his niece, and he was glad to keep it that way. For Felix's sake.

His brother was supposed to be seeing his counsellor today. Lucas could only hope he was keeping his word. His behavior the other day seemed to have snapped him back to awareness. Then again, they'd been down that same road a couple of times.

So he settled for a half-truth. "I'm sure he'll come next time. He had some things he needed to do today."

When he glanced at Darcie a slight pucker formed between her brows before it smoothed away again.

Did she suspect things weren't quite right in the Elliot household? Time to shift her attention.

"Okay, Max, are you ready for me?"

"Just about."

The next several minutes were spent attaching a thick cable to his ankles and an additional safety line to a harness that went around his torso. If something happened to the first elastic band the second one was meant to catch him. He'd done this at least twenty times with no ill-effects. Then again, he'd never had his niece and a woman watching him go over the side. Something inside him poked at him to show off for Darcie—do a spectacular swan dive or something, but that was out of the question. Safety had to come first when it came to Cora.

He moved into position, and Max checked everything once again and then gave him the thumbs-up sign. Lucas counted to three in his head and then...

Over!

He catapulted out into the air, gravity pulling him into a smooth arc as he began his downward trajectory.

The wind whistled in his ears, and he thought he might have heard Cora shout, but it was all lost in the exhilaration of the jump. Although, as the elastic began to grab and slow his descent, he wondered if even this could top that kiss he'd shared with Darcie.

Damn.

The bungee yanked him halfway back up before letting him fall again. But the closer he got to the end of his jump, the more irritated he became. This had once filled his senses like nothing else ever could. And where he'd been happy to share it with her a couple of days ago, he was now not so sure that he'd done the right thing.

His bouncing halted, but unfortunately his wavering thoughts kept right on careening up and down, the whine of the motor as Max slowly lowered him down to the water failing to drown them out for once. Then he hit the pool and let his buoyancy carry him back to the surface, where he unhooked himself from the bungees and ankle straps, and did a slow side crawl to the edge of the pool.

He looked up and saw two faces looking down at him. One filled with an elation he recognized from years of seeing that same expression. One filled with uncertainty, as if the woman he'd known for less than a year had sensed what had been in his head as he'd done the dive.

This was not her fault. It was his own damn exhaustion and worry about Felix catching up with him. It had to be that. It couldn't be that Darcie had somehow struck a chord inside him that was still reverberating two days later.

If it was…then somehow he had to figure out a way to silence whatever she'd started.

Lucas was in the water at the far side of the pool. Waiting for her to jump so he could help her unfasten the bungees. Max told her he'd set the tension so that she wouldn't drop as far as Lucas had before it caught her up. Then the winch would let out the line until she slid into the water. Piece of cake.

Easy for him to say. Lucas hadn't come up to give her a pep talk or anything. He'd remained at the bottom, radioing up from a walkie-talkie on the side of the pool that he'd stay down and help Darcie.

Maybe it was just as well that he hadn't come back up because everything on her body was trembling. Even her hair follicles seemed to be vibrating in terror. She wasn't afraid of heights, but something about jumping and hoping an elastic cord would somehow stop her from hurtling headfirst into the water was a scary prospect.

"You can do it, Darcie." Cora's cheerful voice broke into her thoughts.

Not willing to let the girl see how scared she was, she pasted on a smile she hoped looked halfway real. "You'll be okay up here?"

"Oh, yeah. I'm going to take pictures of you as you go over."

Perfect. Just what she needed. For this moment to be recorded for all to see. She would have to find a discreet way to ask Max not to put it up on his wall of fame. Where Lucas's image appeared in several different sets of swim trunks his face was always filled with that same look of exultation, eyes closed as if taking in every second of the jump.

Speaking of jumps, she'd better go before someone got tired of waiting and pushed her over. "Okay, Cora. Count to three, and I'll jump."

"Woo-hoo!" The child yelled down to Lucas. "Get ready, here she comes. One...two...*three*!"

Darcie held her arms out from her sides and jumped as far away from the tower as she could, just as Max had instructed her. The fabric buckles of the ankle harness were where her every thought was centered right now, and she squeezed her eyes shut tight. She fell... and fell. Suddenly, she felt a firm tug that turned her so she was facing the water—at least she assumed so since she still couldn't bring herself to look. A squeal left her throat before she could stop it as she bounced several times, still with her head pointed straight down. Then she came to a halt.

Hanging. Upside down. In midair. Just like a bat.

She chanced a glance down and saw that Lucas was there, right below her. The sight of him made her pounding heart calm slightly as a mechanical hum sounded from the tower above her. Slowly, she started moving downward at a steady rate. Coming closer and closer to those familiar features.

His arms stretched up as she came within reach and he put a hand around her shoulders, keeping her from plunging headlong into the water. Her body made a curve before his other arm wrapped around her hips. He went under, still holding her. That's when she realized he was treading water and her weight was sending him down. She struggled to free herself, kicking with her legs to keep from drowning the man.

But he didn't come back up. Instead, she felt his hands on one of her ankles, and she stopped paddling to let him undo the carabiner that attached the bungee cord to her legs. She sank beneath the surface and opened her eyes. There he was, fingers undoing the shank that held her ankles together, before moving further up to unclasp the static safety line at her waist.

His eyes were open as well, and they looked into hers. He reached out to finger a strand of her hair that floated between them, making her exhale a stream of bubbles. Then he leaned forward and gave her a quick kiss before grabbing her hands and dragging her upward. A good thing, because suddenly she'd forgotten that she needed to breathe.

Once at the surface she dragged in a couple of ragged breaths while Lucas kept his arm around her waist and waited while she composed herself and prayed for her nerves to settle down just a bit.

"You did it."

"I can hardly believe I jumped." The elation was slow to kick in, but it was there now that she knew she was safely at ground level again.

"I can hardly believe it either." Lucas smiled and leaned in close to her ear. "Well, it looks like you got your first tick mark, Dr. Green. Congratulations."

Since she'd just jumped off a tower into the water, she assumed he was talking about the bungee-jumping item on the list they'd made together.

Which meant he wasn't counting that quick kiss in the water as having completed that other item on her list.

Because he was still waiting on the behind-closed-doors part to happen?

Oh, Lord. And she'd thought bungee-jumping was dangerous. It was tame compared to what her head conjured up.

The prospect of being with Lucas in a quiet, nonpublic place had to qualify as wild and outrageous, right? Because right now she couldn't imagine a scarier prospect than finding herself back in his arms.

CHAPTER FIVE

CORA WAS ASLEEP.

Glancing in the rearview mirror on the way back to the house, a shard of concern worked its way through his chest. He hadn't realized until after he'd helped Darcie from the pool that his niece had been taking pictures of their jumps. He wasn't quite sure what she'd been able to see from the tower, but he hoped that impulsive peck on the lips had been safely hidden beneath the water.

Why had he done that anyway? Kissed her. Again.

Because as he'd seen her sail toward him at the end of that bungee cord she had been so different from the person he'd imagined Darcie Green to be for the last nine and a half months. She'd seemed as free as a bird, tethered only by those safety cords. He'd halfway thought she'd back out of it once the time came. She hadn't.

He was happy for her in a way that was alien to him. And unsettling.

Maybe he should get some things straight with her. Only he didn't want to do that in front of his niece in case she wasn't really asleep.

"Do you mind if we drop Cora off first?"

"Of course not. But I can take a taxi if you want to just drop me off at the hospital."

"Your flat is on the way back, so it's not a problem. You're still at the Delamere place, right?" He'd been to the luxurious penthouse flat for a few parties thrown by Isla and Isabel.

"Yes, I'm there. Are you sure you don't mind?"

"Not at all." He glanced over at her, noting she'd gone back to her prim way of sitting with her hands clasped in her lap. "Did you have fun today?"

After he'd done a couple more jumps—Darcie demurring that once had been more than enough—they'd put on some dry clothes and had then had lunch with Max. That's when Cora had mentioned getting dozens of pictures and that she couldn't wait to show them to him and Darcie.

Showing them to him was one thing. But Darcie?

He was going to preview them first before that happened.

"I did, actually." Her eyes flicked to his and then back to the road in front of them. "I'll probably never get a chance to do anything like that again. Please, tell your friend thank you."

Darcie had already told him multiple times. In fact, she'd seemed to hang on his friend's every word during lunch. He'd been glad in a way, but watching her laugh over something Max had said had also caused a dark squirming of his innards he wouldn't quite call jealousy but it was something he didn't recognize. And didn't like.

"I noticed you exchanged social media information so you can do that."

She frowned and threw him a sharp glance. "Should I not have? He was the one who initiated it."

Yes, he had. And the last thing he wanted was to risk Max's friendship over a woman who would be gone in a couple of months.

He settled for saying the first thing that came to mind. "Max's a nice guy. He doesn't have a lot of experience with women."

Oh, and that sounded awful. Darcie evidently agreed because a dark flush came to her cheeks. "I think it would be better to let me off at the hospital, if you don't mind."

Prim. Uptight. Formal. All things he associated with the Darcie of three months ago. Not the warm, open woman who'd accompanied him today.

He took his hand off the wheel and covered her twined fingers. "I didn't mean that as a cut, Darce. I know you wouldn't do anything to lead him on." Why he'd felt the need to shorten her name all of a sudden he had no idea. But he liked it. Liked the way it rolled off his tongue with ease.

Another reason it would be good to talk to her. Because she was a nice girl. Just like he'd talked about Max being a nice guy. He didn't want to do anything to lead *her* on. And those two kisses they'd shared could have definitely made her think things were headed down the wrong path.

Weren't they?

Absolutely not.

"You're right. I wouldn't lead him—or anyone else—on, or make them think things that weren't true."

The words were said with such conviction that Lucas

glanced at her again and made an educated guess. "Your ex?"

"Yes." She paused for a moment. "Let's just say it's made me careful about how I interact with men."

Wow. Had that been part of those angry sparks that had lit up the maternity ward whenever he'd had dealings with her? He wasn't sure. But one thing he did know, he didn't want to go back to those days.

So maybe he should just cool the warning-her-off speech he'd planned. Wasn't he assuming a lot in thinking she was going to fall all over him because of his two lapses in judgment? Wasn't he being an egotistical jerk to think he was that irresistible?

Good thing the drive over to Felix's house gave him time to think before he did something else stupid.

Speaking of his brother's house… They were nearing the street. He put his hand back on the gear lever and downshifted as he turned at the corner. Five houses went by and they'd arrived.

Once in the driveway, he motioned for Darcie to wait while he got Cora out of the backseat. Unbuckling his niece and easing her from the car, he swung her up into his arms. She peered out of one eye then flicked it shut again.

"Cora, have you been pretending to sleep this whole time?"

"No." The word was mumbled, but there were guilty overtones to it.

Perfect. Good thing he'd decided not to tackle heavier subjects while driving.

And his comment about Max, and practically holding her hand a few minutes ago? Hopefully Cora's eyes had been pasted shut and had missed that.

But knowing his niece…

He gave an inner groan, his mind going back to the camera dangling on a cord around her neck.

Nothing he could do about that at the moment except take her inside and hope she forgot all about it by tomorrow morning.

The first thing he heard when he opened the door was a loud belch from somewhere inside.

Oh, hell. Not now.

He turned to Darcie. "Do you mind waiting here for a minute? I'll be right out."

Proving his point about his niece feigning sleep, her eyes popped open. "Oh, no. She has to come in. I want to take her back to see my room." She held up her camera. "We can look at the pictures I took on my computer."

"Luke? Is that you?" His brother's voice came from the living room, keeping him from commenting on Cora's suggestion. "I've been wondering when you were going to get home."

Felix *sounded* sober. Whether he was or not was another matter. "Yes, it's us."

Stepping in front of Darcie so he could enter first had nothing to do with being rude and everything to do with scoping out the situation. Cora was used to it—in fact, his niece had turned into a mother figure for her broken parent. But it was getting to the point where Lucas was going to have to intervene and take drastic action.

Again.

He set Cora on her feet but held her hand as they

made their way to the living room, Darcie just behind him. There his brother sat in a recliner, staring at the television. Lucas glanced at the floor beside the chair. There was no sign of beer…or any other alcoholic beverage, for that matter. Could he have heard them come home and got rid of it? That burp had sounded pretty damning.

"Hey, girlie, come over here and give Daddy a hug."

Cora rushed over to her father and threw herself into his arms. That's when Lucas noticed the picture. The one of Felix, Cora and Melody taken in this very living room shortly after their daughter's birth. It was on the end table next to Felix and not in its normal spot on the fireplace mantel.

And when his brother's eyes met his they were red-rimmed.

He was drunk…maybe not from alcohol but from the deep grief that he refused to let go of. He held onto it as tightly as he did his liquor.

Damn. Don't do this now, Felix.

Unaware of what was going on, Darcie shifted next to him. His brain hummed as he tried to figure out a way to get her out of there without her realizing something was very wrong. Cora slid from her father's arms and hurried back to Darcie with a smile. "Come see my room."

Darcie's gaze took in Felix and then Lucas, as he stood there, jaw tight, fingers itching to curl into fists at his sides. He forced them to stay still instead. "Sure," she said to the little girl. "Let's go."

The pair trailed off down the hallway, while Lucas stared at his brother. "Have you been drinking?"

"Only one." He reached behind his back and pulled out an empty beer bottle. At least, Lucas hoped it had been empty before he'd secreted it behind him. "Something happened to the rest of them."

Lucas thought he'd dumped all the bottles. Evidently not. "Did you hide this one?"

"Yep." His brother waggled his head. "Good thing, too. Someone must have drunk all the rest of them. I think Chessa might have a drinking problem. Maybe we should fire her."

The childminder wasn't the one with a problem. It was his brother, in all his bitter glory.

"I dumped them. She didn't drink them."

"What?" His brother got to his feet, gripping the bottle in his fist. "You've got no right, Luke."

His voice went up ominously, causing Lucas to glance down the hall where Cora's door was wide open.

"Don't do this, Felix." He kept his own tone low and measured, hoping to lead by example.

"Don't *you* do this." Felix bit out the words. "You have no idea what it's like to lose someone important to you."

Yes, he did. He was watching it happen right before his eyes. Felix was a shell of the man he'd once been. A sad, drunken shell.

He decided to divert the subject if he could. He didn't want Cora or Darcie to hear his brother at his worst— or listen to the tears that would inevitably follow one of his tirades. "Are you taking your medication? You're not supposed to drink with it."

"I'm not."

Lucas wasn't sure if he meant he wasn't taking his

medication or if he wasn't drinking. But since he was now shifting that bottle from one hand to the other, he would have to assume it was the latter. That he was off his antidepressants.

He took another quick look down the hallway then held his hand out for the beer bottle.

His brother surprisingly handed it over without an argument, probably because it was empty. He went over to the recycling bin and tossed it inside, hearing the clink as it landed on other bottles—hopefully the ones Lucas had emptied the other day.

When he went back he knew what he was going to say. "I love you, Felix, and I was hoping I'd never have to say this, but if you can't get your act together, Cora's going to have to come live with me for a while."

His brother shook his head, eyes wide. "You wouldn't take her from me. She's all I have left."

"I don't want to. But I can't leave her here to watch you spiral back down, not when you've worked so hard over the last several months."

Felix sank into his chair. "I know. I need to pull it together, but…" He glanced at the picture of his wife.

With a sigh, Lucas took the picture and put it back in its spot on the mantelpiece just as Cora and Darcie came back into the room.

Darcie's face was pink and her glance went from him to Felix. Her hair was a riot of curls from their day at Max's and the sea air. It framed her face in a way that made his breath catch in his lungs. Lucas glanced at the group of pictures on the ledge over the fireplace.

Was this how his brother had started down that dark

road? An initial attraction that had turned into an obsession that refused to let go, even after Melody's death?

Hell if he knew, but if that's the way it worked, he didn't even want to stop and glance at that road.

Hadn't he already? With both those kisses?

His jaw tightened and he glared at his brother. "Are you going to be okay tonight?"

"Yeah." Except Felix wouldn't quite meet his eyes. "Cora and I are going to be just fine. I've got big plans for us. Pizza and a movie. That one with all the singing and ice and snowmen."

His niece squealed. "I love that movie. You have to sing with me this time, Dad!"

"Yep, we're going to sing." He threw Lucas a defiant glare that dared him to argue with him.

He wouldn't, and his brother knew it. Not right now. But he would soon if Felix couldn't get back on track.

And if he had to take Cora away? What then for Felix?

That was one thing he didn't even want to think about. All he knew was that there came a time when the needs of his niece had to take precedence. And that time was drawing closer every day.

Darcie hadn't slept well. She wasn't sure if it was from looking at those pictures of her and Lucas frolicking in the pool or from the memories of him helping her take her restraints off.

That had to be it, because she certainly hadn't had a lot of restraint when it came to the man. And she needed some. Desperately. At least Cora hadn't captured that kiss they'd shared in the water.

She breathed a prayer of thanks.

Dressing quickly, she scowled at the dark circles beneath her eyes that told a tale of a long, hard night. There'd been those pictures, yes. But there'd also been something about Lucas's brother. He'd seemed just a little "off."

Not that she could pinpoint what made her think that. Cora had seemed happy enough when she'd interacted with him.

Maybe it was her coworker's behavior that had set her on edge and not Felix's.

Lucas had been tight-lipped the whole time he'd talked to his brother, and when she'd been in Cora's room, staring at those damning images, she'd thought she'd heard one of them raise his voice. She wasn't sure who it had been, though.

And it completely obliterated her view of Lucas as a self-indulgent playboy. His face had been deadly serious as he'd faced off with his brother. Were there hard feelings between the pair?

If so, he'd said nothing about it on the way back to her flat. And when she'd invited him up, he'd refused, saying he had an early morning. Well, so did she.

Another thing that had skewed her image of him. What man in his right mind would give up an opportunity to get into a woman's flat and into her pants?

Certainly not the Lucas she thought she knew.

Then again, she'd thought Cora was a full-grown woman back then. She didn't remember hearing Lucas talk about any other women over the months she'd known him. If anything, it was the other way around. Women talked about him. Wore false eyelashes for him. Threw themselves at him.

He hadn't taken the bait once that she knew of.

Maybe he's just not interested in you, dummy. He could have an unspoken rule about dating co-workers.

And kissing them? Did he have a rule against that too?

Not that she could tell. And she knew of at least a couple of the female species who would kill to have been in her shoes on either of those occasions.

Dwelling on this would get her nowhere. She tossed down the last of her tea with a sigh and went to finish dressing. At this rate, it was going to be one very long, depressing day.

Darcie made it to the maternity ward and signed in with just minutes to spare. Her eyes automatically tracked to the sign-in sheet, looking for Lucas's name. The space was blank. Strange. He wasn't here yet.

After all that blubbering about having an early day today? Irritation marched into her belly and kicked at its sides a couple of times. Maybe she'd been wrong after all. Maybe he did take the bait from time to time…just not when she was the one dangling it.

Fine. She wasn't going to wait around for him to check in.

Even as she thought it, she stood there and brooded some more, while the clock crept to three minutes past the hour, and the second hand began its downward arc, reminding her of Lucas's bungee jump yesterday. And, like yesterday, he was headed straight for the bottom… of her respect.

He was officially late. Again.

What was with the man? He never seemed irresponsible when you talked to him. But his actions? Another story.

Even as she thought it, Lucas came skidding around the corner, hair in glorious disarray, face sporting a dark layer of stubble. He took one glance at her and then took the pen and signed in. Five minutes late. Not enough to throw a fit about but he'd obviously not been home.

"Where were you?"

He flicked a glance her way then one brow went up in that familiar nonchalant manner that made her molars grind. "Keeping tabs on me, are you?"

She wanted to hurl at him, "You're late, and I want an explanation!" She wanted something other than his normal flippant response—the one that went along with the MMU's view of him: a charming playboy who took nothing seriously.

He'd diagnosed Margie Terrington, though, when she hadn't.

Because everyone in Victoria knew what redback bite symptoms were.

Except her.

"No, of course not. I just…" For some reason she couldn't get the words out of her mouth, not while tears hovered around the periphery of her heart.

She would not beg him for an explanation. Or ask him to reassure her that he wasn't this rumpled couldn't-care-less man who stood before her, as delicious as he looked.

He stepped closer. "I know I'm late. And I'm going to be later still once I go back and shower. But I'll make it quick." His jaw tightened. "All I can do, Darcie, is say I'm sorry."

Still not an answer. But at least all that glib cheekiness was gone.

She glanced at the patient board. "It's still quiet. I'll let Isla know you're here and that she can go home."

"Thanks." Warm fingers slid across her cheek and his glance dipped to her mouth before coming back up to her face.

Heat flashed up her spine. He wouldn't. Not here at work.

Before she could pull back—or remain locked in place, which was what her body wanted her to do—he withdrew his hand and took a step back.

"It would help me a lot if you didn't go all pink every time you saw me—peace treaty or not, a man's only got so much willpower."

"I don't go pink!" Even as she said it, heat flamed up her neck and pooled in her cheeks, proving her a liar. It also broke the bubble of anger that had gathered around her.

Lucas laughed and tapped her nose. "Like I said…" He let the sentence trail away and then headed for the locker area, dragging both hands through his hair and whistling as he went.

Whistling!

Passing him in the hallway, Isla turned to glance at his retreating back before her eyes came to meet hers. Warmth again flooded her face as her friend drew near. "Well, I see he got here." She looked closer. "Why are you so red?"

"I—I…" What could she say, except deny it again?

"Oh, God. You two aren't…" Isla lowered her voice

"…doing it, are you? I know I suggested he take you to the beach, but—"

Darcie reared back. "Of course not," she said in a loud whisper.

"Then why does the man look like he just rolled out of someone's bed? And why are we whispering? There's no one around."

Darcie cleared her throat and walked to the nurses' station. "We're whispering because I don't want any ugly rumors floating around about my personal life."

"Personal life?" Isla rubbed her belly. "You actually have one?"

The words might have stung had they not come from her friend. But Isla was right. "No. Can you blame me?"

Tessa came from a room with a chart in hand. She'd evidently overheard the last part of Darcie's declaration because she said, "You need to get out there and live it up a bit. Melbourne has some awesome nightclubs. Maybe we could make it a group outing."

"I don't know…"

Isla took up the cry. "Yes! You have to go at least once. I can't believe I didn't take you."

"You were kind of busy, remember?" An understatement if there ever was one.

Her friend laughed, hand still on her burgeoning stomach. "Maybe just a little. But, seriously, you can't leave Australia without seeing at least a little of the nightlife."

The three of them were still joking about it when Lucas appeared less than ten minutes later. Wow, the man was fast, she'd give him that. His hair was damp from his shower and he'd changed into fresh clothes.

"What are we talking about, ladies?"

"Oh…nothing." Even as she said it the slow flush rose in her face like clockwork. One side of his mouth lifted but, thank God, he said nothing about it this time.

Isla nudged her. "Darcie hasn't been to any of the nightspots. None. Zip. Can you believe it?"

"It seems there's quite a lot she hasn't experienced yet."

Lucas said it with a totally straight face, but she glanced sharply at him.

Tessa cocked her head, drumming her short fingernails on the counter. "Maybe I can get a group together to go to the Night Owl tonight. They have brilliant music and dancing. How does that sound, Darcie?"

"Well, I…" She didn't dance if she could help it. Another thing that had worn thin with Robert, who had loved it.

"If Darcie's going to make a checklist of things to do while in Australia, that should definitely go on it."

Great, just what she needed, to have him remind her of his challenge—that she pick things that were outside her comfort zone. Clubbing was definitely one of those. Not that any of them had suggested making the rounds and getting drunk.

She tried one last time. "I have to work tomorrow."

Lucas parried with, "We'll watch our step and make sure you're not arrested."

"Arrested!"

Isla put a hand on her arm. "He's kidding. You should go, Darcie. Especially since Lucas seems to be offering his services as a bouncer. You know, in case a thousand guys start hitting on you. I, unfortunately, am not allowed to have any fun for another month or so, even if Alessi would agree to let me go."

Darcie snuck a glance at Lucas, who didn't look at all put out with the idea of tagging along.

The nurse picked up a chart with a grin. "I have to go back to work now, unlike some of you. I'll ask around and whoever wants to come can meet up at the entrance of the hospital at eight, okay? Wear something sparkly."

And with that, Tessa and Lucas both walked away without giving her a chance to refuse. And the hunky midwife had left without actually confirming that he would be there—protecting her from unwanted advances.

Unfortunately, if he did come, Darcie had no idea who was going to save her from him—or from herself.

CHAPTER SIX

SHE'D WORN SOMETHING SPARKLY. And green. And clingy as hell.

That dress was probably banned in ten countries. There was nothing vulgar about it, but the neckline scooped far enough down that a hint of creamy curves peeked over the top of it. And it was snug around her hips and the sweet curve of her backside, exposing an endless length of bare leg. He'd been trying not to stare as the group of them had taken off from the hospital and headed toward the railway station. But, holy hell, it was hard.

"Did you go shopping?" Because he just couldn't see Darcie pulling something like this out of her wardrobe. Not that he was complaining. No, he was salivating. And thinking about all the men at that club who were going to see her in this dress was doing a number on his gut.

"No. Isla loaned it to me. I didn't bring anything suitable for a night on the town."

Suitable. That was one word for it. What it was suitable for was the question. Because in his mind he could see himself peeling the thing down her shoulders and right past all those sexy curves. They might just get arrested after all.

Why had he agreed to come again?

Oh, yes. To ward off any unwanted advances. If that was the case, he was going to have his hands full. Because he might end up having to fight off his own advances if he couldn't get his damned libido under control. Right now it was raging and growling and doing all it could to edge closer to this woman.

Thank God, the train ride was a short one. And there were seats this time, instead of having to stand and have her bump against him repeatedly. Within another few minutes they arrived at the Night Owl, a club frequented by young professionals looking to let their hair down.

The second the doors opened the music hit him between the eyes. Loud, with a driving beat, blast after blast of sound pumped out into the night air. Despite his cocky words earlier in the day, Lucas had not gone to a club since his early days at medical school. Life had been too hectic, and after Melody had died he just hadn't had much else on his mind except his brother and Cora.

Ten people in all had come with them. The rest of the group went in, but when Darcie started to pass through the door she backed up as if changing her mind, only to crash into his chest. Her backside nestled against him for a split second before she jerked away again.

His internal systems immediately went haywire.

That decided it. He wanted to be here. With her. For whatever reason.

Maybe it was just to escape the highs and lows that had become a normal part of life these last years. He'd enjoyed the bungee-jumping trip far too much. He was ready to repeat the energetic day. But in all-adult company this time. The club would do that and more.

Strangely, the noise would insulate them, keep their words from being overheard by those around them.

When she again hesitated he leaned down. "It's okay, Darce. I'm right here with you."

There was that short version of her name again, sliding right past his lips like it belonged there. He didn't know why that kept happening, but it did the trick. She stepped through the door. And as if he'd fallen down the rabbit hole in that old children's book, the inside of the club morphed into something from another place and time.

Darkness bathed the occupants, except for brief snatches of light that flooded his pupils. The extremes made it hard to focus on anything for more than a second at a time so bodies became puppets, moving in jolts and jerks as if controlled by outside forces. The sensation was surreal. Anything that happened in the club tonight would take on a dreamlike quality: had it happened, or hadn't it? Maybe that was for the best.

Tessa came back and grabbed Darcie by the arm, dragging her away and making a drinking motion with her hand, since it was probably impossible for her to yell above the noise.

When had it become noise? At one time in his life he would have been yelling for the DJ to turn the sound up. Not any more. He squinted, trying to see where the group from the hospital had gone. When he trained his eyes to capture the second-long flashes emitted by the strobe he could just make out the dim overhead lights of the bar at the far side of the room. At least those weren't blinking on and off.

A few minutes later he was there, squeezed between Darcie and some guy on her left—who shot him a look that could only be described as a glare. The man picked up his drink and moved on to another woman a few seats away. Tessa laughed and saluted him with her drink, while the glass in front of Darcie contained something that looked fruity and cold, with plenty of crushed ice—and probably a shot of something strong. The bartender came over with a quizzical lift of his brows.

"Just a lemonade," he yelled above the music.

Darcie threw him a wide-eyed glance. "I thought we were supposed to be living dangerously."

"I still have to get you home in one piece, so it's better for me to play it safe. At least for tonight." Lucas had had enough of Felix's drinking problems to last a lifetime. Except for that swig of beer he'd taken in his brother's kitchen, he hadn't touched the stuff in almost two years.

Some of their party had broken off into pairs and were already out on the dance floor—he squinted again—if that could be called dancing. The body parts moved, but they were disjointed…staccato. Although maybe that had to do with the lights blinking on and off.

Darcie put her straw to her mouth and took a sip of her drink then stirred the concoction while glancing around at the nightclub. The Night Owl was living up to its name, although it seemed a little early for the die-hard crowd. How much more packed could the place get?

"Are these kinds of things big in Australia?" she shouted.

This was ridiculous. They were both going to be hoarse by the time they got to work tomorrow if they kept this up. He drew her closer and leaned down to her ear. "I'm not a big nightclub person."

She tilted back to look at him then moved back in. "You bungee jump, but you don't go out drinking with the guys?"

Her warm breath washed across his ear, carrying the scent of her drink. Strawberries. Or mangoes. Okay, so maybe this wasn't going to be the disaster he was imagining because he liked having her close like this.

The guy from the seat next to him had evidently struck out with woman number two, because he was back. Bodily inserting himself between the two of them and turning his back to Lucas.

"Dance?"

He couldn't blame the guy. Darcie was beautiful. But if anyone was going to dance with her, it was going to be him.

Standing, he poked the intruder in the shoulder to get his attention. The man—a body-builder type with bulges and lumps that bordered on unnatural—didn't budge. So Lucas moved out and around until he was facing the competition.

Darcie was already shaking her head to the offer. Instead of taking the hint, the jerk held out his hand.

Lucas stared him straight in the eye. "She's with me, mate. So try somewhere else." Taking her hand, he said, "Come on, gorgeous. Bring your drink."

She grabbed her glass and went along with him, throwing the other man an apologetic look. What the hell? Had she wanted to dance with him?

This time it was Lucas who hesitated. He stopped and glanced down at her.

"Here, try some," she said, holding her beverage up to him. "It's really good."

As much as he did not want to try some girly-girl drink, he noted the creep from the bar was still glowering their way. Probably hoping to corner her alone. To send another message, he took the glass from her and sipped from the straw…and made a face. He couldn't help it. That wasn't a drink. That was some kind of smoothie or something. But the act of putting his mouth where her lips had been—where they had applied suction and…

He took another sip. A bigger one this time and let it wash down his throat. Not so bad the second time around.

Handing it back to her, he towed her further out onto the floor, where dark forms kicked and flapped and buckled, only to come up for more. It reminded him more of a fight scene from a movie than actual dancing.

Flashes of green from her eyes met his. "I'm not much of a dancer."

There was something about the way she said it. As if she expected him to be upset. Hardly.

She couldn't be any worse than what was going on around him. "Let's pretend the music is slow and not worry about what everyone else is doing." He'd had to swoop in again to be heard. "Can you dance with your glass in your hand?"

"No. Help me finish it." She took another drink, the contents of the large goblet dropping a quarter of an inch, then held it out to him again.

He was going to pay for this later, when the memories came back to haunt him in his sleep. But he drank anyway. Relished the slight taste of her on the straw.

When the glass was empty he motioned for her to wait and then deposited it on the nearest table, ignoring the surprised looks from its occupants. Then he strode back to Darcie and took her right hand in his, his other arm settling across her hips and pulling her close. When his attention swept the bar for the man who'd hit on her, he didn't see him. Good. Because tonight there would be no cutting in.

Darcie was all his. At least for a few hours.

If Cora didn't call.

Closing his eyes and settling her against him, he allowed his senses to absorb the feel of her curves, the scent of her hair and the way it slid like fine silk beneath his chin.

He tuned out the music…and tuned in Darcie instead. Only then did he allow his feet to sway, taking quarter-inch steps and allowing his inner rhythm to take over. Her arm crept up, her hand splaying across the skin on the back of his neck, fingers pushing into the hair at his nape.

Decadent.

Isla was right. There were some things that just shouldn't be missed. And dancing with Darcie was one of them.

She shifted against him with a sigh. "This is much better than what they're doing."

"Who?" His eyes cracked open, letting the chaotic scene back into his head.

"Everyone. I don't normally like to dance. But this feels okay."

"Yes, it does."

The song ended and the room paused for three or four seconds, while Lucas cursed silently. Then, as if the universe had read his mind, another song came on. This was slow and soothing and not quite as loud. The atmosphere shifted. The strobe went off in favor of dim, steady lighting.

Arms twined together and single dancers edged off the floor to let the couples have a turn.

"Is this better?" he murmured into her ear.

"Mmm, yes."

Lucas's hand tightened on her back, thumb skimming up her spine and drawing his palm along with it until it was between her shoulder blades, before gliding back down to her waist.

Hell, this was nice. Maybe a little too nice.

Darcie must have sensed it too because the fingertips that were against the lower part of his scalp brushed back and forth, sending a frisson of raw sensation arrowing down to his groin.

He willed away the rush of need that followed, trying to think about anything else but the pulsing that was beginning to make itself known in not-so-subtle ways.

Football. Kayaking. Hiking.

He dragged various activities through his head and forced his brain to come up with five important items about each one, before moving on to the next. Anything to keep from having to step back a pace or two in order to hide her effect on him.

Because he didn't want to go. Not until this song was over and done. And maybe not even then.

There. Things were subsiding. Slowly. But as long as she didn't…

Her fingertips dragged downward, emerging from his hair and sliding sideways across the bare skin of his neck.

"Darce, are you trying to make me crazy?" Because if he didn't say something, she was going to end up with one hell of a surprise.

Her cheek moved away from his chest and she glanced up at him. "I wasn't trying to. Why, am I succeeding?"

Something about the way she'd said that. As if surprised. Or curious. Or a whole lot of things. None of them good because it just stirred him to say more stupid things. They'd all agreed to leave separately, so they could each decide when they'd had enough. But no way was he letting Darcie leave there on her own.

"Yes." He let that one word speak for him, because it was true.

"So I can cross this off my list, right?"

"Driving me crazy?"

"No." She gave a soft laugh. "I was talking about coming to a nightclub."

His brows went up, and he realized without that god-awful strobe light he could finally see her without the additional shock on his senses. Being this close to her was as heady as laying her down on the sand at the beach had been. "I thought you might be angling to finally cross something else off your list."

Her tongue came out, moistening that full lower lip. "What's that?"

She was going to make him say it, wasn't she? "Kissing an Aussie."

"But I thought you said that had to be behind closed doors in order to count." The breathiness of her response made him smile.

"It does. But that can be arranged."

Her fingers at the back of his neck tightened, and her eyes closed for a second.

Was she going to turn him down? His body started to groan and swear at him for screwing this up. Maybe he should limit it to just the kiss. But, hell, he didn't want just a kiss. He wanted to carry her down some dark hallway and toss her on a bed…expose every luscious inch of her. And *then* kiss her.

When her eyelids parted again she gave a nod. "Then yes. But only if it's a wild and outrageous kiss."

He couldn't resist. He leaned down and nipped the jawline next to her ear. "Trust me. I can make that happen."

The song ended, and Lucas realized he and Darcie were no longer dancing. In fact, they were just standing there in each other's arms, staring at each other.

"Let's go back to Isla's flat."

"What?" He pulled back, thinking he'd surely misunderstood. He wanted to be alone with her, not visit Isla and Alessandro.

She laughed, unwinding her arm from around his neck and grabbing his hand as she made her way off the dance floor. "I mean the Delamere flat, where I'm staying. Alone."

That was more like it. Besides, that end of town was closer than his own place. And his barely furnished flat left little to be desired as far as what she was probably used to. "That sounds like a plan. Lead on."

Darcie was somehow able to find her keys in the tiny glittery purse that she'd slung over her shoulder as they'd left the Night Owl and arrived at the large opulent building Charles Delamere owned. She punched the code into the box by the front door and heard the click as it unlocked. She'd seen it so many times the place didn't even register any more, but with Lucas standing there behind her she suddenly felt self-conscious as they made their way across the marble foyer.

"You've been here before, right?" She didn't want him to get the idea that she was rich or anything. But she'd never thought anything less of Isla for living here, so why would she think Lucas was any different?

Maybe because it mattered what he thought, and she wasn't quite sure why.

"I have. Isla liked to entertain, so I've been here several times."

Entertain. As in a group? Or just Lucas? "Oh, um…"

"We were never involved," he murmured, as if sensing her thoughts.

"Oh, I didn't think—"

"Didn't you? You thought I might be involved with a whole horde of females at one time."

She had. And when had she moved so far away from that initial opinion she'd held of him? Maybe when she'd met Cora and seen how much he cared about his niece. And maybe—when she put all those phone calls into context—they'd become sweet. Whatever it was, she no longer believed many of the things she'd once thought.

"People change," she murmured.

His hand tightened on hers for a second and his footsteps faltered.

Had she said something wrong?

"Yes, they do."

They stopped in front of the lift and Darcie punched the button to call it. Lucas leaned a shoulder against the wall next to her and studied her face, a slight frown between his brows. Right on cue, heat surged into her cheeks.

His mood seemed to clear and he smiled. "I don't think I've ever seen a woman blush as much as you do."

"I can't help it. It's just the way I'm made."

His eyes skimmed down the rest of her, pausing at the neckline of Isla's slinky dress. "I'm kind of partial to the way you're made."

Her face grew even hotter and he chuckled. Then the lift arrived, saving her from having to respond to his comment.

They both got on, and Darcie nodded at the camera tucked into the corner of the lift, hoping he'd understand her meaning.

He did, because he leaned down, his warm breath washing over her cheek. "Don't worry, gorgeous. I don't want an audience this time. Although later…"

When her eyes widened, his hand went to her lower back, fingertips skimming up her spine until he reached her nape. One finger made tiny circles there beneath the curtain of her hair. Pure need spiraled through her as he added a second finger, the pair trailing down and around the back of her dress, which was scooped like the front of it was. To the camera, it would appear as if they were both just standing quietly, but inside her chest her heart was jumping and things were heating up.

A fine layer of perspiration broke out on her upper lip as she struggled not to close her eyes or utter the soft sounds that were bubbling up in her throat. Was there a microphone connected to that camera?

Up, up they went, racing toward the penthouse while Darcie's legs turned to jelly, and the need to touch him back began growing in her chest. In her belly. In her hands.

She curled her fingers into her palms to keep them from reaching for him.

"Do you like that?" he whispered.

Was he joking? Couldn't he tell? She glanced at their reflection in the mirror across from them and noted her nipples were puckered, showing even through the fabric of her strapless bra and her dress, although both were thin.

Ping.

The lift slowed, and Lucas stopped stroking her neck, his warm hand wrapping around her nape instead. When the doors opened, she practically fell out onto the dark glossy floor of the entrance to the flat. Hands shaking, she tried to hit the lock with her key and missed the first time, only to have Lucas's fingers cover hers and guide them to the keyhole, unlocking and opening the door in one smooth movement.

They went inside. "D-do you want a tour?"

"Mmm…yes, but not of the flat." He took the keys

from her hand and the purse from her shoulder and put them both on the slate surface of the entry table.

Her teeth dug into her lower lip as Lucas came back and put his hands on her shoulders, thumbs edging just beneath the fabric covering them. This was a man who bungee-jumped and practically made love to her on an open beach. Who teased and tormented her senses on the dance floor and again in the lift. He didn't want a feeble tour or a half-hearted response from whatever woman he was with.

Robert's face as Tabitha had thrown herself into his arms was branded in her mind. That was what her ex-fiancé had wanted. Not a mild-mannered woman who was far too "safe."

Was Lucas going to find her wanting as well? Would he regret having put all this effort into getting her into bed?

That brought up another question. Was that why he'd done everything he had…the trip to the beach, the list, the nightclub? To sleep with her? Her insecurities grew.

She had no illusions that this was anything but a one-night stand. She'd made it clear that she didn't want anything more than that either. But maybe she should make it clear that she probably wasn't as wildly experienced as some of the women he'd been with.

"I—I'm not…" She licked her lips as Lucas went still. "I'm probably not very good at…" Her voice died away a second time, so she had to use her hand to made swirly motions in the air and hope he got the gist of her meaning.

He tightened his grip on her shoulders slightly. "Please, tell me you're not a virgin."

"No!" The denial came out as a squeak, so she cleared her throat. "My fiancé just found me a bit…dull in that respect."

Lucas didn't move for several seconds, but a muscle pulsing in his cheek made her squirm. Was he wondering how to get out of the flat without hurting her feelings?

"You don't have to stay if you don't want to." There. She'd given him a way to escape.

He shook his head. "I'm not planning on going anywhere, unless you decide to throw me out." He then gave a smile that could only be described as rueful. "My experience with you has been anything but dull."

She remembered his curse when he'd seen her name on that rotation list. Actually, she had been more outspoken with him than she was with most people. But only because he'd irritated her with his attitude and his tardiness. Okay, so maybe she wasn't dull at work. But here? "I'm not very adventurous."

He leaned down and gave her a slow kiss. One that started off soft and easy and gradually built…his hand sliding into her hair and gathering the strands in his fist. When he pulled back again she was breathless and right back to where she'd been in the lift—melting with desire and wanting nothing more than for him to drag her down those three steps to the living area and take her right there on the couch.

"Then you won't mind if I'm adventurous enough for both of us."

The pressure of being someone she wasn't lifted. She could do that. She could let Lucas call the shots and introduce her to things she'd never tried before—

just like he had standing on that high tower, and again after she'd landed in the pool.

This man lit her senses up like no one ever had. "No. I won't mind."

"Well, then." He began bunching her dress in his fists, gathering more and more material in them until the hemline was at the very tops of her thighs. "We won't need this." Up and over her head went the dress, which had no zipper, the stretchy material allowing him to strip it off her body with ease. He turned and carried the garment across the space, going lightly down the steps and placing it over one of the leather chairs in the living room.

When she started to follow him, he held up his hand to signal her to wait. He slowly made his way back up, his eyes on her the whole time. "You're beautiful, Darce. I don't know what your ex told you, but 'dull' is not a word I would ever use to describe you."

He reached for her hands as a warm flush crept up her body. It only increased when he carried her hands behind her back and moved in to kiss her again. This one slow and lingering, his lips brushing across hers, the friction driving her crazy. "Where's your bedroom, sweetheart?"

"Down the hall. First door to the right."

"Down the hall we go, then." Before she could move he released her hands and swept her into his arms as if she weighed nothing.

He arrived at her room and edged her through the door, stopping for a second as if to take in the space. Although she was sleeping in Isabel's old room, she'd boxed up the other woman's mementos and substituted a few things she'd brought with her. But other than that the space was devoid of a lot of personal items other than the bed and dresser. There were built-ins that were still almost empty.

Walking over to the queen-size bed that had her wondering if it would hold Lucas's frame, he glanced down at her, eyes unreadable. "You never planned on sticking around, did you?"

She was surprised by the question. Everyone at the hospital knew she was only here for a year. After that she'd be leaving. Had he expected her to fill the room with stuff, only to have to get rid of it all a few short months later? And that's what it was looking like at this point: a few short months. Her time in Australia had flown by. Much quicker than she'd thought it would. But it had done what she'd intended it to do—erased the pain of Robert and Tabitha's betrayal. "You knew I was only here for a year."

His muscles relaxed, as if she'd given the correct response. Except she didn't know what the real question was. That he didn't want her to stick around, because of the conflict that had flared between them periodically? Or that he was making sure she wasn't going to place any more importance on tonight than he planned to? He didn't have to worry on that account. She'd already bought her return ticket months ago, right after their first big blow-up.

She blinked up at him. "Are you sure you want to stay?"

"You keep asking me that as if you hope I'll change my mind." He dropped her on the bed and then followed her down. "I won't."

She wound her arms around his neck. "Well, okay, then. As long as we're both clear on what happens on the other side, we should be good."

"Let's worry about right now. And then we can deal with the other stuff tomorrow." With that, his mouth came down, blotting out everything except for the fact that this was exactly where Darcie wanted to be. In this man's arms.

CHAPTER SEVEN

HE WAS GOING to make this a night she would remember.

Not because he was that good but because her words had picked at a sore spot within him. No, he didn't want any permanent relationships, but he was stung by how easy she seemed to think it would be to walk away from him. An idiotic response, considering his own attitude, but he'd never been a rational man when it came to Darcie.

Her bra had no straps to peel down so he settled for following the course of an imaginary strap with his fingers, making sure his short nails kept light contact with her skin as they made their way across her shoulders.

Her reaction was to arch a few centimeters off the silk duvet cover. His flesh reacted in kind. Arching up and away from his body, only to be stopped by the fabric of his dress trousers. That would soon be remedied. But not quite yet.

He continued down her arms, going past the crook of her elbows and only stopping when he reached her wrists, which he caught up in both of his hands. He carried them over her head and rested them there, catching sight of bright green eyes as they stared at his face. He wanted her hands out of the way for what he did next.

Her lips were parted and glossy from his kisses, so he leaned in for another quick taste, glorying in the way they clung to his and followed him up an inch or two as he moved away. He gave a pained laugh.

Dull? Hell, her ex was an idiot. This woman was responsive, giving, and sexy as they came. She hadn't put any limits on their time together. When he'd said he was going to be adventurous enough for both of them, her glance had heated instantly.

Which brought him back to his point. He wanted to make this good. Wanted to leave her with no doubt that she was exciting and desirable. Not just to him but to plenty of other men. He'd caught Max's glances at her during the bungee jump. And the guy at the bar? Oh, he'd been interested all right. The thought made his blood pressure shoot up, just as it had at the Night Owl.

Hooking one of his legs between hers, he edged her thighs apart, keeping his foot just behind her ankle in case she was tempted to squeeze them shut again. She didn't even try. That in itself made Lucas's flesh surge, putting up some new demands. He was willing to oblige some of them…but others would have to wait.

He let his fingers slide over the sweet curves peeking just above her bra. Her skin was smooth and incredibly soft. He wanted more. Keeping his leg between hers, he reached beneath her body and searched for the clasp. Found it. Flicked it open.

He then dropped the garment over the side of the bed, and drank in the view before him.

Heavenly. In every way.

Her nipples were drawn up tight—pink and perfect.

Darcie's eyes were open now. She made no move to cover herself with her hands, although her breathing ratcheted up a notch.

That was as far as he got before he could stand it no longer. He leaned down and tasted her, drawing one peak into his mouth and letting his tongue wander over it.

She moaned and arched higher, pushing herself into his touch.

Yes. This was what he needed. He applied more pressure, using her response as a gauge for how much friction she wanted from him.

Hell if she didn't ask him to up the ante even more. When his teeth scraped over her, her hands came down on his head, but instead of pulling him away her fingers buried themselves in his hair and she pushed hard against him.

He came up panting, body raging, wanting to end it all right here, right now. Instead, he let his mouth cover hers, tongue plunging inside again and again, while she maintained her grip on his hair.

Pulling away in a rush, he ripped her undies down and found her hot and wet and ready. He kissed her once again, letting his index finger sink deep into her. Just like he was about to. He got off the bed.

"Do. Not. Move." He growled the words, stripping in record time, letting the sight of her flushed body drive him to action—to find the condom and rip into it, sheathing himself.

Then he was back with her, over her. Finding her. Sliding home to a place where pleasure and madness fought for supremacy.

He set up a slow, easy rhythm that was all for her, ignoring his own wants and needs.

"Lucas." His name was whispered. Shaky. A silent plea he couldn't ignore.

"I'm here, gorgeous." He edged out and then pushed deep.

Darcie responded with a long drawn-out moan, lifting her hips, her hands going to his shoulders and holding on.

Kissing and licking the length of her neck, he allowed her tight heat to wash over him in a wave, careful to hang onto whatever control he still had. He wanted this to last.

And that surprised him.

He usually saw to his partner's pleasure first and then concentrated on his own. He had it down to a science almost. But here he was, breaking his own rules. She hadn't climaxed. And he didn't want her to. Not yet. He wanted to lose himself when she did—wanted to watch the exact second she came apart. He could only do that if he knew when…

He rolled over, carrying her with him until she was on top, straddling his hips. Her eyes jerked open, and she looked at him uncertainly.

"You set the pace, Darcie. Do what feels good to you."

While I watch.

She hesitated for a second then her instincts seemed to take over. She braced her hands on his thighs, just behind her butt and lifted up and came back down as if seeing how it felt. Then her eyes fluttered shut, teeth digging into her bottom lip as she moved over him a second time. Then a third. Again and again, she lowered herself onto him and rose back up. His own personal angel, set on propelling them both toward paradise.

Until Lucas began to ache from holding back.

It was time.

Pressing his palm against her lower belly, he allowed his thumb to find that sensitive place between her thighs. Her head went back, little whimpers coming from her throat and spilling into the air around him. Sexy sounds. Earthy and full of need.

Her movements grew jerky, hands tightening on his thighs.

"Yes, sweetheart, that's it," he gritted. "Let it all go."

With that, Darcie's whole body stiffened, her insides flaring for a split second before clamping down hard on his erection and exploding into a series of spasms that rocked his world, that made him grab her hips and pump wildly, washing her orgasm down with his own. He poured every emotion he had into the act, until there was nothing left.

And yet he was still full. Full of Darcie. Full of those luscious aftershocks that had him pulling her down hard onto him, eyes closed as he absorbed all of it and more.

When he looked up again her eyes were open. Looking at him. A trembling question in those bright green depths.

She had doubts?

He drew her down until she was lying across his chest, her face nestled against his neck. "You okay?"

"Mmm-hmm." A hesitation. "You?"

"Perfect. Absolutely perfect." He leaned down and

kissed the top of her head. "And you're about to cross one thing off your list."

"The kiss?"

He should say yes. End it once and for all. It would be on a good note. One they could both smile about years from now. But he didn't want to. Not with his body already beginning to reset itself. So he said instead, "Not yet. I'll tell you when."

With that he rolled her back beneath him and pressed his mouth to hers.

Darcie had been walking around in a daze.

Beginning with the moment she'd woken up in an empty bed. For some reason, she'd thought Lucas would wake her to say goodbye if he decided to leave. He hadn't. But after the second lovemaking session she'd been exhausted. And replete. And something about going to sleep with his arm anchoring her close to his body had given her a sense of comfort she hadn't felt in a long time.

How long had he stayed once she'd drifted off? A few minutes? An hour?

The only thing that had made her smile—since she'd been squirming with embarrassment over some of her actions—had been that Lucas had ticked the "kiss a non-triangular Aussie" box and drawn an arrow out to a smiley face. *A smiley face.* She'd never known a man to use one before.

And the fact that he'd rolled out of her bed and actually felt like smiling made a lump come to her throat. She'd assumed with Robert it had been her problem... that he'd been rejecting her. Maybe he'd been rejecting them as a couple. Because although Lucas had used the word "uptight" when he'd grumbled about that roster, he hadn't given any indication last night that he still found her that way.

Instead, he'd smiled.

She kept twisting that fact round and round in her head. It had to have meant he was as satisfied as she was, right?

Grabbing the clipboard for her next patient, she glanced at the name. Margie Terrington, their red-back bite patient. She glanced at her mobile phone, wondering if she should call Lucas in to join her for the consultation, but she was leery. She hadn't actually spoken to him yet today. Why ruin her mood before she had to?

She pushed through the door, only to stop short. Lucas was already in the room. But, then, why was the chart...?

He glanced at her with an undecipherable expression. "I thought you might eventually make it to work today."

Eventually make it? She'd been twenty minutes early, just like most days. Which meant he'd been...

Even earlier.

The very corners of his mouth went up, making her heart lift along with them, but she was careful not to let on to her patient that Lucas was teasing her. "I did indeed." She greeted Margie and flipped through her chart, asking a few questions.

Lucas sat and listened to the back and forth for a minute or two before asking his own question. "Any problems from the antivenin?"

"None." The expectant mum rubbed her belly. "I

can't thank you both enough for figuring out what was wrong."

"Thank Lucas, he was the one who realized you'd been bitten."

The young woman shuddered. "My husband tore the rest of the house apart to make sure there weren't any more of them."

They finished checking her over, letting her listen to the baby's heartbeat to reassure her that all was indeed well after the scare the previous week. "Did your mum come to Australia? With your husband working, I know it'll be a great help to have her here. We could all use a little support." As Darcie well knew from her parents' support after what Robert had done.

They'd been thrilled that she'd been able to go to Australia to get away from everything that had happened. She'd barely prevented her dad from punching her ex-fiancé right in the nose. But she'd grabbed his arm at the last moment. Everyone had parted semiamicably. And the only heart that had been broken that day had been hers. She'd been left in the wedding chapel all alone after everyone had left—her mum seeing to all the last-minute explanations and canceling the venue for the honeymoon.

"Yes, she arrived just a few days ago," Margie said. "She already loves it here. And, yes, we could all use the support of family. After our other…loss…I wondered if I would ever be happy again. I thought I'd never get over it."

Lucas stood with a suddenness that made both women look at him. He glanced at Darcie and then away, muttering that he needed to check on another patient.

She frowned.

That look wasn't anything that resembled a smiley face. And she had no idea who that "other patient" could be because there wasn't anyone listed on the schedule board for another hour. There were a couple of patients in rooms, and she'd noticed one poor woman was curled on her side, sucking down nitrous oxide with a rather desperate air, but they all had other midwives attending them. After saying goodbye to Margie, she went into the hallway and glanced down the corridor, but there was no sign of him. Darcie had hoped to talk to him about how they were going to treat last night.

Already one of the other nurses had cornered her and asked why she'd left the nightclub so early. She'd feigned a headache and said she'd caught the train back to her flat. Not a total lie. But she certainly wasn't going to tell anyone she'd dragged Lucas home with her. She couldn't even bring herself to admit all they'd done together, much less admit it to anyone else. It would be much better if they had some kind of joint cover story to hand out to anyone who asked. Present a united front, as it were.

Even if they weren't united.

Oh, well. Stepping outside the hospital to get a breath of fresh air, she heard her name being called. Not by Lucas but by a child. Darcie swung round in time to see Cora and her dad coming toward them on the footpath. Cora broke into a run and gave her a fierce hug as soon as she reached her, Felix trailing along behind. When he finally caught up he looked a bit shamefaced and maybe even a little shaken up. "Do you know where my brother is?"

"I don't. We just finished up with a patient, though, so he's here somewhere." Darcie didn't want to admit that she had no idea where he'd gone or why. Her stomach was beginning to do a slow dive to the bottom of her abdominal cavity, though.

"I can stay here with Darcie, Dad. She won't mind, will you?"

Felix scratched the back of his neck. "I don't know, Cora. I think we should just go home."

"But you can't! You promised me, and you promised Uncle Luke." Cora's voice came across shrill and upset.

If anything, her father looked even more unsure. "I know, but Chessa is sick and I'm not leaving you home alone."

Darcie didn't have any idea what was going on, but whatever it was sounded important, judging from Cora's overly bright eyes. Tears? Looking to defuse the situation, she said, "Why don't I try to reach his mobile and see where he is?"

But when she tried to do that, the phone went right to voicemail. Strange. Unless he had it off so he wouldn't have to talk to her. His behavior in Margie's room had set her alarm bells ringing earlier. And now this. Her stomach dropped even further. She settled for leaving a message. "Hello, Lucas, it's Darcie." Why she felt compelled to explain who she was when he would know from the caller ID was beyond her. She went on, "Felix and Cora are here at the south entrance. Would you mind stopping round if you get this within the next few minutes?"

She pressed the disconnect button, only to have Cora tell her, "We tried to ring him too, but he didn't answer."

That didn't sound like Lucas. He doted on his niece. "I could keep her here with me for a while. I have an office where she could hang out until Lucas turns up."

A look of profound gratitude went through Felix's eyes. "Are you sure it's no trouble? I have an appointment and our childminder is ill."

"It's fine. Leave it to me." She took Cora by the hand. "We'll get on famously until then."

Felix looked uncertain for all of five seconds then he nodded. "Okay, I appreciate it."

"Bye, Daddy," Cora said. "Maybe Uncle Luke can drive me home and get me an ice lolly on the way."

Darcie's heart twisted. So much for hoping he might want to come home with her. Again.

What? Are you insane?

Evidently, because her mind had, in fact, already traveled down that path and was trying to figure out a way to make it come true.

Giving Felix her mobile number and waving him off with what she hoped was a cheerful toss of her head, she made her way back inside the hospital, Cora following close behind.

Once in her office, the little girl found a pull-apart model of a baby in a pregnant belly that Darcie kept to show her patients. She'd forgotten it was on her desk when she'd offered to bring Cora here. "I'm not sure your dad would want you looking at that."

"Oh, I know all about how babies are born. Uncle Luke's a midwife. I have to know."

Darcie couldn't stop the smile. "You do, do you? And why is that?"

"Because I'm going to be a midwife too. Did you know that Uncle Luke helped my mum have me? She couldn't make it to a hospital."

No, she hadn't known, because Lucas hadn't talked about anything personal, she realized. In fact, he knew some pretty intimate stuff about her, while she knew almost nothing about him. Like whether or not his parents were still alive. Or why he'd gone into midwifery in the first place.

Because it was none of her business.

Careful not to pump the girl for information, she settled for a noncommittal response that she hoped would end the conversation.

It didn't. "Mummy died of cancer."

That she *did* know. "I'm sorry, Cora."

"I don't remember much about her. But I do remember she always smelled nice…like chocolate biscuits."

Darcie swallowed hard, forcing down the growing lump in her throat. What would it be like to lose your mother at such a tender age? Her own mum was still her very best friend and confidante. She decided to change the subject once and for all, since neither Felix nor Lucas would appreciate knowing her and Cora's chat had revealed old heartaches. "Speaking of biscuits, Cora, would you like to go down to the café and see if they have something good to eat? I'll just let the nurses know where I'll be."

"Yay!" Cora grabbed her hand and tugged her toward the door. "Does the coffee shop have espresso, do you think?"

She gave the little girl a sharp glance, not sure if she was joking or not. "How about we both stick with hot chocolate?"

"Even better. Daddy sometimes forgets to buy the chocolate powder."

"Then hot chocolate we shall have."

Fifteen minutes later they were in the cafeteria at a table, with Cora imitating the way Darcie drank her chocolate. It made Darcie smile. She could see why Lucas was so very fond of her. The girl was exuberant and full of life, despite the tragedy she'd suffered at such a young age. Then again, children were resilient, a characteristic she often wished was carried into adulthood.

The buzzer on her phone went off and when she looked at the screen her eyes widened. Lucas. He must have got her message. She answered, forcing herself to speak cheerfully, even though her heart was cranking out signals of panic. "Hi."

"May I ask where you are, and why my niece is with you? You're not in your office."

"I...uh..." Oh, God, it hadn't been her imagination in Margie's room. He *was* upset with her for some reason. Only she had no idea why or what she could have done. "We're in the cafeteria. Felix said he tried to ring you, but you didn't answer."

That was really the crux of the matter. Why Lucas had failed to answer anyone's calls.

"I forgot to charge my battery after…" He paused, then forged ahead, "I got home. I had to get the extra charger from my vehicle in the car park."

Oh, well, that answered the question about where he'd gone and why he hadn't picked up his mobile. It didn't answer why he was acting the way he was. "Okay. Well, Felix said the childminder is ill and he had an appointment to keep. He asked if I could watch Cora for a few minutes."

Had Felix not left him a message, like she had?

"I'll be right down to get her."

She tried to smooth things over. "Why don't you join us instead? We're drinking hot chocolate and eating biscuits."

He mumbled something under his breath that she couldn't hear before he came back with, "One of us should stay on the ward."

It was a slow morning and there were several other midwives on duty. Surely he didn't mind sharing her break time?

She simply said, though, "Whatever you think is best. I'll see you when you get here." Then she disconnected before he could say anything else. The last thing she wanted to do was get into an argument with him just when she thought they'd turned a corner.

Turned a corner? Sleeping with him was so much more than that.

Was that what this was all about? Did he suddenly regret what they'd done? Or was he just afraid she was going to become clingy and expect something from him he wasn't willing to give?

She suddenly felt like a fool. Played with and then discarded, like she would have expected him to do with other women. And why *not* her? She was no better than anyone else. Certainly not in Lucas's eyes.

"Darcie, are you okay?" Cora's worried voice broke into her thoughts.

She forced a smile, picking up her hot chocolate and taking a sip of the now-tepid liquid. "Fine. Your uncle is on his way down to have tea with you."

"Shall we order him something, do you think?"

"Oh, I think he can manage that on his own." Another quick smile that made her feel like a total fraud. "And once he gets here I need to get back to work. I have patients that need attending to."

"Can't you stay a little while longer? I know Uncle Luke would want you to."

No, actually he wouldn't. But there was no way she was going to say that to a little girl. "Sorry, love, I wish I could."

The second Lucas arrived Darcie popped up from the table. "See, here she is all safe and sound."

His eyes searched hers for a moment, and she thought she caught a hint of regret in their depths. "I had no doubt she was safe with you."

His hand came out as if to catch her wrist, but Darcie took a step back, going over to Cora and leaning down to kiss the top of her head. "I'm off. Have fun with your uncle."

Then, without a backward glance, she made her way

out of the café, wishing she could grind the last fortnight of their rotation into dust and sweep it into the
nearest bin.

CHAPTER EIGHT

Lucas found her just outside the Teen Mums-to-Be
room.

Isla had the door to the tiny conference room open,
and she and Darcie were discussing ways to promote
the program and give it more visibility. When Isla's
eyes settled on him, however, they widened slightly. "I
think someone wants to talk to you."

Darcie glanced back, and then her chin popped up,
eyes sparkling. "May I help you with something, Mr.
Elliot?"

Her sudden formality struck him right between the
eyes. He wasn't the only who noticed. Isla looked from
one to the other then murmured that she would see Darcie later and left, quietly closing the door behind her.

He'd cursed himself up one side and down the other
for the way he'd spoken to Darcie on the phone yesterday. Margie talking about her miscarriage and wondering if she'd ever be happy again had scrubbed at a raw
spot inside him that just wouldn't go away. Because
he'd wondered the same thing about his brother time
and time again—whether he'd ever be happy again, or if
he'd simply wander the same worn paths for the rest of

his life or, worse, destroy himself and damage Cora in the process. Love and loss seemed to go hand in hand.

But that had been no reason to take it out on Darcie.

Better make this good, mate.

"I wanted to apologize for being short with you yesterday."

"No need. I should have simply asked your brother to take Cora home when he couldn't reach you, appointment or no appointment. I didn't realize you were so against me spending time with her." Her lips pressed together in a straight line.

She was angry.

And gorgeous. Especially now.

He'd settled Cora in his office yesterday while Felix had gone to his therapy session, and between him and the nurses they'd taken turns keeping her occupied. Every time he'd checked in on her she'd chattered nonstop about Darcie. She'd loaded the pictures from their time at Max's bungee-jumping tower onto his computer. One of those shots had taken his breath away. It had been taken just after he'd unhooked her carabiners, just after he'd kissed her. She'd broken through the surface of the water at the same time as he had, brown hair streaming down her back, fingers clutching his.

And their eyes had been locked on each other. He could only hope none of the nurses had seen the picture.

But in that moment he'd realized why he was so against Darcie and Cora spending time together. Because Darcie was too easy to love. Much like Melody had been.

Cora had already grown attached to the obstetrician. That fact made his chest ache. She'd lost her mother, and very possibly her father. This was one little girl who didn't deserve to experience any more hurt. And she would if he wasn't careful. Because Darcie would be leaving the country. Soon.

He'd tried to apologize to her yesterday, but by the time his brother had come to pick Cora up, Darcie had been flooded with patients and unable to stop and talk. At least, that's what she said. And when their shift had ended, she'd left immediately.

"No, you did the right thing," he said. "I was upset with myself for not getting those calls and leaving you to deal with the whole mess." A partial truth. But if his mobile phone had been charged, he could have avoided all of this.

"Mess?"

Damn, he wasn't explaining himself very well. "Things with my brother are complicated at the moment, and I was worried."

Darcie's brows puckered, but she didn't ask what the complications were. "It was no problem. Cora and I get on quite well."

"Yes, I've noticed."

If he were smart he'd have let things continue the way they had yesterday—with Darcie put out with him—until their rotation ended. But the note of hurt in her voice, when he'd demanded to know where Cora was, had punctured something deep inside. He'd found he just couldn't let her think the worst of him.

Which was why he was here.

She glanced at the door Isla had closed, probably planning her escape. So Lucas blurted out, "Which thing on your list were you thinking of tackling next?"

He'd made a promise. He couldn't very well renege on it, could he? Yes, he damn well could. He was just choosing not to.

"I hadn't given it much thought today."

He should have said goodbye when he'd woken up in her bed, but he'd been too damned shocked to do anything but throw his clothes on and get out of there. He rarely spent the night at a woman's flat, most of the time leaving soon after the physical act was completed. Because the aftermath always felt uncomfortable. Intimate. And holding a woman for hours after having sex with her? Well, that was something a husband or boyfriend did. Lucas didn't want either of those titles attached to his name.

But he didn't want to hurt anyone unnecessarily either. Especially one who'd already been treated badly by someone else. One he'd promised wouldn't have to accomplish her to-do-while-in-Australia list on her own.

Besides, he'd promised Isla as well.

"How about the pier? We could walk along it tonight, see the moon shining on the water." It had been on the tip of his tongue to suggest a trip to the dock where his sailboat was moored, but he had the same internal rule about that as he did about spending the whole night with a woman. He didn't do it.

"That wasn't on my list."

He offered her a smile. "Maybe lists were made to be changed—added to."

She stared up at him for a long second. "Maybe they were. Okay, Lucas. The pier. Tonight."

Relief swept over him, not only because he wasn't breaking his promise to show her the sights—and the pier at night was one of his favorites—but that she was back to calling him by his first name. He liked the sound of it on her lips.

Especially in that breathy little voice that—

Back to business, Lucas.

"Okay, then, do you want to meet after our shift?"

"Sounds perfect."

Just as Darcie reached for the door handle of the teen mums' room, Tristan Hamilton, MMU's neonatal cardiothoracic surgeon, came sprinting down the hallway. "Flick's in labor."

Isla pushed the door from the other side, making it known that the rooms were not soundproof. "Are you sure?"

Tristan dragged shaky fingers through his hair. "I'm sure. So is she. She knows the signs."

"It's still early." Lucas said what everyone was probably thinking. Heavily pregnant, Tristan's wife had already been through a lot. So had Tristan. The baby had inherited his father's heart defect—a defect that had required Tristan to undergo a heart transplant when he'd been younger. Thankfully, a specialized team had done surgery on the baby in utero a few weeks ago, repairing the faulty organ and inserting a stent, but the baby was still recovering. The fact that Flick had gone into labor wasn't a good sign. It could mean the baby was in distress. A complication from surgery?

He glanced at Darcie, who nodded. "We're on our way."

Isla, the worry evident on her face, said, "I'll come too."

"No." Darcie moved closer and squeezed the other

woman's hand. "You're needed here. We'll keep you up to date on what's happening."

"Promise?" Lucas noted Isla's hand had gone to the bulge of her own stomach in a protective gesture he recognized.

"I promise."

Then the trio was off, Tristan leading the pack, while Darcie and Lucas followed behind. Once back on the ward, it was obvious which room Flick was in by the bevy of nurses rushing in and out.

The second they entered the space, Flick—already in a hospital gown—cast a terrified glance their way. "They're coming faster, Tristan. Every two minutes now."

While her husband went to hold her hand, Lucas and Darcie hurriedly washed their hands and snapped on gloves. Lucas nodded at Darcie to do the initial exam while he hooked up the monitor.

Without a word being said, she moved into position. "Tell me if you start contracting, Flick, and I'll stop."

Lucas watched the woman's expression, even as he positioned the wide elastic band of the monitor around her waist. Once he switched it on the sound of the baby's heart filled the room, along with a palpable sense of relief. No arrhythmias. No dangerous slowing of the heart rate. Just a blessedly normal *chunga-chunga-chunga-chunga* that came from a healthy fetus.

Darcie's face was a study in concentration as she felt the cervix to judge its state. If Flick was still in the early stages of labor, it might be possible to halt it with medication.

Grim little lines appeared around her mouth as she straightened. "Have you noticed any leakage?"

"The baby's been pressing hard on my bladder so…" Her eyes went to her husband. "The amniotic sac?"

Darcie nodded. "It's trickling. And you're at five centimeters and almost fully effaced. There's no stopping it at this point, Flick. Your baby is coming."

"But his heart…"

Tristan, standing beside his wife, looked stunned. "You'd better get Alessandro down here."

The neonatal specialist was in charge of the hospital's NICU. Once the baby was born, Alessandro would make sure everything was working as it should and that the child's tiny heart was okay.

Darcie asked one of the nurses to put in a call, and then she moved up to stroke Flick's head. "It's going to be all right. You're only a few weeks early."

"Mmm…" Flick's blue eyes closed as she pulled air in through her nose and blew out through her mouth. Tristan leaned closer to help her, while Lucas glanced at the monitor. Contraction. Building.

The baby's heart rate slowed as the uterus clamped down further, squeezing the umbilical cord. Everyone held their breath, but the blips on the screen picked up the pace once the contraction crested and the pressure began to ease.

Lucas came over and said in a low voice, "She's going fast for her first."

A few seconds later Alessandro appeared in the room, along with a few more nurses. He studied Flick's chart and then watched the monitor beside the bed for a minute or two. "Let me know when she's getting close. I'll have everything ready."

He shook Tristan's hand. "Congratulations. It looks like you're going to be a daddy today. Have you got a name picked out for her?"

The baby's sex wasn't a secret any more. Tristan and Flick were having a girl.

"We're still having heated discussions about that," Flick said with a shaky smile. "I hoped we'd have a few more weeks to talk it over."

Her husband laid a hand on her cheek. "Let's go with Laura. I know how much you love that name."

"Are you sure?" Tears appeared in her eyes, but then another contraction hit and her thoughts turned to controlling the pain.

Alessandro's attention turned to the monitor to watch the progression. "Everything looks good so far. Call me when the baby crowns, or if you need me before that." He gave Flick's shoulder a gentle squeeze and then nodded at the rest of them and left the room.

Once labor was in full swing, the room grew crowded with healthcare workers. Flick refused the offer of nitrous oxide, afraid that anything she put into her body at this point would affect the baby, even though the gas was well tolerated and often used to manage labor pain.

"I need to push." Flick's announcement had Darcie at her side in a flash.

She checked the baby's position once again then nodded. "You're all set. Are you ready, Mum?"

"Yes."

They waited for a second as Flick found a comfortable position.

Tension gathered in the back of Lucas's head as he assisted Darcie, while Tristan remained closer to his wife's head, murmuring encouragement.

Lucas saw the climb begin on the monitor. "Okay, Flick, here it comes, take a deep breath and push."

The woman grabbed a lungful of air, closed her eyes and bore down, helping her contracting uterus do its job. Tristan counted to ten in a slow, steady voice and told her to take another breath and push again.

The pushing phase went as quickly as the rest of the labor had gone. Ten pushes, and Darcie signaled that the baby had crowned. "Someone ring Alessandro."

He must have been close by because he entered the room within a minute and stood at the far wall.

"Here we go, Flick."

Another group of pushes as Darcie guided the baby's shoulders. Then the baby was there, cradled in Darcie's hands. She passed the baby to Lucas, and then worked on suctioning the newborn's mouth and nose, the red scar from surgery still very evident on her tiny chest.

A sharp cry split the air, and Lucas smiled as bleary, irritated eyes blinked up at him. Laura cried again, waving clenched fists at him and probably everyone else in the room. "Welcome to the world, baby girl," he murmured.

Tristan cut the cord, and then Alessandro took over, carrying the baby over to a nearby table and belting out orders as he listened to the baby's heart and lungs for several long minutes. There was no time for Lucas to worry about that, because they still had the afterbirth to deliver.

A few minutes later baby Laura was placed on Flick's chest with a clean bill of health.

"I don't foresee any problems." Alessandro smiled down at the new parents. "Her heart sounds strong so the surgery was obviously a success."

Flick grabbed her husband's hand, her eyes on his. "See? Don't you start worrying, Tristan. She's fine."

Lucas knew the man had agonized over the baby's health the entire time, but the problem had been caught and corrected early enough to prevent any major damage to her heart. She would need additional surgery as she grew and her veins and arteries matured but, other than that, she had a great prognosis.

Isla stuck her head into the room. "How are they?"

Flick heard her and motioned her in. "See for yourself."

The head midwife crept closer to where Flick was rubbing her baby's back in slow, soothing circles.

"Good on you. She's beautiful, sweetheart. Congratulations."

Alessandro put his arm around his wife's waist, his hand resting on her pregnant belly. "And now we need to let them get to know one another."

As soon as the room had cleared of most of the nurses, and the baby had successfully latched onto Flick's breast, Tristan leaned down and whispered something in his wife's ear that made her smile, although her face bore evidence of her exhaustion.

Lucas's chest tightened. What if all hadn't gone well in here today? What if something had happened to Flick? It was obvious Tristan was deeply in love with her.

His brother's face swam before him. The times he'd drunk himself into a stupor or lain in bed, unwilling to get up and take care of himself or Cora. On days like that it had been left to Lucas to care for them both.

He glanced over at Darcie and found her looking back at him, although her eyes swung away almost immediately. What would it be like to love a woman and not fear she might one day disappear off the face of the planet?

It was better not to even entertain thoughts like that.

Haven't you already?

No.

He and Darcie had been on a few outings. Spent one night together. That did not a relationship make. And if he kept telling himself that, he could make sure it stayed that way.

He glanced at his watch and realized the end of their shift had come and gone. They should have been off duty an hour ago. A deep tiredness lodged in his bones and suddenly all he wanted to do was sit on that pier with Darcie and stare out over the water.

Just for companionship. Just to have someone to share today's victory with.

He walked over to the happy couple. "Do you need anything else? Something to help you sleep?"

"I don't think any of us are going to have trouble in that area." She kissed the top of her baby's head. "Thank you so much for everything."

Tristan echoed that. "I'm going to stay here with them tonight to make sure everything is okay."

And that was their cue to leave. Darcie must have realized it too because she smiled then walked over and kissed Flick on the cheek. "Take care, young lady. Ring if you need anything. You have my mobile number?"

"Yes. Right now, though, all I want to do is watch her sleep."

Lucas followed Darcie out the door and to the nurses' station. "Are we still on for tonight?"

She pushed a lock of hair behind her ear, glancing at the clock. "Do you still want to? It's after nine."

"If you're not too tired. We can get something to eat on the way."

"I'm fine." She hesitated. "As long as you're sure."

Right now, Lucas had never been more sure of anything in his life.

The moon was huge.

Seated on the side of the pier with her legs dangling over the side, Darcie stared out at the light reflected over the water. "I've never seen anything quite like this."

"I know. It's why I enjoy coming out here from time to time."

She cocked her head in his direction. "I should have made time to do things like this right after I came to Australia. But I wasn't in the mood to do anything besides work."

"Your ex?"

"Yes." This was probably the last thing Lucas wanted to hear while he sat here: her tale of woe. But somehow she found the whole story pouring into the night air. And it felt good. Freeing to actually tell someone besides Isla.

Lucas was silent until she'd finished then said, "Your

ex was a bastard. And your maid of honor…well, she wasn't much of a friend, was she?"

She shrugged. Nine and half months had given her enough distance to see the situation more objectively. Yes, Tabitha and Robert could have handled things differently, but it had been better to learn the truth this side of the wedding vows than to have faced the possibility of cheating and a divorce further on down the line. "I think it was hard for both of them. And I don't think they meant to hurt me. That's probably why our engagement continued for as long as it did. But it would have been easier if they'd been honest with themselves… and with me."

"Being honest with yourself doesn't mean you have to act on your impulses."

She frowned. "So you think it would have been better for Robert to go ahead and marry me?"

"No. Maybe it would have been better for him not to become engaged in the first place."

Interesting. She was seeing a new side to Lucas. "Is that comment speaking to my situation? Or do you simply not believe in marriage?"

"It's not so much that I don't believe in it, I'm just apathetic about the whole institution." He leaned back on his hands and stared at the night sky before looking her way again. "But I didn't bring you here to talk about my philosophies on marriage or anything else. I came to enjoy the view."

"I am enjoying it." She took a deep breath, the salty tang that clung to the air filling her senses and rinsing away the stress of the last two days. "It's lovely. You're a very lucky man to be able to come down here whenever you want and take it all in."

"I am a lucky man."

When she turned to glance at him, he was watching her.

"What?" She pulled her cardigan around herself, unsure whether it was because of the slight chill in the air or because he was making her feel nervous.

His brows went up. "Nothing. I'm just taking it all in."

Her? He was taking her in?

A shot of courage appeared from nowhere. "The view's quite good from where I'm sitting as well."

The breeze picked up a bit, and a gust of air flipped her hair across her cheek and into her eyes. She went to push it back, only to find he'd beaten her to it, his hand teasing the errant locks behind her ear. The light touch sent a shiver through her.

His fingers moved to her nape, threading through the strands there and lifting them so the air currents could pick them up.

Why did everything the man said or did make her insides coil in anticipation? And how could he go from cool and distant to so…here? Present. Insinuating himself into her life and heart in subtle ways that took down all her defenses.

Her mind swept through the events of the day and replayed them. How he'd deferred to her in the delivery room today, letting her take the lead in Flick's delivery while not losing that raw, masculine edge that made him so attractive to her.

And to a thousand other women like her.

Just when she started to thump back to earth his fingers—which were still at the back of her neck—suddenly tangled in her hair, using his light grip to turn her head.

"Your fiancé missed out."

His brown eyes roved over her face, touching on her lips then coming back up. "You're the whole package, Darce. A beauty. Inside and out. And I…"

He let go of her so quickly she had to catch her balance even as he finished his thought, his tone darkening. "And I shouldn't have brought you here."

Where had that come from? One minute he was going on about her hair and how he found her beautiful. The next he was saying he regretted having brought her to the pier.

Hurt—a jagged spear of pain that slashed and tore at everything it came in contact with—caused her voice to wobble. "Then why did you?"

"Because I wanted you to see what I do when I come out to the bay. But all I see right now…is you. And I want to do more than just look."

Everything inside her went numb for a second. Then a swish of realization blew through her, soothing the hurt.

He wanted her. Wanted to touch her. Just like the other night at her flat.

"You can. You can do more."

Before she had time to think or breathe he moved. Fast. His mouth covered hers in a rush of need that was echoed in her. She wanted him. Now. Here. On this pier.

His hand went behind her head as his tongue sought entry. She gave it to him, opening her mouth and letting him sweep inside. He groaned, and the sound was like a balm and a stimulant all at once, although she didn't know how that was possible. Maybe just because of who he was.

Darcie's mouth wasn't the only thing that opened. Her heart did as well, letting him in. Just a crack at first, but then growing wider and wider until he filled her. Surrounded her. Inside and out.

She allowed herself to revel in it, at least for now. Soon she'd have to come back to the real world, but for the moment she would inhabit the land of wish lists and wishful thinking—a place where anything was possible. Where anything could happen.

And, God, she hoped it happened. Soon. Because the need inside her was already too big to be contained.

She pulled back, even though everything was screaming at her to keep going. "Lucas."

"I know." Both hands sank into her hair and he held her still as he ran a line of kisses down her cheekbone, over her jaw, until he reached her ear. "If I don't stop now, I won't."

What? Stop? That's not what she'd meant at all.

"I don't want you to."

A flash of teeth came, followed by, "I don't think you want me to rip your clothes off on a public pier, do you?" A brow lifted. "Unless you're into exhibitionism. Although the thought of having you pressed naked against that bank of windows at your flat—with me inside you—is pretty damned tempting."

Something in her belly went liquid with heat. Not at

the thought of exposing herself to thousands of people but at Lucas—inside her.

"My flat is too far away."

He paused for a moment and then stood and held out his hand. "I know the perfect place."

CHAPTER NINE

"I DIDN'T KNOW you had a boat."

No one did. This was the one place Lucas could come that was totally private. Totally his. Where he could get away from the stresses of the day or—when Felix had been in a particularly bad state—the horrors of his own thoughts. The small sailboat had cost him several months' salary, but it had been money well spent. He would live on it were it not for the fact that he needed to be close to the hospital…and to Cora and Felix.

And he'd never brought anyone here…especially not a woman.

So why Darcie?

He stood with her on the deck as the boat swayed at its mooring. Why was this the first place that had come to mind when he'd realized what she wanted?

It was close. And they both wanted sex. It was the obvious choice. Even as he thought it, he knew that wasn't the reason at all.

She was waiting for an answer, though, so he said, "I like the water, and it's nice to have a place where I can enjoy it."

She smiled, leaning against the railing on the far side of the vessel. "I thought that's what the pier was for."

"Sometimes I want a little more privacy." His lips curled, and knowing she'd probably take the words the wrong way he went on, "For myself. Not for any love triangles."

She eased over to him and ran her fingers from the waistband of his jeans up to his shoulders. "I thought we'd already established you don't do any angles at all."

He didn't do a lot of things. But he liked the feel of her hands on him.

Gripping her waist, he dragged her to him, making the boat rock slightly. "So…do you want to stay topside? Or go down below?"

Her brows went up and a choked laugh sounded. "I assume you're not referring to parts of the body."

"No. Because in that I'm definitely an all-inclusive kind of guy." He leaned down and brushed his cheek against hers. "I meant do you want to stay here on deck or go to the cabin?"

"Okay, that makes more sense."

More than once he'd slept beneath the stars on the boat, letting the sounds and movements of the water lull him to sleep. As cool as it was right now, there was no need for air-conditioning.

Darcie glanced at the dock. "Does anyone ever come out here?"

Rows of other boats surrounded them. The small marina was the place of weekend sailors. But in the middle of a workweek? It was always deserted.

"Just me." He smiled, playing on his earlier theme. "Sorry, no one to watch us but the seagulls."

Even in the dark her face flamed. "That's not what I meant."

"Wasn't it?" His hand slid up her side until it covered her breast. The nipple was already tight and ready. "How brave are you feeling, Darcie?"

He tweaked the bud, glorying in the gasp it drove from her throat.

"Right now? Braver than I was during that bungee jump."

"Let's stay out here, then, where we can see the moon."

His hands went to the hem of her cardigan and shirt and swept them over her head, letting the garments drop onto the plank deck. When he touched her arms they were covered in goose bumps, although her skin felt warm. "Are you cold?"

"No." As if in answer, she undid the buttons of his shirt and yanked it from his jeans, helping him tug free from the long sleeves. She tossed it on top of her clothes. The sight stopped him for a second. But just one. Then he was curving his hands behind her back and finding the clasp on her black silk bra. "Last chance to back out, Darcie."

She leaned up and nipped his shoulder. "Just take it off, will you?"

"My pleasure." He unsnapped the bra, and on impulse dangled it over the railing beside them.

Yes, he liked seeing it there, the inky color contrasting with the sleek chrome. It was his declaration to the universe that she was his for tonight. And he knew something else that would look perfect beside it.

He allowed his fingers to trail over the curves he'd exposed. Just for a second, then he released the snap on his jeans and pushed them down his legs, kicking them to the growing pile of clothes beside him. Then he did the same for her. Much slower, kneeling down, so he could savor every inch of her along the way.

Black silk met his eyes. The same color as her bra. He allowed his palms to trail over her hips as he stood, until the slick fabric met the perfect mounds of her ass. He squeezed, pulling her against him and allowing his stiff flesh to imagine that silk sliding over his bare skin.

He had to know. He pulled away, only to have her reach for him. "Just a second, gorgeous. I'm coming right back."

Reaching down to scoop up his jeans, he retrieved a packet from his wallet and set it on the rail next to her bra. Then off came his boxers. His flesh jerked as he drew her back to him.

He closed his eyes as his naked arousal met the silk of her undies. And it was everything he'd imagined. Slick. Arousing. His hands went to her behind and kneaded as he pumped himself against her, slowly, reveling at the contrast between the silky fabric and the warm skin of her belly.

When he felt hands on his own ass, his lids flew apart. "Hell."

He pushed beneath the elastic, and then, unable to wait any longer, he slid her last remaining item of clothing down her hips, waiting until she stepped free before draping it next to her bra.

Mmm…yes. Just like he'd thought. He liked seeing her displayed there. Liked having her on his boat.

Grabbing the condom, he swept a hand beneath her thighs and her shoulders and hauled her into his arms, where he kissed her for what seemed like forever. This time she gave a little shiver, and he noticed the breeze was a bit cooler than it had been on the pier. Still kissing her, he eased to his knees and then lowered her to the deck, her pale skin looking glorious against the shiny teak planks. The raised edges around the deck provided a windscreen, and, balling up their clothing, he lifted her head so she'd have something to cushion it. "Better?"

"It's all good, Lucas. Nothing could be better."

He grinned down at her. "Wanna bet?"

Kneeling between her legs, he sheathed himself, then let his hands move in light, brushing strokes up her inner thighs, until he reached the heart of her. She was already moist and his fingers wanted to linger and explore, but he knew once he let them he was there to stay. And there were other places he needed to visit.

He lowered himself onto her, supporting his weight with his elbows, then murmured against her lips, "Too heavy?"

"Mmm...no. Too perfect."

That made him smile. He didn't think he'd ever heard a woman refer to him that way before. He liked it.

He'd told her the truth earlier. She was gorgeous, inside and out, sporting an inner glow of health and life that made him wonder how he could have ever thought of her as cold.

She didn't feel cold. She felt warm and vital and he itched to lose himself in her all over again.

But first...

He nuzzled the underside of her breast, savoring the taste of her skin as he came up the rounded side and across until he found her nipple. Drawing it into his mouth, he let his tongue play over the peak, hoping to coax the first of those little sounds he knew she made.

And, yes, it was heady being out here in the open, even though he knew no one could see them unless they climbed aboard and walked to the port side of the boat. But the thought that someone could…and that Darcie was letting him love her beneath the stars…was testament to her trust. One he wasn't sure he deserved.

But he liked it.

He applied more suction, and there it was. A low moan that pulled at his flesh and slid along the surface of his mind like a lazy day in the sun. Or maybe it was more like being in the eye of a storm. A fleeting moment of calm, when you sensed chaos lingering nearby…knew you'd soon be swept up in an unstoppable deluge.

And when that happened, he knew right where he wanted to be. And it wasn't pinning her to the deck where he couldn't see or touch.

He pulled back and climbed to his feet, holding his hand out to her.

"Wh-what?"

"Trust me." He picked up his shirt and helped her slide her arms into it, leaving it open in the front and allowing his fingers to dance over her breasts and then move lower. Touching her and relishing the way her eyes closed when he hit that one certain spot.

Putting his forehead to hers, he stopped to catch his breath for a second. "I want you on the railing."

It was the perfect height. She'd be right on a level with that core part of him. And Darcie's silhouette on the water? There was nothing he'd rather see...experience.

She glanced behind her, where her bra and undies were still draped, and backed up until she was against the chrome, her hands resting on the gleaming surface. "Help me up, then."

Gripping her waist, he lifted her onto the rail, his blue shirttail hanging over the other side, giving them a modicum of privacy, although they didn't need it. Her arms twined around his neck and her legs parted in obvious invitation. He moved in, his chest pressing against the lush fullness of her breasts, his flesh aching to thrust home.

"Hang onto me, Darce." Letting go of her waist, he allowed a couple of inches of space to come between them so he could touch her. Her face. Her breasts. Her belly. And finally that warm, moist spot between her legs that was calling out to him.

"Ahhh..." The sound came when he slid a finger inside her, her feet hooking around the backs of his thighs as if she was afraid he was going to move away. Not damn likely. He was there to stay.

His mind skimmed over that last thought. Discarding it as he added another finger. Went deeper. Used his thumb to find that pleasure center just a few millimeters to the front.

Darcie leaned further back over the side of the boat, her hands going to his shoulders, her legs parting more. This time Lucas was the one who groaned. Splayed out like this, he could see every inch of her, watch the way her breasts moved in time to his fingers as he pressed home and then pulled back.

"Want you. Inside…" The words were separated by short, quick breaths. She was getting close. So very close.

And he didn't want her to go off without him.

There it was. The same sense of need he'd had the last time they'd been together. He moved into position and guided himself home. Paused. Then he thrust hard. Sank deep. His breath shuddered out then air flooded back into his lungs.

Tight. Wet. Hot.

All the things he knew she'd be.

And it was all for him.

He held himself still as she whimpered and strained against him. It wouldn't take much to send him over the edge. He counted. Prayed. Closed his eyes. Until he could take a mental step back.

Only then did he wrap his arms beneath the curve of her butt to hold her close. He eased back, pulling almost free. Remained there for an agonizing second or two before his hips lunged forward and absorbed the sensations all over again. Over and over he drove himself inside her and then retreated.

He leaned forward. Bit her lower lip. Made her squirm against him.

"Please, Lucas. Please, now."

He knew exactly what she was asking for. "Make it happen, gorgeous."

Changing the angle, he reconnected with her, then pushed deep and held firm as she ground her pelvis against him, letting her choose her own speed, her own pressure, all the while cursing in his head as his eyes reopened to watch her face—taking in the tiny, almost desperate bumping of her hips.

His hands tightened on her, barely aware that the vibrations from their movements had sent her undies over the rail and into the water, and that her bra wasn't far behind. He didn't care. Didn't want to stop for anything.

Legs wrapped tight around him, Darcie's movements became frantic, nails digging into his shoulders...for all of five seconds—he knew because he was busy counting—then her head tilted toward the sky, hair streaming down her back, and she cried out in the darkness.

That was it. All it took. Lucas pumped furiously as the tsunami he'd been holding at bay crashed down on top of him. He lost himself in her, legs barely supporting his weight as he rode out his climax, knowing a tidal wave of another kind was not far behind. Coming on him fast.

He stared straight ahead so he wouldn't have to see it, wouldn't have to acknowledge its existence, and found her watching him, her gaze soft and warm.

Accepting.

At that moment the second realization hit him, splashing over his head and making it impossible to breathe. To think.

He loved her.

In spite of everything he'd been through with his brother. In spite of the dangers of letting himself get too close—too emotionally involved—the unthinkable had just become reality. He'd fallen for a woman. And now that he had, there wasn't a damned thing he could do about it.

She could only avoid him for so long.

Two days had passed, and she was still reeling from

what they'd done on Lucas's boat. How he'd buttoned her into her cardigan and slacks—her undergarments nowhere to be found—probably resting on the bottom of the boat slip, waiting on some unsuspecting soul to find them when it was daytime. Mortified, she made Lucas promise he'd go back and see if he could locate them—hoping her argument against pollution had been convincing enough.

They'd been in her locker the next day—how he'd known the combination she had no idea, but she was thankful no one had to see him handing her the plastic bag that contained her errant underwear.

If anything, though, it made her feel even more embarrassed. How had he found them? A net? A gaff from his boat? Or had they just been floating on the surface of the water, trapped between his boat and the dock?

That thought made heat rush into her face. She picked up her pace as she went down the hallway toward the double glass doors of the waiting room, which swished open as soon as she got close. She was supposed to meet Isla for lunch.

But when she arrived she saw her friend deep in conversation with Sean Anderson. Oh, no. Surely he wasn't giving her a hard time again about Isabel. She sped up even more and arrived in time to hear her ask if he'd heard from her sister. The opposite of what Darcie had expected to hear.

"No. And I'm not sure I want to, at this point."

"Really?" her friend asked, giving Darcie a quick glance. "After all that, you're just giving up?"

"I don't know. But I do want some answers. And I don't think I'm going to get them here."

"I'm sorry, Sean. I wish I could help."

Darcie decided to speak up. "Maybe you should consider going to the source."

"Funny you should say that," Sean said. "I decided to take Isla's advice. My contract runs out at the end of the week. I'm flying out as soon as it does."

The two women looked at each other, and Darcie's heart began to thump. Maybe she couldn't fix her own growing problems with Lucas, but maybe Sean could solve his. "So you're going..."

Sean nodded. "To England."

Isla clasped her hands over her belly, knuckles white. "Don't hurt her. Please. You have no idea what she's been through."

"I have no intention of hurting anyone. All I want is the truth about why she left."

Her friend studied him then reached out and touched his arm. "Good luck, Sean. I really mean that."

"Thanks." And with a stiff frame and tight jaw he strode down the hallway toward an uncertain future.

Well, join the club. Who really knew what the future held. Certainly not Darcie, who was busy hiding out and praying that Lucas gave her some time to recover. She needed to figure out what it was she wanted from him before he suggested tackling the next thing on her list.

Because that list had begun to revolve around a common theme, one that was getting her in deeper with each item ticked: Sit on a beach and kiss an Aussie. Bungee jump from a tower and kiss an Aussie. Dance at a club, and make love to an Aussie. Climb on a boat...and open her heart to an Aussie.

Darcie didn't know how much more she could take.

Because her heart was now in real danger, and she was more afraid than she'd ever been in her life...even during that moment when she'd realized Robert didn't love her. He loved someone else.

Because if that happened with Lucas, she didn't want to stick around to see it. The result would be a gaping wound no amount of surgery or medical expertise could repair. It involved who she was at an elemental level. And in opening her heart she feared she'd set herself up for the biggest hurt of her life.

Isla said something, and Darcie swung her attention back to her friend. "I'm sorry. I missed that."

The midwife smiled. A quick curving of lips that looked all too knowing and crafty. "I said, don't look now, but trouble is headed your way."

That was the understatement of the year. Then she realized Isla's eyes were on something behind her.

Darcie turned to look, thinking one of her patients was coming to see her, only to catch sight of the same glass doors she'd just come through swishing open to let in the last person she wanted to see today.

Lucas.

He looked devastating in a dress shirt and black slacks. Her glance went back to the shirt. Blue button-down.

Oh, no. Surely that wasn't the shirt he'd draped around her while they'd...

Warmth splashed into her face and ran down her neck, spreading exponentially the closer he got.

"Hello, ladies."

Instead of sweeping past and continuing on his way, he stopped in front of them.

Isla's smile grew wider. "Darcie, I think I'm going to

have to back out of our lunch date. I need to see Alessi about…tires for his car."

Tires? For his car?

Before she could call her friend on the obvious fib, Isla had retreated back through the doors, leaving her with Lucas and a few folks in the waiting room, who seemed quite interested in the various dramas unfolding in the MMU.

As if he'd noticed as well, he pulled her over to the far wall, well out of earshot. "Felix and Cora are on their way to the park with a picnic lunch. It's not far from the hospital, so I thought you might like to tag along. It's something you should see before you leave the country."

Leave the country. Why did that have an ominous ring to it?

Lucas went on, "From what Isla said, I take it you haven't eaten yet."

Rats. That would have been her first excuse if he approached her. It was why she'd practically begged Isla to have lunch with her for the last two days. And now her friend had turned traitor and abandoned her.

Her eyes met Lucas's face. He seemed softer all of a sudden. As if the weight of the world had been lifted from his shoulders. But what weight? Maybe he was just happy to be having lunch with his niece and his brother. It was obvious he loved that little girl and that she adored him back.

As if sensing her hesitation, he added, "Cora would love to see you. She's been asking about you for days."

Well, that was a change. Before, he hadn't seemed keen on her spending time with his niece.

Her heart settled back in place. The comment about

leaving Australia hadn't meant anything. "I guess it would be all right."

"I'm glad." One finger came out and hooked around hers and the side of his mouth turned up in way that made her stomach flip. "Did you get my little package?"

He was definitely in a cheerful mood today. Did she dare hope it was because of the time they'd spent together over the last three weeks? How strange that something she'd dreaded with every fiber of her being could have turned around so completely.

She decided to add some playfulness of her own. "Little? I thought the package was a decent size. But, then again, I don't have much to compare it to."

"Witch," he murmured. "Maybe you need a refresher. It has been a couple of days after all."

A refresher? He wanted to be with her again?

Maybe she wouldn't wind up on the hurting side of the fence after all. As long as she was careful. And took things slowly. She'd been thinking about seeing if the Victoria had any permanent positions available, but she'd been putting it off because of Lucas. She didn't want to stick around if they were going to end up fighting each other further on down the line.

But right now she didn't see that happening.

"Maybe I've just forgotten." She threw him a saucy smile.

"Mmm...I need to work harder next time, then, to make sure that doesn't happen." The finger around hers gave a light squeeze. "Meet you in the car park in fifteen minutes? I have one more patient to schedule, and then I'll be free."

"Okay," she said. Her spirits soared to heights that were dizzyingly high. A fall from up here could…

She wasn't going to fall. For the first time in a long time she caught a glimpse of something she hadn't expected to feel.

Hope.

Pete the Geek was on a rampage.

Reclining on the blanket that Darcie had somehow scrounged up, Lucas lay on his back, hands behind his head as he watched his niece chasing the dog around their little area of the park. Pete never went far, but seemed intent on having his little bit of fun on this outing, since the cold packed lunch hadn't been on the menu for him.

Darcie sat next to Lucas's shoulder and laughed as Cora just touched Pete's collar, only to have him leap out of reach once again. "He has his timing down to a science, doesn't he?"

"He does at that." He couldn't resist taking one of his hands from behind his head and resting it just behind Darcie's bottom. No one could see. But he just needed to touch her. Not in a sexual sense, although that always hovered in the background where this woman was concerned. But he found he wanted that closeness in more areas. Just for now. In a very little while she would be gone, and while there might be pain in letting her go, at least she would be alive. It wouldn't be like losing someone to death. He could accept loving her within those parameters.

He'd warred with himself for the last two days but

had come up with a compromise he hoped he could live with. He would let himself go with the flow. For the next couple of months.

She sent him a smile in response.

Warm contentment washed through him. Maybe this was why Felix had gone so far off the rails after losing Melody. Lucas had never felt like this about a woman. He loved her. He no longer even tried to deny it. And after staying away from her for two days he'd found he was miserable—and he'd had to find her. Be with her.

For the next two months.

He found himself sending his subconscious little memos. Just so it wouldn't forget. This was a temporary arrangement.

Felix seemed better. His therapy was evidently kicking in. He was fully engaged in what Cora was doing with Pete, really laughing for the first time in years. "Maybe if you tempt him with the ball?"

Cora spun back toward them, while Darcie held out the ball that had landed near her hip a while ago. Leaning down, the little girl flung her arms around Darcie's neck and popped a kiss on her cheek. "I'm so glad you came!"

"I'm glad I did too."

Lucas tensed for a second then forced himself to relax. Darcie and Cora could still keep in contact, even after she flew back to England. There was email and all kinds of social networks. It wouldn't be a drastic break. Just one that would fade away with time.

His niece rushed off with the ball in hand and threw it hard toward Pete, who loped off after the offering with a bark of happiness, scooping it up in his jaws and trotting back toward the blanket.

Lucas smiled and shook his head, his attention going back to Felix.

Only his brother wasn't watching Cora any more. His gaze was on Lucas, his eyes seeming to follow the line of his arm to where it disappeared behind Darcie's back.

Swallowing, he returned his hand to behind his head, and then as an afterthought sat up completely. Darcie glanced at him, head tilted as if she was asking a question. Swamped by a weird premonition, he got to his feet and slapped his brother's shoulder, urging him to come with him to help Cora round up the dog and bring him back to the picnic area.

He watched Felix as they worked, but whatever he thought he'd seen in his brother's face was no longer there. Felix smiled and joked and was finally the one to grab hold of Pete the Geek's collar and snap the leash onto it. Once they were all back at the picnic area he saw that Darcie had packed everything up and was on her feet. "I probably need to get back to the hospital."

That uncertainty he'd caught in her expression from time to time was back.

Because of him.

This was ridiculous. He was imagining demons where none existed. Probably excuses created in the depths of his own mind. There was no reason history had to repeat itself. "I do too. I'll walk you." On impulse, he leaned down and kissed her cheek, watching as they turned that delicious shade of pink he loved so much.

He turned back to say goodbye to Cora, noting his

brother's eyes were on him again. He returned the look this time. "Everything okay?"

"Yep. I need to get Cora home so Chessa doesn't worry. Besides, I have some drawings I need to get to."

Felix had once been a respected architect. When he'd married Melody he kept on working, even though she'd been wealthy enough that he hadn't had to. He'd inherited a fortune after she'd died, but it had meant nothing to him. He'd withdrawn from work and every other area of his life, including Cora. It made Lucas's heart a little bit lighter to see him showing an interest in something he'd once been so passionate about.

"Anything interesting?"

"I don't know yet. I'll have to wait and see what it looks like before I decide."

Kind of like Lucas himself? Waiting to see what things with his brother looked like before going on with his life?

Maybe. He wasn't sure. He still hadn't sorted it all out in his head, but he knew he wanted to spend more time with Darcie. Both during their rotation and after it was over.

For how long? Until she left for England?

He slung an arm around her waist, no longer certain of that, despite his earlier lecture. That drawing hadn't been completed yet. Maybe, like Felix, he should wait to see how things shaped up before deciding things like that.

Felix's eyes were on them again, although a smile stretched his lips. "I'll see you tomorrow, then, right?"

"Definitely." He walked over and kissed the top of

Cora's head then ruffled the fur behind Pete's ears. "Be good, you guys."

"We will, won't we, Pete?"

Lucas gave his brother a half-hug. "You'll be okay taking them home?"

"Of course. I wouldn't have brought them otherwise." His brother's voice was just a little sharper than he'd expected, and Lucas took the time to really look at him. Felix's skin was drawn tight over his cheeks, but he still had that same smile on his face. Maybe he was just tired. He hadn't done outings like this in years. Lucas couldn't expect him to spring from point A to point B in the blink of an eye. It was better not to push for more until his brother was ready.

Just in case, he didn't put his arm back around Darcie's waist. That could wait until his brother and Cora were in the car and out of sight. Besides, he didn't want them to witness him kissing the living daylights out of her right there in the park. Which he intended on doing. Then they could go back to work and act like nothing had ever happened. And hopefully Darcie would be amenable to him driving her home afterward. Enough so that she'd ask him up for coffee?

His brother loaded everything in the car. Cora gave one last wave before she got in and they drove away.

Taking hold of Darcie's hips, he tugged her close.

She grinned up at him. "You know, I think *you* might be the one with exhibitionist tendencies, not me."

"Where you're concerned, anything's possible." With that, he proceeded to do what he'd said he was going to and slanted his mouth over hers, repeating the act until she was clinging to him, and until he was in danger of really showing the world what he felt for this woman. "Time to get back to work."

Her mouth was pink and moist, and her eyes held a delicious glazed sheen. He'd put that there. And he intended to keep it there for as long as possible all through the night.

And then he was going to invite her to come to dinner with him at Felix and Cora's house tomorrow evening. They wouldn't mind, especially since he was the one doing the grilling.

After that? He wrapped his arm around her waist and walked with her the rest of the way to the hospital.

He'd have to see what the drawing looked like further on down the road, but he could afford to give it a little more time to take shape. At least for now.

CHAPTER TEN

LUCAS WASN'T AT WORK.

Darcie did her rounds, trying not to think the worst. He'd been fine at the picnic yesterday. And he'd spent most of last night at her place, making love to her with an intensity and passion that had taken her breath away. After several different places and positions, he'd finally groaned and dragged himself from beneath her covers. "I need to get home so I can be at work on time tomorrow morning." He leaned over and rested his arms on either side of her shoulders, bracketing her in and swooping down for another long kiss. "My rotation partner is a slave driver. She gets all put out when I come in rumpled, wearing the same clothes I had on the day before."

"Maybe that's when she thought you were involved with all sorts of different women."

He'd laughed. "How disappointing it must be to find out what a square I actually am."

"Just the opposite. I was jealous of the way the patients in the MMU always seem to fawn over you. I just wouldn't admit it to myself."

With a laugh, he'd scooped her up and kissed her shoulder. "See you in the morning, gorgeous."

That had been the last she'd heard from him.

She'd walked on cloud nine as she'd got ready for work. Then, when she arrived, she eagerly waited for him to make an appearance and toss her one of those secretive smiles she was coming to love.

But there'd been nothing. No phone calls. No text messages. And nothing on the board to show his schedule had been changed.

Surely he'd made it home safely.

And even though he hadn't said the words, he had to care about her. The way he'd touched her at the park and put his arm around her in full view of his brother and niece had said he wasn't embarrassed to be seen with her.

She cringed at that thought. That was something the Darcie of old would have worried about. Her experience with Robert had shaken her confidence in herself as a woman to the very core. Lucas was slowly building it back up. Kiss by kiss. Touch by touch. He acted like he couldn't get enough of her.

Well, the feeling was mutual.

Today she was not going to let his tardiness get the better of her. She was going to simply enjoy what they'd done last night and not worry about anything else. He'd eventually turn up. He'd probably stopped in to see Cora or something. Or maybe he'd had to drive her to school, which he'd said he'd done on occasion.

He wasn't in bed with someone else. Of that she was sure. Because she was feeling the effects of his loving this morning. It was a delicious ache that reminded her that, no matter who fluttered their lashes at him, Lucas had chosen her.

She sighed and glanced at her watch again. An hour and no word. There was nothing to do but go on with her day and not worry about it. She was tempted to ring his mobile, but was afraid that might seem desperate or needy. So she let it go.

The morning continued to race by at a frenetic pace. Then one o'clock came with no time to break for lunch. She'd just completed one delivery and was heading for the next laboring patient when she saw Isla at the nurses' station. She hurried over.

"Have you heard from Lucas? Or do you know if he's arrived at work yet? I haven't seen him all day."

Her friend blinked at her for a second and then her eyes filled with something akin to horror. "Oh, sweetheart, you haven't heard?"

Only then did she see that Lucas's name had been crossed off today's rota and Isla's name was written in instead. That had to have been done after she'd looked at it this morning.

Darcie's vision went dark for a second or two. "Heard what?"

"Oh…I'm so sorry. I got a call around an hour ago, asking me to step in." She reached out and gripped her hand. "Lucas is in the emergency department…"

Isla's voice faded out in a rush of white noise but the words "alcohol poisoning" and "gastric lavage" came through, before a nurse came out of the room of her next patient. "Mrs. Brandon is feeling the urge to push, and she's panicking. She isn't listening to instruction, Dr. Green."

Somehow, Darcie managed to stumble into the room, and despite her clanging heart she was able to coax the nitrous mouthpiece from between the woman's clamped jaws and get her to focus on pushing at the appropriate times. The baby was a large one, and Darcie had to do some fancy maneuvering to get the baby's shoulders through the narrow space. Then he was out and wailing at the top of his lungs. Darcie wished she could drop onto the nearest chair and join him for a hearty cry. But she couldn't. And it was another hour of praying for a break before one finally came and she could make her way down to Emergency.

Her heart was in her throat. Lucas had alcohol poisoning? How could that be? She'd never seen him touch a drop of the stuff, except for the sips she'd talked him into taking of her drink. And he'd made the most godawful face once he had. She'd convinced herself he was a teetotaler, that he just didn't like alcohol. But maybe she'd got it all wrong. Maybe he was a recovering alcoholic. Or, worse, one who binge-drank for seemingly no reason.

But alcohol poisoning was more than just a couple of drinks. It was a life-threatening toxic buildup that came from downing one drink after another without giving the liver time to filter the stuff out of the blood.

Why hadn't Isla come back to find her as soon as she'd heard the news?

Maybe because she'd been just as swamped as Darcie had been—and just as exhausted. She saw on the patient board that the letters "TMTB" had been scrawled beside two of the names, so her friend had to have been run ragged with those girls—and with all the aftercare that went along with teen pregnancies.

She paused just outside the doors to the emergency

department, unsure what she was going to find. Isla would have surely told her if Lucas was in danger of dying, wouldn't she? Maybe the stomach pumping had done its job and he was already on the road to recovery. Maybe he was simply too ashamed to face her.

As well he should be.

Anger crawled through her veins, pushing aside the worry and fear. If he were an alcoholic, shouldn't he have told her? Refused that offer of a drink she'd given him?

A thought spun through her brain. What if that sip had sent him over the edge? An alcoholic shouldn't drink *any* type of liquor. Ever.

All those late mornings…the rumpled clothes. The surly demeanor when he finally arrived.

God.

She squared her shoulders and stepped on the mat that would open the glass doors and went through. Noise and shouting hit her. The place was just as busy as the MMU had been. Making her way over to the desk and hoping to find a nurse or someone who could provide her with information, she searched the patient board for a familiar name.

Out of the corner of her eye she caught sight of him. Lucas.

He was on his feet, leaning against a wall. She'd recognize those broad shoulders and wavy hair anywhere. But he didn't look right. He was slumped, leaning against the flat surface as if he could barely hold himself up.

The waiting room was crowded, but surely he'd been seen already. Alcohol poisoning was normally run up to the top of the list. Could Isla have exaggerated or made a mistake?

At that moment his eyes met hers.

And what was in them tore apart any thought of exaggeration. There was torment and pain in that red, bleary gaze.

So much pain.

Hurrying over, she stopped next to him.

"Lucas, what's wrong? Are you ill?" she asked.

He didn't answer, just shook his head. His hair was tousled, and two of the bottom buttons of his shirt were undone, as if he'd thrown himself together in a rush.

"I don't understand. Isla said something about alcohol poisoning. She wasn't talking about you?"

"No." Lucas's hands fisted at his sides. "Did you think she was?"

"I didn't know what to think." Confusion swirled around her head. Why did he seem so angry?

"It's not me. It's my brother."

"Felix?" The sound of a siren drowned out his response as an ambulance pulled up to the front entrance. The sound of slamming doors came and then a gurney rushed in with a patient who was obviously in bad shape from the number of healthcare staff heading toward him. When she could finally be heard again she asked, "What happened?"

Two seats opened up as a couple with a child were called back to one of the exam rooms.

She took his hand to lead him over to the chairs so he could sit down before he fell down. He tugged free of her grip but followed her over to the seats. A chill went through her that had nothing to do with Felix's condition as they both sat.

"What happened to Felix?"

He propped his elbows on his knees and stared at the ground. Without looking at her, he said, "He drank himself into a stupor."

"Oh, no." So it was alcohol poisoning. Isla had been right about that. "What about Cora?"

He gave a mirthless laugh. "She's the one who rang me this morning. Felix was out all night, and when he finally made it home he collapsed in the foyer. Chessa had to spend the night at the house because she couldn't reach me. And so here I am."

Her heart squeezed tight. They hadn't been able to reach him because he'd been at her house until almost three that morning, his mobile and car keys deposited on her entry table. "I'm so sorry, Lucas. Will he be okay?"

"I don't know. He may be too far gone this time."

This time?

Things fell into place in the blink of an eye. This was why Felix had seemed off when she'd met him those weeks ago—why he and Lucas had argued. He was the alcoholic, not Lucas.

"He seemed fine at the park."

"He was." Lucas lifted his head long enough to glance in her direction. "At least I thought he was."

That explained something else. Lucas had seemed light and happy. Happier than she'd ever known him to be. She'd assumed it had been because of their budding relationship. But maybe that hadn't been the case at all. Maybe it had been because his brother had been doing so well. Maybe all those affectionate touches and looks had been spillover from what had been going on with Felix.

And last night? Had that simply been an overflow of happiness as well?

Her brain processed another fragment. He hadn't rung her to tell her where he was this morning. Or that his brother was in trouble. He—or someone—had notified Isla instead.

Maybe he hadn't wanted to worry her.

But surely he knew she'd be frantic when he didn't show up for work.

Her thoughts spiraled down from there. He hadn't bothered to tell her the truth about his brother's condition. Or what he'd been dealing with for who knew how long. He'd led her to believe things were fine. With Felix and Cora.

With her.

Just like Robert had done.

When trouble had come to visit, she'd been the last one to find out—and the result had been devastating.

You're jumping to conclusions, Darcie. Give the man a chance to explain.

Only he didn't. He just sat there. She'd had to drag every piece of information out of him the entire time she'd known him. Was this what she wanted? A lifetime full of secrets? Of wondering if things were okay between them?

No.

Something inside her wouldn't let her give up quite so easily, though. Not without trying one last time to reach him.

"He'll be okay." She knew the reassurance was empty.

She had no idea exactly how bad things were. Only Lucas and the doctors knew how much liquor he'd ingested or how much damage had been done to his liver and other organs.

"Will he?"

"What did the doctors say?" She had to keep pushing. To see if he was worth fighting for.

Because she loved him.

Oh, God, she loved him, and she didn't want to have to let him go, unless there was no other option.

"They pumped his stomach. Rehydrated him with fluids and electrolytes. I just have to wait for him to wake up."

She didn't understand. "Will they not let you back to see him?"

"I needed to think about some things. I'll go back in a little while."

"And Cora?"

"She's still with Chessa. We both thought it best not to have her here until we knew something definitive. She's already lost her mum. I don't want her to panic over what might happen to her dad. Unless it actually does."

"It might not come to that." She licked her lips and got up the nerve to slide her hand over his. This time he didn't shake her off. But he also didn't link his fingers through hers or make any effort to acknowledge the contact. "Is there anything I can do to help?"

"If he makes it, he'll have to go to rehab. A residential one this time. I can't trust him to care for Cora at this point."

Which was why he'd been late those other times. Another piece fell into place.

He'd had to take care of his niece when his brother had been too sick or too drunk. And what had she done? She'd yelled at him in front of a roomful of people on one of those days. Guilt washed over her, pummeling her again and again for assuming things that hadn't been true. For not asking him straight out if something was wrong. Maybe she could have helped somehow.

Maybe she still could.

"If you need me to watch Cora, I—"

"No." The word was firm. Resolute. "We'll be fine."

Another chill went through her, and the premonition she'd had earlier came roaring back to haunt her.

He was still going to pretend that things were okay—shutting her out without a moment's hesitation. She removed her hand from his and curled it in her lap.

Lucas sat up, his mouth forming a grim line. "I think I'm going to take some personal time. I have Cora to think about, and I'll need to deal with Felix. I can't do that and work at the same time."

Her heart stalled. "How will you live?"

"I have some savings. And Cora's care comes from a trust fund her mother left for her."

"I see." She licked her lips. "How much time are we talking?"

"A couple of months at the very least. Maybe more." He didn't skip a beat. He'd obviously already thought this through.

She did the calculations and a ball of pain lodged in her chest. He'd be out until after she left Australia and headed back to England. Surely he couldn't mean to drop out of her life as quickly as he'd come into it. Not after everything that had happened between them.

"I could come by after work, help with the cooking."

"I think it would be better if you didn't, Darcie. Please. For everyone's sake."

For everyone's sake. Whose, exactly? His?

"I don't understand."

"Felix is here because he can't get over the death of his wife, despite years of therapy. When he saw you and I together at the park…" He shrugged. "You knew there was never going to be anything permanent between us. At least I thought you did. And right now I have to think about what's best for my family."

His eyes were dull and lifeless. So much so that it made her wonder if he even knew how much he was hurting her with his words.

Then he looked at her, and she saw the truth. He knew. He just didn't care.

The ball grew into a boulder so big she could barely breathe past it. He was dumping her. His brother's illness provided the perfect excuse.

Only, like her ex-fiancé, he didn't have the decency to come to her and tell her until it was as obvious as the nose on her face.

Well, that was okay. She'd survived being jilted at the altar, so she could survive the breakup of something that amounted to a few nights of sex and adventure. He'd wanted to do some wild and outrageous stuff? Well, she'd done enough to last a lifetime. And she didn't have it in her to stick around and watch her world fall apart piece by piece.

One thing she *could* do was make this final break as

easy as possible for the both of them. "I'm truly sorry about Felix, and I hope everything works out with him. But if your decision to leave the MMU has anything to do with me or the time we spent together, this should put your mind at ease. I've decided to go back to England early."

He eyed her for several long seconds before saying, "When did you decide this?"

Right now. Right this second. When I realized I'm good enough to warm your bed at night but not good enough to take up permanent residence in your heart— to share your joys and heartaches.

But she couldn't say that. Not unless she wanted the remnants of her shattered pride to fall away completely and expose everything she'd hoped to hide.

Then the perfect response came to her in a flash, and she snatched at it, before taking a deep breath and looking him straight in the eye. "I decided last night."

CHAPTER ELEVEN

ISLA SLAMMED OPEN the door to his office, green eyes flashing. "What did you do to Darcie?"

Lucas hadn't seen her for the last two days, so he'd assumed she'd already flown home. In fact, that was why he was still at work, tying up loose ends, albeit with shorter hours. Chessa was staying with Cora during the day, and at night he went and slept on the couch.

Felix was still in the hospital, but he was slowly regaining his strength. His brother had admitted what Lucas knew in his heart to be true. That seeing him and Darcie together had reopened wounds that had scabbed over but never fully healed.

And what about Darcie?

He'd hurt her, but he hadn't known what else to do. His brother's life was at stake—because of something he'd done. He couldn't let that happen again.

Besides, hadn't he seen time and time again how love brought you to the brink of disaster and sometimes tossed you over the edge? Everything he'd seen lately had reinforced that. Margie's miscarriage. Tristan and Flick almost losing their baby. His brother almost losing his life.

Isla crossed her arms over her chest, clearly waiting for him to answer her.

"Thank you for knocking before you burst in." When the jibe earned him nothing but a stony stare he planted both his hands on his desk. "I didn't do anything to her, Isla. She said she decided to go back to England earlier than planned."

"Why? Did you sleep with her?"

Hell, if the woman wasn't direct. "I don't see that that's any of your business."

"Maybe not. But I think she was right about you. You're nothing but an arrogant, self-righteous bastard who thinks he can sit above all of us and not dirty his hands with real life and real love. I know...because my husband was once just like you."

"She said that about me?" He tried to ignore the hit to his gut that assessment caused. "As for Alessandro, I bet he didn't have a drunken brother to contend with. Or a niece who needed him."

"And that justifies you hurting Darcie?"

No. Nothing justified that. And he would be damned every moment of his life for what he'd done. But she'd said she was going to leave anyway.

It was a lie, you idiot. You'd practically hung a do-not-disturb sign on your heart and dared anyone to knock. And then once she did, you slammed the door in her face.

Because of Felix.

Really?

Was it because his brother had relapsed—which he'd done on several other occasions without any help from him—or was it because he was too afraid to "dirty his hands", as Isla claimed.

He'd once sat on a beach and dared Darcie to do something wild and outrageous. And she'd risen to the challenge and beyond. And yet here he sat, too afraid to make a list of his own because "loving Darcie" would be at the top of it.

He was terrified of holding his hand out to her for fear of losing her. And the thought of becoming like his brother—a shell of a man…

But what about what Isla had asked? Did any of that excuse what he'd done to Darcie? Because of his own selfish fear?

"No," he said. "It didn't justify it."

Isla seemed to lose her steam. "I didn't expect you to agree with me quite so quickly."

"I know what I did. And I'm not proud of it." If he had it to do all over again, would he? He'd made an impulsive decision while his brother had been fighting for his life—a huge mistake, according to the experts. He should have given himself a day or two before deciding something that would affect both of their lives.

The memory of her laughter, those pink-cheeked smiles…that raw sincerity when she'd offered to help with Cora's care. He'd thrown it all away. He hadn't given a thought to how she might have felt, or how right it seemed to be with her. He'd only thought of himself. And in that process he'd done to her what he'd been so afraid might happen to him. He'd abandoned her. Left her standing all alone.

"Isla, you're a genius. And I'm a fool." He got up

and went around the desk and planted a kiss right on her forehead.

Her face cleared, and she laughed. "I won't tell Alessi you did that. He might knock your teeth right out of your head."

"He knows you're crazy about him…and the whole world knows how he feels about you."

"True. So what are you doing to do about all this other stuff?" She rolled her hand around in the air.

What *was* he going to do? He'd run Darcie off and it wasn't like he could do anything about it. He was here. Having to make sure his brother made it in to rehab as soon as he was released from the hospital. He couldn't just hop on the first flight to England and leave Cora by herself. He was stuck.

"I don't know, actually. I have responsibilities here."

Her mouth curved into a half-smile. "Isn't it lucky, then, that Alessi loves me as much as you say he does?"

Lucas had no idea what that had to do with anything. "Yes, I guess it's lucky for you."

"And for you too. Because he happens to know someone high up at the airline Darcie was scheduled to fly on."

He only caught one word of that whole spiel. "Was?"

"It seems her flight was overbooked, and she was booted to one that leaves tomorrow afternoon."

Hope speared through him, causing him to drop back into his chair. "She's still in Melbourne?"

"For another day. Yes."

"Why the hell didn't you say something before now?"

"Because I wasn't sure you loved her enough to fight for her. And if you don't, she deserves better."

He swallowed. She deserved better anyway. Better than that bastard ex of hers. Better than *him*. "You're right. I'm not good enough for her."

"I might have agreed with you a few minutes ago but I saw your face when the enormity of what you'd done hit you. You were frantically trying to figure out a way to make it right…to get to her. Well, Alessi and I have just given it to you. Don't waste it, Lucas. Because by tomorrow afternoon she'll be gone, and it'll be too late."

He got to his feet. "If she's gone, it'll be because she doesn't want me. Because as of right now I'm going to fight for her with everything I have in me and hope to God she'll forgive me."

Darcie wandered through the empty flat, which was in much the same state as when she'd arrived. There were suitcases sitting neatly side by side, and in her purse was a one-way ticket. She'd come here looking to escape a painful past, only to end up fleeing a new situation that was even worse.

Her feelings for Lucas were light years beyond the ones she'd had for Robert, which maybe explained why he'd found her lacking that certain spark. She had. It had taken Lucas to put a match to it and bring it to life.

Only he'd evidently felt even less for her than her ex had. Because he'd made no pretense of loving her or even wanting a long-term relationship with her. Hadn't he told her that in plain English at the very beginning, when he'd first suggested putting pen to paper and making that list?

She gave a pained laugh. "He did, but you just couldn't

accept that, could you? You had to fall in love with the man, didn't you?"

A knock sounded at the door and Darcie froze, wondering if someone had heard her. The doorman was supposed to ring the interphone if she had a visitor. Her heart thumped back to normal. It was probably just the taxi. She'd asked the airport to send someone if they found her an earlier flight. The sooner she was out of Melbourne the better.

She felt like such a fool and every second she stayed in this flat—in this country—was a horrid reminder of how she'd practically groveled at the man's feet, only to have him knock her offer aside and ask her to leave him alone.

Which was what she was trying to do.

She scrubbed her palms under her eyes, irritated that she had turned into the weepy female she'd vowed never to be again.

Hauling her suitcases to the front door, she went back for her purse and opened the door. "Do you mind getting those? I…"

It took three or four blinks before she realized the man standing at the door wasn't a taxi driver. Or the doorman.

It was Lucas.

Oh, God, why was he here? To make sure she really, really, *really* understood that he didn't want her?

Well, Lucas, I might have been a little slow on the up-take, but once the message sank in it was there to stay.

"I thought you were the taxi driver. How did you get past the doorman?"

"I didn't. He recognized me." He paused. "From before."

Said as if she might not remember their last encounter in this flat. Unfortunately it was burned into her brain with a flamethrower.

She strove for nonchalant. "How's your brother doing?"

"He's out of danger. Looking forward to getting the help he needs. I think being in hospital gave him the shock of a lifetime."

"I'm glad." She was. As hurt and angry as she was at Lucas, she hoped Cora would finally have her father back. "And Cora?"

"She misses you."

Pain sliced through her chest. "Don't. Please."

Lucas glanced to the side where her suitcases sat. "May I come in for a minute?"

"Why?" She didn't think she could take another blow. Not when she was struggling not to memorize every line and crag of that beloved face.

"Because Cora isn't the only one who misses you."

The words took a moment to penetrate her icy heart. Then she started to pick them apart. "You mean Isla and the rest of the staff?"

"Yes, but not just them."

She licked her lips. "Then who?"

Fear buzzed around in her stomach while she waited for him to say something. Anything.

His chest rose as he took a deep breath. "Me. *I* miss you. I don't want you to go."

"You practically offered to pack my bags."

"I was stupid. Scared. My brother is the way he is because he desperately loved his wife. When she died... well, he was never the same. I don't want to end up like that."

She worked through those words. "And you're afraid if you meet someone, you will."

He nodded.

A terrible, wonderful atom of hope split into two. Then three. "Come in."

She stepped aside as he moved into the room and glanced around. Waiting for him to finish and turn back toward her, her brain continued to analyze what it knew. Somehow he'd found out she hadn't left.

Isla.

Darcie had called to tell her that her flight had been delayed. But why would she tell Lucas?

"You say you miss me, that you don't want me to go, but I need something more than that." This time she wasn't willing to settle for less.

He came back and took her hands in his. "I know you do. Which is why I want you to come with me."

"Where?"

"It's a secret. But by the end of it I hope you'll have the answer you need."

The buzzing fear turned into a tornado that whipped through her system and made her doubt. Was he was going to lead her on a merry chase, only to get cold feet again and decide he was better off without her?

Maybe.

So why was that list they'd made a couple of weeks ago stuck in the front pocket of her purse...complete with the smiley face he'd drawn next to the kiss-a-non-triangular-Aussie entry? Because she didn't want to forget. But, like him, she was afraid.

He'd overcome his fear long enough to drive to the flat, though, without knowing what kind of reception he'd get. Didn't she owe it to herself to follow this through to the end? She could always catch that flight tomorrow if it didn't work out.

"Okay, I'll come."

He closed his eyes, the lines between his brows easing. When he opened them again, the brown irises seemed to have warmed to a hue she recognized and loved. A few more atoms split apart, some of them coalescing back together and forming a shape she could almost decipher. He glanced at her clothes. "Can you get those wet?"

"Wet?" Was he going to kill her and toss her lifeless body over the side of his boat? That made her smile. A few more particles merged together. "I think they'll survive."

Twenty minutes later they pulled up to a place she recognized. But it wasn't his boat. "Why are we here?"

"Trust me." He got out of the car and came around to her side and opened the door. She stood on the footpath, staring up at a familiar tower.

"We're going bungee jumping? Now?"

"You're not. I am."

She had no idea what was going on but he'd asked her to trust him. So she walked with him to meet Max, who stood waiting at the entrance. The man pushed his glasses higher on his nose, looking spectacularly pleased with himself for some reason. "Come in. Come in. Everything's ready." He disappeared through the wooden privacy gate.

Lucas murmured, "Remember when you jumped, I waited for you in the pool at the bottom?"

"Yes." She wasn't sure how she got the word out as her throat felt dry and parched.

"I want you to go to the side of the pool and wait for me this time." He gave a half-smile. "Don't ask me why until you've unhooked me."

They went through the gate, a million questions swirling through her mind. Max led her down to the pool, while Lucas climbed the steps to the tower.

She gasped. The water was crystal clear, just as before…but the surface was littered with rose petals. Thousands of them in every color imaginable—red, purple, yellow, white, pink.

Max didn't explain, he just asked her to wait there. "Lucas knows how to unhook himself, but he wants you to go into the water and do it for him this time."

"I don't know how."

The engineer gave her a knowing smile. "He says you do. Just do what your heart tells you."

If she did that, Lucas wouldn't be diving head-first into a pool. They'd be hashing this whole thing out on the couch in her flat. Or in bed, depending on how well the discussion went.

But then Max was gone, joining Lucas in this crazy game of who knew what.

He appeared at the top. His shirt was off. He must have worn swimming trunks underneath his jeans because his tanned legs were on display. He looked strong and powerful. But from the words he'd said back at the flat, he'd hinted he was anything but.

But, then, neither was she. She had her own fears to struggle through. And if they couldn't do it together, then they needed to work on them as separate individuals.

Except those atoms were still dividing. Still joining. She peered, trying to make out what it was becoming. Then, just as Lucas dived far out into the air, arms spread apart, she saw it. It was his face, and the expression on it was similar to the one he had when he looked at Cora. When he looked at his brother.

Love. And fear.

A mixture of two emotions that were intertwined so tightly it was impossible to completely separate them. She knew, because the two were battling it out within her heart as well.

Lucas hurtled toward the pool before being jerked back at the last second, just as he'd been the previous time. The air displaced by his fall made the petals sift over the surface of the water, like ice skaters twirling in colorful costumes. Then the winch began to whine as it slowly lowered Lucas closer to the water. Time for her to get in.

She slipped into the pool, surprised to find some kind of footing where they'd had to tread water before. It felt like wood, but it was high enough that she didn't have to swim, she could simply walk toward him in chest-high water. When she looked up at him, she found his eyes on her. In their depths was a question. She swallowed, emotion bubbling up in her throat and threatening to escape as a sob. She loved this man. Loved him with all her heart. And she was willing to take him as he was, fears and all, if that's what he wanted.

God, she hoped that was what he wanted.

He didn't say anything, but when he was close

enough to touch she gave him a quick kiss on the lips
just before his head disappeared beneath the surface,
followed by the rest of him. Soon he was hidden from
view by the layer of flower petals. Momentary panic
went through her. How was she supposed to unhook
him? Max hadn't shown her, and Lucas hadn't said anything at all.

Just do what your heart tells you.

Darcie ducked beneath the surface and found him
lying on the boards three feet below, the petals shad-
ing the area. He could just stand up if he wanted to…
it was shallow. But he didn't. She pushed herself down
and followed the cord that held his ankles. Unsnapped
it. Then the one attached to the harness at his back. It
stuck for a second and she wiggled it, suddenly scared
he wouldn't come up if she couldn't get it off. There.
The hook released.

He was free.

Lucas grabbed hold of her waist and hauled her to the
surface, breaking through the layer of velvety petals.

The question he'd told her to ask once he'd completed
the jump came out before she could stop it. "Why?"

He pushed damp strands of hair off her face. "Do you
remember what it felt like to take that leap?"

She nodded.

"What did you feel?" he murmured, his arm now
around her waist.

She thought for a moment, trying to gather her jum-
bled thoughts. "I was so scared. I didn't want to go
through with it, and I felt like screaming the whole way
down. But once I reached the pool, and you unhooked

me, there was this sense of exhilaration… I can't even describe it."

He nodded. "I know. Because I felt the same things as I sat on the beach with you and started making that list. Terrified. Like I'd lost my stomach, my heart and my head all at once. I fell, and I haven't stopped falling. But I was too afraid to finish it. To let you come alongside me and undo those ropes."

Her eyes watered. She knew exactly what he was talking about. "I feel it too," she whispered. "The fear."

"I love you, Darcie. It took me a while to understand what I'd find once I reached the bottom of that jump— to get past my fear and open my eyes, to really look at what was waiting for me. It was you."

She threw herself into his arms and lifted her lips up for his kiss. It was long and slow and thorough. Once she could breathe again she laid her head on his shoulder. "I love you too, Lucas. You're right, it was scary and making the decision to go over the edge wasn't an easy one. But it was worth it. All of it."

"Yes, it was."

"Hey, Uncle Luke," a voice came from the top of the tower. "When is it my turn to jump?"

Cora stood peering over the edge at them, and even from this distance Darcie could see the little girl's infectious smile.

Laughing, she nipped the bottom of his jaw. "Good thing I didn't leave you there to drown. You were awfully sure of yourself."

"No. I wasn't sure at all. But I hoped."

She hugged him tight. "Aren't you going to answer her question? When can she jump?"

Lucas kissed her cheek, and then shouted back up, "Not for many, many years, sweetheart."

EPILOGUE

WELCOME HOME!

The words, scrawled in pink childish letters and flanked by a heart on either side, greeted them as they opened the door to Lucas's flat.

Three weeks on a beach, and Darcie was still as white as the paper banner. She didn't care. Besides, they hadn't actually spent all that much time sunbathing while in Tahiti. A fact that made her smile.

"Aw, I think I know who wrote that." Darcie twined her arms around her new husband's neck. "But at least we're all alone, because I have something I want to—"

The panicky sound of a throat clearing came from behind the black leather couch, followed by a yip. And then two. A child giggled.

"Oops." Darcie's face heated, as she whispered into his ear. "Not so alone after all."

Lucas made a face at her, just as people came pouring from seemingly every room of the place. The kitchen, the two bedrooms, the veranda. And finally, from behind the couch, appeared Cora, Pete the Geek, Chessa…and Felix.

Cora and Pete launched themselves at the newlyweds

and her poor husband *oomphed* as the dog—apparently forgetting everything he'd learned—careened into his side, nearly knocking him down. Darcie barely managed to keep from falling herself.

"Oh, my gosh!" Darcie knelt to hug Cora, peering at the mass of people around them. It looked like most of the MMU staff had turned up for their return—which begged the question: who was minding the maternity unit?

Isla came over and planted a kiss on her cheek as Darcie stood, keeping hold of Cora's hand.

"How was the honeymoon?" her friend asked.

She returned her friend's hug. "Spectacular. How's the baby?"

"Growing like a little weed." She motioned over at Alessandro, who was cradling their infant in his arms. "I barely get to hold him. Flick says Tristan is the same way."

It certainly appeared so, since Tristan had a baby carrier strapped to his chest with his daughter safely ensconced inside it. Flick waved at her.

Darcie gazed around at the people she'd come to know and love over the past year and her eyes threatened to well up, although she somehow forced back the tide. Lucas was still a little spooked by tears. He'd overcome a lot of his fears, but every once in a while he looked at her as if afraid she might disappear into the ether.

And she might. But that's not how she planned to live her life. And she certainly wasn't going to let her husband dwell on it either.

Then her eyes widened as her gaze skimmed the rest of the room.

There, still standing behind the couch, were Felix and Chessa. And the childminder had a certain pink tinge to her cheeks that looked familiar. And— Oh… *Oh!* Felix's arm was slung casually around the woman's waist. It looked like she and Lucas hadn't been the only ones who'd been busy over the past couple of months.

Felix had completed his rehab program a few weeks before the wedding and had been on the straight and narrow ever since, according to the texts they'd got from Chessa. But she hadn't mentioned anything about a budding romance.

As if noticing her attention was elsewhere, Lucas glanced up from the group of people he was chatting with and caught her eye. She nodded in Felix's direction. She saw the moment he digested what he was seeing. His Adam's apple dipped. And then he was moving, catching his brother up in a fierce hug that was full of happiness.

And hope.

It was the best gift anyone could have given him— seeing his brother on the cusp of a bright new future. And little did Lucas know that another surprise awaited him. One she'd postponed telling him until just the right moment.

That moment was now. He could handle it. They both could.

When the tears came this time she didn't stop them, feeling Isla's arm come around her waist and squeeze. "It's wonderful, isn't it?"

"Yes."

Before she could say anything else he was back, grabbing her to him, his breathing rough and unsteady.

"Lucas." Her fingers buried themselves in the hair at the back of his head, praying she was doing the right thing as she leaned up to whisper, "I know it's early, but our friends aren't the only ones having babies."

He leaned back and looked at her for a long second, a question in his eyes. She gave a single nod.

"I love you," was all he said, before he drew her back against him, burying his face in her neck.

And when she felt moisture against her skin, she knew it was going to be okay. Her big-hearted husband was finally ready to accept that the world could be a good place. It brought sadness at times, yes, but it was also full of kindness and laughter and contentment.

All because they'd dared to do something outrageous and wild and completely dangerous: they'd fallen in love.

* * * * *

This is the final story in the fabulous
MIDWIVES ON-CALL *series.*
Make sure you've picked up all 8 books!

Join our *EXCLUSIVE* eBook club

FROM JUST £1.99 A MONTH!

Never miss a book again with our hassle-free eBook subscription.

★ Pick how many titles you want from each series with our flexible subscription

★ Your titles are delivered to your device on the first of every month

★ Zero risk, zero obligation!

There really is nothing standing in the way of you and your favourite books!

Start your eBook subscription today at www.millsandboon.co.uk/subscribe

MILLS & BOON®

MEDICAL ROMANCE™

THE ULTIMATE IN ROMANTIC MEDICAL DRAMA

A sneak peek at next month's titles...

In stores from 7th August 2015:

- **Hot Doc from Her Past** – Tina Beckett *and*
  Surgeons, Rivals...Lovers – Amalie Berlin

- **Best Friend to Perfect Bride** – Jennifer Taylor *and*
  Resisting Her Rebel Doc – Joanna Neil

- **A Baby to Bind Them** – Susanne Hampton

- **Doctor...to Duchess?** – Annie O'Neil

Available at WHSmith, Tesco, Asda, Eason, Amazon and Apple

Just can't wait?
Buy our books online a month before they hit the shops!
visit www.millsandboon.co.uk

These books are also available in eBook format!

0715/03